Aimee Molloy is the author of the *New York Times* non-fiction bestseller *However Long the Night*, as well as the co-author of several other books, including *Rosewater*, which was made into a movie by Jon Stewart. Film rights for *The Perfect Mother* have been optioned by Sony/Tri Star with Kerry Washington set to star in and produce the adaptation. Aimee lives in Brooklyn with her family.

THE PERFECT MOTHER

AIMEE MOLLOY

sphere

SPHERE

First published in the United States in 2018 by Harper,
an imprint of Harper Collins
First published in Great Britain in 2018 by Sphere
This paperback edition published in 2019 by Sphere

1 3 5 7 9 10 8 6 4 2

A CIP catalogue record for this book
is available from the British Library.

ISBN 978-0-7515-7034-2

Printed and bound in Great Britain by
Clays Ltd, Elcograf S.p.A

Papers used by Sphere are from well-managed forests
and other responsible sources.

MIX
Paper from
responsible sources
FSC® C104740

Sphere
An imprint of
Little, Brown Book Group
Carmelite House
50 Victoria Embankment
London EC4Y ODZ

An Hachette UK Company
www.hachette.co.uk

www.littlebrown.co.uk

To Mark

THE
PERFECT
MOTHER

Three blind mice, three blind mice,
See how they run, see how they run!

PROLOGUE
MOTHER'S DAY
MAY 14

Joshua.

I wake, feverish. The skylight above me pulses with rain, and I spider my fingers across the sheets, remembering I'm alone. I close my eyes and find my way back to sleep, until I'm woken again, engulfed by a deep, sudden pain. I've been waking with a sick feeling every morning since he left, but I know right away this is different.

Something's wrong.

It hurts to walk, and I crawl from the bed, across the floor, which is gritty with sand and dust. I find my phone in the living room but I don't know who to call. He's the only one I want to speak to. I need to tell him what's happening and hear him say that everything will be fine. I need to remind him, just one more time, how much I love him.

But he won't answer. Or worse, he will, and he'll seethe into the phone, telling me he won't continue to put up with this, warning me that if I ever call him again, he'll—

The pain grips my back so hard I can't breathe. I wait for it to pass, for the moment of reprieve I've been promised, but it doesn't come. This isn't what the books said would happen, nothing like what the doctor told me to expect. They said it'll be gradual. That I'll know what to do. I'll time things. I'll sit on the stoop-sale yoga ball I bought. I'll stay home as long as possible, to avoid the machines, the drugs, all the things they do at the hospital to make a baby come before a body is ready.

I'm not ready. It's two weeks before my due date, and I'm not ready.

I focus on the phone. It's not his number I dial, but hers, the doula—a pierced woman named Albany I've met just twice.

I'm attending to a birth and cannot take your call. If you are—

I crawl with my laptop to the bathroom and sit on the chilly tiles, a damp washcloth on my neck, the slim computer resting on the bulging outline of my son. I open my e-mail and begin a new message to them, the May Mothers.

I'm wondering if this is normal. My hands tremble as I type. I feel nauseous. The pain is intense. It's happening too quickly.

They won't respond. They're out to dinner, eating something spicy to hasten their own labor, stealing sips from their husbands' beer, enjoying a quiet evening together, something experienced mothers have warned us never to expect again. They won't see my e-mail until morning.

My e-mail chimes right away. Sweet Francie. It's starting! she writes. Time the contractions and have your husband keep steady pressure on your lower back.

How's it going? Nell writes. Twenty minutes have passed. Still feeling it?

I'm on my side. I have trouble typing. *Yes.*

The room goes black, and when the light comes—ten minutes later, an hour later, I have no idea—I feel a gray ache blooming from a bump on my forehead. I crawl back to the living room, hearing a noise, an animal howling, before I realize the sound is coming from me. *Joshua.*

I make it to the couch and rest my back against the cushions. I reach down between my legs. Blood.

I pull a thin rain jacket over my nightgown. Somehow, I make my way down the stairs.

Why haven't I packed the bag? The May Mothers have all written so much about what to pack in the bag, and yet mine is still in the bedroom closet, empty. No iPod with relaxing music inside, no coconut water, no peppermint oil for the nausea. Not even one printed copy of my birth plan. I cradle my stomach under a misty streetlight until the car service arrives and I climb into the clammy back seat, trying not to notice the troubled look on the driver's face.

I forgot the going-home outfit I bought for the baby.

At the hospital, someone directs me to the sixth floor, where I'm told to wait in the triage room. "Please," I finally say to the woman behind the desk. "I feel very cold and dizzy. Can you call my doctor?"

It's not my doctor's night. It's another woman from the practice, one I've never met. I'm overcome with fear as I take a seat, where I begin to leak liquid that smells like earth, like the backyard mud my mother and I used to comb for worms when I was six, onto the green plastic chair.

I go into the hallway, determined to keep moving, to stay upright, picturing his face when I told him. He was angry, insisting I'd tricked him. Demanding I get rid of the baby. *This will ruin everything*, he said. *My marriage. My reputation. You can't do this to me.*

I won't let you.

I didn't tell him I'd already seen the blinking green light of the heartbeat, that I'd heard the rhythm, a quickly spinning jump rope, emanating from the speakers in the ceiling. I didn't tell him I've never wanted anything as much as I want this baby.

Sturdy wrists lift me from the floor. Grace. That's what it says on her name tag. Grace leads me to a room, her hands around my waist, and tells me to lie down on the bed. I fight. I don't want to lie on the bed. I want to know the baby is all right. I want the pain to subside.

"I want the epidural," I say.

"I'm sorry," says Grace. "It's too late."

I seize her hands, roughed by too much soap and hospital water. "No, please. Too late?"

"For the epidural." I think I hear footsteps in the hallway, rushing toward my room.

I think I hear him calling for me.

I give in and lie down. It's him. It's Joshua, calling to me through the darkness. The doctor's here. She's speaking to me, and they're wrapping something around my bicep, sticking a needle smoothly under my skin, at the bend of my arm, like the blades of skates over ice. They're asking who's come with me, where my husband is. The room spins around me, and I can smell it. The liquid seeping from me. Like earth and mud. My bones are splitting. I'm on fire. It can't be right.

I feel the pressure. I feel the fire. I feel my body, my baby, breaking in two.

I close my eyes.

I push.

CHAPTER ONE
FOURTEEN MONTHS LATER

TO: May Mothers
FROM: Your friends at The Village
DATE: July 4
SUBJECT: Today's advice

YOUR TODDLER: FOURTEEN MONTHS

In honor of the holiday, today's advice is about independence. Do you notice that your formerly fearless little guy is suddenly afraid of everything when you're out of sight? The neighbor's adorable dog is now a terrifying predator. The shadow on the ceiling has become an armless ghoul. It's normal for your toddler to begin to sense danger in his world, and it's now your job to help him navigate these fears, letting him know he's safe, and that even if you're out of sight, Mommy will always be there to protect him, no matter what.

How fast the time goes.

That's what people were always telling us, at least; the strangers' hands on our bellies, saying how careful we must be to enjoy the time. How it'll all be over in a blink of an eye. How before we know it, they'll be walking, talking, leaving us.

It's been four hundred and eleven days, and time hasn't gone fast at all. I've been trying to imagine what Dr. H would say. Sometimes I close my eyes and picture myself in his office, my time almost up, the next patient eagerly tapping a toe in the waiting room. *You have a tendency to ruminate on things,* he'd say. *But, interestingly, never the positive aspects of your life. Let's think about those.*

The positive things.

My mother's face, how peaceful she looked at times, when it was just the two of us, in the car running errands; on our way to the lake.

The light in the mornings. The feel of the rain.

Those lazy spring afternoons, sitting in the park, the baby somersaulting inside me, my swollen feet bursting from my sandals like bruised peaches. Back before all the trouble started, when Midas hadn't yet become *Baby Midas*, everyone's latest cause, when he was just another newborn boy in Brooklyn, one among a million, no more or less extraordinary than the dozen or so other babies with bright futures and peculiar names asleep in the inner circle of a May Mothers meeting.

The May Mothers. My mommy group. I've never liked that term. *Mommy.* It's so fraught, so political. We weren't *mommies.* We were mothers. People. Women who just happened to ovulate on the same schedule and then give birth the same month. Strangers who chose—for the good of the babies, for the sake of our sanity—to become friends.

We signed up through The Village website—"Brooklyn parents' most precious resource™"—getting to know one another over e-mail months before we met, long before we gave birth, dissecting our new lot in life in a level of detail our real friends would never tolerate. About finding out we were pregnant. Our clever way of telling our mothers. Trading ideas for baby names and concerns about our pelvic floors. It was Francie who suggested we get together in person, on the first day of spring, and we all carried ourselves to the park that March morning, under the weight of our third-trimester bellies. Sitting in the shade, the smell of newly awakened grass in the air, we were happy to be together, to finally put faces to the names. We continued to meet, registering for the same birthing classes, the same CPR course, cat-cowing next to one another at the same yoga studio. Then, in May, the babies began to arrive, just as expected, just in time for Brooklyn's hottest summer in recorded history.

You did it! we wrote, responding to the latest birth announcement, cooing like seasoned grandmothers over the attached photo of a tiny infant wrapped in a blue-and-pink hospital blanket.

Those cheeks!

Welcome to the world, little one!

Some in our group wouldn't feel safe leaving the house for weeks, while others couldn't wait to come together, to show off the baby. (They were all so new to us still that we didn't refer to them by their names—not as Midas, Will, Poppy, but simply as "the baby.") Freed for a few months from our jobs, if not concerns about our careers, we got together twice a week, always in the park, usually under the willow tree near the baseball diamonds, if someone was lucky enough to get there first and claim the coveted spot. The group changed a lot in the beginning. New people came, while others I'd grown used to seeing went—the mommy-group skeptics, the older mothers who couldn't stomach the collective anxiety, those already departing to the expensive suburbs of Maplewood and Westchester. But I could always count on the three regulars to be there.

First, there was Francie. If our group had a mascot, someone to glue themselves in feathers and lead our team in three cheers for motherhood, it was her. Miss Eager-to-Be-Liked, to not screw anything up, so plump with hope and rich Southern carbs.

And then Colette, everyone's girl crush, our trusted friend. One of the pretty ones, with her auburn shampoo-commercial hair, her Colorado-bred effortlessness and unmedicated home birth—the perfect female, topped in powdered sugar.

And finally Nell: British, cool, eschewing the books and the expert advice. So trust-your-instincts. So I-really-shouldn't. (I really shouldn't have that chocolate-chip muffin. Those chips. That third gin and tonic.) But there was something else about Nell, something below the salty exterior I spotted from day one: she, like me, was a woman with a secret.

I was never going to be a regular, but I went as often as I could bear to, trudging first my pregnant body and then my stroller down the hill to the park. I'd sit on my blanket, the stroller parked near the others in the triangular patches of shade under the willow tree, feeling myself grow numb as I listened to their ideas on parenting, on the very specific way certain things needed to be done. Exclusive breastfeeding. Keen attention to sleep cues. Wearing the baby at every opportunity, like he was a statement piece splurged for at Bloomingdale's.

It's no wonder I eventually started loathing them. Really, who can stand to listen to that level of certainty? To sit through the judgment?

What if you can't keep up with it all? What if you're not breastfeeding? What if, for instance, your milk has practically dried up, no matter how many Chinese herbs you ingest, or all the hours you spend attached to a pump in the middle of the night? What if you've been worn down by the exhaustion, and all the time and money you've spent learning to decipher sleep cues? What if you simply don't have the energy to bring a snack to share?

Colette brought the muffins. Every single time—twenty-four mini muffins from the expensive bakery that had recently opened where the tapas place had been. She'd unfasten the paper box and pass them around, over the bodies of the babies. "Winnie, Nell, Scarlett, help yourselves," she'd say. "They're out of this world."

So many around the circle politely declined, citing the weight they still had to lose, pulling out their carrot sticks and apple slices, but not me. My own stomach was already as flat and taut as it had been before I got pregnant. I can thank my mother for that. Good genes—that's what people have always said about me. They're talking about the fact that I am tall and thin, that I have a nearly symmetrical face. What they are not talking about are the *other* genes I've inherited. The ones bestowed to me not by my equally symmetrical mother, but from my exceptionally bipolar dad.

Joshua's genes are no better. I would talk to him about this sometimes, asking if it worried him, the DNA he has to work hard to outsmart. His own crazy father: the brilliant doctor, so warm and charming with patients. The violent alcoholic behind closed doors.

Joshua didn't like it when I spoke about his dad, though, and I learned to keep quiet about him. Of course I didn't mention any of this—my genes, Joshua, his dad—to the May Mothers. I didn't tell them how hard everything was without Joshua. How much I loved him. How I would have given up everything—everything—to be with him again. Even for just one night.

I couldn't tell them that. I couldn't tell anyone that. Not even Dr. H, shrink extraordinaire, who'd shuttered his office just when I needed him most, heading to the West Coast with his wife and three kids. I didn't have anyone else, and so yes, in the beginning I went to their meetings, hoping to find something in common with them; something in our shared experience of motherhood that might help lift the darkness of those first few months, which everyone always said were the hardest. *It'll get easier,* the health experts wrote. *Give it time.*

Well, things *didn't* get easier. I've been blamed for what happened that Fourth of July night. But not a day goes by that I don't remind myself of the truth.

It's not my fault. It's theirs.

It's because of them that Midas went missing, and I lost everything. Even now, a year later, I sit alone in this prison cell, fingering the hard, jagged scar at my abdomen, thinking how differently everything might have turned out if it weren't for them.

If I hadn't signed up for their group. If they'd chosen another date, or another bar, or someone other than Alma to babysit that night. If the thing with the phone hadn't occurred.

If only the words Nell spoke that day—her head tilted toward the sky, her features swallowed by the sun—hadn't been so prescient: *Bad things happen in heat like this.*

CHAPTER TWO
ONE YEAR EARLIER

> **TO:** May Mothers
> **FROM:** Your friends at The Village
> **DATE:** June 30
> **SUBJECT:** Today's advice
> <u>**YOUR BABY: DAY 47**</u>
> Most of you should have gotten into the swing of breastfeeding during the last six weeks, but for those still struggling—don't give up! Breast milk is by far the best thing you can give your baby. If you're experiencing any difficulty, pay attention to your diet. Dairy, gluten, and caffeine can decrease your supply. And if you have pain or discomfort, consider hiring a lactation consultant to help work through the issues. It could be the best money you'll ever spend.

"What is *that* supposed to mean, bad things happen in heat like this?" Francie asks, her curls frizzy around her neck, her face troubled.

Nell swats away a fly with the newspaper she's using to fan herself. "It's eighty-seven degrees," she says. "In Brooklyn. In June. At *ten* in the morning."

"So?"

"So maybe that's normal in Texas—"

"I'm from Tennessee."

"—but it's not normal here."

A hot wind blows the edge of the blanket, covering Francie's son's face. "Well, you shouldn't say things like that," Francie says, lifting the baby to her shoulder. "I'm superstitious."

Nell puts down the newspaper and unzips her diaper bag. "It's something Sebastian says. He grew up in Haiti. They're more accustomed than us Americans to paying attention to the planet, you could say."

Francie raises her eyebrows. "But you're British."

"Everything okay over there?" Colette calls to Scarlett, who is standing among the cluster of strollers in the shade, babies asleep inside. Scarlett ties the corners of a thin cotton blanket over the handles of her stroller and returns to the circle.

"I thought the baby was awake," she says, reclaiming her spot next to Francie and taking a bottle of hand sanitizer from her bag. "It was a long night, so please, nobody go near him. What did I miss?"

"The world is ending, apparently," Francie says, sucking the chocolate off a pretzel, the one indulgence she has come to allow herself.

"True," Nell says. "But I have just the antidote." She holds up the bottle of wine she'd taken from her diaper bag.

"You brought *wine*?" Colette smiles, twisting her hair into a bun as Nell unscrews the cap.

"Not just any wine. The best vinho verde twelve dollars can buy at nine thirty in the morning." She pours two inches into a small plastic cup from the stack in her diaper bag, and extends it to Colette. "Drink fast. It's kind of warm."

"Not me," Yuko says, circling the blanket, bouncing her daughter at her chest. "Yoga later."

"Me neither," says Francie. "I'm nursing."

"Oh, horseshit," says Nell. "We're *all* nursing." She raises her hand to clarify. "Unless you're not. Unless you go home and draw the curtains and secretly administer formula. That's fine too. Either way, a little wine isn't going to hurt."

"That's not what the books say," Francie says.

Nell rolls her eyes. "Francie, stop reading the propaganda. It's *fine*. In England, most of my friends drank a little bit, right through their pregnancy."

Colette offers Francie a reassuring nod. "Have a drink if you want. It's not going to hurt Will."

"Really?" Francie looks at Nell. "Okay, fine. But just a little."

"Me too. To celebrate," Scarlett says, reaching for the next cup. "Did I mention this? We're about to close on a house. In Westchester."

Francie groans. "You too? Why is everyone moving to the suburbs all of a sudden?"

"I'd rather move farther upstate, to be honest, but Professor Husband just got tenure at Columbia and needs to be close." Scarlett glances around the group. "No offense, I know a lot of people love it, but I can't imagine raising a kid in this city. Since the baby, all I see is how filthy it is here. I want him to know clean air and trees."

"Not me," says Nell. "I want my baby raised in squalor."

Francie sips her wine. "I wish we could afford to move to Westchester."

"Winnie?" Nell asks. "Wine?"

Winnie is staring off into the distance, watching a young couple throwing a Frisbee back and forth on the long meadow, a border collie running dizzily between them. She doesn't seem to hear Nell. "Winnie, love. Come back to us."

"Sorry," Winnie says, smiling at Nell and then glancing down at Midas, who is beginning to stir awake in the crook of her legs, his hands tucked against his ears. "What did you say?"

Nell extends a cup across the circle. "Do you want a little wine?"

Winnie lifts Midas to her chest and peers at Nell, her mouth buried in his black hair. "No. I shouldn't."

"Why not?"

"Alcohol doesn't always agree with me."

"What's wrong with you people?" Nell tips a stream of wine into her cup and rescrews the top. A large tattoo of a hummingbird—wispy and pastel—emerges from under the sleeve of her black T-shirt. She takes a sip. "God, that's bloody awful. Oh, listen to this. I went out without the baby yesterday, to get a coffee. A woman looked at my stomach, congratulated me, and asked me when I was due."

"That's obnoxious," Yuko says. "What did you tell her?"

Nell laughs. "November."

Francie looks at Winnie, who is again staring out across the lawn, a stiffness to her face. "You okay?"

"I'm fine." She tucks a strand of hair behind her ear. "This heat's just getting to me."

"Speaking of which, can we discuss another meeting place?" Yuko asks, laying her son on the blanket and hunting inside her bag for a clean diaper. "It's only going to get hotter. The babies will melt out here."

"We could go to the library," Francie suggests. "They have an empty room in the back we could reserve."

"Well, that sounds dreadful," Nell says.

"Have any of you been to that new beer garden, near the big playground?" Colette asks. "Charlie and I went the other day, and there were a few mom groups there with their babies. Maybe we should do that once in a while. We could meet for lunch."

"And sangrias," says Nell, her eyes lighting up. "Or better yet, why don't we do something like that at night? Go out *without* the babies."

"Without the babies?" Francie asks.

"Yeah. I'm going back to work next week. I'm dying to have a little fun while I still can."

"I don't think so," Francie says.

"Why not?"

"The baby's just seven weeks old."

"So?"

"So isn't that a little young to leave him? Plus, he's impossible in the evenings. We are, apparently, at the height of cluster feeding."

"Have your husband take care of him," Scarlett says. "It's important for them to bond during these early months."

"My husband?" Francie asks, her brow furrowed.

"Yes," Nell says. "You know, Lowell? The man whose ejaculate conceived one-half of your baby?"

Francie winces. "Nell. Gross." She looks at Winnie. "Would you go?"

Winnie folds Midas into the Moby Wrap at her chest and collects his blanket. "I'm not sure."

"Oh, come on," Colette says. "It'll be good for us to have a break from the babies."

Winnie stands, her petal pink sundress cascading to her ankles. "I don't have a babysitter for Midas yet."

"What about your—"

"Shit," Winnie says, glancing at the thin silver watch on her wrist. "It's later than I thought. I have to run."

"Where are you going?" Francie asks.

Winnie puts on a pair of large sunglasses and a wide-brimmed cotton sun hat that shades her face and shoulders. "You know, a million errands. See you next time."

Everyone on the blanket watches Winnie walk across the lawn and up the hill, her black hair loose around her shoulders, her dress fluttering at her heels.

When she disappears under the arch, Francie sighs. "I feel bad for her."

Nell laughs. "You feel bad for *Winnie*? Why, because she's so gorgeous? Or wait, it's how thin she is."

"She's a single mom."

Colette swallows her wine. "What? How do you know that?"

"She told me."

"You're kidding. When?"

"A few days ago. I stopped at the Spot for the air-conditioning and a scone. Will had a fit while I was standing in line. I was mortified, and then Winnie appeared. Midas was asleep in the stroller, and she took Will and held him to her chest. He calmed down right away."

Nell's eyes narrow. "I knew those boobs were magic. Just looking at them has calmed *me* down a few times."

"We hung out for a little while. It was nice. She's so quiet, right? But she told me she's single."

"She just offered that?" Nell asks.

"Yeah, sort of."

"Who's the dad?"

"I didn't ask. I've noticed she doesn't wear a wedding ring, but asking outright? It felt intrusive." Francie's expression turns wistful. "She also told me I'm doing a great job with Will. It was sweet. We don't say that to each other enough. Will can be so difficult." Francie breaks a pretzel in half. "I feel like I'm failing at this most of the time. It's nice to hear that maybe I'm not."

"Oh, Francie, don't be silly," Colette says. "Will's great. You're doing fine. None of us know what we're doing."

"Isn't it strange we didn't know that about her?" asks Yuko. "That she's single?"

"Not really." Nell sets her wine beside her and pulls down the stretched collar of her T-shirt. She lifts her daughter, Beatrice, to her breast and begins to feed her. "All we talk about are things related to *the babies*."

"Having a *husband*?" Francie says. "That's kind of related to *the babies*. God, can you imagine? Doing this alone? How lonely."

"I'd die," Colette says. "If Charlie didn't take some of the night feedings, make sure we have diapers, I'd lose my mind."

"Me too, but—" Scarlett starts to speak but then stops herself.

"What?" Colette asks.

"No, nothing."

"No, Scarlett, what?" Francie is staring at her. "What were you going to say?"

Scarlett pauses for a moment. "Okay, fine. I'm worried there's something else going on."

"What do you mean?"

"I don't want to betray anything she's told me, but we've taken a few walks together. We're neighbors, and we seem to travel the same route when we're trying to get the babies to nap. I wouldn't tell you this if I didn't think I needed to, but she's depressed."

"She told you that?" Colette asks.

"She's hinted at it. She's overwhelmed. Doesn't have anyone helping her. She also told me that Midas is a very colicky baby. He can cry for hours."

"Colicky?" Francie asks in disbelief. "*Will* is colicky. Midas seems so easy."

"A friend of mine in London was diagnosed with severe postpartum depression," Nell says. "She felt too ashamed about the thoughts she was having to tell anyone, until her husband forced her to get help."

"I don't know," Colette says. "Winnie doesn't seem depressed to me. It's probably just the baby blues. Who among us hasn't experienced that from time to time?"

"Hey, guys."

They all look up to see Token standing above them, the rise of an infant inside the sling across his chest. He wipes his forehead on the sleeve of his T-shirt. "God, it's hot." He steps out of his sneakers and spreads the blanket he's pulled from his diaper bag on the ground next to Colette's. "Autumn's really fighting her morning nap. I've been walking for an hour to get her to sleep." He sits. "Are you guys drinking wine?"

"We are," says Nell. "Want some?"

"Sure do. Is it any good?"

"Good enough to do the trick."

Francie's gaze remains on Scarlett. "We have to do something, right? Maybe we should organize something for her, give her some time to relax, away from the baby."

"For who?" Token asks.

"Winnie."

Token pauses, his cup suspended halfway to his mouth. "What's wrong with Winnie?"

Francie glances at him. "Nothing's wrong with her. We were just saying maybe she could use a break for a night."

Yuko frowns. "But wait. Maybe she can't afford to. As a single mom? With a sitter, drinks, and dinner, it could be a two-hundred-dollar night."

"I doubt that's an issue," Francie says. "Have you noticed the clothes she wears? She doesn't strike me as someone worried about money. The issue is finding a babysitter."

"I'll ask Alma if she can do it," says Nell.

"Alma?"

Nell's face brightens. "Oh, I forgot to tell you guys. I finally found someone. She's starting tomorrow for a few hours, and then full-time when I'm back at work next week. She's *amazing*. I'll offer to pay her for the night. My departing gift to Winnie." Nell reaches for her phone on the blanket and checks her calendar. "How about the night of July fourth?" She glances up at the group. "Or do you all stay home and recite the Pledge of Allegiance that night?"

"I do," says Colette. "But I'll make an exception this year."

"I'm game," Token says.

"Me too," Francie says. "Yuko? Scarlett?"

"Sure," says Yuko.

Scarlett frowns. "I think my in-laws are coming to see the new house. But I'd hate for you to plan this around me. Who knows how long I'll be in Brooklyn."

"I'll send out an e-mail to all the May Mothers," Nell says. "We'll make a night of it. I'll find someplace fun to go."

"Good," Francie says. "Just make sure you convince Winnie to come."

Nell lays Beatrice on the blanket in front of her. "This will be great. A few hours out. A slice of freedom." She lifts her cup and downs the last of her wine. "Nothing we'll regret. Just one drink."

CHAPTER THREE
JULY 4

TO: May Mothers
FROM: Your friends at The Village
DATE: July 4
SUBJECT: Today's advice
YOUR BABY: DAY 51
This seventh week, your baby should start to master muscle control—kicking, wiggling, and holding her head up, nice and strong. As she grows increasingly physical and in tune with her environment, don't hold back on doling out kisses, smiles, and a few *hip hip hoorays!* showing her how proud Mommy is of all the big leaps she's taking.

8:23 p.m.

The air is heavy with alcohol and heat, the music loud enough to spark an instant headache. It thumps from the speakers, mixing with swells of young laughter. Twentysomethings back in town from college gather at the bar, fingering their parents' credit cards; by the bocce ball court, to wait their turn to throw a ball down a sandy lane; in a dimly lit side room, dancing close together near a shirtless man spinning records.

Nell squeezes her way through the crowd and spots them on the deck out back. Token is sliding together a few tables, hunting for extra chairs. Francie, wearing a black cotton dress showcasing a shocking display of cleavage, is making the rounds, hugging everyone hello: Yuko; Gemma; Colette, who looks even prettier than usual, her shiny hair loose down her back, her lips stained bright pink. A cloud of other women gather nearby, many of whom Nell doesn't recognize, who haven't attended a meeting in a while, whose names she'll never remember.

"Hi," Nell says, approaching Token. He wears the standard Token uniform—a faded T-shirt printed with the name of a band Nell has never heard of, shorts, and scuffed Converse sneakers. "This bar is a bit dodgy, no?"

"It sure is."

"Who picked it?"

"You."

"Oh, right. It's a little rowdier than I expected." She scans the crowd for a waitress, uneasy with how closely Token seems to be examining her. He takes a sip of beer, which leaves a trail of foam on his upper lip. Nell resists the urge to wipe it away with her thumb. "Where'd you get that drink?"

"You have to go to the bar," Token says, leaning in close. "There's no table service right now." Francie is beside them suddenly. Her eyelids glimmer with silver eye shadow.

"Where's Winnie?"

"Hi, Francie. I'm brilliant, thanks for asking."

"Sorry," Francie says. "Hi and all that. But is she coming?"

"Yes. She should be here soon," Nell says, skeptical that Winnie will actually show up. Two e-mails and a phone call, and Winnie still declined to come, saying only that she was unavailable. And then, late last night, Nell got the text, saying she'd changed her mind.

I want to join you, Winnie wrote. Can Alma still babysit?

"I'm assuming she's getting Midas settled with Alma," Nell tells Francie.

"Okay, good. I'll keep an eye out for her."

"And I'll go get a drink." Nell makes her way back inside, toward the bar. She orders a gin and tonic, thinking back to the argument she'd had last week with Sebastian. She'd stood in their bathroom, brushing her teeth, and told Sebastian she'd gone against his wishes and offered Alma the job.

"Nell." There was irritation in his voice.

"What?" She watched him in the mirror.

"We talked about this. I really wish you hadn't done that."

"Why?"

"You know why." He paused. "She's illegal."

She spat into the sink. "You mean undocumented."

"It's not worth the risk."

"To what? Our burgeoning political careers?" Nell rinsed her mouth and stepped past him, walking to the kitchen to turn on the kettle. "I'm pretty sure my career in politics ended in Michael Markham's backyard when I was fifteen."

"You know that's not what I mean. You know you have to be careful—"

She feels a tap on her shoulder as Colette scoots beside her, signaling for the bartender. "You look great," Colette says, glancing down at Nell's shoulder. "And have I told you how much I love that gorgeous tattoo?"

"Wanna know something?" Nell leans in and lifts the bottom of her shirt. "These are maternity pants. The baby is two months old, and I'm *still* wearing maternity pants."

Colette laughs. "The grand reward of pregnancy: discovering wide elastic waistbands." She looks beyond Nell. "Oh, good. She's here."

Nell turns and sees Winnie standing alone near the entrance. She's wearing a fitted yellow dress, which shows off the smooth shine of her neck and breastbones, and a surprisingly flat stomach for a woman who gave birth seven weeks earlier. She seems to be inspecting the crowd around her.

"She looks . . . worried," Nell says. "Right?"

"You think?" Colette is watching her. "Well, who can blame her? It's got to be hard leaving the baby with a stranger for the first time. I still haven't done it."

Nell waves to get Winnie's attention before taking her drink and following Colette back to their table outside, past a group of young men that reek of weed.

"Hi," Winnie says, forcing her way through the throng on the deck, a drink in her hand.

"Everything go okay?" Nell asks.

"Yes. Midas was already asleep when Alma arrived."

"Don't worry about a thing," Nell says. "She's a real pro."

They take their seats and clink glasses—"To May Mothers!" Francie yells over the music—and pledge not to speak of the babies.

"What on earth will we talk about, then?" Token asks dryly. "Our *own* interests?"

"What are those?" Yuko asks.

"Anyone reading any good books?"

"I just got that new sleep-training book," says Francie. "*Twelve Weeks to Peace*."

"Have you guys read that other one everyone's talking about?" Gemma asks. "*The French Approach*, or something?"

"I don't think this counts as not talking about the babies," Nell says. "Colette, help us out here. What are you reading?"

"Nothing. I can't read when I'm writing a book. It messes with my head too much."

"You're writing a book?"

Colette glances away from Nell, as if she hadn't intended to disclose that information.

"Wait," Nell says. "We've been friends for four months, and you're just coming around to sharing this news now?"

Colette shrugs. "Talk of our work hasn't really come up."

"What kind of book?" asks a woman toward the end of the

table, her nails painted neon orange—the one, Nell believes, who has twins.

"A memoir."

"At your age? Impressive."

Colette rolls her eyes. "Not really. The memoir's not mine. I'm a ghostwriter."

"What do you mean?" Francie asks. "Like, you're writing a famous person's book?"

"Sort of. I wish I could say who, but—" Colette waves her hand and looks toward Winnie who, Nell has noticed, has been staring down at her phone since sitting down. "Everything okay?" Colette asks her.

Winnie clicks off the screen. "Yes, fine."

Nell takes note of Winnie's fingernails, bitten to the quick, and the thinly veiled look of concern under her smile. Even before Scarlett told them Winnie had admitted to feeling over-whelmed, Nell was aware how distracted Winnie often appeared, how down she seemed on occasion, how she was beginning to miss so many meetings.

A waiter with a shaved head and a line of stud earrings above one eyebrow approaches the table. "Table service is open, ladies. What'll it be?"

Nell rests her hand on Winnie's arm. "What are you drinking? This round's on me."

Winnie smiles. "Iced tea."

Nell sits back in her chair. "Iced tea?"

"Yeah. They have good iced tea. Unsweetened."

"*Good* unsweetened iced tea? There's not even such a thing." She raises her eyebrows. "I don't want to get all before-the-tenth-grade-school-dance on you, but tonight is about getting a proper drink."

"I'm fine," Winnie says, glancing at the waiter. "Just the iced tea."

"Suit yourself," Nell says, raising her glass. "Another gin and tonic for me. Who knows when I'll be able to get another night out like this."

"I don't know how you're going to do it," Francie says after the waiter finishes taking orders and leaves. "Go back to work *next week*."

"Oh, don't be silly," Nell says. "It'll be fine. I'm antsy to get back to work, in fact." She looks away, hoping nobody can sense the truth: she's sick about the thought of cutting short her maternity leave in just five more days. She's not ready to leave the baby, not yet, but she doesn't have a choice. Her company, the Simon French Corporation, the nation's largest magazine publisher, is forcing her back.

"Of course, we're not *forcing* you back, Nell," Ian said when he called from the office three weeks ago to "check in" on things. "It's just that well, you're the chief technology officer, and this switch to the new security system is the entire reason we hired you." He paused. "You're the only person who can do this. The timing is bad, but this is important."

Important? Nell wanted to ask Ian, her cowlicked cartoon character of a boss. Ian of the ironically preppy belts—navy blue with pink whales, bright green with woven pineapples. *What* was important? Making sure nobody hacked into their secure files? Keeping away the shadowy Russian operatives intent on gaining access to the painfully dull interview with Catherine Ferris, some reality television star, uncovering her heavily guarded top secret tips to clear skin (two tablespoons of fish oil every morning, a cup of jasmine tea each night)?

Nell peers down the table at the crowd of women, their faces slack with pity. "Oh, come on, ladies," she says. "It's good for babies to see their mothers going off to work. It makes them self-reliant." *And what am I supposed to do?* she wants to ask. She can't risk being replaced, not with how much it costs to live in New

York, not with the rent on their two-bedroom apartment two blocks from the park, not with their student loans. She makes more than twice what Sebastian earns as an assistant curator at MoMA, and it's her salary that allows them a life in New York. She can't jeopardize everything for four more weeks of unpaid maternity leave.

"I went to Whole Foods yesterday," Colette says, her stack of gold bracelets catching the light. "The cashier told me she was given just four weeks off after having her baby. Unpaid, of course."

"That's against the law," Yuko says. "They have to hold her job for three months."

"I told her that. But she just shrugged."

"I have a friend who lives in Copenhagen," Gemma says. "She got eighteen months of leave after she had her son. *Paid*."

"In Canada," Colette says, "they have to hold a woman's job for a year. In fact, the US is the only country besides Papua New Guinea that doesn't mandate paid leave. The *United States*. The country of family values."

Nell takes a drink, feeling the alcohol going to work on her muscles. "Do you think if we remind people that babies were fetuses not so long ago, more will be inclined to support maternity leave?"

"Listen to this," Yuko says, reading aloud from her phone. "Finland: seventeen weeks paid leave. Australia: eighteen weeks. Japan: fourteen weeks. America: zero weeks."

The song changes, Billy Idol's "Rebel Yell" blasts from the speakers. Nell points a finger in the air and sings along. "*She don't like slavery. She won't sit and beg. But when I'm tired and lonely, she sees me to bed*. This should be the anthem of motherhood," she says. "Our fight song. *I walked the ward with you, babe. A thousand miles with you. I dried your tears of pain, babe. A million times for you*."

Nell notices Winnie looking at the phone in her lap again and reaches down, takes it from her hands, and places it on the table.

"Come on, dance with me," she says, standing up and tugging Winnie to her feet. "*I'd give you all and have none babe, justa justa justa just to have you here by me, because—* Here we go!" Nell clutches Winnie's hand as the volume surges, as every woman at the table explodes into song at the refrain. "*In the midnight hour, we need more, more, more. With a rebel yell, we cry more, more, more.*"

Nell laughs and raises her glass. "Slash the patriarchy!" she yells.

Winnie smiles and then gently pulls her hand from Nell's and looks away from the table, past Nell, beyond the crowd pressing around them, as the flash of someone's camera, for just a moment, lights the features of her perfect face.

9:17 p.m.

At the bar, Colette has to holler twice to be heard—a whiskey on the rocks—thinking about making it a double, her hips moving to the music. The bartender slides the drink toward her, and she takes a long sip. It's been months since she's been out like this, enjoying a drink with friends, neither tending to Poppy nor worrying about the book and its quickly approaching deadline. Most nights at this time she'd be sitting with her laptop in bed (the room she envisioned as her home office when Charlie's parents bought them the apartment two years earlier has since become the nursery), staring at a blank page, feeling exhausted and inept. *How did I used to write?* she wonders. She completed an entire book—the memoir of Emmanuel Dubois, the aging supermodel—in sixteen weeks, but since she had Poppy, words have become like wisps of air, outpacing her brain's ability to capture them.

She takes another sip, savoring the warmth of the whiskey in her throat, and feels a hand on her lower back. She turns to see Token.

"Hey," he says. She moves aside, and he slips between her and a woman in a straw cowboy hat who is vying for the bartender's attention. "It's a million degrees out there."

"No kidding. You want a drink?"

"Sorry, what?"

She leans in closer to him. "Can I get you a drink?"

"I'm good." He holds up his glass, half full. "I saw you come inside. Thought I'd say hi, take in the air-conditioning."

She smiles and then looks away. She's been with Charlie for fifteen years, an entire lifetime it seems, but Token is just the type of guy she would have once been attracted to: quiet, unassuming, and probably surprisingly good in bed. Nell is sure he's gay ("I heard it myself," Nell said. "He used the word *partner*."), but Colette doubts it. She's been watching him these past several weeks, since he arrived at a May Mothers meeting alongside Winnie. Colette can tell by the way Token looks at Winnie sometimes, his tendency to touch her arm when they speak, that he's unquestionably straight.

"So," he says. "You can't tell us whose book you're writing, but can you tell me how it's going? I can't imagine having to write a book *and* manage a newborn."

Colette considers lying and telling him the story she's been telling Charlie—*it's fine, I'm managing*—but she decides, instead, to admit the truth. "It's awful. I accepted the job two weeks before discovering I was pregnant." She grimaces playfully. "The baby wasn't exactly planned."

He holds her gaze and nods. "You going to pull it off?"

Colette shrugs, and her hair comes loose from its knot, spilling over her shoulders and down her back. "When I'm writing, I feel a need to be with Poppy. And when I'm with her, all I think about is that I need to be writing. But I assured the editor *and* the mayor that the baby isn't going to interfere with meeting the deadline in four weeks. Wanna know the truth? I'm at least a month behind."

He raises his eyebrows. "The mayor? As in Mayor Teb Shepherd?"

Colette feels a hot stitch of regret. "I'm usually good at keeping secrets. Blame it on this dark, delicious whiskey. But yeah, I'm writing his second memoir."

Token nods. "Like everyone else in the world, I read his first." He takes a slow drink of his beer. "You write that one, too?"

She nods.

"I'm impressed."

"Don't tell the others, okay? I don't even know why I mentioned it back there. This is a pretty hard-core stay-at-home-mom crowd. My situation is complicated."

"Don't worry." He leans in. "I'm good at keeping secrets, too." A man behind him pushes forward, pressing Token up against Colette. He nods toward the deck. "Shall we?"

They walk back outside and take their seats just as Francie starts to ding her glass with a knife. "I hate to break up the conversation," Francie says. "But it's time."

"For what?" Nell asks.

Francie turns toward Winnie. "Winnie?"

Winnie lifts her gaze from the phone in her lap. "Yes?"

"It's your turn."

"My turn?" She seems caught off guard by the attention of the table. "For what?"

"To tell your birth story." Colette likes Francie. She's so good-natured and young—from the looks of it, probably not yet thirty—a triple exclamation point of a woman. But Colette wishes she'd let up on this ritual. It was Scarlett's idea, back when they were all still pregnant, to start each meeting with someone sharing their birth plan. After the babies were born, the practice morphed into long, detailed stories of people's birth experiences, and there is very little point in denying what it really is. A competition. Who performed their opening act of motherhood best? Who was the fiercest? Who among them (the C-section moms) had failed? Colette has been hoping the group might soon drop the whole thing, and yet she can't deny feeling curious to hear what Winnie has to say.

But Winnie just glances around the table. "You know what? I'm going to take Nell's advice. I'm going to get a drink. A proper one." She nods at Token's empty glass. "Want to join me?"

"Sure," Token says.

Colette watches them leave and then turns to catch some of the conversations happening around her—doing her best to stay engaged, surprised at how quickly she's finished her second drink, wondering if she should get one more. She rises to use the restroom. On the way, she catches sight of Winnie standing at the bar. She's speaking to a guy—an astonishingly handsome one. He's wearing a bright red baseball cap, and he's leaning in, talking into her ear. Token is nowhere to be seen. Colette senses that she should avert her eyes, that she's witnessing something she isn't supposed to see. But she doesn't look away. Instead, she steps around a couple in front of her to get a better look. The guy's hand is on Winnie's waist and he's fingering the tie of her dress. He whispers something, and she pulls back, staring him in the eye, annoyed. Something about him, the way he's positioning his body so close to hers, something about her expression—

"You good?" Nell asks. She's appeared in front of Colette, blocking her view of Winnie, a menu in her hand.

"Fine. On my way to the bathroom."

"I mean, are you hungry? I can order you something."

"No, thanks," Colette says. "I ate." Nell walks toward the waitress station, and Colette looks back at the bar.

They're gone.

She scans the crowd and then moves toward the bathroom, snaking through the people at the bocce ball court to take her place in line behind a trio of young women wearing nearly identical outfits, texting on their phones. Colette shakes her head. He's someone Winnie knows, she decides. The uneasiness she feels is the result of the whiskey and exhaustion; just her mind playing a trick, like it has a few times these last few days, like this morning, when she absentmindedly poured coffee into one of Poppy's bottles.

She finishes in the bathroom and goes outside to the sidewalk to call Charlie, who tells her Poppy is asleep and he's working on the latest revisions to his novel. "Take your time," he says. "Everything's under control here." Returning to the table, she sits down beside Francie and sees the phone, tucked next to the sticky mason jars of hot sauce in front of where Token had been sitting.

"Where's Token?" she asks Francie, who is putting her own phone into her bag.

"He left."

"You're kidding. When?"

"A minute ago. It was weird. He rushed out. Said something came up at home."

"That's odd. I was outside, calling Charlie. I didn't see him." Colette reaches for the phone. "He left this."

Nell returns, balancing two plates of steaming french fries. "What kind of bar doesn't serve vinegar with their fries?" she asks, taking her seat. "That would be a federal offense in England." Nell notices Colette. "Seriously? First Winnie and now you, glued to your phone. Did we come out tonight for the sole purpose of staring at our mobiles?"

"It's not hers," Francie says, pushing away the plate of french fries and reaching for her water. "It's Token's. He left it."

"Actually, no. It's Winnie's." Colette flips the phone around, showing them the photo of Midas wallpapering the screen. "There's a key here, too. Inside the case."

"Where is she?" Francie asks. "She hasn't come back from getting that drink."

Colette swipes the screen, which lights up with a fuzzy video, glowing bright algae-green. "Wait, what is *this*?" She turns the phone toward Nell and Francie again. "Is that Midas's bedroom?"

Francie snatches the phone from Colette's hand. "It's a video. That's his crib."

"Lemme see," Nell says. Francie hesitates. "Francie, let me see it. I think it's that app." Nell licks the salt from her fingers and takes the phone from Francie. "It is. I know the person who developed this."

"You do?" Francie asks. "How?"

"I worked with him in DC after college, doing data security. It's a good idea. You can watch the baby monitor on your phone, as long as you're on Wi-Fi."

"I've heard of this," Francie says. "Peek-a-Boo! I was thinking of getting it, but it's like twenty-five bucks or something. For an app? That's insane."

"What's insane is that this is what she's been looking at," Nell says. "A grainy video of Midas's crib."

"I don't see what's wrong with that," Francie says.

"What's the point of paying a babysitter if you're going to watch the baby all night?" Nell asks.

"It's her first time leaving him. Give her a break," Francie says. "Really though, where is she?"

"She was talking to some guy," Colette says. "A ridiculously hot one."

"I saw that too," says Francie. "He walked right up to her, when she went to the bar. But that was like fifteen minutes ago."

Francie cranes her neck to scan the crowd. "He was a little forward. Did you see how he was touching her? I'm going to go find her. She probably wants to have her phone with her."

Francie reaches out her hand, but Nell cradles the phone to her chest. "She's a single mom, away from her baby for the first time. Let the woman have some fun."

"Nell," Colette says, glancing at the glass in front of Nell, wondering how many drinks she's had. "Don't be weird. She's going to want her phone."

"Just a sec." Nell swipes the screen.

"What are you doing?" Francie asks.

"Having what I'm sure is a wholly terrible idea."

"What?" Colette asks.

Nell is silent as she swipes, presses, and then turns off the screen. "Done."

"What did you do?"

"I deleted the app. The Peek-a-Boo! thing. It's gone."

"Nell!" says Francie, covering her mouth.

"Oh, please. Let's be real. We're here tonight for *her*. So she can unwind, get a break. Staring at the baby doesn't qualify as either of those things." Nell reaches down to put Winnie's phone in her purse. "It's fine. It's for her own good. It will take her two minutes to reinstall it if she wants to."

Colette is aware of a growing ache behind her eyes—the music, the crowd building around them on the deck, what Nell just did. She's ready to go home.

"At least give me her phone," Francie says. "Her key's in there. Let me hold it until she comes back to the table."

"I got it. Relax." Nell turns her back to Colette and leans toward the women on the other side of her. "What are you guys talking about?"

"My sister," one says. "She's thirty weeks and just found out she has a prolapsed uterus. It sucks. She has to get a labial hitch."

"What on earth is a labial hitch?"

"I know," Nell says, a little too loudly. "You stick it in your vagina. There's a hook on the end, for pulling the stroller. Makes grocery shopping and trips to the Laundromat easier." She rattles the ice cubes in her glass and swallows the last of her drink. "I'll be right back." She stands, singing under her breath, and walks toward the bar. "*I want more, more, more. More more more.*"

10:04 p.m.

"I think she needs less, less, less," Francie says to Colette, waving away a cloud of smoke from people lighting cigarettes at the deck railing, in front of the No Smoking sign. She waits as long as she can bear before peeking at her phone inside her bag. It's been twelve minutes, and Lowell still hasn't responded to the text she sent him. The night is only growing more humid—a heavy humidity unlike anything she experienced in Tennessee—and her head is beginning to throb. Day three without caffeine, and she's feeling it. She's been dying for even a sip of coffee, but she can't do it. Everything she's been reading says the very best thing to do if your milk supply is decreasing is to give up caffeine. Will's been so irritable and unhappy these past few days. He's never been an easy baby—the nurse who answers the nonemergency line at the pediatrician's office keeps telling Francie it's a classic case of colic. That it will pass around the fifth week. But Will is seven weeks and two days, and it's only getting worse. It's not colic, she's decided. He's irritable because she's run out of milk and is starving him. Certainly she can give up caffeine if it will help.

She decides to text Lowell one more time, knowing he'll tell her to stop obsessing about the baby and have fun. But she hasn't been able to stop thinking about Will since she left the apartment, sure he's spent the last two hours screaming inconsolably, the way he sometimes does in the evenings, making himself sick.

Everything okay? Did you get my last few messages? She hits send and feels immediately relieved to see the three dots signaling that Lowell is responding. She waits, clutching her phone.

Do you want the good news or bad?

A blast of fear courses through her body. What happened? She sends the message and waits. Lowell, answer me. What's the bad news?

Three dots. Nothing. Three dots. The Cardinals suck.

She exhales. Don't do that please. How's the baby?

That's the good news. Sleeping. Took the bottle and passed out.

Francie feels a twinge of worry. She told Lowell to give Will the bottle of formula she'd prepared *only* if the baby was upset. It was Will's first time ever having formula. She's been setting her alarm the last few mornings, hoping to wake before him to pump extra milk, but she's gotten hardly anything, not even half an ounce.

She types Does that mean he was very upset, but then someone sits on the chair next to her. She looks up, hoping it's Winnie returning to the table. But it's Colette.

"I just did a quick round of the bar," Colette says. "I can't find Winnie."

Francie drops her phone into her purse. "It's so strange. She can't still be talking to that guy."

"Why not?" Colette asks. "She *is* single. Maybe she went home with him."

"Went *home* with him? She wouldn't do that."

"Why not?"

"Because she wouldn't leave without her phone and key. And because she has to get home to Midas."

"I don't know. The others are beginning to leave. I kind of want to go too."

"We can't leave without her," Francie says, looking increasingly concerned. "And now where on earth is Nell?"

A group of young women comes noisily onto the deck, lighting each other's cigarettes off a shared lighter, planting themselves on the laps of young men claiming the chairs left vacant by the May Mothers who've since gone home to their babies. "I'm going to look for her," Francie says.

Inside, she circles the bar, checking the side room, weaving her way around dancing couples, the beat of the bass thudding inside her chest. Winnie isn't there. She isn't by the bocce ball courts either, or on the sidewalk out front, or, as far as Francie can tell from peering under the stalls, in the bathroom. She pauses at the mirror; two glasses of champagne have left her lightheaded. She sponges a wet paper towel along her neck and returns to the table, nearly bumping into Nell on the way.

"There you are. Where have you been?" Francie notices a wobble to Nell's step, a darkness in her eyes.

Nell holds up a glass. "Getting a drink."

"This whole time? Were you with Winnie?"

"Winnie? No. I haven't seen her since, well, you know."

"No, what do you mean? Since when?"

"Since before. When I saw her."

Francie takes Nell's elbow. "Come on."

Colette is alone at the table. "Where is everyone?" Nell asks.

"Everyone left. It's time to go."

"Already?"

"Yes," Colette says. "Can I have Winnie's phone?"

"Her phone?" Nell sits down. "Right. Her phone." She lifts her purse but then drops it, the contents spilling onto the floor. "Shit," she says, dropping clumsily to her knees. She tosses a scuffed wallet and a travel pack of wet wipes back inside. "This bloody purse. It's too big."

Francie crouches down and retrieves a sunglasses case. "Is it in there?"

"No," Nell says. She pinches the bridge of her nose. "I wish they'd turn the music down. My head is killing me."

"Call Winnie's number and see if we hear it ringing," Colette suggests as Francie and Nell rise to stand, Nell holding on to the table to steady herself.

"She didn't come back here and take it, right? One of us would have seen her." Francie looks around the room again. "Do you think she went home? That would be such a bummer. I really wanted her to have a fun night."

"Winnie told Alma she'd be back by ten thirty," Nell says. "She has a one-year-old and doesn't like to babysit at night."

The waiter approaches. "Another round?"

"No," says Nell, waving him away. "No more drinks."

"We're all still walking home together, right?" Francie says. "I know it's not far, but I don't want to walk home alone."

"I'm ready," Colette says. "I've had one too many, and I have to work tomorrow."

A phone rings from inside Nell's purse. "Oh thank god," Francie says. "Is that Winnie's phone?"

Nell is again fishing inside her bag. "No, that's mine." She closes one eye and squints at the screen. "That's weird. *Hello?*" She puts her finger to her ear. "Slow down, I can't hear you." Nell is silent, listening. And then something changes in her expression.

"What?" Francie asks. "Who is it?"

Nell is nodding slowly.

"Nell," Francie says. "Say someth—"

But before she can finish, Nell opens her mouth, her voice strangled with terror, the sound coming out like a moan. "*Noooooooo.*"

10:32 p.m.

"What do you mean, Midas is gone?"

"I don't know. That's what Alma said."

"Gone where?"

"I don't *know.* Gone. He's not in his crib."

"Not in his crib?"

"Yes."

"What does that mean?"

"I don't know. She went to check on him, and his crib was empty. It was hard to understand her. She's a mess."

"Is Winnie there? She must have gone home and taken him somewhere."

"No. Alma called her, but it went to voice mail. Where the *hell* is her phone?"

"Did Alma contact the police?"

"Yes. They haven't arrived yet. She's there, waiting."

Francie grabs her bag. "Come on. Let's go."

10:51 p.m.

The sound of their feet beating the pavement and their gasps for breath echo through the streets, which are uncharacteristically deserted, everyone away for the holiday weekend, or gathered along the river, collecting overtired children and empty coolers of beer, having waited longer than they'd expected for the fireworks to begin.

"Up here," Colette yells, steps ahead of Nell and Francie. "One more block."

She stops in front of an ornate Gothic building on the corner. The address plate, No. 50, throbs red and blue from the flashing lights of a police car parked nearby. "Is this her building?" Francie asks.

"Number fifty?" Nell's out of breath; her words are slurred. "That's the address she asked me to give Alma."

Colette climbs the L-shaped stoop to the front door. She searches for a row of buzzers. "There's just one doorbell. What is her apartment number?"

"Wait, look." Francie is pointing and then running around

the corner to a landscaped path that leads to a red door, left slightly ajar, on the side of the building.

Colette and Nell are close behind as Francie steps quietly into an entrance foyer. A dozen oversize Rothkoesque paintings hang on the pale gray walls, the ceilings are at least twenty feet high, and four wide marble steps lead to a hallway, down which they can hear someone sobbing.

"Oh my god," Nell says. "This entire building is her house."

They follow the sound, making their way down the hall and into a large chef's kitchen, off which is a skylit staircase. A uniformed police officer, his name badge reading CABRERA, stands on the steps, listening to a crackling radio attached at his shoulder.

"Who are you?"

"Winnie's friends," Colette says. "Is she here?"

"Get out," he says, visibly annoyed.

"Can we just—" Francie says.

"Out," he says, probing his pockets for his ringing cell phone and turning abruptly to rush up the stairs. "This is a crime scene."

They ignore him and continue on into a large living room. When they enter, they see her.

Winnie has curled into herself on a chair in front of a wall of night-blackened glass, her arms wrapped around her knees, a blanket the color of cream draped over her shoulders. Her eyes are vacant as she tugs at her lower lip. A detective is sitting a few feet away, writing in a notebook, a forgotten takeout coffee on the floor beside him.

"It was the pasta," Alma is saying from the other end of the room, out of earshot of Winnie, her words stuttered by sobs. She sits on a soft leather sectional, clutching a rosary in one hand, pausing every so often to close her eyes and wave a handful of crumpled tissues at the ceiling, offering a prayer in a Spanish none of them can understand. She ate too much of the baked ziti she brought from home. It made her lethargic, and she took her phone to the sofa to say good night to her baby, at home with Alma's sister. She must have fallen asleep—that's so unlike her, she insists, throwing a shamefaced glance at Winnie, but her daughter was up four times the night before, teething. When she woke up, she checked the monitor. The crib looked empty.

"You heard nothing?" a second detective is asking. His scruffy gray eyebrows threaten to take over his forehead, and he wears a college ring on one of his thick fingers. An NYPD badge with his name in block letters—STEPHEN SCHWARTZ— dangles from a thin chain around his neck, swinging back and forth, just barely, like the pendulum on a dying clock.

"Nothing," Alma says, and then starts to sob again.

"Nothing like footsteps? No crying?"

"Nothing. No crying." Schwartz takes the box of Kleenex from the table and extends it to her. Alma pulls, sending a poof of tissue dust into the air around his face. "The monitor. It was right there." She wipes her eyes and points to where the detective is sitting. "Right there where you're sitting. The whole time."

"And the monitor was on?"

"Yes."

"You didn't turn it off?"

"No. I didn't touch it, except to check it a few times."

"What did you see when you checked it?"

"The baby. He was sleeping. It wasn't until I woke up that I realized he was gone."

"And what did you do when you first noticed?"

"What did I do?"

"Yeah. Did you check the window in his room? Did you look around the house? Check upstairs?"

"No. I told you. I ran back here for my cell phone. It was on the table. I called Winnie but she didn't answer."

"And then what?"

"And then I called Nell."

"Did you drink anything?"

"Drink anything? Of course not. Other than the iced tea Winnie made for me."

"She made you iced tea," Schwartz says, writing something in his notebook. He lowers his voice. "And where did you say the mother was again?"

"Out."

"Out, right. But did she tell you where, exactly?"

"I forget. She wrote it down. Out drinking."

He looks up, his eyebrows raised. "Out drinking, you said?"

"Final warning, ladies," says the police officer named Cabrera from the stairwell, walking past them with a woman in a police jacket. "Find your way out. Don't make me tell you again."

"We're going," Colette says. Francie and Nell follow her back down the hall, back into the foyer, back out onto the silent sidewalk. But not before they all walk over to Winnie, squeezing her hand. Not before they hug her so long they bring home the scent of her shampoo. Not before Francie kneels down to take Winnie's face in her hands, their eyes inches apart. "They'll find him, Winnie. They will. We'll all have Midas back. *I promise.*" And not before they stand at the rail of her terrace, gazing out across Brooklyn at millions of windows, behind which babies sleep, safe and sound—the inhabitants possibly looking back at them, three shattered mothers, their hair whipping in the hot July wind, their hearts full of dread.

CHAPTER FOUR
DAY ONE

> **TO:** May Mothers
> **FROM:** Your friends at The Village
> **DATE:** July 5
> **SUBJECT:** Today's advice
>
> <u>YOUR BABY: DAY 52</u>
>
> How many times have you heard *this* advice: sleep when the baby sleeps. We know it might seem tiring (ha!) to hear it, but it's true. Some moms find it difficult to relax when the little one does, so here are some tips: Avoid caffeine and sugary drinks. Practice some of the breathing exercises you perfected in preparation for giving birth. Try a glass of warm milk, a square of cheese, or even a little turkey breast before bed—these foods contain tryptophan, which will help encourage a good night's sleep.

Francie stands in her tiny kitchen, lost in front of an open cupboard that's shaded pink with the rising sun, resisting the urge to drink the errant Diet Coke she spotted in the fridge. She can't have slept more than two hours last night, between finally falling asleep on Lowell's shoulder, and waking up in a panic. She dreamed she'd left Will in the grocery store, asleep in his stroller by the yogurt case. It took her so long to choose from among the eight types of yogurts, all the different flavors, and by the time she realized what she'd done, she was halfway home. She raced back to the store, her muscles weak, her clothes damp with sweat. When she lifted the hood of the stroller, it was empty. Will was gone.

The dream jerked her upright, and she lurched toward the cosleeper. It was only after she pressed her palm to Will's chest, feeling the soft rise and fall of his breath, that she could trust it was a dream. Will was still there, asleep beside her. But the commotion had startled him awake with a cry so desperate she doesn't know how Lowell slept through it. It then took two hours of walking him around the living room, up and down the narrow hall, shushing him, rocking him, nursing him through the pain in her right breast, before he finally fell back asleep, rotating a slow circle in the baby swing, his fingers curled like parentheses around his eyes.

She, meanwhile, was wide awake. For the last two hours, she's been pacing the living room, seven steps back and forth, ice cubes melting in one of the baby's washcloths on the back of her neck, seeing Winnie's face as she spoke to the detective the night before. Francie is still trying to piece together the events of the evening and make sense of what happened. Winnie arrived. She seemed quiet but not unhappy. Francie suggested she tell her birth story, and then she and Token went to the bar for a drink. Winnie was talking to that guy. And then, suddenly, she was gone.

Francie is plagued with guilt. If only she hadn't lost sight of Winnie. If only she hadn't handed Winnie's phone to Nell. She's furious with herself for trusting Nell with that phone—Nell, who was clearly drunk by the end of the night. Francie couldn't have been the only one to notice the way she spilled the french fries on her lap, the cloudiness of her eyes, never mind the fact that she brought wine to the May Mothers meeting last week.

Francie opens the refrigerator for the eggs, and searches for the green pepper she swore she bought. Lowell is always telling her to stop with the what-ifs, but *what if*? What if she had insisted, like she'd wanted to, on keeping the phone? What if Nell hadn't been able to delete the Peek-a-Boo! app? Francie would have kept the phone on the table, right in front of her—she's sure that's what she would have done. And then maybe the movement in Midas's room would have sprung the screen to life, and she would have seen Midas in his crib, and then a person standing over him. She would have told Nell to call Alma, which would have woken her up. She would have called the police. Midas would still be—

She feels a hand on her waist, on the thick roll of flesh above the elastic of her pajamas, and she recoils so quickly she drops the eggs, emptying the entire carton onto her feet, the yolks leaking between her toes.

"Sorry," Lowell says. "I didn't mean to scare you."

The scent of Irish Spring soap rises from his skin. "I didn't hear you get up." Three of the eggs have broken on the counter, and Francie wonders for a moment if she can salvage them, pick out the pieces of shell and scramble them with some milk. She can't bear the idea of the grocery store. Not today. Not the narrow, crowded aisles or the endless checkout lines, not the long walk home in this heat with a baby strapped to her chest, her thighs chafing under her last clean skirt, shopping bags swinging painfully from both forearms. Lowell goes to the closet for the mop as she wipes the threads of egg yolk from her feet with a paper towel. It's only then she notices he's dressed for the office. "Are you leaving right now?"

"In a few minutes."

"But it's not even seven. I thought we could have breakfast together."

He nudges her toes out of the way with the mop. "I'm sorry. I have to prepare for tomorrow."

"What's tomorrow?"

He raises his eyebrows. "You're kidding."

Of course. The meeting. He's been preoccupied with it for days—the final round of interviews; a renovation of a former church into a boutique hotel. How could she have forgotten? The job would be his biggest contract, more money than they've made since Lowell decided two years ago to quit the firm in Knoxville and move to New York—a city she had never even *visited*—to start a private practice with a friend from architecture school. She tried to get him to reconsider. ("They need buildings designed right here in Tennessee," she kept telling him.) But this was his dream, he said, so of course she'd agreed to move. "Plus," he reasoned, "the hospitals in New York are the best. Maybe the IVF thing will work better there."

"Sorry. Of course I remember." She wipes her hands on her shirt—a baggy tank top she wore throughout the pregnancy, now stained with cream cheese and brittle beads of breast milk—and takes the mop from Lowell. "We really need this job. Are you ready for it?"

He nods and steps past her to open the refrigerator. "Almost. You okay?"

"The story's in the paper."

He stops. "Already?"

"Yeah, the *New York Post*." She'd found it on her phone while nursing the baby at 3:00 a.m., behind the click of a small headline: KIDNAPPING CONCERN FOR MISSING BROOKLYN BABY. "It was a short article. The police are saying there was no sign of forced entry. They didn't mention Winnie's name, but of course it's her."

"It's got to be a misunderstanding. Maybe his dad came to get him."

"What dad? There is no dad."

"Really?" He makes a face. "She's the virgin Mary?"

"No. I mean—if that was the case, they would have written that. They're treating it like a case of child abduction."

"Don't worry, France. They'll find him." He touches her arm. "It's probably a mix-up. A family member or something. It usually is." He slides two bruised bananas from the bowl on the counter into the outer pocket of his laptop case. "Try not to think about it. I'll be back for lunch."

She kisses him good-bye, trying not to betray her disappointment that he has to work. Leaving her alone, in the wake of this terrible news.

He's doing it for us, she reminds herself as she rinses the empty beer bottle he left on the counter the night before. He works all the time to pay the rent. Cover their health insurance. Buy the eggs she's just wasted. Of course he has to work long hours, never mind his desire to spend more time with the baby, with the two of them. And she has to understand. After all, she was the one who convinced him to use the wedding money his parents gave them on IVF, and then, after the first round failed, begged him to ask his brother, the successful anesthesiologist in Memphis, for a loan to try again.

The sound of the door closing behind Lowell wakes Will. She lifts his warm body from the swing before he can cry, and carries him down the hall to their bedroom, on to the makeshift changing table she'd fashioned on top of their dresser. The morning stretches interminably in front of her—at least five hours to kill before Lowell will come home for lunch. Why hasn't she planned something? What she really wants is to e-mail the May Mothers, ask if anyone is free for an impromptu meetup. She wants to be with them, together with the babies under the willow tree, talking about Midas, processing what happened. But that's not an option. Last night, after leaving Winnie's, Colette convinced them that it wasn't their place to tell the group; that they should wait for Winnie to share the news. And Francie knows that even if the others happen to have seen that *New York Post* article, even if they've read that a baby has been abducted in

Brooklyn, they'll never think for a moment that it could be their neighborhood; that it is actually one of *them*.

In fact, Francie saw that while she was with Colette and Nell at Winnie's, Yuko was at home, creating a photo album on the May Mothers Facebook page—A NIGHT OUT—inviting people to upload their photos from the Jolly Llama. Francie couldn't bear to open it, to see the images of everyone enjoying themselves while Midas was being snatched from his crib, stolen away from his mother.

She carries Will to the living room, stepping around a basket spilling over with dirty clothes and burp cloths. She has more than enough laundry to do to fill the morning, she decides, just as her phone rings.

"Hello." The word comes out too eager. She doesn't recognize the number and thinks—hopes—that it's Winnie calling to say Midas has been found. Lowell was right. It was just a mix-up. But it's not Winnie.

"Hello, Mary Frances. It's your mother."

Francie freezes. "Mom. Hi." She takes the remote and mutes the television. There's silence on the other end of the phone. "Sorry," she says. "I didn't recognize your number."

"I got a cell phone."

"You did?" Francie can't believe it. Marilyn Cletis, the woman who prohibited music in her house, sewed all of their clothes, the person who kept a cow to provide raw milk for her children—this woman now has a *cell phone*?

"Yes. A friend from church convinced me it was time. I can even text on it."

"That's great, Mom."

"I got the birth announcement you sent. Cute photo. But . . ."

"What?"

"Kalani?"

"Yes. William Kalani. I told you that. We're calling him Will."

"Is that a black name?"

Francie snickers before she can stop herself. "A black name? No. It's Hawaiian." She heard it on their honeymoon. It means "sent from the heavens." It's the perfect name for her son.

"Oh. I thought maybe it was a New York thing." She can hear her mother putting away dishes. "I told your grandfather. I'm not sure he understood completely, but he did seem honored you chose William."

Francie has been unwilling to tell her the baby is not, in fact, named after Marilyn's largely absent father, but after Lowell, whose middle name is William. Francie lays Will gently on the play mat, under the jingling band of farm animals, and stands in front of the window fan, waving her shirt away from her body. "I'm sorry I haven't had time to call recently," she says. "Things are a little hectic."

"You don't have to tell me. I was a mother once, too." Marilyn pauses, but Francie is unsure how to respond. "How's the baby?"

"Good," Francie says. "Mostly. I'm having some trouble nursing. He doesn't seem to be getting enough food."

"So give him formula. Put a little baby cereal in it."

"Oh. They don't really use that anymore. And I'm trying not to—"

"People at church have been praying for you. Cora Lee asked me how the birth went and I realized I don't know. You never told me."

"I didn't?" Francie feels herself lighten. "It was perfect. I was able to do it naturally, without any pain medication." It wasn't easy. About a thousand times during the nine-hour labor she'd wanted to give up and get the epidural, but she powered through it, walking circles around the hospital room, slow dancing with Lowell through the pain. She can't help but notice the admiring way Lowell now looks at her sometimes: not as his five-foot-three-inch average-looking wife with the thick thighs and unruly curls going prematurely gray at thirty-one, but as an unstoppable, fire-breathing warrior, giving birth to a healthy seven-pound son, and on Mother's Day, no less.

"Naturally? What does that mean? You didn't have an epidural?"

"No. Not even one Advil."

Silence. "On purpose?"

"Yes."

"Why would you do something like that?"

Francie closes her eyes, feeling ten years old again. She keeps her voice steady. "Because I wanted—Lowell and I wanted the most natural birth experience. Unmedicated births are now—"

Marilyn chuckles. "Oh, Mary Frances, that's so like you. You can't do anything like everyone else." Francie is surprised to feel tears burning the back of her throat. "Anyway, I'm calling because I have something for William. A christening dress." Marilyn pauses. "And I'd like to come visit."

"Visit?" She didn't think Marilyn would ever come to New York. She's never stepped foot out of Tennessee. "You don't have to do that, Mom. Lowell and I are saving for plane tickets home for you to meet Will."

"The baptism is probably soon. I could look into a flight, next weekend perhaps? You'll need help, I imagine."

"I'm sorry, Mom. Next weekend doesn't work." She racks her brain for a plausible excuse. "Lowell has a big interview. He's working all the time, and he'd feel bad if he couldn't spend time with you. Plus, the May Mothers. We're—"

"The May Mothers?"

"It's a group of friends I've made. A mommy group." Francie can only imagine how her mother would judge them all: Nell, with the large, garish tattoo covering her shoulder. Yuko, breastfeeding without cover in the coffee shop, in front of other women's husbands. Token, a gay stay-at-home dad. "But this terrible thing happened—"

"He'll need this gown. It was yours, and before that, it was mine." Her mother waits. She knows what she's doing. She knows Francie won't be baptizing him. She's forcing her to lie. "When is the baptism?"

"We're not quite sure yet. Like I said, Lowell's working a lot right now." Despite the fan, the sweat rises on Francie's back. She turns away from the window, glancing at Will on his mat, at the muted television set, trying to figure out what to say.

And then her heart stops.

It's Winnie. On TV. Not the Winnie she knows, though. This one is much younger—a teenager. She's standing on a stage, wearing a gold strapless gown, her hair tied back in a loose chignon, hanging on to the arm of a nearly identical older woman who must be her mother. Another image appears: Winnie in a blush-colored leotard and long tulle skirt, ballet slippers laced to her knees. Francie picks up the television remote from the counter and increases the volume.

"—Gwendolyn Ross is best known for her role in the cult television series *Bluebird*, which aired in the early nineties."

"Mary Frances?"

"I'm sorry, Mom. I have to go. The baby is awake."

She places the phone on the table. The reporter is standing on a leafy sidewalk, bright yellow police tape visible behind her. Francie moves closer to the TV. The building she's standing in front of. It's Winnie's.

"Sources within the police department are keeping information tightly guarded at this point, saying only that they are, in fact, treating this as a case of child abduction, and that all leads are being pursued. The baby has been missing now for nearly nine hours. Zara Secor, reporting live from Brooklyn."

"Thanks, Zara. Now, on to another bit of disheartening news. The climate change summit has come to—"

Francie goes to her bedside table for her laptop. *Bluebird*. Someone, Gemma perhaps, once mentioned that Winnie was an actress, but half the people Francie has met since moving to New York claim to be actors. She didn't know *this* was what Gemma meant. Winnie is famous. The star of a television show in the early 1990s about a young ballerina auditioning for an apprentice spot in the New York City Ballet. Winnie—who went by the name Gwendolyn—was the ballerina. She was the girl they called Bluebird.

Francie had no idea. She would have been eleven years old when *Bluebird* aired, and it was exactly the type of show—with hints of teenage sexuality, an interracial relationship—that her mother would never have allowed in the house. She opens Wikipedia and finds Winnie's page. Classically trained at the School of American Ballet, a summer at the Royal Ballet School. A family foundation, in her mother's name, that provided scholarships to young dancers.

Francie shouldn't be surprised. She knew the moment she saw Winnie at the first May Mothers meeting four months earlier that there was something special about her. Francie can still picture it. Gemma was telling the group she'd paid to bank her son's umbilical cord blood—a process Francie had never heard of. "It's expensive, but it can save their life if they ever, knock on wood, have a life-threatening disease," Gemma was saying when people began to shift their attention to a spot across the lawn, to the woman walking toward them, the bump of her pregnancy rising under her short turquoise dress, a wide silver bracelet on each wrist. Everyone scooted aside to make room for her, adjusting blankets, shifting babies, and she took the spot right next to Francie. Francie tugged at her shorts and the damp cotton that clung to her midsection as she watched Winnie settle into place, folding her long legs underneath her.

"I'm Winnie," she said, her fingers resting on the slope of her belly, just below her breasts. "Sorry to be so late."

Francie had a hard time keeping her eyes off her, taking in just how beautiful she was. The face of magazine covers and catwalks: the splatter of freckles across the bridge of her nose, the faultless olive skin that had no need for the concealer Francie has been swearing by for the last decade or so.

And then the moment the two of them shared at the coffee shop. Francie was deeply embarrassed by Will's sudden outburst, conscious of the judging stares of the two young men working on laptops near the window, the scowl from the girl behind the counter, waiting for Francie, too frazzled to choose her drink. Winnie seemed to appear from nowhere, unfazed by Will's crying, lifting him from Francie's arms and walking figure eights around the tables, patting his bottom, whispering into his ear, getting him to settle.

"How did you do that?" Francie asked, after joining her at a table in the corner. "I feel like I'm the only one who has no idea what I'm doing."

"Don't be silly," Winnie said. "These May Mothers try very hard to make it look easy, but don't let them fool you." She had a sly look in her eyes, as if she and Francie were lifelong friends, sharing a secret. "This isn't easy for *any* of them. Trust me."

It's more than an hour later, after Will has finally fallen asleep in the cosleeper, the vacuum cleaner running nearby, upright and stationary, to calm him, that Francie comes across the obituary of Audrey Ross, Winnie's mother. She was killed on Winnie's eighteenth birthday, on her way to the store for ice cream. Her death was written up in several national newspapers, for not only was Audrey Ross the mother of Gwendolyn Ross, the famous young actress, she was also an heir to her father's multimillion-dollar real estate business, one of the largest in the nation.

It makes so much sense. Winnie's house. Her clothes. The expensive stroller Francie envied; the same one she examined with longing at Babies "R" Us, until she saw it cost nearly as much as what Lowell and she pay in a month's rent. She finds one photo of the funeral: Winnie and her father walking into a country church near their weekend house in upstate New York, not far from where Audrey Ross was killed. It was a freak accident. The brakes had failed, without explanation. Audrey's car careened down a hill, through a guardrail, plunging eighty feet into a ravine below. Winnie quit *Bluebird* a few months later. That show was canceled soon after.

Francie can't believe it when she hears the distant church bells chiming the arrival of noon, rousing her from the computer. She closes the laptop, wincing at the sight of the untouched pile of laundry, and goes to the kitchen to start lunch. Drained and bleary-eyed, she knows she needs to get into the right frame of mind for Lowell's return. He'll be exhausted and hungry, eager to see her. But she can't deny the heaviness in the pit of her stomach, thinking about all Winnie has lost, everything she has accomplished—a successful acting career, the star of her own show, a happy relationship with a musician, who she mentioned in the one interview she granted after her mother's death.

"I've been relying on Daniel," she said, referring to her boyfriend, when a reporter asked how she was dealing with everything. "He's the only thing getting me through the grief."

And all by seventeen.

Francie starts the water for the macaroni and can't help but picture what she, herself, was doing at that age: singing in the church choir, teaching Sunday school, allowing Mr. Colburn, the science teacher, to lift her skirt and put his fingers inside her in the lab during study hall. At least that was how it started. It didn't take long before he was doing it in his car after school, parked behind the former Payless shoe store in the strip mall, and then in his house, a dingy one-bedroom the volunteer program paid for. It was some Catholic thing. Ivy Leaguers spend the year after graduation teaching at an underprivileged high school, somewhere in the sticks of America, like Our Lady of Perpetual Help, Francie's high school in Estherville, Tennessee. It was in that apartment that she had her first taste of red wine, her first hit of marijuana. It was also there that Mr. Colburn—James, as she dared to call him when they were alone—held her down and removed her volleyball uniform despite her protests.

Francie hears Lowell's heavy footfall on the stairs as she scrapes the last bits of tuna fish from the can into the bowl. She wipes her hands on her shorts and hurries to the bathroom to check herself in the mirror, tame the frizz from her hair, and apply a spritz of floral body spray to each wrist. Before Lowell even has a chance to insert his key, she's opening the door—"Guess what? Winnie was on the news. She's a famous actress—"

But then she notices the dark stubble on the man's face, the wide girth of his waist, the bulge of a gun at his hip. Francie stops, her words hanging in the air as she looks up into the gray eyes of this stranger, blank under the brim of an *NYPD* hat.

———

"Nell." Nell feels a hand on her arm. "You need to wake up."

Nell, the police are here.

It's fifteen years earlier, and she's standing in her apartment in DC, opening the curtains, seeing the dark sedan parked across the street, a man in a black T-shirt and sunglasses leaning against it, lighting a cigarette, his eyes trained on her window.

"Nell." Sebastian is jostling her shoulder, dissolving the memory. "Wake up."

Her mouth is sour, and she tries to sit up but her head is pounding. Sebastian sets a mug of coffee on the bedside table and strokes the hair from her eyes.

"The police are here."

She sits up. "Are you serious? Why?"

"They want to talk to you. About last night."

Last night.

It comes flooding back to her. Winnie. Midas. Walking home, waking Sebastian, telling him what happened before falling into a sporadic, tortured sleep.

"They're waiting in the living room."

She eases out of bed, catching a glimpse of herself in the mirror above the dresser, still in the shirt she wore the night before. Mascara is smeared under her eyes, and her lips are like raisins, crusted with dried lipstick. "Where's the baby?"

"Asleep."

Nell picks up the mug. The coffee singes the back of her throat. "Okay. I'm coming."

The room twists as she walks into the master bathroom. She turns on the faucet, waiting for the water to get as cold as possible, and splashes it onto her face. She presses her eyes closed.

What happened?

The beginning of the night she can remember. Sipping a glass of wine while getting ready to go out. Arriving and sitting out back. The heat from the bodies around her, the conversations. She can feel the fizz of the first drink, the gin in her mouth. Billy Idol. She held Winnie's phone, slid it into her purse. And then— Nell can't recall the details. Only that Francie and Colette were worried about Winnie. They didn't know where she was. Nell looked for Winnie's phone. It was gone.

Sebastian is setting a plate of chocolate digestives his mother had sent from England on the coffee table in front of the detective when Nell walks into the living room, wearing yoga pants and a thin cotton tunic she took from the top of the laundry basket. The detective is in his early forties and handsome, with soulful brown eyes, the dark shadow of a new beard on his face, a faint resemblance to Tom Cruise. He has a large tattoo of an eagle on his right forearm, the number 1775.

"Marine Corps," he says, turning his arm so she can see it better. "The year we were founded. Served for six years." He nods at her right shoulder. "A hummingbird?"

"Yeah." Her voice is like gravel. "A calliope hummingbird, to be exact. Represents escape. And freedom."

His palm is clammy against hers. "Detective Mark Hoyt. Sorry to bother you at home." Behind him stands a man with unruly gray eyebrows, and it comes back to her. Stephen Schwartz. He was the one talking to Alma at Winnie's apartment. Hoyt reaches for a cookie from the armchair and then lifts the plate to Schwartz, who takes three.

"Sorry," Schwartz says. "Busy night. Missed my breakfast."

"We're trying to get a picture of what happened last night," Hoyt says, setting the plate back on the table before meeting Nell's eyes. "Talking to some of you who were with Winnie Ross."

Nell takes a seat on the couch, her head throbbing. "Okay." She notices the camera set up on a spindly tripod. Schwartz steps behind it and presses a button. "You okay with us recording this?" Hoyt asks. "It's the new protocol at the department."

"Sure. Can I get a glass of water before we start?"

Hoyt examines her and smirks. "Rough night?"

She doesn't return the smile. "Every night with a newborn is a rough night."

"I'll get water for you," Sebastian says.

"So, this May Mothers group," Hoyt says. "Can you tell us a little bit about it?"

She clears the rasp from her throat and focuses. "It's, you know, a mum's group. We all have babies the same age. We've been meeting for about four months, since we were pregnant."

"At this bar? The Jolly Llama?"

A shallow laugh escapes her. "No. We meet at the park."

"And whose idea was all this? To meet."

"Francie's."

Schwartz glances at his notebook. "Mary Frances Givens?"

"Yes. Well, not to start the group. We all signed up for it through The Village, the parent website. But Francie suggested the regular meetings." The thought of going into the kitchen to pour a glass of red wine flashes through her mind—it's the only thing that might stop the room from spinning—and she presses her palms hard against the coffee mug in her hands.

"Uh-huh." Hoyt nods. "And what do you do at these meetings?"

"Oh, you know. New mum stuff."

He raises his eyebrows. "Like?"

"Obsess about the babies. Look adoringly upon the babies. Obsess more about the babies."

Hoyt smiles. "Ms. Ross come to all of these meetings?"

"A lot of them. Mostly in the beginning." Nell pictures Winnie walking toward the circle, usually fifteen minutes late, taking her seat, enveloping them in the scent of soft, expensive perfume—exactly the way one would imagine a woman who looks like her would smell.

"Did she talk much about herself?"

"Not really."

Hoyt grins. "You know she was an actress?"

Nell stops the mug inches from her mouth. "She's an actress?"

"She was. Star of a big cult television show twenty-some years ago. *Bluebird*?"

"I had no idea."

"You ever watch it?"

She remembers the girls at her high school talking about that show, always gushing about how cutting-edge it was, the risks it took—a gay character, a teenage pregnancy. "I heard of it, but

I never watched it. More into math than TV at that age, to be honest."

Schwartz steps forward for another cookie. "And you're the one who hired Alma Romero to babysit that night."

It hadn't come out as a question. "Yes."

Hoyt takes a sip of his coffee and nods at Sebastian, who has returned with Nell's water. "Very good, thanks." He keeps the mug in his hands. "You insisted Mrs. Romero watch Midas so Ms. Ross could go out?"

"I don't know if I insisted—"

"Couldn't she have found her own sitter?"

"Yes, but—"

"And also, in an e-mail you sent, you offered to pay Alma, if Winnie agreed to come out?"

Nell takes the water and swallows half of it. "It's silly now," she says. "But at the time, none of us knew about Winnie's money."

"Uh-huh. Where did you find Mrs. Romero?"

"I got her name in the classified section of The Village."

"And how long did you know her before offering her the job of caring for your baby?"

Nell thought the interview would last no more than an hour—Alma was, in fact, the sixth potential nanny Nell had spoken to. None of the other women were right, and then Alma arrived, all sunshine and laughter. She stayed nearly the entire afternoon, sitting with Nell in the living room, drinking tea, sharing the big bag of M&Ms Alma kept in her purse, passing Beatrice back and forth. Alma told Nell about her village in Honduras, where she'd been a midwife, delivering her first baby at the age of twelve. About coming to the United States three years earlier, slipping alone into the United States, across a shallow stretch of the Rio Grande, six months pregnant, doing whatever it would take to give her son a better life.

Before leaving, Alma offered to take Beatrice while Nell showered and enjoyed a few minutes to herself. When Nell lay down on the bed, her legs clean-shaven for the first time since giving birth, she could hear Alma over the monitor, singing to the baby in Spanish. She woke with a start two hours later and rushed down the hall to the nursery. Beatrice was fast asleep on Alma's chest, her tiny fingers grasping Alma's thumb, Alma's romance novel forgotten on her knee. "Five hours or so," Nell says to Hoyt.

"Did you check her references?" he asks.

"Yes."

"Run a criminal background check?"

"No."

"No? That's a little surprising."

"Is it?"

"My wife thought about hiring a nanny once." He shoots Schwartz a haughty look. "Man, she did so many background checks on those women, I told her I should stay home and she should go to work for the FBI." He looks back at Nell. "But who can blame her? It can be terrifying. The things you read."

"I wasn't worried," Nell says. "I've never known a criminal to perform 'Itsy Bitsy Spider' in two languages. But maybe that's just me."

"And what is your understanding of her immigration status?" Hoyt asks.

"Her immigration status?" Nell pauses, careful to keep her eyes off Sebastian. "We didn't discuss it."

Sebastian takes a seat beside Nell on the sofa, and the movement of the cushion sets off a wave of nausea. "I don't understand," Sebastian says, leaning forward, his elbows resting on his knees. "Why are you asking these questions? You can't think Alma had anything to do with this."

"Just trying to dot our t's. Cross our eyes." Hoyt chuckles at the blunder and consults his notebook. "What about when you got to the bar? Notice anything strange? People coming or going that seemed out of the ordinary?"

"No, we mostly kept to ourselves. We were out back, on the patio."

"And Winnie stayed with the group the whole time?"

Suddenly, Nell sees herself. She's standing at the sink of the women's bathroom, breathing in the fetid smell of urine and bleach, drinking water from her cupped hands, her vision cloudy. Darkness crosses behind her in the mirror.

"Ms. Mackey?"

"We'd been there for about an hour, I think, when Winnie went to the bar." The words echo in her ears. "Token went with her. That was the last anyone saw of her."

"There's a mom in your group named Token?"

"No. He's a man. A dad."

She can feel someone's hands on her, pulling at her shirt, fingers digging into her shoulder. Hot breath at her neck.

Schwartz's eyebrows rise again. "A dad? In your mommy group?"

"Yes. I think he's gay."

He nods, and Hoyt marks something in his notebook. "Token. What is that? An Indian name?"

"No. He's white. It's a nickname. I called him that at one of the first meetings because he was the only bloke—you know, the token male. It stuck. I don't even remember his real name, to be honest. I'm not sure anyone does."

Sebastian laughs nervously and reaches for Nell's hand. "She's notoriously bad with names."

"Can you give me a minute? I have to use the loo." Nell stands, her hand on Sebastian's shoulder to steady herself, and walks down the hall to their bedroom and then into the bathroom, closing the door behind her, looking into the mirror. It was just a dream. It had to be.

She crouches on the floor in front of the toilet. It's been a few years since she's had one of those nightmares—the kind that once jarred her awake on a nearly nightly basis. Being followed. People waiting for her around the next corner. It has to be that. She would have remembered if someone had been with her in the bathroom, touching her.

She hears Beatrice crying, and then a knock at the door. It's Sebastian. "Nell. You okay?" She sees her shirt from the night before, in a ball on the floor where she left it. Sebastian knocks harder. "Nell."

"Be right out." She picks up the shirt. It's ripped along the seam of her right shoulder.

She apologizes to Hoyt when she returns to the living room.

"No problem. Just a few more, and then we can get out of your hair. What do you know about the father?"

"Winnie's father?" Nell asks, glancing at the video camera. "Nothing."

"No, ma'am. Midas's father."

"Oh. Nothing. I only recently found out she was single." The heat is building around her. "I had Winnie's phone for a while, but then I couldn't find it. Her key was in the phone case." She swallows. "Did someone find it? Is that how they got in?"

"That's all part of what we're trying to figure out," Hoyt says.

"How much did you have to drink last night?"

She looks at Schwartz, who asked the question. "How much?"

"Yes."

"I don't know. Two drinks, maybe? I hardly touched the second."

"Were you drunk?"

She knows she should just tell them the truth. She knows the risk of lying to the police. "No," she says, her stomach in knots. "Of course I wasn't drunk."

Sebastian appears in front of her, circling the coffee table, refilling everyone's mug. She steals a look at him. At his cap of brown curls, his lean soccer boy's body, imagining him the first time she saw him: sitting at the opposite end of a moody London bar, sipping a Guinness in the shifting light of late Sunday afternoon, sketching in a Moleskine notebook, the face of a man intent on his art. His eyes were kind when he approached her later, asking if the seat beside her was taken, if he might buy them another round.

Nell clenches her palms in her lap as she tries to concentrate on Hoyt's next question, but her gaze is drawn back to Sebastian as he slowly paces the living room, their daughter cradled in the nook of his arm, seeing an entirely different face than the one she remembers from that day six years earlier. The face of a man, terrified and worried.

A man having the same panicked thought as she. *Please. Not this. Not again.*

CHAPTER FIVE
DAY TWO

> **TO:** May Mothers
> **FROM:** Your friends at The Village
> **DATE:** July 6
> **SUBJECT:** Today's advice
> <u>YOUR BABY: DAY 53</u>
> Thinking about co-sleeping? It's not too late. While it may not be for everyone, the benefits are numerous. Co-sleeping babies tend to sleep more. It makes breastfeeding easier, helping to keep up mom's milk supply. And most of all, co-sleeping creates a very special bond. Plus, who doesn't love a good middle-of-the-night snuggle or two?

It's sweltering on the subway platform, and crowded—people lean out over the tracks, trying to spot the lights of an arriving train. The man to Colette's left chews a soft stick of beef jerky, the expensive kind making its way into the grocery stores in the neighborhood. The two women to her right are speaking too loudly, oversize designer bags hanging from their elbows, their cell phones clutched in their hands.

"I have a friend who swims with hers. Would you do that?"

"In the ocean?"

"Yes."

"Never." The girl gazes at the splayed fingers of her left hand

and adjusts the large, brilliant diamond ring. "I don't even like to shower with mine, to be honest."

Colette wanders farther down the platform and stops at the newsstand, where a man in a turban stands, breathing in subway fumes all day, doling out bottled water and rattling containers of Tic Tacs. Winnie's face looms from the cover of the *New York Post*: a photo from years ago. She's wearing a long coat and sunglasses, her face cast toward the street. Colette should probably be surprised to see it, but she's not. The story is on the brink of becoming national news since Winnie released the video yesterday pleading for Midas's return.

Colette watched it at least a dozen times last night in bed, Poppy sleeping peacefully beside her. Charlie was working, and she'd given up on her own sleep after an hour of lying in the dark, her thoughts trapped in a hamster wheel of worry. In the video, Winnie sat on a gray upholstered armchair in front of her terrace windows. She looked so pretty: her pulled-back hair, the strong cut of her jaw, her long, thin neck against a simple black crepe blouse.

"Please," Winnie said, gazing into the camera, her voice breaking the word in two, "please don't hurt my baby. Please, whoever you are, please give him back to me."

Colette hears the squeaking brakes of an approaching train and digs two quarters from the bottom of her bag. Inside the crowded car, she tries to keep her balance among the undulating throng of people pressing against her as she opens the paper to the article. The byline belongs to a reporter named Elliott Falk; the headline reads:

OH GHOSH!

People are beginning to shake their heads about Police Commissioner Rohan Ghosh's handling of the investigation of Midas Ross, seven weeks of age, who has been missing for two days. The baby's disappearance on July 4 was first reported by his babysitter, Alma Romero. The *Post* has confirmed that it took officers more than twenty-three minutes to respond to Romero's 911 call, which they blame on the department's strain due to Fourth of July security, and an accident near the Brooklyn Bridge involving two city buses, in which dozens were injured, including two young children and a young mother, currently in critical condition. After arriving at the Ross residence, police failed to properly secure the crime scene, perhaps even allowing people who may have been inside the home to exit via a door left unattended.

The baby's mother, the former actress Gwendolyn Ross, was out for the evening with members of her so-called mommy group.

Colette pauses; returns to the sentence: . . . *people who may have been inside the home to exit via a door left unattended.*

Is that possible? Was the person who took Midas still inside when the police officers arrived? Is that why the side door of Winnie's building was open?

A few photos accompany the article. In one, Midas is lying on his back on a sheepskin rug next to a small plastic giraffe, staring into the camera, his skin porcelain, his brown eyes so shiny they look polished. In the photo below it, Winnie is on a blanket in the park, cradling Midas in her arms. Colette's breath catches as she realizes it's the photo she gave Detective Mark Hoyt yesterday, when he showed up at her apartment in the late afternoon, after Charlie had taken Poppy out running with him and she was preparing dinner.

"What do you know about her background?" Hoyt asked her. "What kind of details did she share about herself?"

There was something that seemed vaguely familiar about Winnie, Colette admitted. But it had been more than twenty years since she was on television, and Colette hadn't made the connection between Winnie and Gwendolyn Ross, although she'd watched the show periodically. Sometimes, while the other girls at her school were getting together with bottles of wine and joints stolen from someone's parents, Colette would convince her mother—on the rare weekend Rosemary wasn't traveling for work—to join her on the couch, their faces sticky with the egg-white-and-honey mask Colette had read about in *Seventeen* magazine, a bowl of popcorn on the couch between them, watching *Bluebird*.

The train arrives at Colette's stop, and she climbs the stairs and makes her way through City Hall Park, past a crowd of tourists taking photos in front of the fountain. There was one interaction she had with Winnie that Colette hadn't mentioned to Mark Hoyt, which she had remembered just the night before.

It was the afternoon she and Winnie walked home together, after the very first May Mothers meeting. They'd taken their time, strolling along the park wall, staying in the shade. Colette can still smell the roasting nuts from the vendor at the corner, where Winnie stopped to buy a bag of cashews. It was here that Colette admitted, without planning to, how terrified she was when she learned she was pregnant.

"I called the whole thing a mistake, for months," Colette said. "I'm excited now, but it's been a process. I was not ready for her."

Winnie's expression was stark when she looked at Colette. "I can understand that."

"You can?" Colette asked, feeling flush with relief. Since joining May Mothers, she'd felt like an outsider—if not a total impostor—among the other women, who all seemed as if they'd spent their whole lives just waiting to become moms. Who'd spent years charting their cycles, taking their temperatures, their legs suspended in the air above them after sex, hoping this month was their time. Women like Yuko, who'd gone off the pill the night of her engagement. Scarlett, who'd become vegan, believing it would better prepare her body for pregnancy and birth. And Francie, who had shared, very early on in their meetings, the pain of enduring two miscarriages, finally conceiving after two rounds of IVF that left them thousands of dollars in debt.

"What's your story?" Colette asked Winnie. But she waved away the question.

"We'll save that for another time," she said, rifling through her wallet. An older woman in front of them turned, a paper cup of roasted nuts in her hands. She smiled, noticing the rise of their bellies. The woman placed her free hand on Winnie's arm. "You have no idea what you two are in for," she said, her eyes moist. "The world's most wonderful gift."

"That was sweet," Colette said, after the woman walked away.

"You think so?" Winnie wasn't looking at her, though. She was staring past her, beyond the stone wall, into the park. "Why does everybody like to tell new mothers what we're about to gain? Why does nobody want to talk about what we have to lose?"

As she climbs the steps of City Hall, Colette's thoughts turn to the caption she'd read under Midas's photo: *The baby's Sophie the Giraffe, a plastic squeak toy from France popular with American parents, and a blue baby's blanket are also missing. The police are asking anyone with information to call 1-800-NYPDTIP.*

Whoever took Midas, why would they take those things? It's good news, Colette decides, stepping into the elevator. After all, only a person who loves him—or at least someone who doesn't intend to hurt him—would think to also take his favorite blanket and toy.

The question trails her as the elevator doors open on the fourth floor. The lobby is uncommonly quiet, and Allison is at her desk, staring at her computer. She looks up at the sound of Colette's heels clicking on the marble floor.

"Good afternoon," Allison says, and Colette sees the images on Allison's screen—a high chair, a car seat, a blue plastic tub in the shape of a whale.

"Let me guess," Colette says. "Baby registry?" Allison told Colette about her pregnancy a week earlier, in strict confidence. "I'm only eight weeks, so don't tell anyone," she said. "Especially Mayor Shepherd. He's got enough to worry about with his election, and this book."

"This is crazy," Allison says now, leaning in close. "I can't believe all the stuff you need when you have a baby."

Colette glances at the computer screen. "You really don't need all this. The kid will survive being cleaned with a room-temperature baby wipe."

"That's what my sister said," Allison says. "I guess I should trust the experts. Thanks. And guess what? He's running late."

"You're kidding." Colette raises her eyebrows in feigned surprise. "Mayor Shepherd is running late?"

Allison laughs. "He said you should drink all of his coffee. As punishment. I just made a fresh pot, and there's some pastries in there from his early meeting."

"Thanks," Colette says, suddenly aware of her hunger. She's eaten very little since the french fries at the Jolly Llama two nights earlier, too consumed with worry about Midas to think about food.

The mayor's office is peaceful when she enters. Although she's been coming here for the last several months, she can't help but feel impressed each time. The large windows offering a view of the Brooklyn Bridge, the working fireplace, the desk that once belonged to James Baldwin—a gift from the family—it's a far cry from the windowless principal's office at Public School 212 in the Bronx where she and Teb had spent endless hours together four years earlier, working on his first memoir over takeout beer and burritos from the local taqueria. The book had done better than anyone expected, bringing front-page reviews, magazine profiles, a national speaking tour, and then, a year later, a successful run for the mayorship of New York. His publisher had offered him a fortune for a sequel focused on his relationship with his mother, a civil rights activist who'd marched with Martin Luther King Jr. on Selma.

Colette pours herself a mug of coffee and takes a seat at the round table overlooking City Hall Park, trying not to feel annoyed at having to wait for him—yet again. She should take advantage of the time alone, time she can use to make progress on the new material she's meant to deliver in a few days. She removes her laptop from her bag and opens the manuscript, skimming the chapters she sent Aaron Neeley, Teb's chief of staff, the afternoon before. Her skin pricks with embarrassment. The pages are terrible. The writing is stilted and childish, the dialogue almost unreadable.

She hears her phone beep with a new e-mail and reaches for it, grateful for the distraction. It's Francie. She's been in frequent contact with Nell and Francie over the last two days, sharing articles about "Baby Midas," as he was quickly becoming known in the press, checking in, asking if anyone has heard from Winnie yet.

Colette e-mailed Winnie the day before, and a few hours later, she responded.

Who has my baby? How am I going to survive this?

Colette wrote back immediately, asking if she wanted company, offering to drop off some groceries. But Winnie still hasn't responded to Colette's e-mail, or the text message she sent a few hours later.

Did you guys see this? Francie wrote. Attached to her e-mail is a link to a crime blog—one of many that comprised an entire online world of amateur sleuths Colette hadn't known existed before this: people who seemed to devote a surprising amount of time trying to unravel unsolved crimes. Colette reads the post:

> *A neighbor said she passed a woman near Winnie's apartment around 9:30 that night. She was walking down the hill carrying a crying baby that could have been Midas's age.*

A new message from Nell arrives immediately. People are aware this is Brooklyn, right? They levy fines against women who live here and are not, at some point, seen carrying a crying baby.

"Hey, Colette. Sorry about the wait." Colette clicks her e-mail closed. Aaron Neeley is standing in the door. His shirt is wrinkled, and there's a line of dark stubble at his chin that he missed while shaving.

"Everything okay?" she asks.

Aaron carries a stack of folders at his chest and places them, one by one, onto Teb's desk. "Yeah, he's meeting with Ghosh. This abduction thing. What a nightmare." He glances at her. "I'm assuming you heard about it?"

She clears her throat. She should explain the situation—she should tell Aaron that Winnie is a friend of hers, that she was there that night—but something tells her to wait, to speak to Teb about it privately. She knows what it might mean for him if it gets out that someone close to him is linked to this. "Yeah."

"How old is Patty now?"

"Poppy. Almost eight weeks."

Aaron shakes his head. "The twins are seven. I can't even imagine."

"What's the latest?" Colette asks.

"Oh, I don't know. Ghosh is on the defensive. One of the officers—some young kid, a week out of police academy—really screwed things up. Didn't use gloves, left his fingerprints all over the place. It's a real mess." Aaron sighs and then looks up at Colette. "Anyway, the mayor shouldn't be long. Looking forward to discussing the stuff you sent yesterday. We're getting down to the wire, huh?"

"We sure are." She turns toward her screen as Aaron leaves. Meeting with Rohan Ghosh. Ghosh and the mayor were friends at SUNY Purchase, and when Teb tapped Ghosh from his post as Cleveland's deputy commissioner, everyone claimed it was a classic case of nepotism. Ghosh was largely considered the least experienced person to serve in the top position at the NYPD.

Colette opens the manuscript again, doing her best to stay focused. Seeing the folders Aaron left on Teb's desk, though, she wonders if they include his notes on the chapters she submitted yesterday. She stands and walks to the credenza for a Danish, glancing down at the stack. She stops, having to look twice to make sure she's correctly read the name printed in wiry black handwriting on the tab of a manila folder on the top of the pile.

Ross, Midas.

Colette walks to the door and pushes it closed a few inches. Back at Teb's desk, the Danish clutched in her hand, she opens the folder and peeks inside. There's a photograph of a man. He's tall and thin. He wears a hooded sweatshirt and is handing something to a store clerk. There's another, taken from the same security camera, as he turns away from the counter, his face in profile. Then he's walking toward the door and glancing up, straight into the camera. She fingers through the papers underneath: copies of handwritten notes; a photo of Midas's crib, with mint-green sheets and a decal of thin, delicate birds taking flight on the wall above it. And then another of the man, this one crisp and in color. He's of Middle Eastern descent, and he's staring into the camera, sunglasses perched atop his head, balancing a baby on his forearm. The baby is partially covered with a blanket.

She lifts the photograph for a closer look, but then hears footsteps outside the door. She quickly returns it to the stack, closes the folder, and rushes back to the table. The steps pass by outside Teb's office, and she looks down at her notes—Teb's story about finally confronting his mother's abusive boyfriend—but she can't get the image out of her mind. The man's smile. His hands. How they cupped that baby's skull.

Who has my baby? How am I going to survive this?

Before she can consider what she's doing, Colette takes her purse from the chair beside her, walks to Teb's desk, and places the folder in her bag. She walks calmly into the hall and down the corridor to the copy room, where she shuts the door and turns the lock. The sweat of her palms smears the ink of the stamp on the top of each paper—HIGHLY CONFIDENTIAL—as she pages through the stack, knowing how significantly she's breaching her contract with Teb. According to the confidentiality agreement she's signed, she can't access any information he hasn't specifically shared with her. She can't speak to anyone about the things she's learned during the course of her work. She can't even admit to anyone—"no relative, friend, member of the public"—that she's the person who writes his books.

There's a knock on the door.

"Hello?" It's Allison. The doorknob turns. "Is someone in there?"

Colette shoves the papers back into the folder and sets it under a box on a shelf above the copier. She grabs her bag from the floor and digs inside, unbuttoning the top four buttons of her shirt, revealing the upper edge of her nursing bra. She steadies her breathing before cracking open the door.

"Sorry." She offers Allison an apologetic smile and holds up her manual breast pump. "The mayor's still not there, and I need to pump. The bathroom's a little gross. That makes it difficult."

Allison's forehead wrinkles in embarrassment. "Oh my god,

I'm so sorry to disturb you. Of course. I'll keep an eye out for you."

"You're the best." Colette relocks the door, and waits a few moments before reaching for the folder again. Ten minutes later, she's back in the hall, walking slowly toward Allison. "See what you have to look forward to?"

In Teb's office, she returns the folder to the pile. She's just sat down and opened the lid of her laptop when Teb walks in. He's without his suit jacket, and his shirtsleeves are rolled to his elbows, the cotton stretching across the taut muscles of his back.

"You hate me?" he asks, throwing a notebook onto his desk. His smile is wide and radiant—the smile now gracing billboards across the nation as part of the "True Heroes" ad campaign for Ralph Lauren—no signs of the difficult meeting he's come from.

"No, of course not, Mayor."

He grimaces. "How many times do I have to tell you not to call me that? It sounds too weird, coming from you."

"Sorry. No, I don't hate you, Teb Marcus Amedeo Shepherd."

"Whoa. No need to go crazy." He flips through the folders Aaron left and then places them on the credenza beside his desk. "I have some bad news."

Her heart seizes. "About Midas?"

"Midas?"

She shakes her head. "Midas Ross. That baby in the news. Aaron said you were with Ghosh. I thought you were going to say—"

"I was wondering if this was going to get to you. That baby's the same age as Poppy." He turns his back to her and pours himself a cup of coffee. "What kind of monster would take a baby?"

"Do you have any—"

He waves his hand, dismissing the question. "No, the bad news is not about him. It's about you and me." He turns toward her, and she braces herself. "I have to cancel on you. I didn't get a chance to read what you sent yesterday, and now I have another meeting."

The tension in her chest dissolves with relief. She doesn't have to spend the next hour talking about this awful book. She can get out of here, try to make sense of what she's just read.

"Teb—" She makes sure the word comes out annoyed.

"I know," he says. "I'm an asshole. I'm sorry. Can you come by tomorrow?"

She begins to pack up her laptop and notebook. "Sure."

"No. Wait. I'm out on Long Island all day for a fund raiser. The day after?"

She nods. "Whatever you need."

"Thanks, C." He sits behind his desk, scrolling through his cell phone. "How's my baby?"

"Adorable."

"Yeah? She giving her mother any trouble? Because if she is, I'll have a talk with her."

"I'm not sure even you are convincing enough, but feel free to tell her she better start sleeping through the night."

He keeps his eyes on his phone and reaches out his hand. "Let me see." He looks up. "I need to see a recent photo."

Her phone is in her bag. Teb stands up, and she turns her back to him. She cautiously unzips her purse just as Aaron appears at the door.

"Excuse me, sir, but they're waiting for you. They don't have much longer."

"Okay, I gotcha." Teb takes a long drink of coffee and then sets the mug back on the credenza, next to the folders. "Text some to me," he says, reaching to touch her arm on the way out.

Colette says good-bye to Allison, and once outside, she walks quickly through the crowds, through air perfumed with the earthy scent of charred pretzel oil, and toward the subway. Inside the train, she takes an empty seat at the back of the chilly car. Ten minutes later, as the train emerges from the tunnel on to the Brooklyn Bridge, she watches the stream of pedestrians trudging down the pathway under the hot July sun. She takes out her phone, the tears stinging as she types.

Are you guys free tomorrow morning to come to my place? I have something I need to tell you.

CHAPTER SIX
NIGHT TWO

I don't know what to do.

I'm trying to keep in mind the thing the doula told me: Deep breathing initiates the parasympathetic nervous system, the rest-and-relax state. But it's not working. My chest is too stiff, and I can't get enough oxygen. I need to get out of here, breathe some fresh air, but the journalists are outside, circling, waiting to ask me questions. That guy from the *Post,* Elliott What's-his-name, with his shlubby clothes and cheap haircut and oily skin, making his mother so proud to see his name in print. He's there all the time, talking to the neighbors. Where were you that night? What do you think happened? What can you tell me about *the mother?*

I pace. Up and down the hall, instinctively avoiding the creaky sixth floorboard in front of the nursery. I keep the curtains closed. I don't want anyone to know I'm here. I don't want one more visit from a detective, asking if I can talk, wondering if there's anything else I can add.

I have nothing to add. How can I, when I remember so little—when the details of that night come and go, like a rapid blur of static events.

I remember reading Nell's e-mail, suggesting a night out, a few hours away from the babies.

I remember thinking no, of course I won't go to that. But then I kept re-reading the e-mail, considering it. Nell was so persistent. Everyone come, and especially Winnie. We won't take no for an answer.

Fine, I hastily decided. I won't give no for an answer. I'll give yes for an answer! And why not? I deserved a night out as much as anyone. I deserved to have fun. Why did I always have to be the one person staying home, obsessing about a baby, when every other mother in the world seems to have no problem going out, celebrating a holiday, having a drink or two? They're somehow able to effortlessly navigate this new world. So calm. So confident. So fucking perfect.

Why *couldn't* I be more like them?

I got dressed. I remember that. I remember choosing the dress that cinches me at the waist like a strong pair of hands. I remember walking into the bar, spotting them, tired eyes rimmed in kohl liner, black circles tempered under too much concealer, lips shimmering with the lipstick they hadn't worn in months.

"Rebel Yell." I sang along, danced, part of them, all members of the same exclusive tribe. I remember feeling ill all of a sudden, like I needed to get out of there. But then that guy appeared out of nowhere. Offering to buy me a drink, with his deep ocean eyes, his full lips. Guys like him: they've gotten me into trouble my whole fucking life.

I remember very little after that.

Sometimes, when I close my eyes and try to sleep, I can see myself walking along the park, staying in the shadows. I prayed.

Dear Lord, please give me Joshua back. I'll do anything.

"Are you all right?"

I'd taken a seat on the bench, and a man was standing in front of me, a dog at his ankles, his face shadowed by the streetlamp behind him. I still don't know if he was real, or another hallucination.

Why did he leave me? I wanted to yell at this man. *I don't deserve this, not after everything I did for him.*

"I'm fine," I told the man with the dog after he sat down on the bench beside me, his thigh touching mine, his arm draped across the bench behind me. "Thank you. I just need to talk to someone."

That's all I wanted to do. Really. Just *talk* to Joshua. Tell him that being with him is the only thing that's ever mattered to me. Let him know about the letters I've been writing him, maybe offer to read one or two, so he'd know exactly how I feel, and how much I still want him. How sorry I am for anything I may have done wrong.

No, Detective, I'm sorry. I can't tell you any of this.

Sorry, chubby Elliott reporter guy. I have nothing else to add.

My hand is shaking as I write this. I feel weak and confused. I tried so hard to be a good mother. I did my best, really I did.

My god, what have I done?

CHAPTER SEVEN
DAY THREE

TO: May Mothers

FROM: Your friends at The Village

DATE: July 7

SUBJECT: Today's advice

YOUR BABY: DAY 54

Let's talk tummy time! Placing your baby on her belly is critical—even if it's just for ten minutes every few hours or so. Time on her tummy will help strengthen her stomach and neck muscles, and by now, while on her belly, she should be reaching for toys, your fingers, or even your nose. (Might also be time to invest in those baby nail clippers!)

Francie catches her crimped reflection in the brushed silver of the elevator doors, avoiding the way the straps of the Moby Wrap accentuate her muffin top; how short she is next to Nell, who stands next to her, at least four inches taller, pulling off the daring blond pixie, the sprawling tattoo. Francie smooths down her curls, wishing she'd had time to wash her hair, or at least apply a coat of mascara and lip gloss. But this morning has been particularly rough. Will woke up at five o'clock, crying for an hour, refusing to nurse.

Francie leans forward and peeks down her shirt, at the slices of potatoes she stuck inside her bra earlier this morning.

Nell glances at her. "You making hash browns in there?"

"No." Francie adjusts the potatoes to cover the hot, red lump. "Scarlett told me to do this." Convinced she had a clogged duct, Francie went to Scarlett for advice. She is one of *those* moms— the ones who seem to naturally know exactly what to do, always e-mailing the group with helpful tips: twelve chamomile tea bags in the bath to cure Yuko's baby's diaper rash, a review of the new swaddle on back order at the baby boutique near the Starbucks.

I'm glad you asked, because I have just the trick, Scarlett wrote to Francie last night, in response to her frantic request for help. First, NO CAFFEINE. Second, a layer of organic potatoes inside the bra for three hours each morning. I know it sounds odd, but it should bring immediate relief. It has been five hours of potatoes, though, and Francie's breast still burns. She's berating herself for going against her better judgment and buying the nonorganic potatoes early this morning, just to save three dollars. She should have heeded Scarlett's exact advice and splurged. That's probably why it isn't working.

The elevator doors open, and they make their way to 3A, where Colette opens the door before they can even knock. Francie blushes at the sight of Colette, who is topless, her full breasts spilling from a lacy pink bra, her arms and belly a constellation of cinnamon freckles.

"Sorry," Colette says, tying her hair back, the hard dots of fresh hair growth visible at her armpits. "The baby just spit up all over my last clean shirt." She ushers them into the living room. "I folded clothes this morning, and when I went to put them away, Charlie told me I'd just folded two hampers full of dirty laundry. I could have murdered someone."

"Really?" Francie says, but she's too enraptured by Colette's apartment to have heard what she said. Other than Winnie's, she's never been inside such a nice New York apartment. The shiny wood floors. The living room big enough to fit two couches *and* two armchairs. The dining table under the wall of large windows, with space to sit ten. This room alone is bigger than Francie's entire apartment, which is so small they can't have anyone over for dinner; where she has to keep the baby's clothes in plastic bins in the corner of their only bedroom; where she has to nurse in the living room, in view of the residents of the luxury building that recently went up across the street. Lowell has been after her to consider a bigger place, farther out in Brooklyn, perhaps even Queens, but Francie won't hear of it, not with the school district they're in. They need to suck it up, for the baby, for the neighborhood, for the promise of a quality education.

"How'd it go?" Colette asks Nell.

Nell drops heavily onto the couch. "Awful." She e-mailed them yesterday, saying she'd fired Alma and was dropping Beatrice off at her first day at Happy Baby Daycare, to get her used to it for a few hours today before starting there full-time in two days, when she returns to work. "Hysterical crying. It was a total scene. All the other moms were staring."

"Did they know how to comfort Beatrice?" Francie asks.

"Not Beatrice," Nell says. "Me." She wipes her nose with the wet, crumpled Kleenex in her fist. "I made a bloody fool of myself."

Colette sits beside Nell and puts an arm around her, but Francie feels frozen in place. How can Nell do this? Leave her *baby*, all day, in the care of total strangers? The best thing you can do, for at least the first six months, is to hold the baby as much as possible. A day-care worker or nanny isn't going to do that. Sometimes, while feeding Will, Francie will get on her phone and read the most recent posts at isawyournanny.com, a forum for parents to post sightings of the things they witness nannies doing to children—ignoring them, yelling at them, talking on their phone while the child plays alone.

"It's going to be fine, right?" Nell asks, digging in her purse for a clean tissue. "They won't break her?"

"Of course it'll be fine," Colette says. "Millions of women do this every day."

"I know." Nell nods. "And for what we're paying at that place, I expect I'll return later this afternoon to find her with buffed nails, cucumber slices on her eyes, a chalice of milk at her elbow." She wipes her eyes, leaving a smear of black mascara along her right cheek. "I feel so bad about firing Alma, but what was I supposed to do? She's being hounded by journalists. I don't want Beatrice around that."

"It's disgusting," Colette says. "Charlie brought home the paper this morning. There's a photo of her at the playground with her daughter. They ran her out of the place."

"I'm a wreck," Nell says. "I'm at Sebastian's throat all day. Everything he says annoys me. And the baby's waking every few hours again."

Colette goes to the kitchen, taking a paper dessert box from the counter. "Not much help, but I got chocolate-chip muffins today. Thought you could use one of these." She puts the muffins on a plate and sets them on the coffee table before heading down the hall toward the bedrooms in the back. "I need to find a shirt. Coffee's made, if you want it."

Nell takes a seat on the couch. "Not me. I've had four cups already."

Francie walks into the kitchen, which is separated from the living room by a large butcher's-block island. She slides her hand along the smooth wood and the spotless white countertop to the double farmhouse sink. She pauses before opening the refrigerator, examining the array of Polaroids stuck to the door. Poppy, lying on a soft pink bedspread, propped up on a nursing pillow. Colette and a tall, handsome man Francie assumes is Charlie, their tan, toned arms clasped around each other's waists, Colette's long auburn hair beach-blown and wild, her face spattered with a map of fresh freckles. A note in male handwriting, curled and paled by the sunlight streaming in the large window nearby:

> *Attention all kitchen utensils, unfinished books, "useless childhood artifacts," and general household objects: take heed. Colette Yates is nesting. None of you are safe.*

Colette appears in a man's white T-shirt that swallows her. "You know her?" Nell asks Colette. Nell's standing in front of a bookshelf, holding a framed photograph in her hand.

Colette glances at Nell and then walks into the kitchen to pour a cup of coffee. "Yes."

"How?"

"She's my mom."

"You're joking."

"Who?" Francie says. Nell turns the photograph, and Francie walks to take a closer look. It's an image of an older woman with a crisp white bob, standing on a paddleboard, her arms raised triumphantly overhead.

"Rosemary Carpenter." By the stunned look on Nell's face, it's apparent Francie is supposed to know who that is.

"I'm sorry, but I don't know her."

"She started WFE," Nell says.

Francie is shocked. "The wrestling organization?"

Colette and Nell laugh, and Francie's face warms with embarrassment.

"No," Nell says. "Women for Equality. The feminist organization."

"Actually, it *is* kind of like a wrestling organization," Colette says.

Nell puts the photograph back. "My mom gave me a signed copy of her book for my high school graduation."

"Funny," Colette says. "So did mine."

Francie is unsure of what she's supposed to say, wondering why it is that everyone in New York City seems either to be a famous person or know one. Winnie. Colette's mother. The only famous person Francie ever met before moving to New York was the owner of the largest chain of car dealerships in western Tennessee, whose family portrait she assisted with at the photography studio where she worked.

"What was that like?" Nell asks Colette.

"You mean, being the daughter of the woman known to coin the phrase 'The only thing worse for a woman than making herself dependent on a man—'"

Nell finishes her sentence: "'—is to have a child dependent on her.'"

"How awful," Francie says before she can help herself.

"It was complicated, but we can't get into that right now. Charlie will be back soon, and I have something I need to share with you."

"Is it about Midas?" Francie asks.

"Yes."

"Good. I've been doing a lot of thinking about things." Francie releases Will from the Moby Wrap and sets him on the floor before taking the notebook from her diaper bag. She kneels on the soft area rug and opens the notebook to the timeline she's made of the night, including who was there, and what time they left. "I've been trying to piece together a clear chain of events, see if there might be someone who can fill in the holes. Where was Winnie? What time did she leave? Who, if anyone, did she leave with?"

Nell sits on the floor beside Francie.

"The police work on this—something isn't right," Francie says. "Lowell's uncle is in law enforcement. I've been reading the news to him, and he's appalled by how many mistakes the police have made. Did you see this?" Francie searches her bag for the article by Elliott Falk she printed from the *New York Post*'s website this morning. "Apparently someone opened the windows in Midas's room and moved his crib sheets before photographs were taken."

"And did you read the article yesterday?" Colette asks. "Suggesting the person who took Midas could have been *inside the house* when the police arrived?"

"I know, I saw that too," Nell says. "Is that why the door was open when we got there?"

"Let's start with how someone got in." Francie sits back. "Nell, I have to ask you again. Have you given any more thought to her key and phone? Any idea at all what may have happened? They couldn't have just *disappeared*."

Nell keeps her gaze on Francie's notebook. "I don't know. I put her phone in my purse. I know I did. You guys watched me."

"When you dropped your purse, and things scattered, do you think the phone fell out? Maybe it slid under a nearby table?"

"I dropped my purse?"

"Don't you remember?" Francie tries to keep the irritation from her voice. "When you were trying to find Winnie's phone?"

"Right," Nell says, but Francie can hear the uncertainty. "I don't think her phone fell out."

"Walk me through what you do remember," Francie says.

Nell presses her hands to her eyes. "I went to the waitress station to order the fries. A little while later, I went to the bar for a drink with Scarlett. We came back—"

"No, you're wrong." Francie *knew* it. Nell was even drunker than she'd thought. "Scarlett wasn't there."

"She wasn't?"

Francie feels a fresh flood of remorse. *Why* had she trusted Nell with Winnie's phone? She was well aware that Nell had had too much to drink. Why hadn't she been smarter? "No.

Look." She shoves the notebook closer to Nell and points at the list of names. "Scarlett didn't come."

"Okay, Francie, relax. I'm getting the name wrong," Nell says, her tone defensive. "I told you guys, I'm *terrible* with names. Who's the woman who came but left pretty quickly? The Pilates one. We went to get a drink together."

"Gemma? Wearing a blue tank top and jeans?"

"Yes, Gemma. It was her."

"And then what?" Francie asks.

"And that's it. I went to the loo. I came back to the table, we all chatted for a while, and then Alma called."

"You're sure?" Francie asks. "You didn't ask anyone to hold your purse? You didn't lose sight of it at any point?"

"Francie, take a breath," Colette says. "You're going to pass out."

Francie sits back on her heels. "I just can't make sense of any of this. Where was Winnie when Alma called? And when did she get back to her house that night? And did you see what Patricia Faith said on *The Faith Hour* this morning?"

Nell lets out an irritated sigh. "Patricia Faith. I despise that woman. How does being a former Miss California qualify you for a one-hour talk show on cable television?"

"Do you know what her beauty contest talent was?" Colette asks. "Social commentary."

"Please," Nell says. "What? Did she stand on a stage in a bikini, arguing in favor of arming schoolchildren?"

"You can see the foam brewing at her mouth," Colette says. "A rich baby stolen away. The mother, a beautiful, once-famous actress, and now a single mom. She's going to make her network a fortune."

"I know, but guys," Francie says, "did you see what she said this morning? They know about us. That we got in."

Nell gasps and grabs Francie's wrist. "What do you mean?"

The color has drained from her face. "She talked about us? By name?"

"Not by name," Francie says, standing and picking up Will, who's begun to fuss. "She called us 'friends of Gwendolyn Ross.' Said we were allowed in to an active crime scene."

Francie couldn't deny the odd jolt she felt hearing the words, knowing it was her—Francie Givens from Estherville, Tennessee, population 6,360—being referred to by Patricia Faith (however namelessly) as a friend of Winnie Ross. She toes an article from the stack, sliding it closer to Nell. "It got picked up by the press."

Nell reads aloud. "'As first reported by TV personality Patricia Faith, three friends of Gwendolyn Ross, not identified by name, apparently arrived at the Ross residence, letting themselves in, until they were forcibly removed by an officer with the NYPD.'"

"Forcibly removed?" Colette says. "That's a little much."

"I know," Francie says. "But that's not the worst part." The worst part was what else Patricia Faith said—the same thing Francie had read elsewhere—the information that now ties her stomach in knots. When it comes to determining whether an abducted baby will be found alive, the first twenty-four hours are *critical*. "If the police screwed this up as bad as these articles suggest, do you realize what that could mean?" She can't think about it—the idea that Midas could be in even greater danger because of some incompetent policemen.

Colette puts her coffee cup on the table in front of her. Something in her expression makes Francie stop bouncing Will. "What is it?" Francie asks.

"Okay, listen. I feel weird sharing this, but I have some new information. About Midas."

"What do you mean?" Francie asks. "I've been reading everything. If it's been reported—"

"It hasn't been reported. I found it through my job."

"Your job?"

"Yeah. That memoir I'm writing? It's Teb Shepherd's."

"You're kidding," Nell says. "*Mayor* Shepherd?"

"Yes. I'm his ghostwriter."

"Why does he need a ghostwriter? His first book was amazing."

"*I* wrote his first book," Colette says.

"You?" Francie says. Even she knows about that book. It's all anyone could talk about for months—the beautifully written memoir by Teb Shepherd, the young, devastatingly handsome principal at a high school in the South Bronx. Lowell stayed up all night reading it; his mother's book club discussed it. Business was still booming at the Greek diner Shepherd wrote about frequenting near his mother's apartment in Washington Heights, groups of middle-aged women standing in line, hoping to spot him at a table in the back, eating his standard Saturday-morning order: a toasted corn muffin and a side of bacon.

"It's what I do," Colette says. "I write books that other people say they wrote. I'm not allowed to tell you that, so you can imagine how much I'm not supposed to tell you this. But I was at the mayor's office yesterday, and I found Midas's file. From the investigation."

"You're joking," Nell says. "And what? You looked at it?"

"Worse." Colette kneels on the floor and reaches under the couch, sliding out a thick manila folder. "I made copies."

"Oh my god," Francie says. "Does anyone know you did this?"

"Nobody. I could get in serious trouble. I didn't even tell Charlie. I'm so far behind on this book, I couldn't admit how much time I spent last night, when he thought I was working, reading what's in here."

"Does the mayor know you're friends with Winnie?"

"No. I was going to tell him, but after I took this file, it felt too dicey. Now I can't. He'll wonder why I didn't tell him from the beginning."

Francie can't look away from the file in Colette's hands. "What's in it?"

"It appears to be recent reports, specific things they want Teb to see. If you look—" The doorbell rings. "Shit." Colette waits a moment. "I'm gonna ignore that. It's probably a package for Charlie. They'll leave it downstairs."

"Actually, I think it's Token," Francie says.

Colette shoots Francie an irritated look. "You invited Token?"

He e-mailed Francie earlier this morning, asking if she wanted to join him for a coffee at the Spot. It was so strange. He's never asked her to do something, just the two of them, and she knows so little about him. She'll never forget her astonishment, back in early June, when she rushed down the hill toward the willow tree, ten minutes late to the May Mothers meeting, and noticed a man in the circle. He was sitting beside Winnie, whispering into her ear. Winnie listened, amused, and then they broke into laughter. Francie guessed that he was Winnie's husband (although he wasn't nearly as attractive as she would have guessed Winnie's husband would be). He wore a frayed sky-blue baseball cap, the exact color of his eyes, and dressed like so many of the men in Brooklyn—a faded T-shirt and shorts, scuffed sneakers, aviator sunglasses stuck into the collar of his shirt. But as Francie took her seat, she noticed the sling across his chest, a baby curled inside. He wasn't Winnie's husband. He was a dad.

"I'm a SAD," he said a little later, as a way of introduction.

"You're sad?" Nell said. "Good. You'll fit right in."

"No," he said. "Not sad. *A* SAD."

"A sad?" Nell peered at him. "Is that a thing?"

"A Stay-at-Home-Dad. An S-A-H-D. Man, that joke usually works." He smiled and shrugged. "My partner works in fashion, and travels a lot. I don't pay the bills and get to stay home with Autumn. Doing my best not to screw her up."

He became a regular almost immediately, but never offered more than a few details about himself—nothing significant enough for Francie to even recall. Francie still doesn't understand where he went that night at the Jolly Llama, after disappearing from the table, and so this morning, when he e-mailed her about getting together, she told him the truth—that she and Nell were going to Colette's—and invited him to join, hoping to pry some information out of him. "He asked if he could come," Francie says quietly, hearing his footsteps in the hallway outside Colette's apartment. "I didn't know we were going to be talking about *this*."

"Hey," Token says when Colette opens the door. He looks terrible: unshaven, his T-shirt damp with sweat. Francie is surprised to see he isn't wearing the sling in which he always carries Autumn. "The baby's with my mom," he says, before Francie can ask.

"Why did you come, then?" Francie catches her accusatory tone. "I mean, if I had a break from the baby, I'd be sleeping."

Token sits on the couch. "I wanted to see you guys." He rests his forehead in his hands, and Francie notices the patches of gray spreading from his temples. "I'm so worried about Midas. Everything that's happened—you're the only ones I can really talk to about it."

Colette pours Token a cup of coffee and sits back on the floor. "Okay, so, about that," she says. "Token. All of you. What I'm about to tell you—you can't tell *anyone*." She opens the folder and places three photographs on the floor. "They have a potential suspect."

Token jerks his head up. "They have a suspect?"

"Yeah, this guy. His name is Bodhi Mogaro. They think he's connected."

Francie kneels beside Colette. The man in the photograph has deep-russet eyes and light-brown skin; his black hair is shaved nearly to his scalp.

"What do they have on him?" Token asks.

"He was seen around Winnie's building twice. On July 3, he bought beer and cigarettes from the bodega across the street. Used a debit card. It's how they know his name. The clerk remembers him as being uneasy. Said he then went and sat on a nearby bench, along the park wall, watching her building. Casing it, apparently. The next night he was spotted in front of her building again, acting erratically. Yelling into his phone."

"The night Midas was taken?" Nell says.

"Yes."

"He lives in Detroit," Token says, reading a paper he's pulled from the folder, the sunlight streaming through the window onto his patch of couch, washing out his features so that Francie can't read his expression.

"Yeah," Colette says. "He flew into New York on the third of July. Had a flight back on the fifth, but he didn't board. They don't know where he is."

"What do you mean they don't know where he is?" Francie asks.

"I mean, the police can't find him. He's disappeared."

"Jesus," Nell says.

"Do they think he's holding Midas for ransom?" Francie asks. "Actresses probably deal with this stuff all the time. But Lowell told me that if this were about ransom, they would have asked for it by now." She's still convinced Lowell could be wrong. After all, Lowell's uncle—and his one source on law enforcement—is a sheriff back home in Estherville. What would he know about a case this big, with a once-famous actress, a multimillionaire, the daughter of a well-connected developer?

"There's no mention of ransom. At least not in this file."

"You see he's originally from Yemen?" Nell asks.

"Yeah, but he's been here for twelve years," Colette says. "I searched him online. There's not much. He has a Facebook page, but it's private, and everything's written in Arabic. I did find someone with that name who is a mechanic for a company near Detroit that rents out private jets to rich clients. That's got to be him."

Airplanes? "He has access to airplanes?" Francie says.

Poppy cries from somewhere down the hall. "I called Winnie again," Colette says, standing up. "It's the third time. She's not responding."

Nell rubs her eyes. "And the scene around her apartment, with the cameras and journalists. It's out of hand. Some asshole tried to stop me when I walked by on the way here, asked if I live nearby, if I have a comment."

More than a few of Winnie's neighbors have already given interviews, asked what they know about her, if they'd noticed anything suspicious that night. It sickens Francie how many people are willing to chime in, to say whatever it takes to see their names in print: that Winnie seems quiet, a little aloof. That they've never seen her with a man. That they've been curious, they have to admit, who "the father" is.

Token stands, pacing slowly to the window, peering across the street into the park. "They're going to turn this into a fucking circus," he says. "You can feel it."

Colette walks down the hall toward Poppy's cries, and Francie continues to study the contents of the folder, scanning Mark Hoyt's notes. She doesn't want to say anything, but she's also been by Winnie's building a few times in the past three days, in the evenings, after the journalists have left. Will grows so fussy around seven each night, before Lowell is home to help. It's hard to be in the apartment when he's crying like that, trapped with the heat. She's been taking him for a walk up the hill.

She often takes a seat on the bench across the street from Winnie's building. It's been dark inside her house. But last night, as the sky grew dim with nightfall and the mosquitos buzzed in her hair, she pressed Will hard against her chest, whispering in his ear, pleading for some quiet, sure she saw someone moving inside.

CHAPTER EIGHT
DAY FOUR

TO: May Mothers

FROM: Your friends at The Village

DATE: July 8

SUBJECT: Today's advice

<u>YOUR BABY: DAY 55</u>

Think your partner's smile is heart-melting? Just wait. A baby's first smile arrives at about the same time in all cultures, so if it hasn't happened yet, prepare to be rewarded for all your loving care with a beaming, toothless, just-for-you smile. This will probably make you leap with joy (even if you've just had your worst night *ever*).

Nell browses the rack of dresses that hang like boneless bodies from the thin steel pole. She checks her watch—she still has another two hours before she can pick up Beatrice from the day care. A young woman approaches, a cherry smile painted above astonishingly white teeth. "You want me to start a room?" She wears a black fabric rose pinned in her blond curls, and a shirt so short it reveals the sharp edges of her rib cage.

"No, I'm ready now," Nell says, following her to the back of the store, to a small dressing room separated from the racks of clothes by the same thin floral curtain Nell has considered buying at IKEA.

"Let me know if you need another size," the girl says, sliding the curtain closed. Nell takes off her shorts and shirt, tears building for the third time this morning. She can't believe she has to return to work tomorrow, leaving Beatrice in the care of strangers for nine hours a day. She had to beg Sebastian to be the one to call Alma and tell her they'd decided it would be better, at least for right now, to put Beatrice into day care. Alma was a wreck. Nell listened at Sebastian's ear as Alma said how sorry she was, how she hasn't been able to sleep, how the journalists keep calling and showing up at her apartment, that she's been questioned three times already by the police.

"They're asking me everything, again and again. What did I see? What did I hear? How was the mother acting? The priest is here. I'm praying for forgiveness."

Nell tries to close the gap between the curtain and the wall before pulling on a pair of pants. Two sizes up from what she wore before getting pregnant, and she can't get them over her thighs. The blouse she tries next is no better. It cuts off circulation in her arms, and is too tight across her breasts. Sweat slicks her lower back as she pulls a formless black shift dress over her head. She's annoyed to see there's no mirror in the dressing room, and she quietly opens the curtain, locating the floor-length mirror near the sale rack. Within seconds, the girl is on her.

"That looks nice." Nell doesn't respond, hoping her silence will compel the girl back to the front of the store, but instead she tilts her head to the side, her small-bird features creased in thought as she chews her bottom lip. "Know what this dress needs?"

"A sixty-percent markdown?"

The girl laughs. "A statement necklace. Something to bring attention up, toward your neck. Away from the things you want to hide."

"What if the thing I want to hide is my neck?"

The girl holds up a finger and turns on the chunky heel of her ankle boot. "Let me see what we have."

Nell returns to the dressing room anxious and frustrated—about the girl, about how bad she looks in the dress—questioning why she's felt so unsettled since seeing those photos of Bodhi Mogaro yesterday afternoon. She discards the dress in a heap with the other clothes before fleeing first the dressing room and then the store, the jingle of the bell reverberating behind her. She snakes through the people on the sidewalk, unsure of where she's going, past the other boutiques she'd planned to visit for work clothes, for something that will actually fit her body now, fourteen pounds heavier. But she can't deal. Not today. Not with another store. Another dress. Another size-two sales clerk, smelling of hair products and cinnamon gum.

Was it him?

Was Bodhi Mogaro at the bar that night?

She can't get the questions out of her mind.

Is he the one who ripped her shirt? Is it him that she sees when she closes her eyes, the blurry figure behind her in the bathroom, a pair of hands on her shoulders?

Did he follow her, fight her for Winnie's key, all without her remembering it?

No.

The idea is ludicrous. She steps around two boys on a scooter and a young mom buying a pig-tailed toddler a paper cup of rainbow sherbet from an ice cream cart. She would have remembered that; her mind is playing tricks. She's worn down with sleep deprivation and worry. Last night she paced the living room for hours, combing her brain, trying to fill in the blank spots from that night.

If only the press would report something to help her. There's been no mention of Bodhi Mogaro, not even a hint that the police have zeroed in on a suspect. Instead, all the newscasters and pundits want to talk about are the mistakes the police are making. This morning, Elliott Falk wrote in the *New York Post* that Officer James Cabrera, who Nell recognized as the guy who told them to leave Winnie's house, has been put on paid leave, blamed for leaving the door unlocked, for allowing people to enter Winnie's home before evidence could be collected. Sources are reporting that he will probably be fired.

Good, Francie e-mailed. *They should fire him. Someone needs to be held responsible for screwing up this investigation.*

Patricia Faith is having a field day, calling for Commissioner Ghosh's immediate resignation, laying the blame for everything squarely at the feet of Mayor Shepherd, for choosing his incompetent friend to lead the police department, for caring more about appearing on billboards for fashion labels than about protecting innocent children. "Am I crazy?" Patricia Faith asked. "Or is it almost like this mayor doesn't want to see this case solved?"

Nell stops at the corner and waits for the light, the heat like a woolen blanket shrouding her body, people brushing her arms as they hurry by. A white plane of sunlight reflects off a wall of windows on the bank across the street. She closes her eyes.

A memory comes back to her. She's standing at the bar, a cold drink in her hand. *More, more, more.* Someone is singing those words to her. She feels a chin on her neck, lips on her ear.

She squeezes her eyes tighter, feeling hands on her waist. Someone is holding her arms.

I want more, more, more.

She opens her eyes and begins to run.

———

The man sitting at the end of the bar is in his early thirties. He wears a black T-shirt and camo shorts, and both arms are covered in sleeves of black-and-gray tattoos. He's sipping a pint of beer and glancing at the soccer match on one of the large television screens hanging above the rows of liquor bottles, a pen dangling above a copy of the *New York Times* crossword puzzle. The only other person there is the bartender, who leans over a sink, washing glasses. He shakes the soap from his wrists as Nell approaches. "What can I get you?"

"A club soda."

She swallows half of it before sliding off the stool and making her way through the bar, the air dense with bleach and beer, to the patio out back. She moves a chair to the spot she occupied that night and tries to re-create the scene in her mind. Colette and Francie are across from her. Winnie is to her right. Token—at least for a little while—is somewhere in the mix. She closes her eyes and sees Winnie, sipping iced tea, stealing peeks at the phone in her lap.

When Nell opens her eyes, the man at the bar is watching her. She closes her eyes again, this time seeing herself. She feels the heat and the pounding music. The crowd grows around them. She takes Winnie's phone from Francie.

She deletes the app.

Why? Why did she do that? Hadn't she learned her lesson? One impulsive decision can destroy an entire life. If anyone should know that, it's her.

She stands and paces the empty patio.

Think, think, think.

She goes inside, past the jukebox, past the bocce ball court, now dark and deserted. Up to the waitress station, where she ordered the fries. She took them to the table, eventually going with Gemma, or whoever it was, for another drink.

Nell's eyes flash open. *The cigarette.* She scans the room, spotting the door along the far wall, near the bathrooms. She sets her drink on the bar. The door to the smoking patio is unlocked, and she steps into a small gravel area filled with wobbly bar tables and stools, surrounded by a fence strung with Christmas lights. *Quiet please. Respect our neighbors.* She can smell the smoke in her hair, her tongue heavy with nicotine and tar. She's talking to someone, asking for a fag, forgetting not to use the British term, hearing him laugh. That was why she felt so sick the next day, the cigarette. It had been more than a year since she'd smoked, since she and Sebastian decided to try for a baby.

She paces, picturing a man, fuzzy at the edges, extending the pack of cigarettes, the *click click* of the lighter before it caught. He had dark eyes, and she'd told him why she was there. "I'm part of a mommy group," she said, drawing out the last two words, as if she were admitting to something too outrageous to be true. "Me. In a mommy group. Can you *believe* that?" She feels a hand on her arm, laughter in her hair as the heat builds around her.

"Another club soda?" the bartender asks when she goes back inside.

"Yes," Nell says. "And splash some vodka in this one."

He slides the drink toward her, and the fizz rises from the first sip, tickling her tongue.

"Oh shit." The bartender is looking up at the closest television, set to the local news. He reaches for the remote. "Not this again."

The woman on the screen is wearing a sleeveless black blouse and a bright yellow skirt, her forehead pinched in concern. Nell examines the woman's surroundings, and then she stands and walks to the window. Across the street, she sees it—the bumblebee yellow of the woman's clothes, the light of the camera, a news van parked nearby.

The bartender increases the volume, and the woman's voice jumps from the speakers near the ceiling. "*The baby has been missing for four days, and with no news of a suspect, the case is looking grim. Sources tell us that this morning the nanny, Alma Romero, originally from Honduras, was brought in for additional questioning. The police are also asking anyone who may have any helpful information to call the number listed here on the screen.*" The woman turns and gestures toward the entrance to the bar. "*As you know, Jonah, at the time of the baby's abduction, his mother, the former actress Gwendolyn Ross, was out at a bar with members of her mommy group. This bar, the Jolly Llama, is located—*"

The screen goes black. The bartender has thrown the remote next to the sink, knocking over a drying beer mug. "Here we go again. Every time we're on the news, we get another round of teenagers coming in, passing me fake IDs, wanting to see the 'famous' Baby Midas bar someone wrote about on Facebook." He plunges his arms back into the suds. "Those assholes don't tip."

Through the window, Nell watches the reporter crossing the street with her cameraman. She digs for the ten-dollar bill in her bag, leaves it on the bar, and is hurrying through the side door to the smoking area as the reporter enters, introducing herself to the bartender. "I'm Kelly Marie Stenson with CBS local news and I'm wondering if I can ask—"

Nell carries a bar stool to the fence. She climbs on top of it and grips the coil wire, pulling herself up, hoisting a leg over the top. Her palms are damp and she loses her grip, her sandals slipping in the wire. She falls to the other side, landing hard on the pavement of the parking lot next door. Feeling the taste of blood from where she's bitten her lip, seeing the razor cuts on the heels of her hands and knees, she stands and hurries through the parking lot out to the sidewalk, feeling a hard shoulder of a man bump into her side. "Jackass," she yells. "Watch where you're walking."

Up the hill, back toward the park, she slows her pace. As she crosses the street, she senses someone walking close behind, shadowing her steps, and it all comes back to her. People waiting around the corner, watching her, trying to document her every move. She breaks into a tender, awkward run again, ignoring the ache in her C-section incision and the pain spreading along her inner-right thigh; across the street, down the block, and toward the day care. She has another hour before picking up Beatrice, and yet she forces herself to keep up the pace, her feet burning in her thin sandals. Within ten minutes, she's arrived. She peers into the window between the cutout sunflowers and butterflies taped to the glass. Two women are kneeling on the floor in front of a bouncy chair, leaning toward the baby strapped into it. One of them is pressing the baby's chest. The women—they look in distress. The baby is choking. Nell moves to get a different angle. The baby they're kneeling in front of is Beatrice.

Nell dashes to the door, twisting the handle, but it's locked. She bangs on the glass, slamming her fists, imagining Beatrice inside, choking on an object carelessly left within her reach, her face turning blue. Finally the lock clicks open. Nell runs down the hall and throws open the door, meeting the startled look of a young woman in ripped jeans and a T-shirt printed with a pink cupcake and the words HAPPY BABY DAYCARE.

"Ms. Mackey. You're—"

She rushes past her, dropping to the floor next to the two women. Nell reaches for her baby, hearing her phone chiming in her bag as she registers the look on her daughter's face.

Beatrice is beaming.

Nell turns to the woman. The thing in her hand: it's a phone. She was taking a photo.

"Look at that gorgeous smile," the woman says, grinning down at Beatrice.

"Smile?"

"Yes."

"That's not gas?"

The woman laughs, and Nell's phone chimes again. "Not this time. That's a smile. You haven't seen her do that before?"

"No," Nell says. "I've been waiting for it." She kneels back on her heels, reaching for her phone, the tears smarting her eyes, her breath catching as she reads Francie's message.

They found him.

———

I want my mother.

Colette breaks into a final sprint as she reaches the top of the hill. She is too old to be having the thought, and yet she keeps imagining it: sitting with her mother at the large kitchen table at their home in Colorado, the dogs at their feet, the glass doors thrown open to the yard as her father fixes them drinks and Colette tells her mother everything. About how worried she is Midas will never be found. About taking the file from Teb's office and making copies and showing them to Nell and Francie. About the deep regret she's been feeling over her decision to share the information with Token, whom she barely knows. She wants to admit how embarrassingly bad her writing has been, and tell her about this morning, at the doctor's office for her second postnatal checkup, sobbing in the room with Dr. Bereck, admitting how overwhelmed and anxious she feels, how much trouble she's having getting to sleep.

"What are you feeling most anxious about?" Dr. Bereck asked.

"Everything, but Poppy mostly. I'm worried something is wrong with her." Colette has been trying without success to ignore her concerns—that Poppy's limbs seem weak, that she still hasn't mastered holding her head up fully, that she sometimes struggles to make eye contact. "When I'm around the other babies in my mom group—I don't know. They seem different. Stronger," Colette said, finally giving herself permission to cry. "And I get these daily updates from The Village. She's not hitting the milestones they say she should be."

"First of all, stop reading those," Dr. Bereck said. "They assume all babies are going to develop at exactly the same rate. That's not how this works."

"I know, but still. I can't stand the idea of it. Charlie says I'm crazy. That she's fine. But I'm her mother. I can feel it. Something might be wrong."

Colette wants to tell her own mother these things, but she can't. She doesn't even know where she is. The last time they spoke, ten minutes over a staticky phone line more than two weeks ago, Rosemary was in the San Blas Islands off the coast of Panama, conducting research on one of the last remaining matriarchal societies. Colette's father, recently retired as the chair of biology at UC Boulder, had accompanied her. ("As a member of a matriarchal family, I feel I'll fit in well," he said when her parents called to tell her they'd be going away for three months, leaving a week after Poppy was due.)

Colette is breathless as Alberto, the doorman, opens the door for her, and when she gets out of the elevator on the third floor, stopping to unlace her sneakers, she can hear Charlie inside the apartment, in the kitchen, speaking to someone on the phone.

He drops the phone from his ear when she enters. "Wow," he mouths. "You look hot."

She glances in the mirror over the table in the hall. Her hair is soaked, her freckles crimson, the layer of sunscreen she applied on her way out of the doctor's office chalks her skin. It's the first time she's gone for a run since giving birth, and she had to stop and walk several times. "I'm assuming you mean as in very warm," she says to Charlie.

"No," he whispers. "I mean as in hot." He kisses her hand and then speaks into the phone. "We can make that work. I just can't let these things get in the way of finishing the new book." He pours a cup of coffee and hands it to Colette. "And I probably shouldn't miss any major holidays. Doubt the baby would ever forgive me for that."

"Nor the baby's mother," Colette says, assuming he's on the phone with his publicist, discussing another invitation to speak somewhere. He finished his book tour two months earlier, but the requests for additional cities keep coming. She pours a glass of water and notices that the dining table—a vintage farm table Charlie bought them last Christmas—is set for two, with her grandmother's dishes and their linen napkins. A handful of bright blue bodega daisies, some of the petals flaccid and wilting, are arranged in a stainless-steel travel mug in the center of the table.

She takes a grape from the bowl at Charlie's elbow and wraps her arms around his waist, pressing her cheek into the familiar hollow between his shoulder blades, taking in his scent—Speed Stick and roasted garlic—hearing *Womb Noises* floating from the monitor on the shelf. She allows herself to feel the easy joy of the moment. The warmth of Charlie's body. Poppy asleep in the nursery. The rhythm of the apartment. If only she could stay right here, in this exact moment, forever.

Colette unclasps herself and sees the book—*Becoming a Family*—on the counter beside the coffeepot. She takes her coffee and the book and slides onto a stool at the island as Charlie chops a thick bunch of parsley in quick, sure bursts, the phone pressed between his shoulder and ear. She opens to the early section on pregnancy, glancing through Charlie's notes in the margins, the corners he's turned back to mark certain pages.

Nine weeks: the baby is the size of a grape.

How to prepare your birth partner.

Things to avoid: raw fish and undercooked meat, excessive exercise, hot baths.

Colette feels the lump in the base of her throat as she reads the words, remembering those early weeks. The ache in her breasts as she climbed the stairs. The stomach-turning scent of strangers' soap and perfume on the subway. Getting sick in her publisher's restroom, in the middle of a meeting to discuss the direction of the second book.

The devastating shock at the two pink lines on the plastic pregnancy test.

It was a glitch in her system. An off month. She knew her body well enough to avoid birth control, which had, the few months she was on the pill, left her feeling angry and depressed. (Charlie had joked with her, saying if all women responded to the pill the way she did, he understood its effectiveness. It made women so miserable, nobody wanted to have sex with them.) She'd gone to see Dr. Bereck, needing confirmation. Bodies change, Dr. Bereck said. Cycles slow. She was almost thirty-five. Things were beginning to shift.

Five weeks: the baby is the size of a poppy seed.

Five weeks: the September night she told Charlie she was pregnant. They made love afterward, and he lay alongside her, his chest against her back, his hand on the slope of her waist. "You. A baby. My book," he'd said. "This is everything I've ever wanted." She just lay there, unmoving, trying to imagine it. Pregnancy. A baby. Motherhood.

She couldn't do it. She couldn't imagine any of it. Her imagination was already occupied by other things. The two-month trip to Southeast Asia she and Charlie were planning to take after he finished his second book. The marathon she'd just begun training for. Finally getting out of ghostwriting and publishing another book of her own. Those things she could imagine. But this?

She called her mother the next morning, questioning how she was going to manage, how she'd stay herself, admitting she'd had three whiskeys one night before knowing she was pregnant; that she'd gone on several punishing runs.

"What if I've already hurt the baby?"

"Colette," her mother had said, "when abortions were illegal, women had to throw themselves down the stairs. You're not going to kill your baby by accident."

The memory dissolves as Charlie hangs up and comes to kiss her forehead. She closes the book. "You've scrambled eggs for me?" she says. "What's the occasion?"

"Your doctor's appointment." He nods at the book. "I've consulted the experts, and according to them, we're out of the woods."

"Out of the woods?"

He walks to the built-in wine cooler next to the dishwasher and takes out a bottle of champagne, popping the cork in one quick twist. "Yes. The baby is going to start smiling soon. A schedule will develop as she understands the difference between night and day. Oh, and—" He pours a little champagne into a water glass and tugs her to her feet. "We can have sex again. Drink up, woman."

Her body tenses as Charlie wraps his arms around her lower back, his hips against hers, walking her backward, pressing her against the refrigerator. Sex? The thought repulses her. She's exhausted and spent; her breasts and back ache. She slept fitfully last night, listening to Charlie rustling around the living room after Poppy woke up at midnight, putting on a series of jazz records to soothe her, reading to her from his novel, the chapter in which the young soldier leaves his mother, goes off to fight the war. Colette knew she should have gotten out of bed and offered to nurse Poppy, which would have instantly put her to sleep, but she was too exhausted to bring herself to do it, to drag herself up from under the weight of the blankets in the air-conditioned room, from her thoughts of Midas. Of Winnie. Of Bodhi Mogaro. Did he have Midas? Was the baby still alive?

Colette gently nudges Charlie away. "You're aware I have to leave soon, right? I'm meeting Teb."

Charlie freezes and closes his eyes before touching his forehead to hers. "You're meeting Teb."

"You forgot."

"I forgot."

"Today's your day with the baby," Colette says. "I had her yesterday. And I told you, he had to reschedule last time—"

"No, I know. It slipped my mind. Poppy was up three times last night. I'm exhausted."

"I'm sorry," Colette says. "But tonight's my night, and you'll get a break from her most of tomorrow."

He sighs and releases his hold on her. "You have to pump more. I used the milk in the freezer."

"I did. This morning. It's in there."

"And we need to talk about all this."

"All what?"

"This thing we're doing, splitting child care fifty-fifty. It's not working."

She feels instantly irritated. "I can't give up any more time," she says, trying to keep her voice steady, scooping a lump of scrambled eggs from the skillet into her mouth. "I've fallen a little behind on Teb's book." She hasn't told him the extent of it: how sure she is that she'll never meet the deadline, or how off her writing has been. She's too overwhelmed to admit how hard she's finding it, trying to manage everything, how she's aware they're out of laundry detergent and the showerhead is leaking, the sound of it driving her mad, and how she just made Poppy an appointment with the pediatrician tomorrow, at Dr. Bereck's suggestion.

"I'm not asking you to take on the child care, Colette. I'm saying we need to hire a nanny." His expression softens. "I know you're scared. This Midas thing is awful. But we can't have it both ways. We can't both try to hold down full-time work, have a newborn, and not have some help." He takes her hands. "It's not like we can't afford it. We can use some of my parents' money."

She pulls her hand away. "I don't want to hire a nanny, Charlie." She can't bear the thought of it, leaving the baby with a stranger. She walks past him toward the bedroom, lifting her damp T-shirt over her head.

"Well, then, what are we supposed to do?" He follows her into the bathroom. "If you won't agree to hire a sitter, you have to pick up the slack."

She turns on the shower, lifting the pink plastic baby tub from the floor of the bathtub, averting her gaze from the large clump of hair in the drain she shed during yesterday's shower. "But that's not what we agreed to."

"I understand that. But having a kid is a little more difficult than either of us expected. We need to reevaluate it. My book is due in two months."

"And mine is due in one."

"I know, baby." His jaw is clenched. "But you know what's riding on mine."

"I have to get ready." She closes the door, then showers slowly, scouring her body with a new salt scrub she bought on a whim at the grocery store yesterday, trying to rinse away her frustration, the exhaustion. When she re-emerges from the bedroom in a clean blouse and skirt twenty minutes later, Charlie is in his office with the door closed. She steals into the nursery, the darkened room echoing with the cetacean calls of the *Womb Noises* CD, the air filled with the scent of her daughter. Colette can't resist the urge to lean into the crib, to touch Poppy's cheek and brush aside the threadlike hairs—as orange as pumpkin pie—from her forehead. A face so much like Colette's mother's.

Deciding not to disturb Charlie, she quietly leaves the apartment, walking toward the subway, where she stays at the end of the platform, away from the newsstand, wanting a few hours' reprieve from the latest headlines about Midas. Once on the train, she closes her eyes, thinking how ridiculous this argument with Charlie is. He's at the height of his career. A huge advance for his debut novel, gushing reviews anointing him one of the most promising new voices in decades, in the midst of finishing his second, highly anticipated book.

And here she is.

On her way to sit at the mayor's office, to wait around for Teb, writing a book he's going to say he wrote himself, earning him a fortune in royalties, too afraid to attempt another book of her own. Her first book, a biography of Victoria Woodhull, the first woman to run for president, was published six years earlier. Colette spent years researching it and was infinitely proud of the work. But its sales were dismal, and while she wrote two subsequent book proposals, no publisher was interested. Too gun-shy to try again, on her agent's advice she began to accept ghostwriting work. Just for a little while, her agent said. Just until a better idea for the next book strikes. That was four years ago.

Her phone dings with a new text message as she climbs the subway stairs at her stop near City Hall, distracting her from the thoughts. It's Charlie.

I've been thinking about something, he wrote.

What's that?

Global warming. What a bummer, huh? She waits. Also, how about a romantic dinner at home tonight? After the baby's asleep.

Sounds nice.

I'll even let you cook.

Colette stops at the coffee cart at the entrance to City Hall Park. "A large black iced coffee," she says to the man inside. "And a glazed doughnut, please."

How generous, she types.

I think so too. What are you going to make?

A soufflé.

Awesome. What kind?

The invisible kind.

But you made that yesterday.

She has another ten minutes before she's scheduled to meet Teb, and she decides to take her coffee to a bench in the park, near a butterfly bush blooming with purple flowers. It would all be so much easier if she could tell Charlie the truth. She wants to stop working. She wants to focus on Poppy. She pulls the doughnut apart, envisioning the life she wants: being only a mother right now. Making sure Poppy is okay. That she's loved, healthy, getting the things she needs.

She casts the idea away. She can't tell Charlie that.

She can't *be* that.

Colette Yates, the daughter of Rosemary Carpenter, *the* Rosemary Carpenter, who made a career writing about the plight of motherhood, the inherent sexism in domestic partnerships, the need for women to avoid dependence on a man. *She* was going to choose to be a stay-at-home mom?

Colette finishes the doughnut and opens her e-mail, knowing she has to gather herself and prepare for her meeting with Teb. There's a new message from Aaron Neeley, with notes on the chapters they're meant to discuss today.

You're not really getting this part—the emotional toll Margeaux's death had on the mayor. The timeline here is all screwed up. Go back and dig up the Esquire profile. That writer got it right.

Colette raises her face to the sky, feeling the sun's warmth on her skin, and hears the chime of an incoming text. She tries not to think about Aaron's message, or the hour she'll have to spend talking about this book, or the image of Winnie sitting alone in her apartment, Midas's crib empty, surrounded by reminders of his absence. All she wants to think about, at least for another five minutes, is the sun on her face, dinner with Charlie, the pediatrician's appointment tomorrow, where she'll hear everything is fine. Poppy is normal. Her fears are unfounded.

She reaches for her phone to see what Charlie has written. But the message isn't from Charlie.

It's from Francie.

———

Colette tries to appear composed as she greets Allison.

"Go on in and get settled," Allison says. "He's finishing up another meeting."

Inside Teb's office, she sits at the large round table and opens her laptop.

They found him. That's all Francie's text said.

She types the address of the *New York Post* website, bracing herself for devastating news. The article is on the home page.

SUSPECT IN MIDAS ROSS ABDUCTION FOUND IN PENNSYLVANIA

Colette exhales, resting her forehead on her palm. Francie didn't mean Midas. She meant Bodhi Mogaro.

A 24-year-old Yemeni man believed to be linked to the abduction of Midas Ross was arrested early this morning in Tobyhanna, Pennsylvania, two hours west of New York City.

The police pulled him over for trespassing after his parked

car was spotted on the grounds of the Tobyhanna Army Depot, which houses surveillance equipment used by the Department of Defense. The police confirm they have been searching for Mogaro for two days, after eyewitnesses spotted him around Gwendolyn Ross's residence on the night of July 4, at the time of her son's abduction. A bag containing nearly $25,000 in cash was discovered in the trunk of Mogaro's car, a 2015 Ford Focus, rented from JFK early in the morning on July 5.

$25,000 in cash.

Colette reads the sentence again. Why would he have that money?

The Department of Homeland Security has become involved, investigating why Mogaro may have been trying to break into the Army Depot, while also trying to determine if any military personnel may have been working in collusion with Mogaro. Mogaro's wife, a professor of economics at Wayne State University, did not respond to several requests for comment.

Colette's phone beeps again. It's Nell. What does this mean?

"Colette." Allison is standing in the door. "Sorry to interrupt your writing, but the mayor's running a few minutes late."

Colette nods. "Okay," she says, barely getting the word out. "Thanks."

"And I should let you know. The copy machine broke." Allison lowers her voice. "The repairman won't be here for another hour, if you need to use the room. I can make a sign. Nobody will disturb you."

Colette glances down at the article. "Good timing," she says. "I was just about to see if the bathroom is empty."

Allison's smile is wide. "Give me a minute."

Colette takes her bag from under the chair and walks to the credenza beside the mayor's desk. The file is still there, heavier in her hands than it was two days earlier. Allison flashes a thumbs-up from her desk as Colette walks to the copy room, clicking the lock into place behind her. As she lifts the file from her bag, something falls from it, landing at her feet. A flash drive. She sets it on the copy machine and pages quickly through the papers inside the file, scanning for Bodhi Mogaro's name. In her haste she slices the crease of her thumb and forefinger, leaving a painful wisp of a paper cut, and a trail of her blood on the top page.

"Shit," she whispers, rubbing the blood across the words "Membership list: May Mothers."

She flips through copies of the questionnaire she had to fill out when signing up for May Mothers through the Village website. She sees Nell's profile. Yuko's. Scarlett's. Francie's. How did the police get access to these?

She sees hers.

She takes it from the stack, looking at the photo she included, from the trip to Sanibel Island she and Charlie took before Poppy was born. The night he proposed, the anniversary of their first date, the first night they'd spent together, waking up the next morning in his Brooklyn Heights apartment, watching the first plane hit the tower. "I will be with you forever," she said that day on the Florida beach, her hair thick with sand and salt water, holding the ring in her hand. "But you know me, Charlie. Marriage isn't my thing." She barely recognizes herself in the photo. Just two years earlier, but she appears so young.

Then it occurs to her: Teb will see this. He'll discover that she knows Winnie. He'll know—if he doesn't know already—that she was there that night. He'll want to know why she didn't tell him.

She looks at the shredder next to the copy machine, and

without a second thought, she feeds the paper into the slit on top. In one rapid motion, slivers emerge from the other end of the machine.

She returns to the folder, flipping through the papers. Photos of the back deck of the Jolly Llama. Photos of Winnie's house. Her kitchen. A lab report Colette can't make sense of. She stops at a transcript of an interview, several pages long.

HOYT: Can you spell your name for me?

MERAUD SPOOL: M-E-R-A-U-D S-P-O-O-L

HOYT: And you're a friend of Ms. Ross?

SPOOL: A former friend. We haven't spoken in years, but we were close when we were young.

HOYT: I know we want to get to the incident with Daniel you witnessed, but before we get to that, tell me about your relationship with Ms. Ross.

SPOOL: We met at the Bluebird auditions. We had a lot in common, and we clicked right away. When my mom and I moved here for the show, Mrs. Ross invited us to stay with them while the apartment we bought was being renovated. We would spend our weekends at their country home, upstate. Winnie and I shared a room. She felt like my sister.

HOYT: Okay.

SPOOL: So, anyway, we both got cast. Winnie, obviously, got the lead.

[Laughter]

HOYT: How did you feel about that?

SPOOL: How did I feel? To be perfectly honest, it stung. For all the girls, not just me. She wasn't the best dancer. But she was the most beautiful.

HOYT: Did she get along well with the other girls?

SPOOL: No, not really. She was awkward.

HOYT: Awkward?

SPOOL: Yeah, like she never really knew how to just be herself. She was always shape-shifting, trying to be what she thought others wanted her to be. Trying to portray whatever image it was that served the situation. But she got more confident after she met Daniel.

HOYT: And where did they meet?

SPOOL: I have no idea, to be honest. Skinny. Acne. It shocked all the other girls that they were dating, but not me, not after I saw the two of them together. They made so much sense. He was a lot like her. Studious. Artsy. They really loved each other. [*Laughter*] I mean, the way we do when we're seventeen. Kid love. Although, at thirty-nine, with three kids and twelve years of marriage, I'm starting to think that that, in fact, is what real love is. This? This is work. Am I talking too much? I'm not sure I'm answering your questions.

HOYT: You're doing fine.

SPOOL: Well, anyway, the show was doing great. Winnie had Daniel. She had me. And then her mom died. And—

HOYT: Yes?

SPOOL: And then things, well— Look, you guys contacted me to ask if you could interview me, and I'm happy to help. I have three sons. I seriously can't imagine what she's going through. But I'm afraid to say the wrong thing.

HOYT: Try not to worry about that. We're just gathering facts.

SPOOL: She went crazy. I mean, who wouldn't? Losing your mom so young. It was horrible. This freak accident, which nobody could explain. Her brakes go out, just as she's driving down a hill? It was so strange. On top of that, the guy was back. Archie Andersen.

Colette pauses. Yesterday, Francie mentioned in an e-mail that Winnie had a stalker, wondering if he had any contact with Winnie since her *Bluebird* days.

SPOOL: He'd disappeared for several months, after the restraining order was issued, but then he showed up at her mom's funeral, making a huge scene, wailing at the front of the church. It was a lot for her.

HOYT: Are you all right?

SPOOL: It's just so sad. Winnie and her mom were so close. Like, the kind of relationship every young girl wants to have with her mother. And then, poof, she was gone. Winnie started to have panic attacks. Terrible crying fits. It reminded me of my stepmom, actually.

HOYT: Your stepmom?

SPOOL: She had just given birth to my half sister at the time. She's, let's say, a number of years younger than my dad. She went nuts afterward. Crying. Unable to sleep. She was eventually hospitalized for a while. Postpartum psychosis.

HOYT: And how did that remind you of Winnie?

SPOOL: Well, Winnie, she— She wasn't herself. And then the incident happened.

HOYT: Tell me about that.

Someone is knocking on the copy room door. Colette thrusts the papers back into the folder and hastily shoves it in her bag, along with the flash drive. "Hang on," she says into the thin crack of light between the door and frame. "Last boob, nearly done." She pulls out her manual pump, unbuttons her shirt to below her bra and opens the door.

It's Aaron Neeley. "Everything okay?" He lowers his eyes to her bra.

Colette fumbles to rebutton her shirt, her face hot with embarrassment. "Yes, fine."

"We're waiting for you."

"Okay, great." She returns the pump to her bag. "All set."

Allison shoots Colette an apologetic look as she follows Aaron back to Teb's office. He's sitting in his chair, reading a printout of the manuscript, his feet propped on his desk, revealing red-and-white polka-dot socks. Aaron gestures at one of the empty chairs in front of the desk. "Give me a second," Teb says.

Colette keeps her bag on her lap and glances at Aaron, and then at the wall behind Teb, which showcases a rotating collection of framed photographs of him posing with various celebrities. A few new ones have been added. Teb with Bette Midler. With a young man recently signed to the New York Mets. With former secretary of state Lachlan Raine, who, it was announced earlier this morning, is likely to be nominated for the Nobel Peace Prize for the work his foundation is doing in Syria.

"Cool, huh?" Teb is watching her.

"Very."

"Met Raine two weeks ago, at my thing at Cipriani's. He's raising millions for my campaign, but man, is that guy crazy. No joke, there wasn't a waitress he didn't hit on."

Colette tries to keep her voice breezy. "I'm shocked."

Teb chuckles. "Yeah, right." He puts down the final sheet of paper. "Okay, C. I have to be honest. I think we're going in the wrong direction in a few places."

She tucks her hair behind her ears, willing herself to appear indifferent. "I understand." Aaron is looking on with a mixture of boredom and weariness. "Can you be more specific?"

Teb leans back in his chair and studies the ceiling. "The first book. Who did that reviewer compare my writing to?" he asks Aaron.

"'Prose like Hemingway. Wit like Sedaris,'" Aaron says.

Colette scoffs. "To be honest, Teb, that was a little much."

"Fine, but this one? It's not going to wow anyone." He looks at Aaron. "Right?"

Aaron blows out a long puff of air. "Yes, sir, I have to agree. I get that we're asking you to write quickly, Colette, but we can't settle for something mediocre. Not with the expectations the mayor set with his first book."

"Okay." She nods. "Let's go through it."

For the next hour, she tries to focus on what they're asking of her, but she's distracted by the weight of the folder in her bag—what if Teb has already gone through it? What if he's seen her membership form? By the muted television in the corner, set to NY1. Colette can't keep her eyes away, and eventually she sees a photo of Bodhi Mogaro flash across the screen, the photo the police must have provided to the press—the same photo she has at home, in the folder under the couch. *Yemeni man in custody for trespassing, possible connection to Midas Ross abduction.* She feels a flood of relief when Allison knocks gently on the door, peeking her head inside.

"Mayor, your next appointment is here. They're waiting in 6B. I've set you up with lunch."

"Great, thanks, Allison." Teb straightens the papers and hands them across the table to Aaron before reaching to check his phone. "This was helpful, right? This will get us all back on track?"

"Absolutely," says Aaron.

Colette gathers her computer and notebook, sliding them inside her bag next to the folder. She walks into the lobby, where one of the young assistants from the press office is leading a public tour, pointing out the art on the walls, guiding the crowd to the large bay window offering a view of the Brooklyn Bridge. Colette snakes through them to the bathroom, waiting just inside the door, watching the hall to Teb's office. When she sees Teb and Aaron heading to their next meeting, she walks toward

Allison, who's on the phone at her desk. "I think I dropped my wallet in there," Colette whispers.

Allison waves her inside. She pretends to inspect the floor around the chair she'd occupied, and then beside Teb's desk, guiding the folder back into its place.

She waves good-bye to Allison, pressing the button at the elevator. Two women scoot inside just before the doors close, coffees and lighters in their hands.

"They say he's from Yemen. A Muslim," one says to the other, in the raspy voice of a longtime smoker. "That can't be good."

The other woman shakes her head. "What I want to know is, where's the mother? Why isn't she giving any interviews? Only a woman with something to hide would refuse to speak to the press."

The women both look at Colette. She smiles and pushes the button for the lobby, her heart thudding, her bag pressed against her chest, the flash drive still inside.

CHAPTER NINE
NIGHT FOUR

I feel better here.

Shaded by the trees and shadows, the brim of a hat. Only two hours from the city, and yet I may as well be an entire world away. Thank god. I wasn't sure I'd be able to leave, but I simply packed the car in the middle of the night and headed out before the sun rose, not a word to anyone, letting myself in before the neighbors were awake, using the key left in the flowerpot.

It was the right choice, to leave the city and come here. I feel stable, lucid. Euphoric, even. To be honest, I haven't felt this good in months. It's probably the good country air, and those pills the doctor gave me before I left the hospital, something to take the edge off.

Okay, I need to get down to business. I don't know why I'm feeling coy about writing this, but . . .

Joshua and I. We're back together.

It's too good to be true, and god how I hate to jinx it, but there you have it. I did it. I went to see him. I thought he was going to be angry with me for showing up like I did, telling him I just needed to say my piece, once and for all. But he wasn't angry. I held myself together and explained how hard it was being without him, and how hopeless and depressed I've been, reminding him how happy we were in the beginning, those long nights in the bath. Lying in bed on Sunday mornings, reading aloud. Shakespeare. Maya Angelou. *A Tree Grows in Brooklyn*.

And you know what? He let me talk. No, he *wanted* to hear these things.

"I'll take care of things," I said. "For you. For us." He smiled. "If I do, will you come home with me?" I moved closer, pulling him toward me, lost in the feel of his skin, his smell, his body pressed against mine. "You need me as much as I need you. You know it."

I can't lie. I'm nervous. I'm having trouble trusting any of my decisions, and this one is no different. But then I keep thinking about that sign hanging in Dr. H's waiting room.

> *Some want it to happen. Some wish it would happen.*
> *Some make it happen.*

It makes me laugh now, remembering my first time meeting Dr. H, how I took that tacky plaque off the wall and carried it inside his office. The room smelled of carpet soap and a lingering trace of woodsy cologne left behind by his last patient. "You're kidding," I said, kicking off my flip-flops and tucking my legs under me, the plaque in my lap.

"What?" he asked, his hands clasped in his lap, benevolence in his eyes. (He's from Milwaukee.) "What am I kidding about?"

"This plaque. What? Were all the cat posters saying HANG IN THERE sold out?"

But that plaque was right. I couldn't sit around for the rest of my life *thinking* about being with Joshua. I couldn't just *wish* to be with him. I had to make it happen, whatever it took.

It's not going to be easy. I think we both know that. We'll stay here for as long as we can, until we figure out where to go next. I'm considering Indonesia, like in that book everyone loved. I'll cut my hair. We'll rent a house on a rice paddy, do yoga, find ourselves. I'll learn to cook.

But the details can wait. Right now, I just want to be here, enjoying the fresh air and warm breeze, with Joshua. This evening I grilled steaks for dinner and opened the most expensive bottle of wine I could find in the cellar. We lay in bed afterward, and after he fell asleep, I couldn't take my eyes off him. I know he'll wake up and wonder where I am, but I'm so content, wrapped in this silk robe, listening to the crickets, gazing out at the starlit fields left behind by people who can't afford to farm any longer.

I will say this: I need to stop reading the news. The media—all of them—they're obsessed with the story. The former actress who had it all.

Money!

Beauty!

A gorgeous new baby!

Patricia Faith is even intent on making something of the date—the *coincidence* of a baby disappearing on the Fourth of July, his mother freed from the burden of motherhood, on Independence Day. The date, like his name, has taken on some sort of symbolic meeting. Midas. The great Greek king who turned everything to gold and then who, at least in Aristotle's telling, starved to death for his "vain prayer." (In other versions, of course, he was rescued at the last moment from certain death.)

But what did I expect? Of course they're obsessed. Entire careers have been built around stories like this. It upsets Joshua that I'm reading about it, but I'm having a hard time pulling myself away. I need to know what people are saying. Where fingers are being pointed. Especially today, now that Bodhi Mogaro was found. People have taken to the comments sections like members of a fevered mob. *A guy caught with $25,000 in cash? Someone just bought himself a seat in the electric chair.*

Children are abducted all the time in Africa and in the inner cities of America, and nobody seems to care about that. Those stories don't make it to the front page of the New York Times.

Why is this newspaper not reporting on the eyewitness accounts of a middle-aged Caucasian man spotted the night of July fourth, sitting on a bench across from her building. It's on all the crime blogs and confirmed by at least two anonymous sources within the NYPD. The guy is a registered sex offender, on probation after molesting a young boy.

I'll admit it. That last piece of information made me smile. I planted it myself. Why? Because somebody is going to pay for what happened, and I'm going to make goddamned sure it's not me.

Anyway, I should allow my mind to rest, to enjoy how peaceful I feel. Or how peaceful I would feel if I wasn't so on edge, if I wasn't imagining, every moment, that I hear my baby crying.

CHAPTER TEN
DAY FIVE

> **TO:** May Mothers
> **FROM:** Your friends at The Village
> **DATE:** July 9
> **SUBJECT:** Today's advice
> <u>**YOUR BABY: DAY 56**</u>
> Happy birthday, baby! Your little one is eight weeks old today. You did it! (It's hard to even remember a time before you became a mother, right?) Time to celebrate these last few weeks of nurturing, feeding, snuggling, and loving your new little wonder. And go ahead, have that piece of cake. You've earned it.

They found a little boy, in New Jersey.

The entire police force of a small beach community had been summoned, but it was a member of the volunteer search team who discovered him. He was a mile down the beach, walking along the reeds looking for shells, two hours after wandering away from his parents in the moment it took his mother to unpack the sandwiches.

A girl in Maine was last seen getting off the school bus near her home. The police searched through the night, created a command post along Route 8; a rescue dog was brought in. The next morning, she was found alive at an uncle's house.

It happens all the time: a kid goes missing, only to be discovered safe and sound not long after. But, Francie notes once more as she scrolls through the stories on the Center for Missing Children's website, these kids were all found within twenty-four hours.

Five days.

It's been five whole days, and the police are saying *nothing*. Not whether they've found any trace of Midas, no word on whether he's safe. They haven't even released any information linking Bodhi Mogaro—who is still being detained on trespassing charges—to the abduction.

Francie takes the bottle from the steamy pot of water on the stove and carries Will to the rocker, a few inches from the window fan. Shading him from the sunlight filtering through the curtains, she nestles him into the crook of her arm and lifts the bottle to his mouth, hoping (she can't deny it) that he's going to refuse the formula, that he'll accept nothing other than her milk, that he'll cry in disgust at the chemical smell. She teases his lips with the gummy orange nipple and he opens his mouth—the thin gray liquid spreading across his bottom lip—and then drinks in quick, nearly frantic gulps.

Francie ignores the twinge of disappointment and reaches for the remote. Oliver Hood is being interviewed on CNN. A civil rights attorney who made a name for himself arguing for the release of six prisoners from Guantanamo, he announced yesterday that he's taken on Bodhi Mogaro's case, pro bono.

"As far as I understand things," the host—a middle-aged man in dark-framed glasses and a bold checked shirt—is saying, "Mogaro is currently being held on trespassing charges. But the real interest is in determining his role in the abduction of Baby Midas. Oliver Hood, what can you tell me?"

Hood is a slight man with large round eyes. "Well, I can tell you a lot of things, but the main thing I want to say is that my client is innocent. He didn't knowingly trespass, and he most certainly didn't have anything to do with the disappearance of

Baby Midas. This is a textbook case of racial profiling. What is the evidence against him? He was seen around Winnie Ross's building, and he's of Middle Eastern descent. That's it."

"Well, if you talk—"

"And it gets worse. I spoke to two detectives who say the man identified by an eyewitness as Bodhi Mogaro the night of July 4, the man said to be walking near Ms. Ross's building, ostensibly at the time of the abduction, yelling into a phone, acting erratically"—Oliver Hood pauses for effect—"is *not* Bodhi Mogaro."

"What do you mean?"

Hood holds up a photo of a man wearing a white surgical coat. "His name is Dr. Raj Chopra, and he's the head of surgery at Brooklyn Methodist Hospital. He was rushing in to work, on his night off, to assist with a bus crash in which two little kids and a young mother were badly injured."

Francie closes her eyes, letting it sink in. Bodhi Mogaro wasn't even there that night? If that's true, it's possible the police have no credible leads.

"Well, some might argue you shouldn't take anything a *detective* is saying about this at face value. Not with the mess they've made of this case. And your claim certainly doesn't explain why Mogaro had that cash in his car."

"I've spoken at length with Bodhi, his wife, and his parents. Bodhi was in Brooklyn to collect money from friends and relatives in the area, to help pay the funeral expenses of an aunt who'd died back in Yemen. It's what they do in the Muslim culture."

The host smirks. "And drink beer and smoke cigarettes, as Bodhi Mogaro was allegedly doing the night of July 3, as he sat on a bench watching Winnie's house? Is that *also* what they do in the Muslim culture?"

Oliver Hood laughs. "Look. Mr. and Mrs. Mogaro are new

parents." He lifts another piece of paper from the desk in front of him and holds it to the camera. Francie gasps. It's the photograph of Bodhi Mogaro she saw at Colette's apartment; the one in which he's smiling widely, a baby resting on his forearms, sunglasses on his head. "This is the so-called kidnapper and his six-week-old son. Did he have a drink and a smoke one night? Yeah, but come on. He's a new dad. Cut the guy some slack."

"And his flight?"

"He missed his flight. He overslept. It was an honest mistake. He couldn't afford another plane ticket, so he rented a car to drive home."

The host squints at Oliver Hood. "He was picked up three days after missing that flight. I don't think it takes three days to drive from Brooklyn to Detroit. Even my wife's eighty-four-year-old granny could make that trip in one day."

"He stopped to see an uncle in New Jersey. Then he got lost on the way. He didn't know he'd driven onto army property. I'm telling you, Chris, the guy is innocent. It's tragic what's happening to him. The police better show some credible evidence and charge him, or they gotta let him go."

"Okay, I have to say, you make an interesting argument. This will certainly be fascinating to watch. Thank you, Oliver Hood. Now, with me via satellite from Santa Monica is my next guest, the author Antonia Framingham." Francie sits forward. She loves this woman. She's become very wealthy from a series of young adult mysteries—Francie has devoured every one of them—and announced yesterday that she was donating $150,000 to the NYPD to help with the investigation. Her own daughter was abducted fifteen years earlier. The police never had a single credible lead.

"Why, Antonia, did you decide to donate this money?" the host asks her.

"Because I know there's nothing worse than a mother losing a child." Francie looks down at Will, at his sparkling eyes gazing up into hers as he drinks from the bottle. "Any mother who has ever lost a child knows—"

Francie mutes the television and sets the remote on the table beside her. The brakes of a bus whine outside her window, and the taste of diesel fumes wafts into the room, settling on her lips. She doesn't want to think about Antonia Framingham's loss. Or about Winnie's loss. She particularly doesn't want to think any more, as she has these last few days—the thoughts careening around her mind—about the loss of her own three children.

The first one, a daughter. She's been seeing it, so clear in her head when she's alone. The white tiled room, the stink of antiseptic, the terrified faces of the other teenage girls waiting on the hard plastic chairs in the reception area. They, at least, were there with someone—equally terrified boys; girlfriends who sat nervously beside them, chewing half of the stick of gum they'd broken apart to share. One girl was even there with her mother, who wore large hoop earrings and clung to her daughter's hand, telling the nurse she didn't care what the rules were, she was going to accompany her daughter into the room. Francie's mom was waiting for her in the car, driving circles around the Big Lots parking lot next door to the clinic, afraid she'd be spotted by someone from church.

"You understand the risks to your body?" a nurse asked Francie after she was finally led to a sterile, chilly room and handed a blue paper gown.

"Yes."

"And you have the father's permission?"

"My father is not around," Francie says. "He left when I was a baby."

"Not *your* father. The baby's."

"Oh." She felt a flash of panic. "Do I need that?"

The nurse looked up. "Not legally. But it would be nice." Francie kept her eyes on the floor. "Can I have the father's name?"

"His name?"

The nurse's pen was suspended over her clipboard. She released a highly irritated sigh. "Yes, his name. I'm assuming you know it?"

Of course she knew his name. James Christopher Colburn. Twenty-two years old. Graduate of St. James University, volunteer with Catholic Volunteers, science teacher at Our Lady of Perpetual Help. She'd stayed after lab and told him, explaining about the morning sickness and the positive pregnancy test. He collected his things, said he had to go, telling her he'd call later that night. The gym teacher was in his place at the front of the classroom the next day. She never saw him again.

"No. I don't know his name."

The nurse shook her head, her stiff blond curls swaying against her shoulders, saying something under her breath as she made a note on the paper. "Sign here, saying you consent to the procedure." She cracked her gum. "Gotta make sure you won't regret it." Francie's hand shook as she signed her name. She wanted to tell the woman that she *didn't* consent to the procedure. She wanted to keep the baby. She could do it, she thought. The baby wasn't due until the summer. She could give birth after graduation, get a job to support them.

But her mother forbade it. "No, Mary Frances. I won't hear of it. There is no room in my life for this," Marilyn said as she roughly kneaded a ball of dough. "Things are difficult enough, raising two daughters on my own. I don't need a baby to feed on top of everything else."

"Are you okay?" Marilyn asked when Francie eased herself into the front seat of her mother's Cutlass an hour after the procedure.

"Fine. It was quick." They never spoke of it again.

The two other babies she lost, the miscarriages—those were equally heartbreaking. The first, just four months after their wedding, was so early it wasn't even real. That, at least, is what the OB in Knoxville had told her. "It's very early, just a collection of cells. Don't worry. Keep trying."

What wasn't real about it? she wanted to ask, as Lowell held her hand that morning in the doctor's office, the ghostly blue ultrasound gel drying on her abdomen. The names she'd picked out? The life she'd been imagining?

The second—two years later, after seventeen tortured months of trying unsuccessfully to get pregnant, and then a round of IVF on her doctor's advice—was the result of an embryo abnormality. "Something we can't explain," the doctor said this time. "It's rare for someone in their twenties to have reproductive issues. But try again. Perhaps you'll have better success on your second attempt."

She could explain it. It was exactly what the nurse at the clinic had warned her about—that her decision would be something she'd come to regret. That there would be consequences. In the days leading up to the appointment, Francie would lie in bed, convinced the baby was a girl, picturing what she would look like, wishing she was strong enough to stand up to her mother, to do whatever it took for her child. To parent this baby the way *she* wanted to. But she didn't do anything. She was powerless.

Francie wipes the tears from the corners of her eyes, and when she glances back at the television, Midas is on the screen. It's a photo of him on his back, his fists at his cheeks, staring into the camera. She reaches for the remote and turns up the volume. Antonia Framingham is holding a tissue to her nose.

"I can't help but picture Midas, the way I used to lie in bed and picture my daughter after she went missing." She sniffs. "It's like I can see him. He's alone somewhere, without his mother, an ache in his tiny heart, wondering where she is. Wondering when she's coming to get him."

Francie turns off the television and throws the remote onto the couch. She's had more than she can handle for the day. She walks to the kitchen, quietly placing the bottle in the sink. The formula has left Will peaceful and sleepy, and she gently fastens him into his stroller, lifting it down the four flights to the foyer, and then out into the heat and up the hill, six blocks to the park. She stops at the bodega for a Diet Coke—her first taste of caffeine in more than a week. By the time she takes a seat on the bench, *her* bench, in front of Winnie's building, her T-shirt is glued to her lower back. She sets the stroller in the shade and reaches into the diaper bag for her camera, blowing the dust from the lens before standing on the bench to see over the stone wall and into the park, sweeping across the meadow to the black willow, where the May Mothers will be meeting in thirty minutes.

She's eager to see everyone again. It's been a little over a week since the group has been together under that tree, and she's felt the loss. The anticipation of the meetings. Her place in the circle among the other mothers, sharing advice, surrounded by the babies. She steps off the bench and trains her camera across the street, panning from a few of the journalists who linger in front of Winnie's building, to the news van parked nearby, and then to a window a few doors down, where, inside, she can make out a series of black-and-white family portraits hanging over a sofa, and several large palm plants that stand in the corner. She turns the zoom lens, getting in closer, until she can read the titles of the books in a neat row on a shelf.

A dog begins to bark, and Francie guides her camera to the sidewalk, to the man with thick glasses. He's in his late forties, and she's seen him here before, walking back and forth in front of Winnie's building, a tiny brown dog on a leash. He's always peering at the windows, as if he's trying to see inside.

Francie can't help but wonder if it's him: Theodore Odgard.

The registered sex offender who lives somewhere on this block. She found his name late last night as she fed Will, scrolling through the sex offender registry on her phone. And perhaps he's the *same* man Francie read about on a crime blog—the one spotted on a bench across from Winnie's building, the night of July Fourth.

Francie watches him through her viewfinder as he pulls his dog along. Just as he passes Winnie's building, her front door opens. Francie's heart quickens—Winnie's there!

She zooms in on the door and is disappointed to see it's not her, but a man. He closes the door behind him and walks gingerly down the stairs. He's older, in his late sixties perhaps, and wears a light-yellow golf shirt, the name HECTOR embroidered on the front pocket. The little dog lunges toward him when he reaches the sidewalk, exploding in a burst of shrill barks. Hector reaches to pet the dog, nodding hello to the man at the end of the leash, to the three journalists who sit nearby on a curb. He then strolls back and forth in front of Winnie's door, his hands clasped behind his back, stopping to finger the flowering bush near the path, snapping off a few withering petals. Francie remains motionless, watching. There's been very little written about Winnie's father, and Francie wonders if this is him. No, she decides, with the way he paces back and forth, he must be a security guard. A retired cop, perhaps, who Winnie hired to protect her house, making sure nobody tries to enter, no journalist rings her bell; shooing along the well-intentioned strangers who've come to leave a bouquet of bodega roses that immediately wither in the heat, or add another Sophie the Giraffe to the long line of Sophies laid side by side on the sidewalk, stretching from one end of Winnie's block to the other.

She finally called Winnie. Three times. Winnie never answered, but Francie left a message each time, telling Winnie she's been thinking of her, offering to bring her groceries, make her a few meals she can stick in the freezer. Francie also wants to tell her how much she's been enjoying *Bluebird*. She found a DVD box set on eBay, all three seasons for just $60—a charge she prays Lowell won't notice on the bank statement next month. She loves it. Winnie is so funny, so natural, such a phenomenal dancer.

Francie is still upset about the way Lowell reacted earlier that morning when she told him about the calls to Winnie.

"I don't think that was smart, France."

"Why not?"

"She probably wants privacy right now. And plus—"

"Plus what?"

"Well, you never know."

"What is that supposed to mean?" she asked him. "Never know what?"

He sighed, and seemed unwilling to say anything else, but Francie pressed him. "Where was she when Midas was taken? And how come there was no sign of forced entry? All I'm saying is, I don't think it's a good idea for you to get too close to her. And I certainly wouldn't want Will to spend any time around her."

Francie was furious. "I don't like what you're insinuating."

Francie watches Hector disappear around the side of Winnie's building, wanting to forget about that conversation. She hears the vibration of her phone in the diaper bag, and strings her camera around her neck. It's Lowell, texting. To apologize, she assumes.

Bad news. Didn't get the renovation job. They went with the other guys.

Francie tucks the phone back into her bag, flooded with worry. That job was their only promise of income. Their rent is due in three weeks. Will rustles in his stroller, and she zips her camera into its case, piloting the stroller toward the park entrance, hoping to lull Will back to sleep, dark thoughts creeping into her brain.

She tries to block them out.

She loves Lowell. He's a good husband, a kind man.

And yet. Why didn't she choose a man more like those so many of the May Mothers ended up with? A man like Charlie, able to buy that fancy apartment on the park, always posting photos of Colette and Poppy on Facebook, alongside sweet messages about how beautiful they both are, how lucky he is. Or Scarlett's husband, a tenured professor who can provide a big house in the suburbs, enough money for her to stay home without worry. She once mentioned that he even made sure to be home by six each night, to sit down to dinner with her, do the bath, help with bedtime. A man nothing like Lowell, who works constantly; who has never, not once, given the baby his bath; whose practice is failing, who's begun to tell her, with increasing frequency, that she has to figure out a way to earn some money. He's the one who came up with the idea that Francie should organize this meeting and volunteer to take photos of the May Mothers' babies, to build a portfolio to start a baby portrait business, a passing interest she mentioned once.

When she arrives at the willow tree fifteen minutes later, slanted under the weight of the diaper and camera bags, her curls are frizzed and damp. Colette is there already, spreading out her blanket. She wears a short light-blue dress, her hair in a fishtail braid down her back. Francie doesn't know how Colette does it; how she always appears so rested and put together. Francie's not even sure she brushed her teeth this morning.

"Have you heard from Nell?" Francie asks her after parking Will's stroller in the shade.

"Not yet." Colette opens the paper box of mini muffins and offers one to Francie. "She's supposed to call me at her lunch break. I hope her first day back is okay."

Token walks up then. He takes off his sunglasses, and his eyes are red-rimmed.

"You okay?" Colette asks.

"Yes," he says, looking away. "My allergies in this heat. It's brutal."

Others begin to arrive, and Francie recognizes none of them. Women she's never seen before, who never cared enough to attend a meeting when free baby photos weren't involved, walk cautiously up to the tree, asking if this is where the May Mothers are meeting. Meanwhile, there's no sign of the women Francie was hoping to see—no Yuko, Scarlett, or Gemma. She tries to tamp down her disappointment as she arranges the props she's brought for the portraits, eventually inviting people to step up for a turn. She's never taken photos of babies before, and she throws herself into it, eager to be distracted from her worries about money, about Lowell, about the image Antonia Framingham painted: Midas, alone, terrified, missing his mother.

"So, I know this is morbid, but can we talk about Midas?" someone asks from the blankets behind her.

"We were at the pediatrician this morning," someone else says. "I waited *ninety* minutes to be seen and my phone died. Anything new?"

Francie tries to shut them out, concentrating on the light, the shadows, on getting the fussy and obstinate baby in front of her to cooperate. "There was an interview this morning with that doctor from Methodist—the one they mistook for Bodhi Mogaro on July 4. He graduated top of his class from Harvard Med. He wasn't 'acting erratically.' He was yelling instructions into the phone to an EMT. The young mother in critical condition? She died last night."

"Oh, how sad."

"This thing with Bodhi Mogaro is equally disturbing," someone else says. "His wife gave an interview. They're making it seem like they just arrived here from Yemen, but they're US citizens. She's from Connecticut."

"My mom doesn't believe a word his wife is saying." Whoever is talking laughs. "Granted, my mom only gets her news from *The Faith Hour*, so I'm not sure she should be trusted."

"I still can't believe any of it." A big sigh. "That this happened to one of *us*."

Brittle pine needles pit Francie's knees as she kneels on the ground, holding her breath against the stench of a nearby garbage can overflowing with paper coffee cups and plastic bags of discarded takeout, feasted on by a swarm of spinning flies. She leans closer to the baby, wishing he'd stay still, the way she imagined they would, the way babies do for that one woman, whatever her name is, who gets them to sleep inside huge flower petals, their heads covered with a cabbage leaf.

"Can you move him a little, please? He's in a shadow."

"I can't get it out of my mind—the idea of getting a call, hearing my baby is gone. My husband and I were supposed to have our first date night last night, but I couldn't do it. I couldn't leave her with a sitter. I read somewhere that the nanny, Alma, is part of a baby-selling ring."

Francie read the same thing yesterday, and immediately texted Nell. Alma? Part of a baby-selling ring? Is that true?

Nell had written back one word: Yes.

Francie called her right away. "Nell, this is awful. How did you—"

"It was right there on her résumé," Nell said. "'Nanny for three years. Mother of two. Member of a baby-selling ring.'" She heard Nell *tsk* on the other end of the phone. "What could I do but hire her? I had to go back to work, and do you have any idea how few nannies there are in Brooklyn these days?"

Francie is still upset that Nell could find humor in any of this. "Nothing about this is amusing, Nell."

"I know, Francie. But the way they're dragging Alma into this whole mess, while breathing fear into every woman with a nanny . . . It's infuriating. She would never do anything to hurt anyone. I *have* to laugh about it. Otherwise I might just go and kill someone."

"Nice job, buddy," Francie says now, to the new little boy on the blanket in front of her. "That's it. Just sit still like that for another minute."

"You see *Us Weekly* yesterday?" Francie's back is to them, and she can't tell who's speaking. Their voices are running together. "An article said Patricia Faith has offered Winnie two million dollars for a sit-down interview."

Francie hears the chime of a new text message, and she pauses to glance at her phone, on the ground near her camera bag. It's Lowell again.

Really sell this business idea. Try to book something right away.

"Well, I heard a company's offered to pay her to do a workout video, for new mothers. Disgusting." Francie's phone beeps again but she ignores it—she can't deal with Lowell right now.

She turns toward the group, her head aching from the sun and heat. "Who's next?" she asks, noticing Colette is staring down at her phone, her brow furrowed. Colette meets Francie's eyes, and her expression is shadowed with concern.

"Look at your phone," Colette says quietly. Francie hastily drops the camera on the blanket. It's a message from Nell.

Turn on the Patricia Faith show. Immediately.

———

Nell's arms are raised over her head and her shirt is lifted, exposing the puckered skin of her stomach spilling over the wide elastic band of her maternity jeans. She has a drink in one hand, and the other holds on to Winnie's wrist. Nell remembers the moment this photograph was taken. It was early in the night.

They were complaining about the lack of paid maternity leave in the US. She'd stood up, singing the words to "Rebel Yell," pulling Winnie to stand. They danced. People sang along. Everyone was laughing.

Who would do this? Who among them would have given this photo to Patricia Faith, whose smug face has replaced Nell on the television screen? She's wearing a sleek, sleeveless black dress and appears to have found the time to freshen her highlights. She stares into the camera so intensely, Nell feels as if Patricia Faith can see her there, sitting alone at a table at the Simon French corporate café, her palms moist, bile inching up her throat.

"So, to recap," she says, her chin resting on her splayed, intertwined fingers, "this morning, we were sent this disturbing photo, showing Gwendolyn Ross the night—perhaps the very moment—her baby, just seven weeks old, was taken from his crib." The camera zooms in on the photograph, to a close-up of Winnie's face. She's looking directly at the camera, her eyes half closed and vacuous, a woozy expression on her face.

"Look at that. She's drunk," Patricia Faith says. "And I'm sorry, but I gotta ask the question. What does a photo like this mean? Does it, and should it, change the story? I know we've been focused on other things. The incompetent mayor and the horrendous police work. Bodhi. Questions about the nanny. But, well, I don't know. A new mother, just a few weeks postpartum, and she leaves her baby at home to act like *this*? Is *this* the definition of modern motherhood?"

The camera pans to one of Patricia Faith's guests: an older man with unblinking black eyes and a graying goatee. "I'm happy to have with me Malcolm Jeders, the head of Calgary Church and a board member of Family America. And Elliott Falk of the *Post*. Thank you, gentlemen, for being here. Malcolm, I want to start with you. What's your take on this?"

"A baby is missing, Patricia. That's tragic. But if you ask me, the chickens are coming home to roost on this idea that women need to 'have it all.' What has that come to mean, exactly? That a few weeks after giving birth, they're out at a bar, moms getting drunk, acting like they're pledging a college sorority?"

"The Jolly Llama," Patricia says. "Or more like the Jolly *Mama*." She smirks at the camera, a clever eyebrow raised over the frames of her bright orange reading glasses. "I agree. Nobody is going to argue that women need to be home rolling meatballs all day. But if I had a child—a *newborn* no less—would I leave that baby to go out to a bar? No sir. When my mother had her first child, her only priority was that baby, and it stayed that way until her youngest started kindergarten. She never would have—"

Four young women carrying paper bowls overflowing with salad noisily take a seat at the table next to Nell, drowning out the sound of the television. Nell picks up her tray and walks to a booth in the corner, under a larger TV, the words in closed caption on the bottom of the screen. Patricia Faith turns to her other guest. "Elliott Falk, nice seeing you again. The women pictured here with Winnie Ross—let's call them the Jolly Mamas, for the sake of convenience. What do we know about them and their role that night?"

"Well, Patricia, so far, the names of these women have not been released. But as we know, Winnie was out with her mommy group. This is a fairly new cultural phenomenon. Let me explain. Historically speaking, women have always depended on a circle of women to help them after giving birth. Of course, they didn't *sign up* to join this circle. It happened naturally. It was their mothers, aunts, sisters. This still happens in the developing world. But today—"

"Nell?" A woman stands at the table, holding a tray of food. Her hair is held back in a sleek ponytail, and her ID badge is turned so Nell can't read her name. Nell's mind races. They attended the same conference, shared a bottle of wine one night over a dinner in LA. "I haven't seen you since you returned from maternity leave. When did you get back?"

"Today."

"Oh, man. And how old's the baby?"

"Eight weeks." Nell looks up at the television.

The woman grimaces. "How's it going?"

"Great."

"Really? It's great leaving your infant so you can come to work? I don't believe you." She takes the seat across from Nell. "My kid is eight months. I'm still plagued with guilt."

Nell nods and swallows hard. She's not going to cry, not in the middle of the company café, not in front of this woman. (She plans to limit that to the fifteen minutes three times a day she'll be spending on the toilet in the handicapped stall, staring at photos of Beatrice as she pumps milk.)

The woman notices. "Oh, Nell. I'm sorry. It'll get better." She shakes a bottle of thick protein drink. "They're supposed to give us a nursing room—"

Nell sees it then. On another screen, in a bank of televisions across the room. The face of former secretary of state Lachlan Raine. He's taking questions from reporters outside his lake home in Vermont, his expression somber. Nell knows that look too well: the slow shake of the head, the practiced expression of remorse.

"I have to go." Nell picks up the tray, her lunch untouched. "I have a meeting in a few minutes."

"Okay. You should know, there's a group of new moms at the company that meets—"

Nell feels lightheaded as she slides the tray beside the others on the metal cart near the garbage cans. A small crowd is gathered at the elevator bank, holding iced coffee drinks and plastic to-go containers. She walks past them into the stairwell, taking the stairs two at a time to the sixth floor. Her cell phone rings as she shuts her office door.

A wave of relief washes over her when she sees the number. It's only Francie.

"Colette and I are here," she says. "We raced to Colette's apartment. Hang on. I'm going to put you on speaker."

Nell sinks onto her desk chair, out of breath. "That photograph of me. Did you see it?"

"Yes."

Nell closes her eyes, seeing the photograph again. The sweat stains under her arms. The maternity band at her waist. The milky fat of her stomach. "Who sent that to her?"

"An opportunistic jerk, that's who," Colette says. "I don't think it was one of us. You can tell from the angle. Whoever took it was on the far end of the deck. And really, Nell, nobody will know it's you. It's way too blurry. You can't make out your face."

"But then why is Lachlan Raine being interviewed?" Nell asks.

"What do you mean?"

"I saw him, on *CNN* or something. Taking questions."

"They say he's being considered for the Nobel Peace Prize. Did you think he was commenting on the photo of you?" Colette laughs. "I know some people are going to treat the image of a mother drinking as a matter of national security, but involving the former secretary of state might be a tad extreme, even for Patricia Faith and her cable news friends."

Nell rests her forehead on her palm, feeling the relief wash over her. There's a light tap on her office window. Ian is standing in the hall, pointing at his watch. Nell holds up a finger to indicate she's on her way.

Francie sounds on the verge of tears. "This keeps getting worse. What are people going to think?"

"Who cares what people think?" Colette says. "We didn't do anything *wrong*."

Nell's desk phone rings. "Shit. Hang on. Sebastian is calling me. The baby woke up with a fever and he's home with her."

He must have seen Patricia Faith's show. He'll be so worried.

"Thank god you answered," he says, his voice strained. "I know you have that meeting, and I was afraid I wouldn't get you."

"I know. I have to go now. Did you see it?"

"See it? See what?"

"The photograph. Patricia Faith."

"No, but—"

"Isn't that why you're calling?"

"No, darling, listen." He lowers his voice, as if someone is listening. "The police are here. They want to speak to you. I think you need to come home."

———

Mark Hoyt stands in Nell's living room, browsing the bookshelf. He's gotten a haircut since his visit four days earlier.

"Ms. Mackey," he says, turning to look at her as she closes the door behind her, laying her bag on the floor next to the couch. She can't tell a thing from his expression. In the taxi on the way home, after telling Ian that Beatrice's fever had spiked and she needed to go home, Nell tried to convince herself that everything is fine, reminding herself she's done nothing wrong. Or at least nothing illegal. And yet she can't deny the rising sense of dread she feels. Does Mark Hoyt know something about that night? Did he discover something that happened, in the moments Nell can't remember?

The sound of someone walking down the hall startles her, and she turns to see Sebastian. "Oh good, you're here," he says, setting a mug of coffee on the table. "You okay?" He whispers the words, but she can sense the uneasiness in his voice.

"Yes. How's Beatrice?"

"Good. Her fever broke. She's sleeping."

"Why don't you take a seat, Ms. Mackey?" Hoyt suggests.

Nell reaches for the coffee Sebastian set down, knowing he likely made it for Hoyt, and sits on the couch. "What brings you here, Detective?"

Hoyt walks slowly to the oversize armchair near the window and perches himself on one of the arms. She resists the urge to tell him to sit properly, that he's going to ruin the frame the way he's sitting. The chair was a wedding gift from her mother, and Nell knows how many overtime hours at the hospital she worked to pay for it.

"Just a few questions," Hoyt says, sliding up the sleeves of his gray cotton T-shirt. "Some loose ends you might be able to help us out with."

"Okay."

"First, how you doing?"

"I'm fine."

He stands and returns to the bookshelf. "Yeah? You're all right?" He lifts a framed photograph from the shelf, one from her wedding day, wiping the dust from the glass with his thumb. "This your dad?"

"Stepdad."

He nods. "Nice dress."

Nell points to the bottom shelf, to the large photo album tucked alongside some of Sebastian's art books. "There's the full album. Says 'Wedding Day' on the binding. If that's why you're here, to look at my wedding pictures."

Hoyt laughs. "No, not quite."

"That's too bad. It was a brilliant wedding. Just sixteen people. My mother-in-law made Haitian food." Hoyt places the photograph on the shelf. His silence feels oppressive. "So, Detective, today was my first day back at work after maternity leave. Not really the ideal time to tell my boss I need to leave early. Plus, my baby came down with her first cold after four hours at a day care. I'm a little knackered. Can we get on with why you're here?"

"I'm really sorry about that." He's shaking his head, his voice tinged with good-cop sympathy. "I thought it would be better for us to go over my questions here, rather than, you know, show up at your office."

"What questions?"

"Still trying to clear up some of the confusion about that night." Sebastian enters the room with another cup of coffee, but Hoyt waves it away. "No thanks. Overcaffeinated." He addresses Nell. "You'll have to forgive me if we've gone over this already. My mind's not as sharp as it once was. But as I understand it, you're the one who organized this night out to the Jolly Llama. Correct?"

"Not really. We all—"

"You were pretty adamant that Winnie Ross join you."

"We all wanted her there."

"But you sent the e-mail to everyone. You wrote something— what was it—'Everyone come, and especially Winnie. We won't take no for an answer.' Or something to that effect. Am I right?"

"I can't remember exactly."

"No?" He takes a notebook from his back pocket and flips it open. "Yes. That was it. Maybe my memory's not as bad as I thought."

Nell nods. "Can't really say the same. I can hardly remember to put on pants these days. A bit sleep-deprived at the moment."

Hoyt grins, a little-boy smile, a look Nell guesses his wife probably finds irresistible. "Let's see. What else? Oh yes." He looks up. "Ms. Ross's video monitor app. Why did you delete that?"

"Why did I—"

"Peek-a-Boo, I believe it's called? Allows a mother to watch the video monitor remotely. You deleted this app from her phone?"

Nell can feel Sebastian's eyes on her. She's been too ashamed to tell him she did that. "It was silly, really. We were just having a bit of a laugh."

"A bit of a laugh?"

"Playing a joke. Winnie was looking at her phone a lot, watching the baby. The point of going out was to be away from the babies. So when she got up to get a drink, and Colette saw she'd left her phone behind on the table—" Nell tries to keep the tremble from her voice. "Of course I'm gutted about it now. Thinking how the night might have ended differently if I hadn't done that." Sebastian takes Nell's hand, easing his fingers between hers. "And really, she could have easily reloaded the app. It wouldn't have taken her more than a minute."

"Is that right?" Hoyt nods, offers a shallow laugh. "Have to admit, I know nothing about how all the gadgets these days work. My eleven-year-old daughter—she's always making fun of me, saying I live in the Dark Ages. Between you and me, I'm pretty sure my daughter thinks the Dark Ages began sometime around 1995. But she can find her way around my wife's laptop with her eyes closed."

Nell doesn't want to hear about this man's daughter or wife. She wants him to leave.

"And why did you call Winnie Ross's cell phone on two separate occasions that night, Ms. Mackey?"

"Why did I—"

"Ms. Ross's cell phone records indicate that between 10:32

and 10:34 p.m.—just around the time of the abduction, we believe—you called her cell phone twice. Or"—he holds up a hand for clarification—"I suppose I should say, someone using your cell phone did."

She feels her palm growing sweaty in Sebastian's grip. Hoyt raises his eyebrows, waiting for an explanation, but she has no explanation. She doesn't remember doing that.

"Why did you call her phone?"

"I was . . . I must have—"

"How many drinks did you have that evening, Ms. Mackey?"

"I already told you. Two."

"Right. And Ms. Ross. Do you know how many drinks she may have had that night?"

"You asked me that the other day." She wills herself to stay measured. "Honestly, who cares?"

"Who cares?"

"Yeah, how is it relevant? I don't think she drank that night. She was having iced tea. And despite what the mob on cable news might be saying, mothers are still allowed to have a drink if they want."

"Alcohol can make her story a little less reliable," Hoyt says, his expression static. "The same goes for you."

Beatrice whimpers from the nursery, and Nell's mind clouds as she tries to decipher the cry. Is the baby's fever back? Is she hungry? She realizes Hoyt is staring at her, waiting for her to say something.

"I missed that," she says. "What was the question?"

"Was anyone near her when she ordered her drink? Anyone who may have had bad intentions. Who may have slipped some-thing in it."

"No, not that I saw." Beatrice whimpers more loudly, send-ing Sebastian jogging down the hall. He closes the nursery door behind him, and Nell turns toward Hoyt. "While we're asking questions, Detective, maybe I can ask a few of you."

Nell sees something flash across his face, but then he steadies his expression. "Shoot."

"Who's talking to the press about Alma?"

"Who's—"

"Yeah, this thing about her being in a baby-selling ring. These whispers that she might have been involved." Nell knows she should rein herself in, but her anger and impatience take over. "Unless there's something very concrete you want to tell me, I will swear on my child's life she had nothing to do with this. You and the people in your department need to stop suggesting otherwise. This could ruin her life." Nell smiles. "She may be an immigrant, but she's still human."

"I've suggested nothing—"

Sebastian steps into the hallway, looking worried. "Her fever's back," he says. "You should probably nurse her."

Nell sighs and presses her eyes with the heels of her hands, trying to contain the ache swelling behind them. "Listen, Detective, it's been great catching up, but my baby needs me. I'm assuming I have the right to ask you to leave?"

Hoyt nods. "Of course you have that right. I'm happy to come back when it's more convenient. I know how it is with kids." He rolls his eyes. "I got three of them."

Nell stands, her legs heavy, and walks to the door. She makes a show of opening it wide. "Then you know how difficult it can be when they're sick."

Hoyt pauses a beat. "Of course, Ms. Mackey. It's not easy. Parenting can be truly overwhelming. Certainly when they're babies." His gaze is intense. "Wouldn't you agree?"

She's silent as Hoyt stands from the chair and walks slowly toward the doorway. He stops in front of Nell and draws a business card from his back pocket.

"This is my direct line," he says, handing it to her. "Call me if you think of anything that might help us. Okay, Ms. Mackey?"

She takes the card. "Yes, fine."

Before she can close the door, he stops it with the toe of his boot, peeking his head back inside, and gives her a curious look. "That *is* your real name, correct? Nell Mackey?"

CHAPTER ELEVEN
DAY SIX

TO: May Mothers
FROM: Your friends at The Village
DATE: July 10
SUBJECT: Today's advice
YOUR BABY: DAY 57
If you haven't already implemented a bedtime routine, we have one question: What on earth are you waiting for? A routine will help the little one know it's time for sleeping, so consider spending as much time as you can rocking, singing, bathing, reading, and/or cuddling. You'll both be ready for a good night's sleep afterward!

The blood runs from the slit in Francie's wrist down her forearm, pooling in the bend of her elbow. She steadies herself against the counter as Lowell rushes toward her, holding the good yellow dish towel, the one with sunflowers. The blood is going to ruin the towel. She'll have to throw it away.

"Jesus," he says, pressing the towel to her wrist.

"I'm sorry."

"It's fine. Hold it tighter."

"But that plate. It was one of your grandmother's."

"Don't worry about it." He wipes the blood from the scuffed linoleum under her feet before picking the pieces of glass out of the sink. After everything is cleaned up, he leans against the counter. "You okay?"

"Fine. It looks worse than it is. That was so weird. The plate slipped through my fingers."

He nods. "I heard you out here last night. What were you doing?"

"I thought I heard Will cry, and then I couldn't get back to sleep. I was just reading some things—"

Lowell shakes his head. "There are people working on this case, Francie. Professionals. If he's out there, they'll find him."

She keeps her eyes down, pressing the wound. "I know."

"You're so anxious and distracted. That's not good for Will."

She spins toward him. "What does *that* mean? Not good for Will?"

"You need to be thinking about him now. About his—"

"Are you serious? Our baby is the *only* thing I think about anymore."

"Francie. Come on. Calm down."

"Calm *down*? No, Lowell, you calm down. The *people* working on this? They're a bunch of incompetent buffoons. You've said so yourself. And what? I'm just supposed to forget that?" She throws the towel on the counter. "This whole Bodhi Mogaro thing? Have you been reading about it? People are coming to his defense. Saying he's being racially profiled. The ACLU is starting to pay attention. They have *nothing* on him. No criminal history. No motive. His wife says he missed the flight because he overslept." She hears the accusation rising in her voice. "She says he doesn't get much sleep, because *he* gets up with their son at night. So *she* can rest."

Lowell is silent, his expression impassive.

"Even Patricia Faith is saying the police are overstepping by keeping him in custody. The guy was lost. That's why he was on that government property. If they had anything on him, they would have charged him by now."

"I wouldn't put too much faith"—he raises his eyebrows and smirks—"in what that woman says."

"It's not funny, Lowell."

"I know it's not, but Francie, you can't do anything about it. I'm serious. You're not sleeping. You're hardly eating." He rests his arms on her shoulders. "I know I'm not allowed to suggest that Midas is dead—"

"Lowell, stop."

"—but guess what? He might be."

She pulls away. "Lowell, *stop*. Don't be so cavalier. It's a baby's life we're—"

"Francie, listen to me. He might be dead, okay. It's awful, but you have to prepare yourself for that news."

"He's NOT dead." She remembers that Will is in earshot, rocking on the bouncy chair in the living room, and she lowers her voice. "I know it."

"How? How do you know it? Bad things happen, France."

Francie closes her eyes, and the memory returns: sitting under the willow tree among the May Mothers just ten days earlier, the sun on her neck, hearing Nell's words. *Bad things happen in heat like this.*

The room tilts around her. "The best thing you can do is take care of yourself," Lowell says, his voice thin and distant in her ears. "It's not good for anyone for you to be losing your shit like this. I'll take today off. I can cancel a meeting."

She looks up at him. "Why?"

"So you can rest."

She savors the idea: climbing into bed, treating herself to a few hours alone. It's been months since she's been by herself for more than fifteen minutes—when Lowell watched the baby so she could run to the shop for a jar of sauce. She should do it. She should allow herself a break from Will and his crying, from thinking about Midas and reading Patricia Faith's website, with its hideous comments and the questions people are beginning to ask about Winnie. Where was she that night? Why isn't she speaking to the press, doing interviews, demanding Midas's return?

But she can't do that. They can't afford Lowell missing a meeting, not after he just lost the job they were counting on.

"No, it's fine," she says. "I planned to take the baby out for a walk. I need to start exercising."

"You sure?"

"Yeah. You're right. I need to take better care of myself. A good brisk walk will help."

Lowell seems to soften. "I'm offering. Last chance to say yes."

"You need to work. I'll be fine."

"Okay, if you're sure." Lowell kisses her forehead. "I'm going to take a shower."

She waits until she hears the shower running to head into the bedroom, closing the door quietly behind her, removing the notebook she buried in the top drawer under the lacy underpants she hasn't worn in months. She flips it open to the list she made of the people who were at the bar that night, and turns to the new list she's been keeping—the names of every possible suspect.

She puts a question mark in front of the first name on the list. *Bodhi Mogaro.*

What if his lawyer is right? What if it really isn't him? She reviews the other options.

Someone related to Winnie's grandfather's business.

Alma. Nell is adamant that Alma played no role, but Francie doesn't know what to believe anymore. Is it really possible that someone came into Winnie's home, took Midas from his crib, and Alma heard *nothing*? Yesterday Francie read that Alma's brother in Tucson was arrested a few years ago for stealing a car. That an uncle back in Honduras had killed someone.

The thing that's really beginning to trouble her, though, is Winnie's stalker. Archie Andersen. She circles his name several times. There wasn't much written about him, and she couldn't find even one photo of him online. It was years ago, before the Internet and Facebook and twenty-four-hour news, and the only definitive information she dredged up was an article in *People* saying that Archie Andersen had showed up at the *Bluebird* studios, making it all the way to the set a few times, forcing Winnie's mother to go to the authorities more than once, to eventually file for a restraining order. At the time he was sixteen years old, convinced he and Winnie were meant to be together. And then he appeared at Winnie's mother's funeral, wailing as if he'd lost his own mom, until he was forcibly removed by Winnie's boyfriend at the time.

Archie would be in his early thirties now. Just like that guy at the Jolly Llama—the one who'd approached Winnie so suddenly, as soon as she was alone at the bar. The last person she was seen with.

Francie e-mailed Nell and Colette a few hours earlier, asking if they thought the police were making a mistake by not looking into Archie Andersen.

I would guess they are considering him, Colette wrote back. Despite what the media has suggested, the police are not that dumb.

But how could Colette be sure? If Mark Hoyt and company were, in fact, getting this Bodhi Mogaro thing wrong, what else might they be screwing up? Francie hears the shower water go quiet and then the curtain gliding open, and she shuts the notebook, sticking it hastily back into the drawer. In the living room, she lifts Will from the bouncy chair, grabbing the diaper bag and Moby Wrap, and calls good-bye to Lowell.

He steps from the bathroom in his boxer shorts, towel-drying his hair as she's walking out the door. "Where you going?"

"May Mothers." She clears her throat. "There's a last-minute meetup at the Spot. Just got the e-mail."

"I'm so glad to hear that, sweetheart." He steps back into the bathroom. "That's exactly what you need."

————

Francie tries to block out the buzzing of an overhead light as she bounces Will back and forth in the chilly, empty waiting area, stopping to browse a table laden with stacks of pamphlets. Countering Terrorism through Information Sharing. LGBTQ Outreach. *If you see something, say something.*

She startles at the sound of a door slamming behind her and turns to see Mark Hoyt walking into the lobby of the police station with a man who has an unkempt beard and shifty eyes and is wearing a black T-shirt and baggy jeans. The man looks at Francie, making eye contact for a split second before he nervously looks away. Hoyt turns to her after the man has left the station. "Mrs. Givens. Sorry to keep you waiting. Why don't you come on back?"

Francie follows him past an officer who sits at a desk behind a pane of glass, studying the sudoku board on the back page of the *Post*, and down a well-lit hall. "Was that guy here to talk about the investigation?" she asks Hoyt.

"No."

"Is he a suspect?"

"No."

The hall is lined with a few small offices, and when they reach Hoyt's, he stands aside, inviting Francie to lead the way in. It belongs on the set of a bad cop show: a battered desk covered in crooked stacks of manila folders, papers spilling out messily. Three paper cups, half full of coffee, are lined next to an archaic desktop computer. A puckered layer of brown-and-green mold lines the top of one of the cups.

"You want some coffee?" he asks.

"No thank you. I've given up caffeine." She nods down at

Will on her chest. "For the baby." She feels a twinge of guilt lying to the police, but she's certainly under no obligation to tell them she's mostly given up nursing. And besides, she'll start crying if she says it out loud.

"I can probably scare up some decaf if you'd like."

"Then yes," she says. "Thank you."

He partially closes the door behind him, and she takes in his office. Mark Allen Hoyt. Born in Bay Ridge, Brooklyn. Grandson and son of cops. Six years with the US Marine Corps. Graduate of the New York City Police Academy. She found his biography online, posted as part of a talk he gave at a Staten Island high school career fair last year. She leans over his desk, examining the stack of folders, assuming they deal with Midas. He can't possibly be working on another case. She timidly reaches across the desk as the door swings open behind her. She snatches back her hand, knocking a coffee cup with her elbow, its contents spilling onto her shins and sandals and the stained carpet below.

It's Stephen Schwartz. "I'm so sorry," she says, reaching into the diaper bag for wet wipes. "I'll clean this up. I didn't mean to—"

"Come with me."

His tone is unfriendly, stern even, which annoys her. Perhaps she shouldn't be snooping around Detective Hoyt's desk, spilling his disgusting, moldy coffee, but Schwartz should be happy to see her. As far as he knows, she may have valuable information to help the investigation, something to assist in actually solving the case and finding Midas alive. But there's not a hint of gratitude in Schwartz's voice as he gestures down the hall. "Leave it. I'll have someone take care of it."

"But Detective Hoyt is on his way back. He's getting me coffee."

Schwartz waves his hand. "Come with me."

She follows him, relieved Will shows no sign of waking. The

formula she's been feeding him has really helped his sleep, and she's hopeful the eight ounces he hungrily drank on a bench outside the police station will keep him down for at least another hour.

Schwartz opens a door at the end of the hall. It's frigid inside and stark, the fluorescent light yellowing the plain white table and four metal folding chairs. Francie catches her reflection in the glass wall opposite her—the growing plane of gray at her roots, her protruding belly—and looks away. Hoyt is sitting in one of the chairs, his legs stretched in front of him, crossed at the ankles. He points to a chair and slides a Styrofoam cup of coffee toward her.

"Have a seat."

"I'm going to keep standing, if that's okay. The baby doesn't really tolerate stillness." Francie picks up the cup, feeling nervous. "A lot of babies don't." She takes a sip of the coffee. It's lukewarm and bitter, swimming with coffee grounds; she resists the urge to spit it back into the cup. Schwartz closes the door and leans against it. "So, Mary Frances Givens. What gives us the pleasure of seeing you this morning?"

She sets the coffee on the table and resumes bouncing Will. "I'd like an update on the investigation."

Hoyt raises his eyebrows. "You'd like an update?"

"Yes. It's been six days since Midas was abducted. I'd like to know where things stand." She fights to keep the apprehension from her voice. "I'd like to know why you haven't found this baby."

Schwartz glances at Hoyt. "Well, you should have told us that sooner," Schwartz says. He pulls back an empty chair, sits down, and draws a small notebook and pencil from his chest pocket. He licks the pencil's tip, his face a study of concern. "Can I have your e-mail address?"

"My e-mail address?"

"Yeah."

"Why?"

"I want to send you the full report. And updates as they come in."

"Text is much more efficient," Hoyt says. "You might want to get her cell."

"Good idea." Schwartz's pencil is poised above the paper, his enormous eyebrows raised expectantly. "What's your cell?"

"You're being funny."

Schwartz snickers and tosses the pencil onto the table. "Yes," he says. "I guess you might say I'm being funny."

She feels her face flushing with anger. "Well, can you at least tell me what's happening with Bodhi Mogaro? Are you going to charge him? Or is it true about the mix-up with that surgeon?"

"Francie," Hoyt says. "You know we can't comment on an active investigation." He takes a sip of his coffee, watching her. "Is this why you came today? To see what we know?"

"Yes. Well . . . I've also been thinking about some things. Things you might want to be aware of." She keeps her eyes on Hoyt. Unlike Schwartz, he wears a wedding band. Maybe he has children himself. "There's a guy who lives a few blocks from Winnie."

"Okay," Hoyt says.

"A registered sex offender."

She's right. Hoyt *is* sympathetic. Something in his face softens when she says this, and he leans forward on his elbows. "Francie, do yourself a favor. Stop reading the crime blogs. It's going to make you crazy."

"No, you don't get it. Apparently, there was a middle-aged white guy sitting on the bench near her house that night, and he's a sex offender. Yes, fine, I read about it on a crime blog, but so what? And you can look it up—where sex offenders live. There's one in the big apartment complex a few blocks away." Francie knows she's talking too fast, and she tries to slow down. "I've been watching her house." She reaches into the front pocket of her diaper bag for the photograph she took and had printed at the pharmacy. "This guy comes by a lot, walking a little dog. He seems to have a weird interest in her building. Like, he's always stopping in front of it, peering into the windows. Almost like he's casing it, to be honest."

"Why have you been watching her house?"

"Well, not watching it, like, through binoculars or anything. I live nearby. I walk by there with the baby. The idea that it's a neighbor who took Midas makes a lot of sense. Think about it. It was Winnie's first time out of the house at night. Her first time away from the baby. It *has* to be someone who knew that. Who was watching her."

"It sounds like *you've* been watching her," Hoyt says.

"What? No. I mean—" She pauses to compose herself. "She's my friend."

"How long have you known her?"

"Awhile. Four months. But we knew each other over e-mail months before that."

"Four months? That's not a whole lot of time."

"Yes, it is. And also, this is different. We're new moms. You wouldn't understand. It's a special kind of friendship."

Hoyt is silent, nodding, expecting her to go on, but she doesn't want to. She doesn't want to explain to this guy what it's like; how the members of May Mothers understand Francie in a way nobody else has. How often they were there for her during her pregnancy, when she was terrified that she would lose this baby, like she'd lost the others. How much they've helped her since Will was born—sending articles, responding to her questions and her reflections on motherhood, helping her battle the isolation.

"I'm not here to talk about friendship," she says to Hoyt. "There's something else I want to tell you. A confession, really." Hoyt glances at the wall of glass, and for a moment she wonders if there's someone behind there, watching them. "Something happened that night, and it's only hitting me now how strange it was."

"And what was that?" Schwartz asks. He sounds bored.

"Do you remember that guy I mentioned when you interviewed me? The guy at the bar, who approached her out of the blue?"

"Yes."

"You should find that guy. Bring him in."

Schwartz leans back, tipping his chair so that it's balanced on the back two legs, and clasps his hands behind his head. "I'm no legal scholar—hardly made it through police academy, if you want to know the truth—but I'm pretty sure approaching a woman and offering to buy her a drink is legal. At least in New York."

"I'm not suggesting those things are illegal, Detective." She's trying her best to keep her voice steady. "I'm suggesting that the behavior is a little suspicious."

Schwartz begins to speak, but Hoyt raises a hand to stop him. "Fine. I'm going to play along. What's suspicious about a guy speaking to a woman at a bar? Isn't that why guys go to bars?"

"Maybe. But—"

"Your friend Winnie is a very beautiful woman."

"Yes. I know. But—" Will squirms at her chest, and Francie realizes she's stopped bouncing. "But I have an idea of who that guy might have been. It didn't dawn on me until this morning, really. This is something you have to pursue."

"What is?" Schwartz asks.

"Are you familiar with the name Archie Andersen? Winnie's stalker?"

Schwartz sighs heavily and stands up, walking toward the door. "I'm going back to work."

She looks at Hoyt after Schwartz has left, feeling a twinge of relief that they're alone. "I really think that guy at the bar could have been Archie Andersen. Have you looked into him?"

Hoyt rubs his eyes. "Francie, you need to know we're doing our job. We're taking this case very seriously."

"Do you have children?" Her voice sounds strained, and she silently berates herself. This is no time to cry.

"Three." He reaches into his back pocket for his wallet, taking out a wrinkled photograph of three little girls standing in a kiddie pool. "I'm old-school. Still like these things on paper. This was a few years ago." He examines the photo more closely, as if he hasn't seen it in some time. He shakes his head. "They really do grow up fast."

"Can you imagine, Detective, how upsetting it would be to lose one of those little girls before they had the chance to grow up? Like Winnie has?" She lifts the diaper bag from the back of the chair, accidentally bumping Will's head with her arm, causing him to wake with a start. His eyelids flutter open and his face grows pink, on the brink of a wail. She feels the sweat pooling around the fabric of the baby carrier, and the sudden need for fresh air. "I've said what I've come to say. I couldn't have lived with myself if I didn't."

She starts for the door, but Hoyt steps in front of her. "Listen, Francie. I meant what I said. We're doing everything we can to find Midas. I want to see that kid alive as much as anyone." She nods and tries to move past him, but he rests a firm hand on her arm. "And you want to know the truth? In cases like this, when a baby goes missing, when there's no sign of forced entry, no revenge motive, we have to start looking in places we don't want to look."

She yanks her arm away and hurries down the hall toward the exit. Will is crying louder, drowning out the buzz of the light, but she can still hear Hoyt's words as she charges toward the lobby.

"I mean it's time to start questioning the motives of people who knew him. I mean, Francie, people close to the family."

CHAPTER TWELVE
NIGHT SIX

My mom always said I was naive. She was, of course, usually referring to an interaction with my father: my most recent decision to forgive him for something he said, or something he did, for the way he came home drunk again, pulling me out of bed by my arm, dislocating my shoulder, telling me to put away my fucking shoes, left in the middle of the hall, trying to kill him.

"He feels bad about it," I'd say the next morning, avoiding her eyes as she held the ice pack to my shoulder. "He didn't mean it."

She'd shake her head. "You're so clever about everything except him." I can see the disappointment in her eyes. "When are you going to learn?"

Maybe she was right. Maybe I'll never learn. The truth is, this is all so much harder than I expected. How stupid of me to think I could simply steal away and be happy. For one thing, I'm bored to death. There's *nothing* to do here. Nothing to occupy my thoughts. And god knows that boredom doesn't suit me. Idle hands and all that.

Joshua is the same way. He's happiest when we're out, walking into town for a turkey sandwich and ice-cold beer from the little shop near the library, or at the secluded swimming hole we discovered, under the bridge, down the wooded path, stretched naked on a rock afterward, drowsy and pink with sun. But I told him today I don't feel safe doing those things any longer. There are people around—walking their dogs, delivering mail—and they're starting to ask me how I'm doing. That's the problem with these country people. They're so nosy. *Go back inside,* I want to tell them. *Go back to your cross-stitch and frozen macaroni and cheese and your twenty-four-hour cable news.* I've been practicing my responses; going over my story again and again with Joshua, trying not to trip up, to come to believe my own lies.

I should be a pro at this by now. I've been lying my whole life.

My mom's not feeling well. It's the flu. She's sorry, but she asked me to call and cancel for her.

Don't be ridiculous, I'm not asking you to leave your wife. I'm not interested in anything more than what we have.

Sperm donor, I'd say, leaning in, smiling as if this person— bad-mannered enough to ask me who the father was after I started showing at five months—was the only one I was trusting with the secret. *Feeling the tug of motherhood, and I can't wait around forever for the perfect guy now, can I?*

But things aren't quite so simple this time. The lies are more complicated, easier to get tangled in. So no more going out, no matter how bored we are. And no complaining about it either. I'm going to make the best of a bad situation. Like I did with dear Father.

I've started already. This morning, Joshua woke up moody and distant. Did I get mad? Did I demand to know what was wrong? Nope. I left him brooding in front of the television and went out into the sunshine, walking the property, collecting the wildflowers that grow near the brook. I brought them inside and pressed them between the pages of cookbooks, like my mom and I used to do. He was in a much better mood when I got back, and after breakfast we went through the house together, throwing away things we don't like—those tattered throw pillows with the scratchy cases, the outdated curtains in our bedroom, the family photos I can't bear to look at any longer—rearranging the place so it feels more like *our* home.

I've also been keeping these journals, like Dr. H recommended. "I think you should write things down," he'd say. "It'll be a place to help process your feelings. A way to feel centered."

I'm doing it, and trying to adopt the right attitude, but I don't like it. I don't want to be writing these things down. I want to be talking to him, on the soft leather couch in his office, a mug of peppermint tea between my palms, a breeze blowing the sheer curtains, the drone of the white noise machine soothing my nerves. I wish he could lead me through the exercises he'd do when I felt particularly anxious, the ones where I close my eyes and envision a happier place.

I want to tell Dr. H where I am and how I've been feeling, and that, honestly, I never meant to kill anyone.

But of course I can't do that. I've looked into it—he'd have to report me to the police. That would be awful for both of us. I want to tell him about the voices I hear at night among the call of the cicadas and crickets. Mark Hoyt, badgering me with questions. *Where were you that night? What do you know?*

It depends on what you mean by where.

Physically: I thought I knew, but I can no longer remember. The night is gone, like it no longer exists. Like it never happened.

Emotionally, spiritually: that I know. I was in hell. Lost. Tortured. Having no idea how to get through this. How to handle it. The overwhelming sadness. The failure. The guilt of being such an imperfect mother.

———

I need to get ahold of myself. The best thing I can do right now is figure out where we're going next, and hurry up and leave. We obviously can't stay here any longer.

Not with what I've just done.

CHAPTER THIRTEEN
DAY SEVEN

TO: May Mothers
FROM: Your friends at The Village
DATE: July 11
SUBJECT: Today's advice

YOUR BABY: DAY 58

Still swaddling your little one? It might be time to stop. While swaddling a newborn can help him feel safe and snug, swaddling is also believed to lead to a higher incidence of SIDS as children become more mobile and learn to roll over. So while the baby may fall asleep in seconds in that swaddle, it's always better to be safe than sorry.

Colette's palms are sticky on the stroller handle and the sun singes the back of her neck, even now, not yet seven in the morning.

"I'm dying," Nell says, red-faced and sweaty. "I can't believe you actually *run* this."

Colette slows to stay in step with Nell. "We're almost there." They make it over the hill and head down the shaded path, under the arch, the wheels of their strollers crunching over the pebbles.

"Do I look any slimmer?" Nell asks when they stop in the large open plaza where a group of toddlers from a summer camp, wearing bathing suits and bright yellow vests, clutch each other's hands and make their way into the park. "Sebastian is expecting me to get naked in front of him again. I'd like my ass to be only one stone heavier than he's accustomed to when that happens."

"Turn around. Let me check."

Nell laughs and turns her backside to Colette, but her expression darkens as she sees something in the distance. "Oh my god," Nell mutters. "Look."

It's Midas.

His face is printed on a banner held by two older women trying to work out how to fix it to the stone wall bordering the park. Colette walks closer, approaching a very overweight woman with gray hair held in a high ponytail. She rests her forearms on the metal bars of a walker. Nearby, a small group of women lay pink carnations in a circle on the hot pavement.

"What are you doing?" Colette asks.

The woman cranes her neck to get a closer look inside the stroller at Poppy, who is sound asleep, her arms raised over her head, tucked close to her ears. "How precious," the woman says. "We're holding a prayer vigil for Baby Midas. It'll begin in an hour or so." Nell appears beside Colette, and the woman hands them each a flyer from a stack on a plastic folding table behind her.

A PRAYER FOR MIDAS

Can a woman forget her nursing child,
that she should have no compassion on the son of her womb?
Even these may forget yet I will not forget you.
—Isaiah 49:15

Colette sees what's printed below the words—CHILD NEGLECT IS A CRIME—and then the photograph. The one Patricia Faith first showed, of Nell and Winnie from the Jolly Llama. The image is merciless: Nell, a drink in her hand, her stomach bared. Winnie, peering into the camera, a vacant look on her face, her eyes half closed.

Colette returns the flyer and takes Nell's hand. "Come on, let's go."

"You should join us," the woman says. "This baby needs all the prayers he can get. And we have a special guest coming." She leans toward them, speaking just above a whisper. "Patricia Faith."

"I don't think so." Colette steers the stroller with one hand, propelling Nell forward with the other. Nell is on the brink of tears by the time they reach the sidewalk outside the park. A young man with a dark beard and—despite the heat—a slouchy winter hat on his head gets out of an idling van at the corner, carrying a television camera.

"That photo." Nell's words are choked. "It's not— It makes us look—"

"Let's go to my apartment," Colette says.

"I have to get ready for work." Tears build in Nell's eyes.

"Just for a few minutes. Charlie's not home. I'll make us coffee." Colette takes Nell's arm, and they begin to walk faster.

"Who are those people?" Nell says as they approach Colette's building a few blocks away. Alberto opens the door for them, and they prod their strollers into the elevator. Nell looks down at the flyer, still clutched in her hand. "What are they asking for?"

"Scarlet letters, I think."

The apartment is quiet. Colette puts on the water to make coffee and cuts the lemon cake she made earlier this morning, after getting up with the baby at five. Nell sits on the couch, clutching Beatrice to her chest. "What is happening?"

"I don't know."

"This is bad. You can feel it. They're going to blame her."

"Yeah, I know." Colette takes a seat at the kitchen island. Her head is throbbing. "I'm just surprised it's taken this long."

"It's rubbish." Nell's breath comes out in a cascade. "All we did—all she did—was go out for an evening."

"Nell, stop. We didn't do anything wrong. Don't even—"

"You're watching this all, right? You can see where Patricia Faith is steering it? Her show yesterday, she kept playing that video of Winnie, the one from the day after Midas was taken, examining every gesture, asking why she hasn't said a word since."

"Yes," Colette says. "We both have to stop watching this crap."

"There's no way Winnie could have—"

Colette presses her temples. "I don't know."

"No, don't say that. She couldn't have done something so evil. We *know* her."

Colette looks at Nell, hesitant. "Do we? Do any of us really know each other?"

"At least enough to know if there was a psycho in our midst. I know how much everyone loves to blame the mother, but I refuse to believe she's responsible for this." She spreads the tears on her cheeks with both hands. "I read this awful article yesterday. It was all about Winnie and the so-called Medea complex, from Greek mythology. The daughter of a king, she avenged her husband's betrayal by killing their children."

"Stop reading this stuff, Nell. I'm serious. No good will come of it."

"The things people wrote about Winnie in the comments. The collective outrage, saying she shouldn't have left her baby with a stranger to go get drunk. That even if Midas is found, he should be taken away from her, that she's not fit to be a mother." Nell stifles a sob. "Don't they know how hard this all is? The pressure of just keeping these babies alive. The task of loving someone like this, and how easy it is to fuck this up, the way we're sure our mothers did." Her voice breaks. "Some days I honestly think I'm going to fall apart. I'm so bloody tired. I know it happens, but can you even imagine? Hurting your own child?"

Colette peers down at Poppy, asleep in the stroller beside her.

"Why did I do it?" Nell says. "Deleting that app. And then I lost her key. I can't—"

"Nell, stop. Don't let these people get in your head. You didn't do anything wrong. None of us did. Even if you did drop her key, it's not like someone found it and said, 'Here's Winnie's key. I guess I'll use it to get inside her apartment and take her baby.' Whatever happened, it was *planned*."

Nell nods. "I keep telling myself that, but by *whom*? Why don't they have any leads? Why haven't her phone and key turned up?" She looks away. "I have to tell you something."

The tone of Nell's voice makes Colette uneasy. "Okay."

"I drank too much."

A quick laugh escapes Colette. "Nell. No shit."

"I said that I had only—"

"Nell, I know. You weren't the only one who drank too much that night. We were out. Away from the babies. It's not a crime to—"

"It was weird," Nell says. "I had a few drinks, but then, suddenly—well, there's a huge chunk of the night I can't remember. That's not like me. Getting that drunk, forgetting things. That doesn't usually happen." She hesitates. "And my shirt was ripped, at my shoulder. I noticed it the next morning. I'm worried something happened that I can't remember."

"Like what?"

"I don't know. It's a sense I have—someone around me, touching me. Maybe whoever has Midas was there that night, looking for her, and took her phone and key from me, and I don't remember. But then I think, no. It can't be. I would remember that, right? I don't know what's true anymore. I'm afraid I'm going crazy." Nell glances at Colette. "And why was she looking at her phone all night, at Midas in his crib? Have you wondered about that?"

Colette nods. "It was like she was waiting for something."

"I want this to be over with," Nell says. "I want to be told that Winnie was somewhere that makes sense. To know that he's alive." She begins to cry harder. "If he's dead, I'll never—" She stops herself and takes a baby wipe from the container on the table and blows her nose, leaving a milky film that glistens on her skin. "I want to know she didn't do this."

"Yeah," Colette says softly, glancing toward the couch in the living room. She stands up. "So do I."

———

Nell slides a stool closer to the island, Beatrice draped over her shoulder. "How long have you had this?"

"Three days."

"And you haven't looked at it?"

"No." Colette ties her hair back with the band from her wrist, and then inserts the flash drive in her computer. A folder appears, with several files listed. "I shouldn't have taken it. I've convinced myself not to look, to just put it back the next time I see Teb."

She clicks open the first file, and a video fills the screen. "Oh my god," Nell says. "It's me." Nell is sitting on a couch next to a man Colette assumes is Sebastian. Her face is pale and her eyes are bloodshot. Colette hits play.

"*You okay with us recording this?*" The voice is Mark Hoyt's. "*It's a new protocol at the department.*"

"*Sure. Can I get a glass of water before we start?*"

"This is that first morning, when they came to my place." Nell leans toward the screen. "God, am I really that fat?"

"Rough night?"

"Every night with a newborn is a rough night."

"Can we please see what else is on here?" Nell asks. "I can't look at myself."

Colette closes the video and clicks open the second file. The video player opens again.

"It's Scarlett," Colette says. "They must have interviewed everybody."

Stephen Schwartz appears from behind the camera and takes a seat across from Scarlett.

"I understand you didn't go out last night."

"No. My husband's family is visiting. I can't believe it. This is awful." Her face is dark with worry. *"I just can't imagine. Do you have any idea what happened?"*

"That's why we're asking questions of people who know Winnie. This man in your group." Schwartz looks down at his notebook. *"Token, I believe you call him?"*

"Yes."

"Do you know him well?"

"No, not really. I attended the meetings a lot while I was pregnant, but we're moving and I'm so busy now. To be honest, I always thought the nickname was childish."

"Ugh," Nell says. "Can we keep going?"

Colette closes the video and opens the third one on the list. "Yuko," Colette says, quickly closing it and going to the next: Gemma sitting at a dining table. A man is standing behind her, holding their son. *"I got there close to eight twenty, I think. I can look at my phone. I texted James when I arrived to check on the baby."*

Colette's stomach sinks. Is her interview with Mark Hoyt on here? Does Teb already know she was there that night? She clicks on the final file in the list, bracing to see herself. She hears Nell's gasp.

It's Winnie. She's at home, sitting in the corner of the sectional couch. Her hair hangs limp at her shoulders, and her eyes are swollen. She stares vacantly at the camera.

"*Did you get any sleep?*" It's the voice of a woman this time.

"*Some.*"

"*Good. Glad to hear it.*" The woman appears from behind the camera. She wears black pants and a pink sleeveless blouse. "*I have just a few follow-up questions and then I'll be on my way. First, I understand you've been seeing a psychiatrist.*"

The woman pulls up an ottoman and takes a seat across from Winnie.

"*That doesn't sound like a question.*"

The woman softens her voice. "*You mentioned it to Detective Hoyt last night.*"

"*Did I?*"

"*You don't remember?*"

"*You're all asking me so many questions. It's hard to keep everything straight.*"

"*How long have you been seeing this doctor?*"

"*A long time.*"

"*For?*"

"*Depression.*" She shrugs. "*Camaraderie. My father sort of forced me to do it, after my mother died.*"

"*And when was the last time he treated you?*"

"*A few months ago.*"

The woman raises her eyebrows. "*Not since giving birth?*"

"*No.*" The detective begins to speak, but Winnie cuts her off. "*I was feeling good after Midas was born. Better than I felt in years.*"

"*Okay. I want to also ask you a little bit about Daniel.*"

Winnie shifts in her seat. "*Daniel? Why?*"

"*You dated in high school. Why did you break up?*"

A cloud crosses Winnie's face. "*I couldn't deal with anything at the time. Including Daniel.*"

"But you stayed close?"

"Yes. He was my first love."

"After he got married. Did you ever have an affair?"

"An affair?"

"I know this is uncomfortable, but I have to—"

"No, we never had an affair. I'm not really sure what—"

Colette hears the sound of a key being inserted into the apartment door.

"Who is that?" Nell whispers.

The door opens and Charlie walks in, balancing two coffees in a carryout tray and a white paper bag.

"Oh, hey," he says, removing his earbuds.

Colette closes her laptop. "Baby, hi." She tries to keep her voice from faltering. "You're back early."

"Turns out they're doing a sing-along at the coffee shop now. I got run out by babies and nannies." He peeks inside the stroller at Poppy, and then back at Colette. "What are you guys watching?"

Colette unclenches her hands in her lap. "A video. About sleep training."

"Oh yeah?"

"Yes, you know," Nell says. "Put the kid in his cot with a can of soup. Lock the door. Come back in a few weeks."

Charlie laughs. "After the night we had, I'll buy the soup." He walks to the kitchen island and sets the coffee and bag on the counter next to Colette's laptop. "I got you an almond croissant and a coffee. And Nell, if I knew you'd be here—"

"I'm fine. Have to leave for work now, actually."

Charlie kisses Colette's forehead. "So do I. See you later."

Colette waits until Charlie closes the door to his office. When she hears jazz coming from the room, she reduces the volume and hits play.

"No, we never had an affair. I'm not really sure what you're getting at with that question."

"I'm sorry, Winnie. I know this is difficult, but we have to ask you these questions in order to get a full picture of the situation."

Tears leak slowly from Winnie's eyes. *"Daniel has been nothing but a good friend to me."*

"I understand." The detective hands Winnie a Kleenex and then leans forward in her chair, her notebook dangling from her hand. *"Let's talk about something else. Tell me, if you don't mind, about where you were last night. After you left the bar."*

"I've already told you."

"Well, you told Detective Hoyt. But I'd like to hear it myself."

Winnie closes her eyes. *"I went to the park."*

"The park."

"Yes. It was my first time alone since giving birth. And that bar—it wasn't where I wanted to be. I went outside and decided to keep walking. I ended up at the park."

"Did anyone see you?"

"I don't know."

"On the way there, maybe? Or inside the park? Did you pass anyone, or speak to anybody?"

"Not that I remember."

"Are you having trouble remembering things?"

"No." Winnie stares at her hands in her lap for a few moments, but then abruptly jerks her head up. *"Did you hear that?"*

"What?"

"It's Midas."

"Midas?"

"Shhhh, listen." Winnie stands, listening to something in the distance. *"There. Did you hear that?"*

"No, what are you—"

"He's crying." Winnie walks off camera. *"I can hear him crying."*

"Winnie—"

She appears on the screen again. *"He's quiet now."* She looks down the hall, toward the nursery. *"But where is it coming from?"*

"Winnie, listen. I want to call your doctor. We think you should make an appointment—"

"I don't need a doctor." She runs her fingers through her hair, gripping it in her fists. *"I need you to find my son. He's crying right now. He wants me. And you're sitting here, asking me the same questions again and again. Why are you even here?"* She walks to the terrace door and opens it. *"Why are you not out there, searching for my baby?"*

The detective stands and walks stiffly toward the camera. *"Let's take a break."* The rest of her words are undecipherable, before the screen goes dark.

Colette is aware of the silence around them and a heavy ache in her chest. "Oh my god," Nell says. "She's lost her mind. Do you . . . Did she—"

————

Nell sits on the toilet seat, attached to the pump. She looks down at her phone and, against her better judgment, closes the photo of Beatrice and types in the address of Patricia Faith's website. The television host is, as Nell expected, broadcasting a live-feed from the park plaza, under the large banner headline: A PRAYER FOR MIDAS.

Nell hesitantly opens the video, and her screen springs to life—an image of Patricia, in a tight floral dress, calling out to a woman walking behind a double stroller. "Excuse me," she calls. "Do you have a minute?" The woman stops, and Patricia scuds gingerly toward her on her three-inch heels. Behind her Nell sees the circle of women, pink carnations in their hands, their heads bowed in prayer. "I'm Patricia Faith, host of *The Faith Hour*."

"Yes," the woman says. "I know."

"We're here today, talking about what some people are calling the Jolly Mama phenomenon."

"I think you're the only one calling it that."

"So you've heard of it?"

"Yes," the woman says. "Unfortunately."

"Wonderful. You're a mother, obviously. You look like someone who loves her child." Patricia raises her eyebrows. "What do you think about the idea of mommy groups meeting at bars, drinking alcohol? Some even do this in the afternoon, bringing along their children, I hear." She discreetly wipes the perspiration from her eyebrow with her finger and points her microphone at the woman.

"I think who gives a shit."

Patricia Faith peeks at the camera and grimaces.

"The kids are not the ones drinking. You do understand that, right, Patricia?"

"Yes, but the parents *are*. With all the places there are to meet, isn't it irresponsible? The night that Midas Ross was taken, his mother was at a bar." She shows the woman the flyer in her hand, with the photo of Nell and Winnie. "Have you seen this? This is the night—"

Nell shuts down the phone and flips off the pump, silencing the droning motor. She hasn't gotten nearly as much milk as she'd hoped, but it's hot and stuffy in the bathroom, and she needs to get back to work. She buttons her shirt, packs the bottle, and waits until the bathroom is empty before making her way out of the stall. She needs a coffee—she's felt unsteady since she left Colette's apartment, that image of Winnie caught in her mind.

Heading down the hallway, she's surprised to see Ian waiting for her, his hands along the top of her door frame, his cowlick curling like a question mark from his forehead—a feature Nell has heard that many of the company's young female employees find irresistible. His belt today: pink flamingos embroidered over a sky-blue background. "Hey," he says as she walks into her office, setting the pump under her desk. "Got a second?"

"Sure." He's with a young woman Nell has met a few times in passing, someone from editorial. She's in her mid-twenties, and she wears a white lace dress over black jeans and orange ballet flats. Her hair is arranged into a perfectly messy bun, and she holds a folder in her hands.

"You know Clare?" Ian asks. Nell nods and straightens her back, aware of the pull of her shirt and the way it puckers between the buttons. She still hasn't found the time to shop for clothes that fit. Ian saunters to the window and perches on the sill, moving aside some of the framed photographs of Beatrice that Nell placed there earlier this morning. "Second day back, huh? How's it going?"

"Brilliant, thanks."

"Yeah? It's okay? Being back at work?"

He's wearing two different-colored socks, which Nell assumes is deliberate. "It's an adjustment. But I'm happy to be back."

"Yeah, I know how it is."

She smiles. No, he doesn't. He's a forty-four-year-old single man, rumored to be dating one of the assistants of *Wedded Wife*, the company's bridal magazine. What does he know about leaving a baby, practically still a newborn, at a day care for nine hours a day?

"I have to say, I'm glad you're back," Ian says. "We've lost so many good people to their babies since I've been here. They take their maternity leave, tell us they'll be back, and then, wham!"

Nell raises her eyebrows. "Wham?"

"Yes, wham. A few days before we expect them to show up at the office, we get the call." His voice gets a little smaller. "'I can't do it. I can't be away from the baby.' I'm glad that's not you."

The image flashes in her mind. Knocking this wanker to the ground, straddling him, grinding his face into the carpet. "Thanks a million, Ian."

"Sure. And now, Clare and I need some help." He gestures at Clare to come forward. "We're disagreeing on a cover and decided to come straight to the expert." Clare removes two printouts from her folder and lays them side by side on Nell's desk. They're mock-ups of this week's *Gossip!*—the company's largest magazine—showing the actress Kate Glass, who recently gave birth. She stands on a beach in two different poses, wearing a bikini top and shorts, holding the American flag, under the bold headline How I Got my Body Back.

"What do you think?" Ian asks Nell.

"What do I think?" Nell is aware that Clare is looking at her expectantly.

"Yeah. As a new mom, how does this resonate with you?"

"Lemme see." Nell picks up the images. "Well, I'm very pleased to hear this."

Ian's head is tilted. "Which part?"

"That she got her body back."

"Crazy, right?" Clare says. "This is just five weeks after she had a kid."

"Wow," Nell says. "That must have been terribly difficult for her. Trying to care for an infant, and all without a body." Nell addresses Clare. "So what happened? Had someone stolen it? Were those abs recovered at a CrossFit in Cleveland by a search party?"

Ian laughs. "Told you she's hilarious," he says to Clare, his gaze on the printouts. "It can be a little silly, I know. But these postpregnancy covers kill it every time. Women love this stuff." He studies the two samples, side by side. "I'm wondering if we should photoshop out that flag she's holding."

"I don't think so."

"No?"

Nell can't help herself. "No. All new mothers typically remember to pack their American flag for a day at the beach."

He laughs again weakly. His impatience is apparent.

"Sorry," Nell says. "It's just . . ." She glances at Clare. "This particular magazine. Not my favorite among the ones we publish."

"I know, I know. But remember. If we didn't have the ad revenue from *Gossip!* we could never publish *Writers and Artists.*"

"Okay, sorry. Let me give it another go." She surveys the images again. "I like this one," she says, holding up the image in her left hand. "And lose the flag. It's ridiculous."

Clare executes a soundless clap, her rose-painted fingernails just in front of her mouth. "I *told* you that's the better photo."

Ian nods as he collects the images, his face pensive. "I don't know. I still think we're making a major mistake."

"A major mistake?" Nell waves her hand dismissively. Having a photo of yourself taken at a bar, drunk and overweight, wearing maternity pants two months after having a child, and then having that photo distributed to the residents of Brooklyn: that's a major mistake. *This* is foolishness. "It'll be fine. The photos are nearly identical."

Ian is shaking his head again. "That's not what I mean." He returns to the window, gazing out at Lower Manhattan, to the Hudson River a few blocks away. "It's a mistake not to go with a cover story on Baby Midas."

Nell keeps her expression blank as Ian turns to look at her.

"But we've gone over it a million times," Clare says. "*Everyone* will do a cover on that. We're banking on getting all the readers who are having Baby Midas fatigue."

"But *nobody* is having Baby Midas fatigue," Ian says. "People don't want to read less. They want to read more." He looks at Nell. "Right? Don't you want to read more?"

"No," Nell says. "What is the point of constantly covering the story? Besides ad revenue, I mean. That family needs—"

"But who is Midas's dad?" Ian is becoming more upset. "Why is she not saying anything about this?"

"I heard it is a sperm donor thing, and—"

"Fine, Clare, fine. But then why not come out and say that? Why not talk to Oprah, like so many moms in her situation have done before?"

"Oprah retired."

"You know what I mean, Nell. It's what we've come to expect, and Gwendolyn Ross *knows* that. She was raised in the press. Why is she being so silent? What is she hiding?"

"Remember, we're doing six pages on her," Clare says gently. "All we're talking about is the cover."

"I understand. But are readers even going to get to that story? Wouldn't it be smarter to stay focused on Midas? It's time to get some answers. We have a stringer out in Queens, trying to get the nanny to talk. From what I hear, she never even *saw* a baby. She didn't go into his room. But that stringer sucks. And this Jolly Mama phenomenon? We could do weeks on that."

"I think we should rise above it," Nell says.

He snaps his head toward her. "Rise *above* it? That's not our job, Nell. Our job is to *create* it."

She knows the argument is futile. "Well, either way, I still agree with Clare about the cover. I'd be more apt to buy the magazine with Kate Glass on it."

Ian sighs. "Okay, fine. Hope you guys are right. Our numbers are down. The lady upstairs isn't happy." He rises from the sill. "Guess we should all get back to work." He walks toward the door and then stops. "Oh, and jeez. I almost forgot, Nell. The other reason I came to talk to you. We're sending you away."

"Away?"

He laughs. "Don't look so scared. I mean we need you to go on a trip at some point in the next two weeks. Four days. To"—he pauses for effect—"the Bahamas. They're considering it for the new server facility, and they want you to go. Meet the key players. Part work, part perk. How does that sound?"

"Four days?"

"Yeah. It's right on the beach."

"Sounds great," Nell says, forcing a smile. "I'll pack my flag."

Nell reads the same paragraph in the training manual for the fourth time, willing herself to concentrate, but the thought inches back in.

Four days away.

She can't think about it. Sebastian's first curated exhibit opens in three weeks. He's been working late every night and won't be able to get back to Brooklyn by six when the day care closes. Who will pick up Beatrice? How will Nell pump enough milk for four days? How will she stand to be away from the baby for that long? She pushes away the thought, the trip, her reality (maybe her mom can use a few vacation days, drive down from Rhode Island), and tries to concentrate, but she's too distracted. She minimizes the pdf.

She'll quit.

She'll go down there, right now, to Ian's office. *Wham!* she'll say. *At least I lasted two days.*

No, she won't go down there. She'll go *up* there, to the eighteenth floor, to see the lady upstairs herself. Adrienne Jacobs, the thirty-five-year-old creative director of the Simon French Corporation, the former fashion blogger, the first woman and youngest person to ever head the ninety-eight-year-old company. The wife of Sebastian's brother. Nell's sister-in-law.

Nell can see it. Marching in there, past Adrienne's assistants, into her windowed office with its pristine white walls, the two white couches, the white rug imported from Turkey that cost more than what Nell earns in a year. *Wham!*

And then what? They can't afford their apartment on Sebastian's salary, or his student loan payments, or the vacation they promised they'd take—their first in four years—over Christmas. For the first time since they began dating, they're doing well financially. Far better than they ever imagined in London, when Sebastian was studying art and she was attending classes toward her master's degree while adjunct-teaching a few classes in cybersecurity at a local college. When they used to eat ramen noodles a few times a week, sneak their own popcorn into the movie theater to save the four quid.

And it's not like she can easily get another job. Not with her employment history, her background, the things she'd have to tell people about herself when applying for a new job.

She's lucky to have this position. She's been telling herself this since her first day at the Simon French Corporation eighteen months ago; since even before that, when Sebastian told Nell about the offer that chilly fall morning, when she walked into their London flat after a day of teaching, her arms heavy with groceries.

"You're joking," she'd said to him, frozen in place.

"No." His eyes were bright with excitement. "Adrienne called here herself while you were out. She's offering you the job. Vice president of technology. In charge of all their online security stuff."

"Online security stuff? Is that the official description?"

"You can go back to doing what you love."

"Sebastian, no. She doesn't have to—"

"This isn't an act of charity, Nell. Adrienne said it herself. 'There's nobody better than Nell.' She wants you on her team. She said she'll take care of everything." He cleared his throat. "And I explained it all to her. That you're going by Nell now."

"I can't work there."

"Why not?"

"Because their main magazine is *Gossip!* And I have standards."

Nell paces her office, remembering the look in Sebastian's

eyes. He'd recently been contacted by MoMA, offered the job he'd been dreaming about, and he was going to turn it down. They couldn't relocate to New York City on what the museum offered, especially since he and Nell had just started trying for a baby. But could she really say no to him? After everything he'd done for her. Never judging her past mistakes. Accepting her for who she was, and not the person others declared her to be. And plus, this was a chance to move back to the United States. To go home. To be closer to her mom.

"Okay, fine," Nell said. "I'll talk to Adrienne."

Sebastian was grinning as he crossed the room, kissing her before taking the bags from her hands. "Thank you. And don't mention the trying-to-get-pregnant thing."

Nell hears her e-mail ding with a new message. She returns to her desk, knowing she has to get back to her work. She clicks open her e-mail, seeing six new messages from the May Mothers. The group's activity has begun to pick up again, following a few days of dormancy after the news about Midas broke, when nobody seemed to know what to say.

Yuko had written with a question. Hi mamas. I need some help. Nicholas woke up with a rash on his back. I'm attaching a photograph. Do I need to worry?

Nell scrolls through the responses.

Looks like a heat rash to me, Gemma replied.

Avoid the doctor! Scarlett wrote. They'll give you something harsh and toxic when all you need for this is calendula cream.

Nell deletes the messages, wondering if Winnie is still receiving the May Mothers e-mails. She pictures her in that video interview, her face gaunt, her eyes flitting around the room. She hears Ian's words.

Who is Midas's dad? What is she hiding? It's time to get some answers.

Nell closes her eyes. For the tenth time since watching the

flash drive interview with Winnie, and the hundredth time since the night Midas was taken, the thought occurs to her: How secure is the Village website? How difficult would it be to get inside, take a look at the questionnaire Winnie filled out when registering for May Mothers—the same questionnaire they all had to fill out? *Your name. Your partner's name. Tell us a little bit about your family.*

Nell stands and closes her office door. Back at her desk, she can feel her heart beating as she opens The Village website and begins to type, hacking her way into the administration page. It takes less than five minutes. It's something she's been a natural at since her first computer science class—an instinct, one professor later said, or, as she likes to think of it, her superpower. In college, she was the first freshman to win a national coding competition, which helped land her the prestigious internship—chosen from more than 8,000 applicants—at the US State Department, working directly for Secretary of State Lachlan Raine.

Nell sees Francie's profile at the top of the list and clicks it open. The photo she'd included is exactly what Nell would have expected: a selfie with Lowell and their ultrasound picture. Nell quickly reads what Francie wrote—she and Lowell met in their hometown in Tennessee, and she followed him to Knoxville, where he studied architecture while she took photography classes and worked as an assistant at a portrait studio, freelancing in her spare time, taking photos of people's cats. "We're somewhat new to New York and I can't wait to meet all the other mommies!" Francie wrote.

Nell closes Francie's profile and skims others, surprised at some of the things she's reading; at how little she really knows these women. Yuko clerked for a state supreme court judge before having her son. Gemma is from Nell's hometown in Rhode Island; she went to the rival high school.

The sudden ringing of her desk phone surprises her, and she closes the website. "Hi, this is Nell Mackey." There's heavy breathing on the other end. "Hello? Who is this?"

"Nell, it's me."

She pushes away from her desk. "Colette?" There's silence, and then Nell hears Colette crying. "Colette, what is it? Are you okay?"

"I'm in the copy room at the mayor's office," she whispers. "I think someone's outside."

"What do you mean? Are you all right?"

"No." She pauses. "I went into the police file. I saw something. It hasn't been reported. I don't know—"

"What, Colette? What is it?"

"They found a body."

———

Francie traces her hand along the pilling fabric of the Ektorp couch, and then continues down the maze, pausing to check the price tag on a rocking chair upholstered in fake white leather. She pats Will's bottom and checks her phone. Colette had a meeting with the mayor this afternoon, and she'd agreed to look inside Midas's file, to see if there's any information about Archie Andersen. Francie is hopeful that after her visit to the police station yesterday, Mark Hoyt has realized they've overlooked something crucial. They should have located Andersen's whereabouts and brought him in for questioning by now.

Francie wanders toward the bedroom furniture. This is her fifth trip to IKEA in two weeks. Lowell has finally installed the window AC unit in their living room—a secondhand one she bought off the Village classifieds—but it's a piece of junk, blowing out putrid, lukewarm air. She's desperate for some relief from the worsening heat, but she can't stand to turn it on—who knows what toxic fumes it might emit? She's been trying to make the best of it, seeking refuge at the library, music classes, and here at IKEA, which Will seems to like. Perhaps it's the shock of fluorescent lighting, or the cavernous feel, as if they'd entered a vast, well-lit womb, but he calms down as soon as they enter, affording her at least forty minutes of relative quiet, allowing her thoughts to calm, a crack of light to open in her brain.

Will begins to fuss in the pillow section, and she picks up the pace, heading to the café. The air is steeped in the stench of meatballs, and she angles a chair toward the window, reaching in her bag for the bottle of water and a packet of formula. She pours the powder into the bottle, and as she shakes it, she notices a young mother sitting beside a stroller, forking a glob of pink salmon into her mouth and staring at the packet of Enfamil on the table in front of Francie.

Francie averts her eyes, feeling the rise of shame and embarrassment as she nudges the nipple into Will's mouth, trying to ignore the woman's stares. She wishes she had the courage to explain to her that she knows breast milk is better, but her milk is gone. Her body can no longer feed him.

Will is nearly finished with the bottle when her phone rings. It's Colette. "Oh good," Francie says, feeling a wave of relief. "I've been waiting for your call."

"I know. I'm sorry."

"Well?" Francie says. "What did you find?"

"Nothing."

"Nothing? Are you sure?"

"Listen, Francie. You have to stop texting me about this. I can't tell you how much trouble I'll be in if anyone here finds out what I did."

"I know, I'm sorry. But I don't get it. Did you look in the file?"

"Yes."

"And?"

"And there's nothing on the Archie guy."

Francie lets out an irritated sigh. "*Nothing?* How is that possible? Is Mark Hoyt not even *slightly* interested in doing his job? Is he really not going to find him and question him?"

"It doesn't mean he hasn't. It just means it's not here, in this file. This isn't everything. Shit. Francie, I have to—"

"Okay, but wait. What about the guy Winnie was talking to in the bar? Is there anything on him?"

"There's nothing new in the file." Francie can hear voices in the background. "I have to go," Colette says and ends the call.

Francie is on the brink of tears as Will finishes the last of the formula, and when she stands, she feels faint. She was too upset to eat this morning, and she considers ordering something, but the thought of the food here turns her stomach. She walks out of the café toward the exit before realizing that she's gone the wrong way. Retracing her steps, she's caught in the complicated grid, unsure which way is out. Will begins to cry, and Francie walks quickly toward the rug section, where she gets caught behind a woman with a stroller who is taking up the entire aisle, walking too slowly.

"Excuse me," Francie says, trying to hurry past, but then she sees the woman's face and stops. "Scarlett."

Scarlett looks at her with a confused expression, and Francie is overcome with awkwardness. Scarlett doesn't recognize her. "It's me, Francie."

Scarlett lets out an embarrassed laugh. "Of course. I'm sorry. My brain froze there for a second. I'd say pregnancy brain, but I guess I have to stop using that excuse." Scarlett glances down at Will, who is wiggling in the carrier, his cries growing louder. "How's the clogged duct? Did the potatoes work?"

"Yes," Francie lies, unable to cope with another piece of advice at the moment.

"I'm so glad. And still no caffeine?"

Francie hesitates. "No, none. Not in a week. How are you?"

"Tired. Between the baby and this move, I haven't had a moment to myself." Scarlett glances under the blanket on top of her stroller and lowers her voice. "He's been sleeping for nearly two hours, thank God."

"Two *hours*? Will has never napped for two hours."

She knits her brow. "Never? Do you make sure he's eaten enough before you put him down?"

"Yes," Francie says. "I think so."

Scarlett nods, and Francie can't help but notice a smugness to her expression. "I've been lucky with this little guy. He's always been a good sleeper."

Francie nods. "Are you shopping for the new house?" she manages.

"Yes." Scarlett fingers the fibers of a nearby rug. "My husband keeps telling me the stuff here is junk. I know he's right. I should really shop somewhere in the city." Francie bounces Will, who has begun to cry more loudly. "How are you? I miss seeing everyone."

"Me too," Francie says, her voice cracking. "It's been hard since what happened to Midas—"

Scarlett closes her eyes. "I'm sick about it. I just can't imagine what Winnie must be going through."

"I know." Before Francie can help it, the tears escape. "To be honest, I'm a little overwhelmed right now. The baby's been up at night a lot, and it's difficult, because Lowell needs his sleep. Our apartment is so small." She laughs. "Certainly no four-bedroom house in the suburbs. And then even after he falls asleep, I stay awake, thinking about Midas. There's got to be some explanation for what happened, right? How they got in, or why someone would want to take a baby." She knows she should stop talking, but the words tumble out. "The police have done such a terrible job, don't you think? Detective Hoyt.

He just doesn't seem to know what he's doing. I refuse to believe Midas is not alive. Colette just called. We've been doing all that we can to figure this out." She wants to tell Scarlett that Colette was her last hope in finding Archie Andersen, that she's searched the Internet so many times to locate him—to see if he ever served time in jail, if he still lives in New York, if he might have been anywhere near Winnie's house that night. Francie pulls a wipe from her diaper bag and blows her nose. "I probably haven't been eating enough, either. Do you want to go get some food, or at least a coffee? I'd love some company—"

When Francie looks back at Scarlett, her body floods with embarrassment. Scarlett is watching her, a horrified expression on her face. Francie glances at the floor, humiliated. *How I must look!* she thinks. Standing in IKEA, wearing a stained and wrinkled top she pulled from the laundry basket, her hair a mess, growing hysterical in the rug section.

"I'm sorry," Francie says. "I don't mean to burden you with—"

"It's fine," Scarlett says. "I'd love to get a coffee." She smiles wanly, her eyes shadowed with pity. "But the movers are coming in an hour to give an estimate."

"Of course," Francie says. "I understand."

"Lunch this week, in the park maybe?" Scarlett says, starting to walk away. "We're back and forth between Brooklyn and the new house for a few more days. I'll e-mail you."

Francie says good-bye and walks in the opposite direction, dropping the package of pink paper napkins she was going to buy in a bin full of plastic salad tongs, eventually finding her way to the checkout lines, weaving between people trying to navigate heavy trolleys overloaded with long cardboard boxes. Out on the steaming sidewalk, she spots a bus idling at the stop across the street and runs for it.

She takes a seat in the back, her head pressed to the window, tamping down the shame. Why on earth did she do that? Scarlett is so put together, so confident—a house in Westchester. Buying new furniture. Yet another mother with an easy baby and a seemingly ideal life. And here she is, sobbing in IKEA with a baby she can't control and a husband who won't agree to buy a new air conditioner for the living room, or a new stroller, even after the brake on the one his aunt bought for them stopped working two days ago. Francie was having visions: losing control of the stroller, Will inside it, seeing it careen down the hill, too fast for her to catch it, and into the street. When Lowell called her from the office yesterday afternoon to check in, she worked herself into a panic, demanding he stop at Target on the way home from work and buy a new stroller immediately. He refused.

The motion of the bus helps to settle Will, and she roots inside her bag for the warm bottle of Diet Coke from this morning and drains it, wondering if she should consider what Lowell suggested last night. They were lying in bed, Will between them, when Lowell told Francie she should go see her doctor. "It was my mom's idea," he said. "I called her today. She thinks there might be something you can take for how anxious you are, and how much you cry now."

"I don't need a pill," Francie said. "I need them to find Midas. I need to help that baby get back with his mother."

A man takes the empty seat beside her and she moves closer to the window. She doesn't want to think anymore—not about Lowell, or Scarlett, or her mother-in-law's judgment. Taking her phone from her bag, she checks the weather—it's going to reach the high nineties for the next few days—before opening Facebook. Her gaze snags on the post at the top of the page—the standing invitation to view "A Night Out," the album Yuko created for the Jolly Llama get-together. Francie still hasn't had the stomach to look, but she clicks on it now, eager for any distraction, and scrolls through the photos people have added. Yuko and Gemma standing at the rail of the deck at the Jolly Llama. Nell and Colette clinking glasses. Francie's breath catches when she comes across a photo of Winnie. She's sitting at the table, her chin resting on her hand. There's another of her, watching the crowd, the sun setting behind her, a strange, almost dreamy expression on her face.

And then Francie sees it, in the background: the splash of bright crimson.

She spreads the photo larger with her fingers. The red baseball cap.

It's the guy Winnie was talking to. He's standing by himself, holding a drink. He's in another photo too, his face clear in the background. And he's not just standing there. He's staring at them, watching them, looking directly at Winnie.

"Excuse me," she says to the man beside her fifteen minutes later when the bus pulls up to her stop. She steps over his legs and hurries from the bus and toward her building, flush with anticipation. The front door is slightly ajar. Francie has asked Lowell at least four times to fix the latch, which hasn't been catching. It's not safe. Inside, the mail is stacked on the wobbly wooden table in the small foyer, and she sees a credit card bill and a large envelope with her name written across it in green block letters. She tucks the credit card bill into her diaper bag, knowing she has to figure out a way to pay for the $100 in baby clothes she ordered from Carter's before Lowell found out he didn't get the renovation job, and ignores the other envelope— the handwriting vaguely resembles her mother's, and she doesn't want to deal with that now, assuming it's the stupid christening dress her mom insisted on sending. She sprints up the three flights of stairs, finally locating her laptop under the recipes she printed earlier this morning. Toeing Will's bouncy chair, she opens Facebook and goes to Yuko's photo album.

Yes.

It's him. The guy Winnie was talking to. Francie examines every photo, seeing if she can spot him in the background. As she does, she can't help but study the photos of Winnie one more time. The faraway look in her eyes. The way she's captured in one photo looking down at her phone. It's strange, but Francie tries not to think about it. She tries to stay focused on the good news.

She now has a plan.

CHAPTER FOURTEEN
DAY EIGHT

TO: May Mothers
FROM: Your friends at The Village
DATE: July 12
SUBJECT: Today's advice
<u>**YOUR BABY: DAY 59**</u>

Chances are, you still have a few extra pounds to lose. Don't let that remaining baby weight get you down. Instead, get up! Grab your stroller (and maybe a few members of your mommy group) and take a brisk walk around the park. Choose vegetables and fruit for snacks. Chew your food slowly. Stay away from carbs. You'll be zipping up those old jeans in no time at all.

Colette sits at the kitchen island, Charlie's hands on her swollen breasts. "Charlie, come on," she says, nudging him away. "Not now. You know I have to work."

"I do know that," he murmurs. "But the baby just fell asleep in the stroller, and you were up late working again. You've earned your state-mandated fifteen-minute coffee break." He glides his hands down her stomach, finding his way into her cotton pajama bottoms, cupping her inner thighs. "Don't make me report a secret employee of the mayor for violating labor laws."

She squirms out of his grip. "Please, Charlie, stop. I need to finish this chapter."

He stands up, sighing. "Baby, you're killing me. It's been three months."

"I know."

"We've gotta turn this around."

She swivels toward him, trying to mask her irritation. "Charlie, I know. But this minute? I'm working. I don't come into your office when you're writing and try to seduce you."

He laughs. "You know what, sweetheart? If you ever feel even slightly inclined to come into my office and seduce me while I'm writing, you should act on it. Immediately. Even if I'm on the phone with my editor. Even if my parents are there. Even if I happen, for whatever reason, to be hosting a meeting with the pope. I will stop the discussion, and I will pleasure you right then and there, in a wholly spectacular fashion."

Colette smiles. "That's good to know."

He nods toward his office down the hall. "You wanna give it a shot? See if I'm telling the truth?"

"Is the pope in there?"

"No."

"Then I'm not interested." She stretches her legs and places her toes on top of his. "I'm sorry. I need to focus. I just used the thesaurus for the word *went*. It's not going well." He extracts his feet, walking to the refrigerator for the bottle of breast milk she prepared earlier. "You leaving?" she asks him.

"Yes."

"Where you taking her?"

"Running."

"I'll take her when I get back. This meeting should be quick." Charlie nods.

"Take the yellow sun hat," Colette says. "The others are too big for her."

"Yep. Know that."

"You have the sunscreen?"

"Yep."

"It's supposed to get even hotter today."

"Yep." Charlie closes the fridge, keeping his back to her. "I know how to take care of my daughter."

"Are you annoyed with me?"

"Yep."

He turns, exasperated. "This is frustrating."

"Are you going to divorce me?"

He can't help but snicker. "Yes, Colette. I am."

"Will you leave me the espresso machine?"

Charlie drops the bottle on the counter and walks over to her. "Nope."

"The French press, at least?"

"Talk to my lawyer."

"You love me?"

"A lot. But god, you're stubborn." He leans down and kisses her forehead. "I'll see you later."

Colette pours a fresh cup of coffee and brings it to the window, peering down at the street, queasy with exhaustion. She spent most of the night on the glider, catching moments of sleep in between nursing Poppy, knowing she should put the baby in her crib, force her to get accustomed to falling asleep on her own, like every expert recommends, letting her cry for a few moments if necessary. But she couldn't bring herself to do it. Every instinct told her to stay with her baby, let Poppy sleep in her arms all night if that's what she needed.

The visit to the pediatrician had not gone well. "She's behind," the doctor said. "It's clear. She's having some muscle weakness in her upper body, a little more pronounced on her right side. And I'm concerned about the way she's holding her head."

"What does it mean?" Colette asked, cradling Poppy to her chest.

"It's too early to tell. All we can do at this point is watch her. Come back in three months."

"*Three months?* Why so long? There's nothing to do before that?"

"Not at this age. We just have to wait and see. Kids can outgrow this."

Charlie appears on the sidewalk downstairs. He adjusts his earbuds and then breaks into a slow jog, steering the stroller toward the entrance to the park. He reacted to the news as she expected he would. Calmly.

"Okay, so we'll bring her back in three months," he said. "If he tells us then that we need to be worried, we'll start worrying."

A car comes careening down the street just as Charlie starts to cross, not waiting for the walk light. Colette holds her breath as he steps back onto the sidewalk, yelling something at the driver. When he jogs across and turns at the stone wall, she closes the curtain, places her coffee on the table, and kneels in front of the couch, feeling underneath for the envelope holding the flash drive.

She zips it into the inner pocket of her bag and lingers in the shower, the water extra cold, trying to clear her head and force herself awake; to purge the thoughts that have been plaguing her since yesterday. They found a body.

The information was scarce—a simple note from Mark Hoyt at the very top of the stack. *Remains were discovered at approximately 5 p.m. yesterday. Sent to lab, identification to be confirmed by 1200 hours tomorrow. Will update asap.*

She closes her eyes under the stream of cold water, reenvisioning the dream she had last night. Winnie was in a field, standing over Midas's lifeless body. Colette walked closer, reaching to take Winnie's arm, but when Winnie turned, Colette saw she'd been wrong. It wasn't Winnie standing over Midas. It was Francie.

She turns off the shower and dresses quickly. When she arrives on the fourth floor of City Hall an hour later, Allison is not at her desk. Colette waits in the lobby for a few minutes before going to Teb's door and peeking inside his empty office. Her footsteps are quiet on the carpet as she walks slowly toward his credenza, fishing inside the pocket of her bag for the flash drive. Just as she's about to place it on the floor under a row of chairs, Allison stands up from behind Teb's desk.

"Hi," she says.

"Oh my god." Colette tightens her grip on the flash drive. "You scared me to death."

"I'm sorry," says Allison, placing her palm on her abdomen. "Whoosh. That made me a little dizzy."

"What are you doing?" Colette asks.

Allison sighs. "Listen, is there a chance anyone came and took something from the mayor's desk while you were in here working?"

"Took something?" Colette clears her throat. "No, not that I remember."

"Shoot."

"What's wrong?"

"Oh, nothing. I swore I put something in here for the mayor, but he can't find it. He's pissed at me."

"I can help you look," Colette says. "What is it?"

Allison waves her hand. "Don't be silly. You have enough to worry about without having to fix a mess I made. But"—she frowns—"I have to ask you to wait outside. I've been told I can't let anyone into his office if he's not here. He probably doesn't mean you, but I'm in enough trouble, so—"

"Of course," Colette says. "I'm happy to wait outside."

Colette follows Allison back into the lobby. Beyond the couches, in front of the large west windows with a view of City Hall Park, a young man is setting up a podium while another waits nearby, looking bored, holding a cardboard seal of the city. Colette takes a seat in one of the leather chairs and drops the flash drive into her bag just as Allison reappears, a large manila envelope in her hand.

"This arrived for you."

Colette's name is written in green block letters on the front of the envelope, followed by the address for City Hall. Who would send mail to her at the mayor's office? Nobody's even supposed to know she comes here.

"When?" Colette asks.

"Late yesterday."

Colette takes the envelope and tucks it into her bag. "Thanks."

"My pleasure. Hopefully you won't have to wait long, but to be honest, it doesn't look good." Allison nods toward the two young men setting up the podium. "Something strange is going on here today."

Allison returns to her desk and Colette settles into her seat, distracted by the envelope. Something tells her she shouldn't open it now. Not here, not with people around.

For the next thirty minutes, Colette flips idly through old issues of the *New Yorker*. At last Colette hears people coming down the hall. Aaron enters the lobby with a woman. She's wearing a dark gray suit, and Colette catches a glimpse of a holstered gun at her waist. There's something familiar about her.

"See you later," the woman says to Allison, and hearing her voice, it hits Colette. It's the detective who interviewed Winnie. The one from the flash drive. She disappears into the elevator as Aaron approaches Colette, his cell phone in one hand and a thick folder in the other. Colette stands up, but he gestures for her to sit back down. "Not yet, sorry. Something's come up. The mayor apologizes. Give us ten more minutes."

"I can come back when it's a better time."

"No, I'm doing my best to get you in," Aaron says, glancing over Colette's shoulder at Joan Ramirez, the mayor's press secretary, who is standing outside the mayor's door. Aaron nods at Joan. "Ten more minutes." He touches Colette's shoulder and turns to go, but as he does, the folder drops from under his arm to the floor, scattering papers around her feet. She stoops to help collect them, reaching under her chair.

Her hand stops midair.

It's a photo of Midas. Colette picks up the photo and examines it. He's wearing a gray-striped onesie and is sucking on his fist. He appears to be lying on a white carpet.

"Colette?"

Aaron is holding out his palm. She stands and gives him the photo.

"Thanks," he says, winking at her. He ushers Joan into the mayor's office, and Colette sits back down, the room spinning around her. She rests her forehead in her hands, fighting the desire to lower her head between her knees, the way she was advised to do by a bus driver in the second grade, who'd noticed her turning green with car sickness in the seat behind him. *Remains were discovered.* That photograph. The detective. The press conference they're setting up for.

Midas is dead.

What else could it be?

She hears Teb's voice and looks up, seeing him walking toward her. She stands, keeping her bag close to her body.

"I have some bad news, Colette," Teb says. His tone is serious. "There's something here I need to deal with. I'm really sorry."

"What is it?" she asks, but then Aaron is there, his cell phone ringing. He reaches into the inside pocket of his suit jacket.

"Yep," Aaron says into the phone. "Okay, good." Aaron hangs up. "Commissioner Ghosh just arrived, sir. He's on his way up." Aaron glances at the podium in front of the windows and then back at Teb. "You might want to change ties. Something a little more solemn."

Teb nods and turns to walk back toward his office. "Sorry, Colette," Aaron says, guiding her toward the elevator, pressing the down button. "I know it must be frustrating when this happens, but sometimes things are beyond our control. Nature of the job." The elevator doors open, and Elliott Falk of the *New York Post* bursts out. "I'll have Allison call you to reschedule," Aaron says. The elevator doors close between them, and when they open again, she runs outside, waving down the nearest taxi. She slams the door shut behind her.

"Where to?"

"Brooklyn," she says, sliding across the hot, cracked leather. "Prospect Park West."

She presses the power button on the television in front of her seat and the screen flickers, filling the cab with loud music, a jingle about buying a mattress. The cabdriver lays on his horn at the entrance to the Brooklyn Bridge. A local morning program is on, in the midst of a cooking program. How to get kids to eat more greens. The driver turns up the radio, competing with the sound of the television. He's listening to the all-news station.

She leans forward. "Did you hear anything about Midas, that baby that was taken?"

"The rich one?"

"Yes."

"He'd dead," the driver says. "An ex-boyfriend killed him, apparently."

"No." The word is choked. "Where did you hear that?"

"My wife. She told me that the other day." He makes a face. "She's obsessed with this story."

Colette's phone beeps. It's Nell.

I NEED to see you. Meet me at 5? The Spot. I'm going to sneak out early, need to get Beatrice at 6.

I can't. Colette types. Not today.

Three dots. Nell's response is immediate. PLEASE. It's important.

Colette places her phone on her lap and closes her eyes. *Remember to breathe.* She pictures the doula kneeling in front of her at the worst moments of her labor, repeating the phrase again and again. *It all comes back to your breath.*

I'm serious, Nell writes. I have to talk to you.

Fine. I'll be there.

"Excuse me," the driver says, fifteen minutes later. "We're here."

Charlie is in the kitchen making a sandwich when she enters the apartment.

"You're back already?"

She drops her bag by the door, mutes his music and then turns on the television, flipping through the stations.

"What are you doing?"

"The mayor is holding a press conference. I think it's about Midas—" When she gets to a cable news program, she sees Teb standing at the podium, holding up his hand to silence the reporters. "The remains were discovered in the woods about four hundred feet from Winnie Ross's home, on her property in upstate New York. Because the body had been badly burned, we elicited the help of the FBI to identify the remains."

"No." Charlie comes to stand beside Colette and he takes her hand. "They found Mid—"

"Shhhhhh."

"We received confirmation this afternoon that the remains belong to Hector Quimby, a longtime employee of the Ross family." Teb consults the notes in front of him. "For the past thirty years, Mr. Quimby has worked as the groundskeeper at the Ross property, as well as maintaining the family's home in Brooklyn, from which Midas was taken on the night of July 4." A photo flashes on the screen. The man is in his late sixties, with gray hair, a gray mustache, and cottony blue eyes. "We do not yet know if there's a connection between Mr. Quimby's death and the abduction of Midas Ross, but we are proceeding with the investigation assuming there is."

"How was the body discovered?" someone calls from the crowd of reporters.

"Investigators with the FBI and NYPD were led to Mr. Quimby's body"—Teb coughs—"excuse me. They were led to Mr. Quimby's body by cadaver dogs sniffing for the scent of Midas Ross."

Colette unwinds her fingers from Charlie's. "I need a second." She walks to the kitchen, picks up her bag, and locks the door behind her in the bathroom. She sits on the toilet and removes the manila envelope, tearing it open. There's no sign of who sent it. No letter. No signature. Just a single sheet of paper.

It's a mug shot.

He's a teenager in the photo. There are no lines around his eyes, no gray in the goatee. He stares into the camera, a defiant expression on his face. The nameplate he holds in front of his chest is lettered with his date of birth and place of arrest. But not what he was charged with. Not even his name.

But of course it's him. Token.

———

Francie sucks in her stomach, aware of a guy approaching, but he strolls past her, taking a seat at the far end of the bar. She checks the time again: 3:32 p.m. He's thirty-two minutes late. Maybe he lied. Maybe he's not coming.

"Another white zinfandel?"

She tugs at the fabric of her low-cut neckline in the wake of the bartender's gaze. "I guess so," she says, glancing down at the text her mother-in-law, Barbara, sent a few minutes ago, with an attached photo of Will lying on a blanket in the park. We're doing great. Hope the photo shoot is going well. Good luck!

Her hand is unsteady as she gives a ten to the bartender, thinking again about the argument she and Lowell had this morning, after he came out of the bedroom to find Francie sitting on the couch, feeding Will a bottle, trying to hold back tears.

"What is it this time?" he asked her.

"What is what?"

"You look upset."

"I'm not."

"Francie—"

"It's nothing. I don't want to talk about it." She can't tell Lowell what's bothering her—how she called Mark Hoyt yesterday to inform him she'd found photographs of the guy who approached Winnie at the Jolly Llama.

"I'm disappointed I had to do this work myself," she said to Hoyt, impressed with the authority in her voice. "But so be it. I will e-mail them to you now, unless, for security purposes, you'd prefer to send an officer over to pick them up personally?"

"Francie, listen to me," Hoyt had said. "You need to back off."

"Back off? Are you—"

"You heard me, Mrs. Givens. Back off. Find something to do. Take that kid to the swings. Or maybe go see your doctor. Make sure everything is okay. Let us do our job."

"Go see my—" A laugh escaped her. "Do you have *any idea* what a shitty job you're doing here? Are you even aware there is a newborn baby counting on you to bring him back to his mother? Go see my doctor? Are you *kidding* me? I don't need another man—"

"Good-bye, Mrs. Givens."

Of course she could never tell this to Lowell, who just stood there, looking at her like she was crazy, his back against the counter, his arms crossed at his chest. "I'm starting to worry about you, Francie."

She feels sick now, thinking about what she said to him after that, how she accused him of being cold and unsympathetic as he got dressed, turning away from his kiss as he made his way out the door to pick up his mother from the airport (Lowell had, apparently, called Barbara and asked her to come from Tennessee for a few days, telling her Francie was overwhelmed and could use some help with the baby, without even discussing it with her first). Francie hates it when they fight. They hardly ever argued before, but now, since the baby, she's annoyed by everything he does. She knows she needs to apologize to him and smooth things over, especially with Barbara staying with them, sleeping on the sofa in the living room, in earshot of every word they exchange. She reaches for her phone, but then she feels a pair of hands around her waist.

She turns, her phone frozen in her hand, stunned by how handsome he is up close: his icy blue eyes; his strong, square jaw; his dark hair under the bright red baseball cap. Before she can even say hello, he lifts her from the stool and draws her close, kissing her in a way she hasn't been kissed in a very long time, helping her forget all about Lowell.

———

He pulls back. "You *are* the woman I'm supposed to meet, correct?"

"Yes. Hello." Francie regrets the nervous crack in her voice.

He drops onto the stool beside her and signals to the bartender, ordering a beer and a shot of whiskey for himself, not offering to replenish her drink. "Sorry I'm late. Something came up." He downs the shot in one easy swallow and follows it with a sip of beer. She reaches for her glass of wine, glancing at him. She was right. He's in his thirties, the same age Archie Andersen would now be. He takes another drink, and she sees the way his hand grips the glass, the pull of his T-shirt at his biceps. He's much bigger than she remembers from when she watched him at the Jolly Llama. "I like your style," he says, wiping his mouth with the back of his hand.

She raises her eyebrows. "My dress, you mean?" His gaze travels over her breasts to her neck, and then to her eyes, framed under the false eyelashes she applied an hour earlier in the bathroom of a nearby Starbucks.

"Well, yeah. That too. But I mean that you didn't waste any time. So many girls wanna e-mail for days before meeting."

Francie's proud of how quickly she was able to devise this scheme, all thanks to Nell. Yesterday, after contacting Mark Hoyt had dead-ended, she e-mailed Nell at work.

I know it's a long shot, but I found some photos of that guy Winnie was talking to at the Jolly Llama, Francie wrote. Any chance we can use these to find out something about this guy?

It took Nell seven minutes to respond. This is all I can find. I put his photo into a face recognition app. He seems nice.

Francie opened the link, and there he was: his photos and accompanying profile at a website called Sex Buddies, a dating site, of sorts. He revealed very little about himself—his height, his weight, and his preference for big-breasted women, but not his name (unless his name was really Doktor Danger).

What are you going to do with this? Nell wrote.

Nothing, Francie replied. Keep it on hand, just in case.

In reality, she spent the next hour applying makeup, taking selfies, trying to look as suggestive as possible, and generating her own dating profile at Sex Buddies. Three e-mails from the fake Gmail account she'd created was all it took to arrange this meeting. Reading through the things people had written on the site left her feeling depressed, and then utterly grateful for Lowell, for the life they have, the beautiful family they've created.

The guy leans toward her. "You smell amazing," he says.

"Thank you. But first, I don't even know your name."

"My name? What do you want my name to be?"

"What do I *want* it to be?"

"Yeah." She can smell tobacco on his breath. "Why don't you choose my name?"

Francie pretends to mull it over for a moment. "I want your name to be Archie."

He laughs. "Like the guy in the cartoon?" She laughs too, trying to mask her disappointment. It can't be him. Unless he's some sort of Oscar-winning actor, he wouldn't have responded so cavalierly if she'd correctly guessed his name. "Archie. I like it."

"Good," she says. Fine, even so, she thinks. He might not be Archie Andersen, but he's still going to be able to answer some critical questions: why he approached Winnie, what they talked about, where Winnie went that night.

"You can be my Veronica," he says. "Now if only we had a Betty."

He glances at something behind her and without a word takes Francie's hand, pulling her off the stool and toward the back of the bar. She struggles to keep pace, wine spilling onto her dress, trying to balance in the heels she's wearing. They walk down a narrow, darkened hall that reeks of urine, and then into an empty back room, with a pool table in one corner and a battered couch in the other.

He leads her to the couch and pulls her toward him, his lips on her ear. "It's more private back here," he mutters and then nudges her backward, until she falls awkwardly onto the couch, splashing most of her wine. He sits beside her and puts a calloused hand on her knee, moving it slowly up her thigh.

"Not quite yet," she whispers, removing his hand. She's filled with relief as two guys enter the room. They head toward the pool table, wearing dusty work boots and tool belts; likely on a lunch break from a nearby construction project. She can't help the thought: what if, by some stroke of horrible luck, they know her? What if they're colleagues of Lowell, guys he's worked with on a building project?

"I have forty minutes before I need to go to work, Veronica," fake Archie says. He seems annoyed. She can't really blame him. Sex Buddies is not exactly known as a place through which people get together at a bar during the day to discuss their shared interests. And she doesn't have much time herself. She's told Nell she'll meet her at the Spot at five; there's something Nell wants to talk to her and Colette about. In the meantime, she has this plan to execute. A plan she was awake thinking about all night.

She stands up, straddling his outstretched legs, and rests her hands on his thighs, her breasts inches from his face, enveloping him in the scent of her perfume. "I'm going to get us another round."

At the bar, Francie fights the urge to look one more time at the photo of Will at the park, feeling another wave of guilt for lying to Lowell and Barbara, telling them she'd placed a classified ad on The Village website and had been hired to shoot a nine-month-old. She carries the drinks back to the couch, doing her best to appear composed and confident as she sits down beside him.

"So. Veronica." His mouth is back near her ear. "What do you want to talk about?"

She takes a long sip of wine and then delivers the words she practiced this morning. "I need this drink. I lost my job."

"That sucks." He removes his baseball cap and strokes her neck with his nose.

"Yeah. I was a waitress. At this really cool place in Brooklyn. The Jolly Llama."

He leans back. "I go there sometimes."

"You're kidding."

"Not kidding. It's a few blocks from my apartment."

"That's weird." She squints and looks at him more closely. "Oh my god, wait a minute. It's *you*."

He frowns at her. "You who?"

"You!" She sets her glass on the sticky table and turns toward him, placing her hand on his knee. "Were you at the Jolly Llama on the fourth of July?"

He thinks about it. "Yeah, actually. How did you know that?"

"You're *that* guy. What are the chances?" She laughs and slaps his knee. "My coworkers are not going to believe this. We've all been talking about you."

He appears stunned. "Me? Why?"

"You're the guy who was talking to that woman. That Winnie woman."

"What's a Winnie woman?"

Francie is surprised at the convincing job he's doing, pretending he doesn't know what she's talking about. "Gwendolyn Ross? The actress? Her kid was abducted?"

"When?"

"Really? Do you not read the newspapers? Watch television?"

"Just sports."

She can't believe it. He really doesn't know. "Do you remember talking to a woman at the bar that night? Pretty? You may have disappeared with her for a little while?"

Finally, a flash of recognition. "*That* woman had her kid abducted?"

"Yes. Her son Midas. He was taken that night."

"Holy shit. I *have* heard about this. The girls at work are always talking about it. Midas. Like the Greek god." He puts his beer on the table and leans forward, laughing. "That is insane. Wait until I tell my friends."

"Why?" Francie asks, conspiratorially. "What will your friends say?"

"They were the ones who dared me to do it."

The amusement drains from her voice. "Do what?"

"Talk to her. Hit on her." He appears dumbfounded. "There were these moms there, out back."

"Yes, I remember them. She was with them."

"My buddies said they'd give me twenty bucks if I hit on one of them. You know, as a joke. Like, who could get with a MILF? I took the bet. The first one I tried denied me before I could even offer the drink, but then she—this Winnie woman—she was into it." He scoffs. "*Really* into it."

Francie takes another sip of her drink. She needs to slow down. The wine is muddling her thoughts. "So you didn't know her before that night?"

"No." He smirks. "But I sure knew her by the end of it."

She softens her voice and peers at him from under her eyelashes. "I'm intrigued."

He's quiet, studying her. He takes the hem of her dress between his fingers and folds it over itself, making her dress shorter, exposing her freshly shaven thighs, shiny with peach-scented lotion. "You sure you want to hear? It's really crazy."

She forces a flirtatious tone into her voice. "I like really crazy."

"Oh yeah, Veronica? Prove it."

"Prove it?"

"Yeah. Let's say I have an incredibly good story for you."

"Okay."

"But you have to earn it." His face is inches from hers. "Kiss me, and I'll tell you."

He leans in and roughly presses his lips against hers, pushing his tongue inside her mouth. He pulls away eventually, leaving a bitter hint of beer in her throat. "I bought her a drink."

Francie raises her eyebrows and then frowns. "That's not really crazy."

"No, that's just the beginning." He traces Francie's collar bone with his thumb. "You want more?"

She nods as he slides his hand under her dress, gently forcing her legs apart. He squeezes her inner thigh, his thumb teasing the edge of her underwear. "Go ahead," she says. Her voice sounds hollow and unfamiliar.

"I asked her to come home with me." One of the construction workers at the pool table glances at them as fake Archie takes Francie's hand and places it in between his legs. Francie can feel he's grown hard, and he guides her hand back and forth over the fabric of his jeans.

"And did she? Go home with you?" she asks. He kisses her. When he pulls away, her vision is hazy. The smell of beer on his breath. The bruising stubble on his chin. It's not him she's seeing—not this man she's calling Archie—but the science teacher. Mr. Colburn.

"No, sadly. She said she had this kid to think about. She was upset about it."

Francie spreads her fingers wider, feeling a sinking sensation as she continues to press down on him. She closes her eyes. "Winnie was upset?"

"Yeah." He forces aside her panties and she feels her arms being pinned down, the scratch of the cheap blanket on top of Mr. Colburn's bed. She feels the urge to scream, but she can't. "She said all she wanted was to go back to my place. Climb on top of me." Her hand moves faster over the fabric of his jeans. "That she hated being stuck at home. Having this baby to worry about all the time."

She whispers into his ear. "She said that? That she hated having a baby?"

"Something like that. We locked ourselves in the bathroom.

I couldn't keep my hands off her body. It was amazing. I told her to at least stay a little longer. Let me get her another drink."

"And?"

"She started yelling at me. Telling me she had to go take care of things. That she wasn't like that. Something about being a good mother." His breath grows shallow on Francie's neck, and she feels his body beginning to tense. "I would have killed to take her home. To shove her down on my bed. To rip off that dress." He removes his hand from between Francie's legs and clutches her wrist, pressing her palm down, forcing it to move faster, his eyes closed, his mouth open. "Winnie. My god. She was so fucking hot." Francie feels the tears seeping from the corners of her eyes as he moans, deep and low, the sound filling the room.

They're watching. Both of the guys at the pool table. Standing motionless, their cues held like pitchforks at their sides. Archie doesn't seem to notice she's crying as he stares up at the ceiling, licking his lips, his head resting on the back of the couch.

"Her kid. Abducted." He shakes his head, sitting up and reaching for the rest of his beer. "I sure hope the police are asking her some questions. That girl was fucking nuts."

———

Nell sits at a table near the window at the Spot, her mug of black tea growing cold in her hand as she scrolls through the photos she took last night of Beatrice; dozens of pictures of her tiny hands, her minute feet, the bottoms yellow like butter, sweet enough to eat.

Nell checks the door again, hoping Colette and Francie are on their way. She's impatient to get to the day care to pick up Beatrice—knowing how ludicrous it is, the number of hours she spends staring at photos of her baby's feet while paying strangers to care for her.

Nell drops her phone in her purse, and when she looks up, Colette is standing at the table, Poppy peeking out from the fabric of a Moby Wrap. Colette's eyes are red and her freckles are stark and lacy against her skin, which is unusually pale. "You okay?" Nell asks.

"Did you see it?" Colette sits heavily on the chair across from Nell. "They identified the body."

Nell nods. "I watched it at work, in the corporate café. Everyone was glued to the television. I thought it was going to be Midas. Ever since you called yesterday, I was sure the body was going to be his."

"I know. Me too." Colette leans in toward Nell. "I have to talk to you about something. I got this thing in the mail—"

Nell spots Francie near the door, squinting up at the chalkboard menu over the counter. "Oh good, she's here," Nell says. Nell stands and waves to Francie, surprised to see she's wearing a tight, low-cut dress, offering a peek of her black lace bra underneath.

"Did you see it?" Francie asks, approaching the table. "The body?" Her mascara runs in smeared arches over her eyes, which are framed in long, false eyelashes, like the thin legs of a spider.

Nell nods. "I saw it. It's—"

She sits down. "And Bodhi Mogaro? They've released him." The news of his release broke earlier that day, in a press conference called by Oliver Hood. Standing on the steps of the jailhouse beside Mogaro, his wife, and his mother, Hood demanded an apology from the police officers involved in the investigation, from Commissioner Rohan Ghosh, from Mayor Shepherd.

"We'll see the NYPD in court," Hood said.

"I really need a coffee," Francie says. "And some water." Nell notices the way her words slur, the sheen of perspiration above Francie's lips.

"Francie, are you drunk?"

Francie throws Nell an irritated look. "No, Nell. I'm not drunk. I'm a nursing mother." She reaches for the water in front of Nell and takes a long drink. "I'm very shaken by this Hector news. I saw it on the way here. Do they have any idea who killed him?"

"No, but listen—" Colette says, but Francie cuts her off.

"He had keys to her building. He could have gotten in. Or let someone else in. They're going to put that together, right? Even an idiot like Mark Hoyt will be able to make that connection?"

"Yes," Nell says. "And they're asking for volunteers to search the property and surrounding areas for Midas. We should go."

Francie's face is pinched. "You mean search for his body."

Colette leans forward. "Listen. I have something I need to tell you—something very disturbing happened today." She takes an envelope from her diaper bag, her name written in green block letters on the front. "This came for me today, at the mayor's office."

Nell sees the block handwriting. The green ink. She reaches into her bag at her feet and retrieves a similar envelope, her name written in the exact same print. "This came for me, at work," Nell says. "It's why I asked to see you. To show you this."

The envelope was in her mail slot when she returned from lunch. She opened it sitting at the head of a conference table, before a meeting to brief the other officers of the company on the impending changes to the security system. She stumbled through her presentation, flustered by what was inside.

Francie's eyes are wide. "Oh my god. I got one of those too. At home, this morning. I didn't open it. What is it?" She snatches Nell's envelope and pulls out the mug shot. "Who sent this?"

"I have no idea," Colette says, her voice just above a whisper.

"Someone who knows I'm working for the mayor. Which is, like, you guys, and Token, who I somehow doubt was the one who sent this."

"What was he arrested for?"

"It doesn't say here," Nell says. "I did some digging, but—"

"Digging?" Francie is staring at Nell. "Where?"

"A few places. I wanted to see what I could find. I mean, why would I be sent this? It's even creepier now. Why were we *all* sent it?" She lowers her voice. "I went into The Village website, to the May Mothers admin page. I broke into it, to see his profile, to learn a little bit more about him."

"How—" Francie's gaze is intent on Nell.

"It doesn't matter. It's something I can do."

"And?" Colette says.

"And nothing. He hardly filled it out. He grew up in Manhattan, which I think we knew. His partner's name is Lou. He didn't even include a photo."

Francie keeps her voice low. "You should go back in. Look at Winnie's profile. See if she says who Midas's dad is."

Nell hesitates and then leans in closer. "I did."

A man bumps roughly into Nell's chair, spilling something on her shoulder. She turns, annoyed, and sees it's someone she recognizes—a man from her building.

"Nell, hi. Sorry about that."

It's the guy who lives one floor down, the one who always has the cuff of his right leg rolled up, at the ready to mount some waiting bike; the one with the frowning wife.

"How you doing?" he asks. "How's the baby?"

"Brilliant, thanks."

The man nods. "Sounds like she's having some trouble sleeping, huh?"

"What do you mean?"

"Lisa and I, we can hear the crying sometimes. Through the ceiling."

"Oh, right. Well—"

"Lisa's actually been doing some research. Do you give the baby a pacifier?"

"A pacifier? Yes."

"Oh. Because Lisa read they can help to stop babies from crying."

"Right," Nell says. "I assume you don't have kids—"

"Or there's these new swaddles. Enchanted SleepSuit, or something. If the baby cries—"

"It's nice of you to be so concerned," Nell says, her patience waning. "But there's no need. The crying last night. It wasn't the baby."

"It wasn't? Who was it?"

"My husband. Sebastian."

"Sebastian?"

"Yes. He was watching *Beaches* again. Gets him every time."

The man offers a lopsided smile. "Right. See you later, Nell."

They all remain silent until he finishes pouring milk and sugar into his coffee at the nearby counter. As soon as he exits the café, Colette leans in toward Nell. "What did Winnie's profile say?"

"It wasn't there," Nell says. "She doesn't have a profile. There's no record of her membership that I could locate."

"What does that mean?"

"I'm not sure, exactly. I'm assuming she canceled it, and the system doesn't keep a record of that. And really, who would blame her? Imagine her opening her e-mail, hoping for some good news about Midas, and then having to wade through sixteen new e-mails about Kegels."

Colette rests her forehead in her hands. "This is getting crazy. I have no idea what we're supposed to do now."

"I do," Francie says. She looks from Colette to Nell, her gaze disturbingly opaque, as if a shade has been drawn across her eyes. "We're going to do whatever it takes to find Midas. We're not giving up on him. Not until we have to. Not until we make sure we've done everything in our power to get him back, where he's meant to be: safe with his mother."

CHAPTER FIFTEEN
NIGHT EIGHT

I've been thinking about something these past few days—that promise I made to myself when I found out I was pregnant. What a moment that was. Hovering above the toilet seat in the Duane Reade pharmacy, too anxious to wait until I got home to take the test, seeing the two bubble-gum-pink lines forming an immediate cross, like the one my mother hung over the door of her bedroom.

I will not, I promised, be one of those mothers.

I won't read all of the books. Stress out about phthalates in my shampoo, pesticides in my creamer. BPA in my takeout Chinese container. I won't ever, not once, stand in the grocery store, talking loudly to my child, hoping everyone hears how understanding I am, how close we are, as if parenting is a fucking piece of performance art.

I won't become a different person.

And then how long did it take me to break that promise?

Three minutes.

Yes, three minutes: the amount of time it took to wind the pregnancy test in toilet paper, stow it in my purse, wash my hands, and go outside. Three minutes, and I was someone else entirely.

A mom.

How did I know? Because I stood at the corner, no cars in sight, and I waited for the walk light. I've never done that before in my life. I can still see myself. A crowd of people hurrying past me, into the empty street, on their way to the gym, to brunch, their to-go coffees slip-sloshing onto their workout clothes, while I stood there, motionless, my palms against my belly, convinced that the moment I stepped off the sidewalk a car was going to barrel down the street out of nowhere, turn the corner, flattening the baby (and me, along with him) against the windshield.

And I never went back. All of a sudden, that's who I was. It was like an escalator materialized under me, lifting me against my will, carrying me to this place where—poof!—everything was something to fear: microwave ovens, manhole covers, dust from the renovation next door. It was all a cause for concern, things I couldn't ignore, lest I risk losing the baby. Have him stolen away.

I tried my best to protect him.

I failed.

———

It's later now. I've just woken from a fitful nap, hoping a little sleep might make me feel better, clear my head. Give me the courage to be more honest.

I'm starting to regret my decision.

There, I said it. It's about time I had the guts to get this all out. Here's more:

This isn't working, this thing between us. I fear that no matter what I do, Joshua will never be happy with me. Our days have been difficult. He's sullen, ignoring me, pushing me away.

He tunes me out, like I'm not even there. Like my feelings don't matter. (I would never say this to him, but I swear, he is *just* like his father.)

This morning I reminded him that this was something we *both* wanted. And then I said a few things I wish I hadn't. Telling him that maybe I made a mistake. That maybe I was better off before. That I'd have to live with what I did for the rest of my life, and I no longer believed it was worth it. I can be so mean sometimes. I shouldn't have said any of that.

I've been trying to see his side of the story. How annoying my constant need to talk about things must be, especially now that they've let Bodhi go. How I haven't figured everything out yet. I've told him all my stories, of course—how *clever* I've always been, testing off the charts as a child, a natural-born problem-solver, as my mother said. And now I think he's waiting for me to be the one to solve this predicament, figure out the right strategy. To make sure we're protected.

But know what else it's time to admit? I'm not clever at all. I am, in fact, a moron.

We can't go to Indonesia. Joshua can't get a passport, obviously. I should have realized this from the beginning—it's exactly the type of thing Dr. H would have helped me with in the past. Seeing the holes in my logic, my inability to make sense of even simple things. So we're back in Brooklyn, back in the bubble, figuring out a new plan, laying low, getting things in order to get out of here.

The May Mothers are everywhere. Sometimes I stand at the window, peering out from behind the curtain, trying to get a bit of sunlight on my face, and I see them. A few hours ago it was Yuko, walking on the shady side of the street, a yoga mat under her arm, earbuds in her ears. Then, not twenty minutes later, Colette. She was with a guy I assumed to be Charlie. Big-time writer Charlie. Poppy was strapped to his chest and he and Colette were holding hands, laughing about something, passing an iced coffee back and forth, her arms heavy with flowers from the farmers' market. The ideal Brooklyn family. So good at making perfect look easy.

What people like them don't get is what seeing scenes like that does to people like *me*. To people who don't have what she does. Joshua and I went for a drive yesterday, and I was looking out the window at a stoplight. I watched this mom in the next car. She was in the front seat, facing forward, her arm reaching into the back seat, holding hands with a little girl strapped into her car seat. It was so simple and beautiful. Little did she know she was breaking my heart. In the city you can feel it, the rhythm of children. The burst of yells and laughter early in the morning, little bodies gathered, running in sprinklers in backyards invisible from the street, arguing over the swings at the playground. Then the lull around noon, when they return home to wash their hands, eat their lunch, and then sleep, quietly, peacefully, slack-jawed and wheezy until they wake a few hours later, springing to life again.

I can't bear to stay inside for much longer, but nor can I bear the idea of running into one of them on the street, of having to make conversation about how I am, where I've been. Having to hear the inevitable question: *My god, what happened to Midas?*

Oh no. Joshua is up. I must go. He really hates to see me cry.

CHAPTER SIXTEEN
DAY NINE

> **TO:** May Mothers
> **FROM:** Your friends at The Village
> DATE: July 13
> SUBJECT: Today's advice
>
> <u>YOUR BABY: DAY 60</u>
>
> Let's talk about . . . sex. Chances are, you've been too tired these last few weeks to give the topic much thought. While it's common to have a low libido after giving birth, there's a good chance things are beginning to feel back to normal in that department. And it's important us new moms don't forget we're also wives. So, it might be time to break open a bottle of wine, turn on some music, and see what happens. (But remember, ladies: BIRTH CONTROL IS YOUR BFF.)

Francie sits on the hot, rough stoop of a brownstone, sucking on a chocolate-covered pretzel, pressing the soft rise of a blister on her heel, her camera resting on her lap.

It makes so much sense, she thinks, once again.

The way he looked at Winnie during the meetings, whispering in her ear, saving her a seat beside him on his blanket. It was like he was obsessed with her. And where did he go, after disappearing so abruptly from the Jolly Llama? Francie should have been focused on this from the beginning, not getting derailed by false leads. Archie Andersen, who somehow seemed to vanish into thin air. Fake Archie Andersen. The thought of that guy repulsed her—his hands on her body, the stench of his breath. She's felt disgusted ever since she excused herself from that couch, telling him she had to use the bathroom and then hightailing it out of the bar.

She hadn't told Nell or Colette she'd met him, or the things he'd said. There was no need to. The guy was a liar. She could tell, the minute she saw him. *Maybe* he was telling the truth about some of it. *Maybe* they had hooked up. And so what? Winnie was single, she could do whatever she wanted. Francie had never slept with anyone other than Lowell (the science teacher didn't count), but she's aware of how things work in the real world. Especially these days, especially in New York, and most certainly for a woman as beautiful as Winnie. But say those things about Midas? About not wanting her own child?

No.

Francie knew women who didn't like their own kids. She grew up with one of them. Winnie was nothing like that.

A door slams across the street. She picks up her camera, zooming in on a woman in yoga pants and a tank top skipping down the stairs of No. 584, the address Nell copied from Token's profile at May Mothers. The woman stops to stretch her hamstrings on the steps and then turns toward the park, breaking into a jog a few buildings down. Francie is growing impatient. She's been sitting on this stoop for more than an hour, and people are beginning to arrive for appointments at the chiropractor's office on the ground floor. Lowell's mother, Barbara, made a hair appointment for noon, and Francie said she'd be back to take the baby long before then. She picks up the camera, promising herself she'll stay just ten more minutes, scrolling through the photos stored on her camera—the babies from the May Mothers get-together five days earlier she still hasn't done anything with, the images of Hector Quimby, wearing the light-yellow golf shirt, standing outside Winnie's building.

Francie closes her eyes, seeing Hector as she watched him from her spot on the bench, his hands clasped behind his back, pacing slowly in front of Winnie's building. Who *was* he? According to Patricia Faith, Hector's body was discovered after his wife called the local police, saying her husband had gone to take care of a few things at the Ross property and hadn't come home. They had been married for fifty-two years. Ten grandkids. A volunteer driver for Meals on Wheels. He'd been working for the Ross family for nearly thirty years, thought of Winnie like a daughter. The forensic evidence suggests he was killed and then his body dragged to the woods, that it had been doused in gasoline and lit on fire.

Francie stands up, returning the camera to her bag, knowing it's time to call it a day and go home. It's too hot to sit here any longer. One good thing about Barbara visiting is that Lowell came home last night with a brand-new air conditioner, after his mother complained about the used one. Francie will go home and turn it on and play with Will for a few hours in the cool apartment. Her stomach rumbles as she trudges down the stairs and turns to walk down the hill back to her apartment, but then she hears something: the door of Token's building closing once again.

It's him.

Autumn is in the sling, and he's putting on a pair of sunglasses, walking down the stairs, turning west toward the park. Francie drapes her bag across her chest and follows him up the hill, trying to ignore the painful rub of the blister, careful to keep a half block behind him. He turns north on Eighth Avenue and walks two blocks, into the Spot. She crosses the street and crouches behind a Volvo station wagon, peeping through the car's windows. When he takes a seat on a bar stool at the window, Francie lifts her camera and watches through the viewfinder as he pages through a newspaper left behind on the counter and stirs his coffee—the double shot of espresso with a touch of steamed milk that he used to bring with him to every meeting.

He drinks his coffee in three smooth sips, makes a phone call, and then heads toward the door. Francie steps behind another car and holds her phone to her ear, pretending to speak to someone. She turns cautiously, seeing him walking up the hill, and follows from the opposite side of the street, trying to remain out of view behind the parked cars between them. It appears he's going to make a right, to head away from his apartment, and Francie begins to cross the street. But suddenly he stops and turns around. She's in the middle of the street, in his line of sight. She pivots and runs back to the sidewalk, but she trips on the curb, trying to protect her camera, feeling the sting on the heels of both hands and a pain in her knee where she hit the pavement.

"Oh dear. Are you okay?" An older woman is standing above her, a small dog wearing slippers on a leash at her heels. "Here, let me help you."

"I'm fine," Francie says, standing. There's a large gash in her knee, and a trail of blood runs down her shin.

"Are you sure? Let me get you a tissue."

"I'm fine," Francie says, waving the woman away. She picks up her bag and turns, spinning straight into Token.

———

Token walks out of the galley kitchen just off the living room, holding an ice pack in one hand and two cups of coffee in the other. "Shit," he says, placing the mugs on the coffee table. "I forgot that unlike me, who lives on the stuff, you're off caffeine."

"Not anymore." Francie takes the mug and ice pack.

"Hang on. Let me get something for that cut. It's pretty bad."

He walks through the French doors at the other end of the room, disappearing into a bedroom. A large-screen television set inside a built-in bookcase is tuned in to *The Faith Hour*, showing the scene of Winnie's property upstate, shot from a helicopter, where more than one hundred people have come to help search the area. Patricia Faith, filming live all week from the ballroom of a Ramada hotel, which has been designated the headquarters of the search, sits at a banquet table talking to the pastor of a nearby church. Patricia seems particularly concerned today.

"The way I see this," she says, "is, there are two options." She holds up one perfectly manicured finger. "Hector Quimby was involved in the disappearance of Baby Midas. Maybe he was paid by someone—let's not speculate who just yet—to take Midas and then dispose of him. And maybe that plan went awry." She holds up another finger. "Or, he's another tragic victim in this already tragic story. Maybe he knew something he wasn't supposed to know. Maybe he had to be silenced."

The pastor shakes his head. "All due respect, Miss Faith, but I've known Hector and Shelly Quimby for nearly forty years. I baptized their children, and their grandchildren. And I will swear on my grandfather's Bible that there is no way that good, warmhearted, *Christian* man had anything to do with the abduction or murder of any baby."

"And what can you tell me about Winnie Ross?" Patricia says, squinting at the pastor. "Her family has owned that house for decades. Did you know any of them?"

The man wipes his mouth with a cotton handkerchief. "No, ma'am, I can't say I did. As far as I know, not one member of the Ross family has ever darkened the door of *any* local church."

Francie turns away from the television, feeling unsteady. To-ken checked her skull, running his fingers through her hair, softly pressing every inch of her head. There was no sign of a bump and yet her head is pounding. She takes in his apartment, which is small and neat. The linen love seat on which she sits flanks a vintage mahogany coffee table, and small framed photographs of city street life hang over a dining table, set with a vase of fresh-cut spray roses. She stands and tiptoes toward the bookshelf, her knee throbbing, and examines a few framed photos of Autumn and Token, Autumn and some woman. The bathroom is just off the living room, and she peeks inside, finding bottles of face cleanser and hair gel lined neatly on a windowsill overlooking a light shaft.

She hears his footsteps shuffling toward her from the bedroom, and she closes the bathroom door. "It was under the changing table," he says, holding up the small tube of Neosporin. "Because where else would it be?" He ushers Francie back toward the couch. "Sit. Let me put some of this on your knee."

"I can do it," she says, taking the tube.

He sits on the chair across from her. "Where were you running to so quick?"

"You know. Getting some exercise." She points down at the soft pooch of her belly. "They say the baby weight melts off with breastfeeding. They lie."

"With your camera bag?"

"Yeah. Trying to start that portrait business. Never know when you're going to run into a potential client."

He nods and glances at the television set. "I don't know why I have this horrible woman on. She's having a field day with the news of Hector's death."

"Hector?"

"Yeah. Hector Quimby. The guy—"

"I know who you're talking about," Francie says. "But you said that like you know him."

Token looks at her. "Did I?"

Francie shifts her gaze. The ice pack stings her knee. "This is a nice apartment," she manages to say, and then sees, through the French doors to the bedroom, three guitars resting on stands. "You play the guitar?"

He shrugs. "Not as much as I used to."

"Um-hmmm." She sips her coffee. "So, tell me about Lou."

An alarm beeps in the kitchen. "Be right back." He returns wearing pot holders and carrying a loaf cake, which he sets on a trivet on the table.

"I went out for a walk, forgetting this was in the oven. Thank god I remembered before I burned down the entire block." He cuts into the cake with a long, thin knife. "To be honest, I'm a shitty baker. But whatever. I'm trying."

"Just a small piece," she says. "Trying to cut down on carbs and sugar."

Token extends a piece to her on a napkin, and they eat in silence for a few moments. Francie notices how his leg twitches, the way he keeps clearing his throat, his eyes flitting to the television screen behind her.

"You know, I've been thinking," Francie says. "You never got to tell your birth story."

"My birth story, huh? Didn't expect I'd get a turn."

"Why not?"

"I wasn't the one who did the work."

"You mean the mom?"

"Yeah." Token laughs and crumbles the napkin in his hands. "The mom."

"Did you adopt?"

"Adopt? No."

"Then how'd you get the baby?"

"How'd I *get* her." He squints at Francie. "Well, you see, Francie, when two people love each other—"

"No, I mean—"

Token laughs. "I'm kidding. Lucille had her."

"Lucille?" She struggles to swallow the cake. "Wait. Lou is Lucille?"

"Yeah. My wife."

"But you're gay."

He sits back in his chair and raises his eyebrows. "I am?"

She chuckles nervously. "You're not?"

"I don't think so."

"Well, how come I never heard you talk about a wife? And the mom group thing. It's not really something—"

He's nodding. "I had a feeling you all thought that. Nope. Straight as can be, and no adoption. We had her the old-fashioned way. Scheduled C-section." He smirks. "That was the plan, at least. Autumn had her own idea. Came a few weeks early, and on the one night I was out of town, playing a gig. Pretty sure Lou's still annoyed at both Autumn and me about that. It was not an easy birth."

"You guys doing okay?"

"Me and Lou? No. Not really." He stands and takes the cake to the dining table, his back to Francie. "You know how it is after you have a kid. You gotta adjust." He turns to face her. "I will say this, if it weren't for May Mothers, I'd be pretty lost. It's isolating, doing this as a guy. But you've all been great. I wasn't sure, you know. A dad, showing up to a mom's group. Let's just say I was a little nervous about it. It's been harder this past week, without the meetings to look forward to. I miss seeing everyone."

"Everyone?" Francie says. "Or Winnie?"

He cocks his head. "Winnie? What do you mean?"

"I mean maybe you don't miss her. Maybe you've been see- ing her since that night. Maybe you know more than you're let- ting on." Francie can't deny how exhilarated she feels, looking him in the eye, speaking the words out loud.

He folds his arms at his chest and leans against one of the dining chairs. He seems unsure of what to say.

"Not only that, but you seem a little obsessed with her." She plants both feet on the ground and places her napkin and the ice pack on the coffee table. "I'm going to come out and say it. We know all about you."

Francie swears she sees his jaw muscles clench. "You know about me?"

"Yes. Your arrest. Your criminal record. That ring a bell?"

"My record?"

"Yeah, that's right." She pauses. "So what did you do?"

A slow smile spreads across his face. "You know all about me, so why don't you tell me."

"Well, that part I don't know. Nell tried to find out, but she didn't succeed."

"Nell tried to find out?"

"Yes."

"How'd she do that?" The panic she thought she'd seen in his face is replaced by something else. Anger.

"I'm not exactly sure, to be honest. She knows how to hack into things. She looked you up. Got into your May Mothers profile." As soon as the words come out, Francie questions saying them. Maybe it's not wise to rat out Nell like that, but she's feeling flustered by the self-righteous tone of his voice, by the way he's looking at her. She straightens her back, prepared to demand an explanation of why he left the bar that night, where he went, what he's hiding. But before she can, he's walking toward her.

"You've all been looking into me? Digging around, have you?"

"Yes, but—"

But before she can get the rest of the words out, he's above her, reaching out, his hand gripped around her wrist, lifting her roughly from the couch.

The baby wails in his arms, and he shushes more loudly, feeling the anger rising inside him. Autumn's heat rash is making her extra fussy; the doctor said it's the result of too much time in the sling in this heat—it's been in the nineties the last three days—but it's the only way she'll nap, and he needs her to nap so he can have a break.

He goes into the kitchen, dropping the entire loaf cake into the garbage can, seeing the expression on Francie's face, how scared she looked when he led her to the door, shoving her into the hallway. He balances the baby on his shoulder and turns the faucet on, the steam rising as he rinses the plate. He miscalculated, thinking he could trust these women. That he could join their group, try to fit in with them, to think—

He slowly inhales, trying to compose himself. He needs sleep. He was awake most of last night, thinking about Winnie, about the message she left him yesterday morning, before the news broke, telling him they'd found Hector's body. He hasn't been able to get in touch with her—she's not answering his calls—and he's unsure what to do. He turns off the water and reaches for a towel in the cabinet under the sink. As he does, he thinks he hears steps outside his apartment. He walks into the living room, listening. Someone is at the door, twisting a key into the lock.

———

"Sweetheart, hi." Dorothy drops her bag on the floor near the front door. "My god, it's hot out today. They said it's a record high—" She stops when she notices the expression on his face and then walks closer to him, hugging him, Autumn between them. "You okay?"

He nods, calmed by her familiar scent, her arms around his back. "I completely forgot you were coming."

She pulls back and takes his face in her hands, studying his eyes. "Is today still good?"

"Yes, of course."

"What's wrong?"

"Nothing, Mom. Don't worry. I'm just tired."

"How's Lucille's trip going?" Dorothy asks, removing her sandals and setting them beside the door before coming to take Autumn from his arms.

"It got extended." He walks into the kitchen, placing the coffee mugs in the sink. "She won't be back until tomorrow now. But it sounds like it's going well." He's glad Dorothy can't see his face. She'd know he's lying.

Lou had called last night from LA, saying her last meeting was postponed a day. He knows that's not the truth, that she's staying behind to have one more night with him. *Cormac.* The fucking boss. The jerk with the CrossFit membership and a personal driver. It's been a year since he found their e-mails, scrolling through her phone while she showered, searching for the dentist's number.

The pet names. The meeting places.

Lou swore it was only a fling, that she'd already ended things. That she was ready to do what he'd been after her about: start trying for a baby.

"Is my granddaughter ready for Grandma Day?"

Dorothy took Autumn on her first Grandma Day when she was just twenty-three days old. Lou had returned to work already. She'd been in the process of closing a major deal when her water broke two weeks before the C-section she'd scheduled, and she wasn't happy about taking off before the account had wrapped up. She said she was going to the office for only a few hours that first day, but she didn't come home until 9:30 p.m., and she's been back to working sixty hours a week ever since. Or she said she was at work.

"You think you should cut back?" he asked Lou a few weeks ago, his voice tinged with fury, letting her know he wasn't going to keep playing along with the charade. "You know, on all of this *work*?"

She bristled and walked out of the room. "And how am I supposed to do that?" she called from their bedroom. "If we didn't have my income . . ."

"You sure you're okay?" his mother asks him now, walking into the living room, Autumn in her arms. She is dressed in a crisp cotton dress with yellow daisies.

"I'm fine, Mom. Really."

"Okay." She straps Autumn into the stroller.

"Did you buy her that dress?"

"I can't help myself." Dorothy walks close to touch his cheek. "What are you going to do?"

"I'm not sure yet."

"Sleep, I hope."

"Yeah, probably." He kisses her forehead. "Thanks, Mom."

He closes the door and waits a few moments before walking into the bedroom, where he opens the drawer of the bedside table and pulls out the envelope. He peeks inside, making sure the papers are still there, and then slips on his sneakers at the window, confirming his mother is out of sight before leaving.

He knows exactly where he's headed and he walks fast, before he can second-guess himself. Fuck Nell, he thinks. Fuck Francie, following him this morning, "hiding" behind that car, watching him drink his coffee at The Spot. Fuck all of them. When he arrives at Winnie's building ten minutes later, he sees that the number of journalists waiting outside has dwindled, many of them no doubt headed upstate to report on the progress of the search.

He keeps his distance, standing across the street, his eyes hidden behind his sunglasses, noticing that dozens of new Sophie giraffes have been added since yesterday, reading the latest messages to Midas—*Praying for Baby Midas. BRING MIDAS HOME*—tacked to the silver linden tree in front of Winnie's building. He glances up at Winnie's windows, picturing what's happening behind the thick silk curtains. He imagines Mark Hoyt in the kitchen, crouching on bended knees next to the island, inspecting a small spot that will turn out to be marinara sauce splashed onto the tile floor ten days earlier; the forensic experts running latex fingers across the windowpane in Midas's room, roaming slowly through Winnie's bedroom, checking, once again, the door to the terrace. He looks at the door, remembering the first time he entered that bedroom.

He turns away from the building and takes the folded envelope from his pocket. It appeared in his mailbox two days earlier. He still doesn't know who sent it, or why, and he'd planned to ignore the papers inside, sure that whoever was behind this had only bad intentions.

He crosses the street and approaches Elliott Falk, who is leaning against the shaded hood of a maroon Subaru, smoking a cigarette.

"You want a story?"

Falk exhales a stream of smoke. "Probably. What's it about?"

"The night Midas was taken. The woman in the photograph that Patricia Faith released. The drunk one, at the Jolly Llama."

Falk's eyes glimmer. "What about her?"

"Her name is Nell Mackey."

"Nell Mackey?"

"Yeah. And you need to look into her."

"Look into her? How come?"

He hands the envelope to Falk. "She's not who she says she is."

Falk flicks the cigarette into the street and pulls out the papers. He lets out a low whistle as he reads what's inside. "Wow, man, thanks."

He tries to respond, but the words are caught in his throat as he turns and walks away, toward the park, his eyes cast toward the ground, a hard pit of shame in his chest.

CHAPTER SEVENTEEN
DAY TEN

TO: May Mothers

FROM: Your friends at The Village

DATE: July 14

SUBJECT: Today's advice

<u>YOUR BABY: DAY 61</u>

Not to alarm you, but you should start to pay attention to the shape of your baby's skull. While "back is best" is the preferred method of sleeping, too much time on her back can cause your little one to develop a soft spot, known as positional plagiocephaly. You can address this by making sure she's getting the required amount of tummy time a day. If the flat spot seems pronounced, be sure to talk to your doctor.

"Ellen! Ellen! Give us a smile!"

"Ellen, do you know what happened to Midas?"

Sebastian blocks their cameras with his arm, pushing roughly through the crowd, shielding Nell.

"Any comment on the photo of you at the Jolly Llama? How drunk were you and Winnie that night?"

"You look great, Ellen! What do you think of Lachlan Raine's Nobel nomination this morning?"

Nell grasps Sebastian's hand, stunned by the flash of the cameras and the constant whir of their shutters. She ducks into the back seat and Sebastian closes the door, waving good-bye from the sidewalk, as she gives the driver the address of her office. He glances in the rearview mirror as she holds her purse in front of the window to obstruct their view, her sunglasses cloudy with tears. "You an actress or something?"

"No. Please go," she pleads.

As they pull away from the curb, the screen on the seat back springs to life, tuned in to a morning program. Three women sit at a table, coffee mugs at their elbows, their faces amused. Nell hates these asinine TVs, recently installed in the back seat of every taxi. How is it, she wonders, that people are too afraid to be alone with themselves to endure even one goddamn car ride through New York City without the distraction of inane "entertainment"? She hears her mother's voice last night on the phone. *Breathe, Nell. Everything is going to be okay.*

Nell reaches to silence the television, just as she hears her name.

"Ellen Aberdeen is back in the news this morning," says one of the women, her hair bleached Barbie blond, her forehead as still as glass. "Last night it was reported by Elliott Falk at the *New York Post* that Aberdeen, now thirty-seven, is living in Brooklyn, working at the Simon French Corporation. She's going by the name Nell Mackey. I guess she's gotten married."

One of the other women chuckles. "That must have been an awkward first date. 'Aren't you the one from the Aberdeen affair?'"

"Can we hang on a minute, please," the third woman says, raising a hand in protest. "She was a twenty-two-year-old intern. He was the sixty-six-year-old secretary of state, and a candidate for president. Why have we named this affair for *her*?"

A photograph bursts onto a wide screen behind their table: the image of Nell from that night at the Jolly Llama. "There's more," the first woman says. "You'll never believe this, but *she's* the woman who was at the bar the night—"

Nell hits the mute button, pressing her eyes with her fists, feeling the panic swell inside her. *No, no, no. Please don't let this be happening again.*

A photograph of Nell and Secretary of State Raine comes next—the original photograph: the two of them on the fire escape, a bottle of tequila between them, Nell's bare feet resting on his thigh. Then others, the same photos that decorated the front pages of newspapers and magazines around the world fifteen years ago. Nell, standing beside her mother on the day she graduated from Georgetown. Alone in the back seat of a taxi, after the news of the affair broke, the hunted look in her eyes on the cover of *Gossip!*

She descends into the darkness, allowing the memories to flow. The lingering regret that she'd fallen for it—for the way Lachlan spoke to her, the way he looked at her the first time they met, when he went down the line, shaking hands with the new interns. The gifts he left in the top drawer of the desk she was given down the hall from his office, beginning a few weeks after she started working for him, after being awarded the State Department internship. She'd applied for it on a whim during her last year at Georgetown, which she'd attended on scholarship. That was the only way she ever could have gotten there. With the money her mom and stepdad made, they never could have afforded the tuition.

"You did it, Ellen," her mother had said when Nell called to tell her she'd been chosen from more than eight thousand applicants. "There's no limit to what you'll do, I know it."

It started with a rare coin from his recent trip to India. Then it was a jewelry box, with a note attached saying he'd seen it in a store window in Paris and thought of her; that he couldn't help but notice how the peridot jewels on the lid matched her eyes. Finally, it was a thin, gold necklace, hung with a pendant *E*.

For Ellen, that card read. *I'll be at the office late tonight. Stop by around 8.*

There were plenty of reasons to say no. He was three times her age. He had a wife and four daughters, his oldest just one year younger than Nell. Kyle, her kind, devoted boyfriend of four years, had recently proposed. But Nell didn't say no. Lachlan had recently announced that he was running for president. She was twenty-two, afraid of not following his instructions, curious about what he wanted.

He was at his desk when she knocked, inviting her inside, telling her to close the door, that he needed help trying to figure out how to print to the new network. He was casual, charming, laughing at his embarrassing lack of technical skills; he was about to order in Indian food, did she like shrimp korma? They ate on the floor, leaning against his desk as armed men in dark suits with the Diplomatic Security Service shuffled back and forth outside the closed door. Raine gave her a taste of his rice pudding and told her stories of being on the mall for the "I Have a Dream" speech, of his recent meeting with the British prime minister, how they'd shared two bottles of wine over dinner and fallen asleep afterward in the private theater at 10 Downing Street, watching *Zoolander*.

The Nose. That's what they called her after their short affair was revealed, after a high school student sold the photograph he'd taken from his roof—Nell and Lachlan sitting on her fire escape. Kyle was away that night, and Nell said yes when Lachlan offered her a ride home in the back of an unmarked sedan. She said yes again when he invited himself inside for a few minutes. "It's always so interesting to see how young people like you live these days," he said as he walked through her small apartment in Dupont Circle, unwinding his tie.

She can still see Kyle's face, the look in his eyes when she returned home the evening the photograph appeared on the front page of the *Washington Post*. Kyle sat at their small dining table in the kitchen, sipping bourbon. Beside him on the floor was a suitcase. Hers.

"You have to leave."

"No, please. Can we talk—"

He held up his hand. "Ellen, stop. I don't want to hear it." His eyes were filled with disgust when he looked at her. "Here? In our bedroom?"

"No," she said. "Never. It happened just once. I didn't know how to say—"

"I don't want to hear it. It's over with us."

She sat down across from him. "But, Kyle. The wedding invitations. They just went out."

"My mom has started calling people, telling them it's off." Kyle finished his drink, walked calmly to the sink, and washed his glass. He set it in the drying rack and then took his coat from the hook near the door. "I talked to Marcy. She said you can stay there. Be gone by the time I get back."

She was let go from the internship three days later, which she learned when a reporter called, asking her for a comment; one of the same reporters who'd called her a home wrecker. A slut. A chunky girl with a big nose and a daddy complex, with not an ounce of concern for this man's wife. Priscilla Raine stood beside her husband at the press conference, stoic as she listened to him express his regret to the American public, his voice full of false contrition; as he went on to admit that he'd been weak, insinuating that Nell had seduced him—that she'd called him "handsome" and offered to work late. Raine draped his arm around Priscilla's thin shoulders, explaining that he'd asked his family for forgiveness, that he was spending time with his minister, that he'd begun to seek treatment for alcohol, and that he would no longer pursue the presidency of the United States. They—the media, the pundits, the gossip magazines—all claimed Nell had bragged to her friends about the affair, saying Lachlan was going to leave Priscilla to be with her. Nell had never said that. She never thought that. Not an ounce of her wanted that.

Honking interrupts her thoughts, and Nell realizes it's coming from her taxi. The driver leans out his window, waving his fist at a young man on a bike. "Move over! What is wrong with you?" The smell of a garbage truck three cars ahead of them consumes the taxi.

It's Alma who told them, who revealed Nell's identity to Mark Hoyt, who then must have told the press. It *has* to be. Nell's been sure of it since the moment she got the phone call from Elliott Falk late yesterday evening, asking her to confirm her identity, telling her the story was going online in ten minutes.

Nell didn't plan to tell Alma about her past, but it all came out, that first meeting, after she knew she was going to offer Alma the job. Nell *had* to tell her. Alma was going to be with Beatrice fifty hours a week. She needed to know, in case the moment Nell has dreaded for the past fifteen years actually came to pass—in case she was found out.

This.

The taxi crosses into Manhattan. She tries to pull herself together, and yet the tears come again. She hates herself. All the work she's done, the steps she's taken to become someone else. The years of therapy, hiding in London, where the accent became a natural part of her, getting a master's degree, working at a small college, teaching people too young to have any idea who she was. Even Sebastian didn't know, not until their eighth date, when she told him everything, convinced he would leave.

But he didn't leave; he pulled her close. "I'm sorry that happened to you," he said.

"I went along with it," Nell said, pulling back from him, looking at his face. "It wasn't all him."

THE PERFECT MOTHER **249**

Sebastian nodded and took her hands. "I know. But you were just a kid."

Nell studies her reflection in the window of the taxi: the short hair, the tattoo, the incredibly pert nose, the sight of which still startles her sometimes, in the mirror in the morning—paid for by the father she hardly saw, who lived in Houston with his second wife and two sons and called a few times a year. None of it matters, these steps to look completely different, to *be* completely different. She's still *her*. She'll *always* be her.

"We're here," the driver says. Nell hands him a twenty-dollar bill, opens the taxi door, and steps onto the sidewalk, back into the strobe of their cameras.

———

Two hours later she sits at her desk, going through the final version of the training manual and picking at the egg-salad sandwich Sebastian packed for her this morning, knowing she can no longer eat in the company café. Not with the way they'll watch her.

There's a light tapping on her office door. "Good morning, Nell." Ian sticks his head inside and then enters. "How you holding up?"

She swivels toward him in her chair and forces a smile. "Oh, you know. It's a little rough right now." Nell is sure the editors at *Gossip!* are upstairs talking about the story, wondering what they should do, how they'll handle writing about her. "It should all blow over in a few days. They'll find fresh blood somewhere else." *The sharks like you*, she means.

"The number of cameras out front this morning when I came in. Quite a crowd."

"I talked to the head of security," she says. "They're seeing what they can do to keep people away from the front of the building."

"They can't do anything. They called me. It's public property." He pauses. "You know how this works, Nell. The cameras have every right to be there."

"Yeah, well." She shrugs. "You never know. There could be a humanitarian crisis somewhere. A stolen election. Maybe a government bombing its own citizens that Americans will want to read about instead of me. We can hope, right?"

Ian leans forward, a bemused expression on his face. "I gotta tell you, and I mean this sincerely—the British accent? *Genius.* I seriously had *no* idea." His smile fades when she doesn't respond. "I'm really sorry to hear about your friend's baby. That must be rough."

Nell nods.

"You were there the night it happened, huh?"

"Yes."

"Were you one of the women who got into her house that night? Before the police secured it?"

Nell nods again.

"Yikes." Ian closes the door. "So, what do you think happened?" He winks. "Anything you want to share? Just between us?"

"Stop with the winking, Ian. Don't even try it."

He sighs and leans against the door. "Okay, Nell, listen. I hate to be the guy to say this, but we think you should take some time off."

"Time off?"

"The strain of all of this, it's got to be getting to you."

"I'm fine. I've survived this before, and I'll survive it again."

"Yeah." He nods. "The thing is, Nell, you haven't really been at your best since your return."

"My best? Ian, give me a break. It's been less than a week."

"That's what I'm doing. Offering you a break. Maybe we asked too much of you, coming back—"

"Ian, I—"

"We'll pay you. Consider it a long-term leave of absence. Extended maternity leave, if you will. For a few months or so. A little more if it'll help."

Nell laughs. "Really? Extended maternity leave? Is this a new company-wide policy? The ladies will be thrilled." Ian smirks, and she tries to dial back her anger. "When would you like my maternity leave to start?"

"Today."

"Today? Ian, the security training is tomorrow. I've been preparing for it. I came back to work early to oversee it."

"We've talked to Eric, and he's going to take over your responsibilities." Ian looks out the window, avoiding her gaze. "He's not going to do the job you would, but we're confident he'll manage, including taking your place tomorrow. Go get the rest you need. Spend some time with Chloe."

"Her name's Beatrice. Look, I know this is inconvenient, but I've done nothing wrong. They found me. Fine. But what happened was fifteen years—"

"Nell," Ian says, meeting her eyes. "I'm sorry."

"Talk to Adrienne."

He bites his lip. "Why?"

"Because she knows. She's known all along. And she doesn't care. You can't make me leave."

"Adrienne's the one who sent me down here. She feels awful about it. We all do. But we can't afford this publicity. It's too much of a distraction."

Nell steels herself. "From what? Writing about it? From deciding which photo to use of me on next week's *Gossip!* cover? Is that what this is about? I could put on a bikini and go get a flag, if that would help."

He keeps his gaze steady on hers. "Let's keep this simple. Please pack your stuff. We can revisit this in a few weeks. See where things stand."

She closes her eyes and sees it: placing her belongings into a box at the State Department. People averting their eyes as she walked toward the elevator. Going outside into the crowd of cameras. The years following, unable to get work, turned down for every job, the expression on the faces of every potential employer. *He gave up a chance at the presidency for* her?

She opens her eyes and looks at Ian. "Nope."

"Nope?"

"Nope. I'm not leaving. You can't fire me."

"Nobody's *firing* anybody—"

"I'm not leaving, Ian. I'll hire an attorney if I have to. But I'm not leaving."

"But, Nell. I'm . . . it's—"

"Excuse me for being rude, Ian, but I have to ask you to leave. Consider it a short-term leave of absence from my office." She turns back to her computer. "I have a training to finish preparing for tomorrow."

Ian opens her door, walking silently back into the hall. Nell stands to close it behind him, noticing the young man dawdling a few feet away, trying to eavesdrop on their conversation, probably hoping to discreetly snap a photo for his stupid Facebook page.

She returns to her desk, reading numbly through the training manual, trying to block it out. Ian. The kid in the hall. The photographers outside. The article she read before Ian came in.

The same morning former Secretary of State Lachlan Raine is nominated for the Nobel Peace Prize, Ellen Aberdeen is linked to the disappearance of Baby Midas. In fact, she's been identified as the intoxicated mother drunkenly dancing at the Jolly Llama on July 4, the night of the abduction.

Nell reaches for her purse on the floor, digging through her wallet, thinking about Alma. She shared a few secrets of her

own the morning Nell admitted the truth about her past: telling
Nell about the guy in Queens who sold her the fake social security cards, the lies her husband told to get the job managing the
Hilton by the airport—details that Nell has been wondering if
the police have uncovered.

She finds the business card Mark Hoyt gave her and dials the
number, staring at a photo of Beatrice on her desk. Hoyt picks
up on the second ring.

Nell hangs up the phone. She dials another number, crum-
bling with tears when she hears the soft hello.

"Mom," she says. "I need you. Can you please come?"

———

Colette slides the emerald back and forth along the thin gold
necklace. She woke up this morning to find the box on Charlie's
empty pillow. *Poppy's birthstone, on her two-month birthday,* the
card read. *Thank you for being such a great mom.*

She picks up her phone. I'm so sorry, Colette types, suppress-
ing the lump in her throat at the thought of the images dom-
inating the news this morning. The photos of Nell as a young
woman; the videos of her walking from the taxi into the Simon
French building earlier that morning, trying to shield her face
with her bag. I wish you'd told me.

The Nose. That was Nell. Colette remembers the scandal
well. Her mother was among the chorus of women's rights
activists who spoke out against what happened, who tried to
deconstruct the situation for what it was: not the story of a pro-
miscuous young girl trying to sleep with her powerful boss that
the media was so eager to present, but the story of a young
woman being preyed upon by a powerful man.

She checks the clock above Allison's desk again, trying to
ignore the tingling in her nipples. This can't be happening: the
first time she's forgotten to pack her breast pump is the one day

she may actually need it. She was so upset watching the news about Nell this morning she had trouble getting herself together, forgetting to pump before leaving. Then she was late to leave and had to run back home for her wallet. And now, she realizes, she's forgotten the manual pump she always carries, leaving it behind on the kitchen island. Plus, Teb is running late after promising he'll be on time. He knows she has to be back home by two o'clock.

It's important we're done on time today, she texted Teb earlier this morning. Charlie has a meeting.

It isn't just any meeting. The editor of the *New York Times Magazine* has invited Charlie to a last-minute lunch, to talk about the possibility of running an exclusive excerpt of Charlie's new novel.

"No, Colette, I can't risk it," Charlie said last night. "If you can't change your meeting with Teb, I'm going to hire a sitter."

"I'll be back," she told him. "I promise. Teb promised. I won't be late."

She picks up her bag and walks to the bathroom, her heels clicking loudly on the wood floors. Someone is in the first stall; she takes a seat on the toilet in the second one and checks her phone. Nell has replied to her message.

Screw them. This destroyed me once. Not this time. Not with Beatrice around to see it.

The woman from the other stall smiles as Colette approaches the sink, but her expression changes when she glances down at Colette's breasts. Colette looks in the mirror. Two wide gray circles are spreading across her white silk blouse. The woman quickly finishes washing her hands, and when she's gone, Colette turns on the hand dryer, holding her blouse under the hot stream of air, but the spots reappear as soon as they dry. The folded toilet paper she sticks inside her bra leaves jagged wrinkles visible beneath her blouse.

She presses her bag to her chest, feeling the sting of her milk continuing to release as she walks back to the lobby. Her phone chimes from inside her bag. It's a text from Charlie. I have to leave. Assuming you're en route. I'm leaving the baby downstairs, with Sonya. It'll be fine. We spoke. You can pick her up there.

"Colette." Allison is standing beside her. "He's ready for you."

Colette silences her phone and keeps her bag clutched in front of her as she heads into Teb's office. Sonya? That girl on the second floor they've met, what, twice, at the building's holiday party? Teb is sitting back in his chair, scrolling through his phone. He nods at one of the leather chairs across from him, and doesn't apologize for the wait. "Have a seat."

"How are you?" she asks.

"Great," he says, but his tone—and his expression—are cool.

"It looks like—" He ignores her and leans forward to press a button on his desk phone.

"Aaron, come in." The door opens almost immediately, as if Aaron was expecting the call. Aaron nods at her and walks to the credenza, lifting the stack of folders onto his lap. She can see Midas's name written on the top folder. "Okay, Colette." Teb's eyes are hard. "We're in big trouble here."

Her stomach drops. They know.

They know she was with Winnie that night, and that she took the file. They tested the blood she'd smeared on the papers after the paper cut a few days ago, and found her DNA. They have somehow discovered that she took the flash drive, which is still at her apartment, stashed inside an old purse in her closet. Milk saturates the crumpled toilet paper, trickling through the fabric of her bra. She tries to figure out where to start—how to explain why she's been hiding the truth from him, the reasons she couldn't resist looking at Midas's file—when Teb speaks.

"This book is awful." Teb is rubbing his eyes.

She exhales. "Okay."

Teb leans back in his chair. "C, what happened? Why is this so bad?"

Why? An unexpected pregnancy. Sleep deprivation. Her worries about Poppy's health. Panic that Midas is dead. "Part of it might be that you're busier now," she says. "It's not like the last time. It's been a little difficult to keep our scheduled meetings—"

Teb shakes his head. "No. That's not the issue. The issue is that this doesn't sound like something I wrote."

"Well, you didn't write it."

Aaron shoots Colette a look as Teb swivels slowly toward her in his chair.

"What do you mean?"

Her mouth has gone dry; she wishes she'd packed a bottle of water. "I mean you didn't write this book, Teb. I did."

"Colette." There's caution in Aaron's tone. "I'm not sure—"

"I'm sorry," she says. "Of course I'm happy to rework the book, but we need to set up a schedule to talk more about some of these experiences you want to include. With all due respect, Teb, it's been hard to sit down with you."

"I think what the mayor means," Aaron says, "is that this isn't working."

"I get it. So let's talk about how to fix it."

Aaron begins to speak, but Teb cuts him off. "I'm sorry to say this, C. But we have to bring in another writer."

"Another writer?"

Aaron leans forward in his chair. "We've spoken to the editor," Aaron says. "We're hiring someone else to fix the book. Someone with a bigger name. That guy from *Esquire*."

"You're kidding. You've already arranged this? Without talking to me?"

"Come on, Colette," Aaron says, pinching the bridge of his nose. "This book is going to be an integral part of the mayor's race for re-election. You know that. We can't bring what you've written to the publisher *or* the voters. We're in a ton of shit with this baby-abduction thing. That crazy real estate guy is throwing money at our opponent. We're barely hanging on here."

She searches for the right response, and then says nothing. It's done.

She doesn't have to pretend any longer that she can manage the baby and this work. She'll get to stay home with Poppy.

"You're sure about this?" She addresses Teb, but Aaron is the one to answer.

"I'm afraid so, Colette." His phone beeps. "And we, unfortunately, need to go." Teb is staring out the window, unwilling to look at her. "The banking people are here," Aaron says, buttoning his jacket, gesturing toward the door. "Colette, thank you so much." His manner is light, as if they're wrapping up a conversation in which they've decided on brunch plans. "The mayor has really enjoyed working with you."

She stands, expecting Teb to say something, but he remains silent. She walks out of his office, toward the elevator. Her head is swimming. What happens now? What will this mean for her career? She should call the editor, or her agent; she needs to explain herself.

But then she pictures Poppy, alone with a woman she doesn't know.

She races past the elevator, down the four flights of stairs. Outside, there are no taxis in sight, and she runs as fast as she can across City Hall Park, down the stairs to the subway. A train is on the platform, and the doors are beginning to close as she swipes through the turnstile. She gets there just in time to stick her arm between them, and they close on her elbow. The doors open a few inches, and before they can close again, she pries them apart with both hands, wide enough to slip inside and take one of the last empty seats. The woman next to her smells of hair spray, and Colette catches the eye of an older woman with a pile of orange plastic shopping bags on the floor between her feet. The woman *tsk*s loudly. "Slowing everyone else down," she says, scowling. Colette looks away. Her elbow is throbbing.

Rap music blares from the headphones of a man sitting across from her, and she presses her fingers to her ears, trying to think of how to explain this to Charlie. He doesn't know how badly the book has been going, how much she's been struggling. What is he going to say? Colette opens her eyes, seeing that the man across from her is holding open a copy of the *New York Post*, the photograph of Nell from the Jolly Llama on its cover.

The air fills with the sound of squealing brakes and the sudden wail of a baby. The woman beside her clutches Colette's thigh as the train jolts to an abrupt stop, and an older man near the door falls to the floor.

"I'm sorry," the woman next to her says, removing her hand. A young couple is helping to lift the man, and people are glancing up from their phones, scanning each other's faces as a stunned hush settles over the subway car. The older woman with the shopping bags *tsk*s again and begins to say something, but her words are swallowed by the voice of the conductor. "Police to the tracks. If you can hear me, police to the lower-level tracks near the F platform. We have a person on the tracks." There's a moment of static and then: "He's strapped to something."

The power is cut, silencing the air-conditioning, cutting the lights; a ghostly quiet settles over the car. Colette feels the shift around her as people turn to their cell phones, as she does, knowing she won't have service.

I have to get home to Poppy.

The door at the end of the car skids open. "You didn't think this was coming?" The guy wears jean shorts and a thin white tank top revealing wiry, muscular arms. He walks briskly through the car toward the door at the opposite end, weaving between the people standing in the aisles. "You didn't think we'd see a suicide bomber in New York, with this jackass as our president?"

The panic builds in her chest. She sees Poppy's face, how she looked in the middle of the night, nursing, her deep blue eyes naked with love, staring up at Colette. Colette is incredulous, still, that she can feel a love this bottomless, like the abandoned quarry she was too afraid to jump into as a child, the one that later swallowed up a boy from her high school, his body never found. She takes her phone from her lap and types a text to Charlie. She won't be able to send it without service, but if someone finds her phone, if it survives the explosion . . .

I love you more than anything. Poppy. Please let her know—

The lights flash back on, and then the jolt of the AC hits. "Ladies and gentlemen, this is the conductor. We're going to open the doors in the front car. Make your way forward to exit. Be as quick and orderly as you can."

Colette stands, entering the silent stream of people making their way down the crowded aisle. In the next car, a teenage girl is sitting alone at a window seat, holding her phone in her hand, a tear sliding down her cheek. She wears argyle tights, with a rip in one knee, and a gold stud glitters at the bend of one nostril. Colette touches her arm, and the girl looks up at her.

"I need to call my mom, but I don't have any service."

"Come on," Colette says, taking the girl by the arm. "Walk with me." She keeps her hand on the girl's elbow, guiding her forward. When they get to the first car, she's relieved to see that the front half is in a station; they won't have to walk along the tracks. She waits her turn to exit, and then she and the girl begin to run with the rest of the crowd, down the platform, through the turnstiles, and up the stairs. The girl disappears in a swarm of people, and Colette sprints away from the subway entrance. On the next block she sees someone exiting a cab and dashes toward it, stepping in front of a man about to climb in the back seat.

"I'm sorry," she says. "I need to get home."

She slams the door against the horrible names the man is calling her, the sound of his fists banging the window. "Brooklyn," she says to the driver, giving him her address. "Please hurry."

She closes her eyes, and it seems like hours have passed when they arrive at her building. The sky is drained of light, and her legs are weak as she goes inside, approaching the doorman's desk. "I need Sonya's apartment number."

On the second floor she tries to compose herself, and then knocks gently on Sonya's door. There's no answer. She keeps banging, so hard her fists ache.

"Hello? Sonya?" The door across the hall opens. It's a man in his late twenties, a small dog nipping at his heels behind him, classical music playing in the background.

"What are you doing?" he asks, easing the dog back into the apartment with a bare heel.

"She's not answering her door. She has my baby. I live upstairs."

"She left."

"Left?"

"Yeah, I heard her go out. You can hear everything through these walls."

"What time?"

"I don't know. Twenty minutes ago?"

Twenty minutes? Did Charlie have milk to leave her? Did he give her the sunscreen? Colette doesn't know this woman's phone number. She's not even sure of her last name.

She turns and runs up the stairs, taking the steps two by two. She'll call Charlie, disturb his meeting, demand he come home and help look for the baby. She hunts for her phone in her bag and enters the key into the lock.

Charlie.

He's there, lying on the floor next to Poppy, who is reaching for her toes on the play mat at his side. Colette drops her bag and rushes to the baby, lifting her from the mat, kissing her face so eagerly, Poppy whimpers with annoyance. Charlie's breath is raspy; he's fallen asleep. Poppy nuzzles the warm skin of Colette's chest, rooting for milk. Colette feels the full weight of her exhaustion, the room shifting around her. She closes her eyes, imagining lying down next to Charlie, curling against him, and telling him everything. About what happened on the subway, about losing the job. About the terror she's been feeling, the desperate need to know that Midas is still alive. She wants to tell him about her guilt over being away from the baby, about how hard she's been working trying to hold it all together. She wants to wake him up and tell him she can't wait three months until Poppy's next appointment to start worrying. She's already terrified.

But she's too afraid. Afraid that if she begins, she'll start to cry and never stop, that she'll be swallowed by her sadness, her fear, how overwhelmed she is, how certain she is that everything she has is slipping away.

"Do you have to do that right here, in front of me like that?" The sound of Charlie's voice sends a jolt through her body. He's awake.

"Do what?"

"That. Be all over her." She doesn't say anything. She doesn't have the words to respond. "It's not easy watching how affectionate you are with her when you pull away every time I touch you."

"Charlie, no. Please. I thought—you have the—"

"I didn't go."

"Why?"

He stands and walks down the hall toward his office. "I knew how upset you would be if I left the baby. I didn't want to do that to you."

She follows him, reaching for his arm, but he pulls away. "Not now, Colette. I need some time."

"Charlie. I'm sorry. Listen, there's some things—"

But he's already closed the door.

CHAPTER EIGHTEEN
DAY ELEVEN

> **TO:** May Mothers
> **FROM:** Your friends at The Village
> **DATE:** July 15
> **SUBJECT:** Today's advice
> <u>YOUR BABY: DAY 62</u>
> We've all had a few particularly frazzled days, even moments of feeling sad and overwhelmed. Those feelings should be lifting by now as you and your little one settle into a routine. But if you—or someone you love—are beginning to wonder if what you're feeling is more than the baby blues, don't let embarrassment or pride keep you from talking to your doctor. Getting help for yourself can sometimes be the best thing you can do for your baby.

Francie strolls slowly through the narrow fiction aisle in the bookstore at the back of the Spot, Charlie's debut novel in her hands, trying to convince herself that everything is going to be fine, that Nell will get through this. Francie had no idea about any of the things the newscasters were saying about Nell. She wasn't even aware of the scandal—the presidential candidate who dropped out of the race after having an affair with a twenty-two-year-old State Department intern. Francie was sixteen when it happened, and her mom wasn't the type to expose her family to political sex scandals (or anything to do with a Democratic politician, good or bad).

And then there is Token. The way he roughly led her out of his apartment two days ago without offering any explanation of his arrest, raising only more questions.

The worst, however, is what happened this morning. Francie walks to the front of the store to pay for Charlie's book, feeling another wave of queasiness as she envisions the moment. Barbara was sitting on the sofa, watching television, waiting for Francie, who had offered to make Barbara the runny egg sandwich she ate every morning. Francie was doing her best to tune out her mother-in-law, who was going on about gossip from back home. How her friend's niece just had her fourth child, a darling little girl. How there was a new nail salon that opened in town, where Barbara had gotten her nails done for the trip. How it was staffed by four women who were probably in the country illegally. *Orientals.*

Francie heard Colette's name just as the toaster popped. She turned to look at the TV, seeing Colette on the screen, jogging down the sidewalk near her apartment building, red-faced and breathless. "Leave me alone," Colette said, hurrying past the cameras, her arms shielding her face. "I have no comment."

"Colette Yates is the daughter of Rosemary Carpenter, the well-known women's rights activist," the reporter said. "She's also romantically involved with the novelist Charlie Ambrose, with whom she had a child two months ago." Colette was one of the women with Winnie at the bar that night, the reporter went on to say, and while a source reported that Colette was close to Mayor Shepherd, he wouldn't comment on the story. And then suddenly they were talking about her—Francie. They even had a photo of her, one from the night at the Jolly Llama, her face pressed against Nell's.

The reporter added that Francie was a stay-at-home mother, and the moment that Lowell walked into the kitchen, Francie heard Barbara's gasp. "Her husband, Lowell Givens, is one of the principal owners of Givens and Light Architects, a young Brooklyn firm."

"This is awful," Barbara said, ignoring Francie, looking straight at Lowell. "What is this going to mean for your business?"

Francie hands the money to the clerk, knowing she shouldn't be buying Charlie's book, that she should have waited to get it from the library. But the library doesn't open until noon, and her apartment is so small, and she needed to get out, away from Barbara and the look on her face. The judgment. The disappointment.

Francie takes her change and turns to look for a table. And then she sees her, on the sidewalk outside.

She wears sunglasses and a long, shapeless jacket, and her hair is tucked under a baseball cap, but Francie knows it's her.

"Winnie!"

The word escapes Francie more loudly than she expected, silencing the crowd waiting for their coffee. Francie careens through them, running out the door, out onto the sidewalk. "Winnie! Wait, Winnie!"

Pressing Will against her chest, she jogs awkwardly after Winnie, who is walking quickly up the hill. "Winnie, wait, please!" She doesn't understand why Winnie isn't stopping. Will begins to whine as Francie breaks into a run after her, reaching her just before she arrives at her building. Winnie is scrambling inside her bag for her keys. "Winnie, please. I need to talk to you. I've been so worried." Francie tries to catch her breath. "Have you gotten my messages? I'm so sorry we—"

A car screeches to a halt, the two front tires veering onto the sidewalk a few feet away. A short, overweight man wearing a fedora and plaid shorts jumps from the driver's seat, grabbing for the bulky camera around his neck. "Gwendolyn! Look this way. How are you? Gwendolyn!"

Winnie rushes to insert her key into the door, and Francie

follows her, stumbling over the step and into the cool, darkened foyer. Winnie presses the door closed on the man's fists, and Francie trails her up the four marble stairs and down the hall, the flash of his camera lighting the walls. Thick silk curtains are drawn in the living room, and Francie is overcome by the staleness of the air and the stench of decomposing food. Winnie wrenches open the curtains on the terrace doors, and it takes Francie a minute to adjust to the shock of sunlight. Two large rugs are rolled into coils, propped up against the far wall. Packing boxes are piled haphazardly in the corner. Food containers are scattered on the table and floor; an empty bottle of wine lies on its side near the doors to the terrace. Francie can't help but notice the two wineglasses nearby, next to a pink silk robe, discarded in a ball.

Winnie removes her jacket. She looks skeletal. "I've gotten your messages. I'm sorry. I haven't had the energy to call you back."

Francie stands in the center of the room, patting Will's bottom, trying to catch her breath. "Winnie. I don't know what to say. Are you—are you moving?"

"Moving?" Winnie says.

Francie gestures at the rolled-up rug, the packing boxes. "The boxes—"

"Oh." Winnie's eyes flit around the room. "The team of detectives did all this. In the days after . . ." She allows the thought to trail off. "I saw what happened to Nell. And now you and Colette. You're in the news."

"Us? Don't worry about us. How are you? I can't—"

"I'm fine."

"Fine?" Francie has trouble finding any other words, stunned by how different Winnie appears. So gaunt. Hollow. Nothing like the woman Francie admired so much, just a few months ago, when Francie first noticed her walking across the lawn toward the willow tree, ripe with pregnancy. Nothing at all like the beautiful, kind woman who'd sat across from Francie that day at the Spot, or the fresh-faced girl in the *Bluebird* DVDs Francie has watched again and again.

"What do you want me to say, Francie?" Winnie says. "My baby is gone. There's nothing I can say to describe what I'm going through."

Francie feels the tears beginning to well in her eyes. *I understand*, she wants to say. *More than you know, I understand what it's like to lose a child.* But she doesn't dare. "Is there anything I can do to help? Anything you need? Do you have any idea what happened?" The words are tumbling out too quickly.

Winnie turns toward the terrace doors. "Of course I don't know what happened."

"I've been giving it a lot of thought," Francie says. "I can't believe how much the police have screwed this up. At first I was sure it was Bodhi Mogaro. I believed them, you know. And then I began to think about other possibilities. Like that guy you were talking to at the bar."

Winnie turns to look at her, a glimmer of *something*, Francie can't place it, in her eyes. Or maybe it's her face, and the way she's speaking. It seems so stilted, empty.

"The guy at the bar?"

"The one who came up to you that night. The one who you— The one you had a drink with."

"I didn't have a drink with anyone that night."

Will settles, resting his head on Francie's chest, and she has to battle an urge to leave. Why is Winnie lying to her? "Then where were you? After you left the table?"

Winnie avoids Francie's eyes, and then appears not to hear what she'd said. Instead she turns and walks to the kitchen, returning with a bottle of wine and two plastic cups. She pours the wine, handing a cup to Francie. Francie accepts it, but she doesn't move, seeing Winnie at the last May Mothers meeting in the park, her lips in Midas's hair, waving away the wine Nell offered. *No thanks. Alcohol doesn't always agree with me.*

"I went to the park," Winnie says.

"The park? Why?"

"To visit my mom." The cup trembles in Winnie's hand.

"Your mom? But Winnie, your mom is dead."

Winnie shoots Francie a look. "Thank you, Francie. I'm aware of that." She takes a drink of her wine. "There's a dogwood tree there that my dad and I brought from our property upstate. We planted it in the park one night, at my mom's favorite spot, near the long meadow. It's this secret thing I've always had, a place to feel close to her. I went there that night."

"Why?"

"I miss her." Winnie opens the door to the terrace and steps onto the wide balcony. Francie follows. The shrill laughter of children playing in a sandbox in the backyard of a day-care center a few buildings down pierces the heavy air around them. Pots of dead herbs line the rail. "It's not a great alibi."

"Alibi? What do you mean?"

"That I was at the park. Nobody saw me. I know what people are saying. I know where—" She takes another mouthful of wine. "I would never hurt my baby."

Francie remembers the cup in her hand and takes a sip, trying to swallow, despite the growing lump in her throat.

"I thought the worst thing that would ever happen was losing my mom. I was wrong." Francie reaches for Winnie's arm, but she moves away. "I don't want any more questions. I can't think rationally, linearly. Time is running in circles." Her face appears to harden as she notices something in the distance. Francie looks and sees a woman standing on a small balcony across the backyard, a baby resting on a blanket on her shoulder, watering a box of pink zinnias. The woman places the watering can on the ground and prunes some of the plants before stepping inside, closing the door behind her.

"Mothers and babies. You're everywhere. I hope you appreciate everything you have." Winnie tips back the cup of wine, swallowing the last of it, and then peers down at Will. "I don't want to be rude, Francie, but I can't really deal with—"

Francie is flooded with regret. Why didn't she think of this? Of how selfish and insensitive it was to force Winnie to see Will. How difficult it must be for Winnie each day, surrounded by the sight of mothers with their children. She understands now why Winnie ran away from her outside the coffee shop.

"I'm sorry, Winnie," Francie says. "I should have been more considerate." They walk inside, and Francie closes the terrace door. Winnie's back is turned to Francie as she ascends the stairs.

"You can let yourself out."

"If there's anything you need—" Francie pauses. "He's alive, Winnie. I can feel it. Please. Don't give up hope. I haven't."

Winnie turns the corner at the top, disappearing down a hall.

Francie walks unsteadily through the living room, past another stack of moving boxes—saddened by the idea of strangers combing through Winnie's house, their hands on her possessions—and opens the door to the sidewalk. She walks, unsure of where she's going, becoming aware of the sound of steps running toward her. The guy in the fedora is rushing from the corner, his camera covering his face. "Hey! Mary Frances! What did Winnie say—" The shutter of his camera clicks relentlessly, and he yells out questions, but Francie pays him no attention as she keeps walking, her head bent toward the sidewalk, her arms shielding her baby, her mind foggy.

"What are you doing?" Lowell asks Francie later that evening. She's sitting on the living room floor, her stomach in knots, placing lavender-scented candles in a circle around Will, who lies on the blanket in front of her.

She tries to keep her voice steady. "I'm practicing *hygge*."

Lowell nods. "Oh yeah? What's that?"

"It's all the rage in Denmark." Francie blows into her mug of tasteless chamomile tea, aware of the way Lowell is looking at her. Watching her. "It means 'being cozy.' It's why those people are so calm and happy. I thought it might help Will's mood."

"That's a good idea." Lowell sits on the sofa and opens a beer. "And how's your mood?"

Francie puts a fresh pair of cotton socks onto Will's feet. The article said it was best to surround oneself with sheepskin, but she didn't dare spend the money on the rug she found online, knowing these Carters' cotton socks will have to do. "My mood? Fine. Why?"

"What do you mean why? Can't I ask my wife how she's feeling?"

"Well your mom told me this afternoon she thinks our floors are unhygienic. And that I should wash them with bleach." Francie keeps her voice low. Barbara is in the bathroom, soaking in her nightly bath, her face set in a mud mask, listening to talk radio on her iPod.

"What'd you say?"

"Nothing. But I can't use bleach on these floors. *Bleach*? Around a *baby*? I feel like she's finding fault with our apartment. With half the things I do."

"Francie." His face clouds. "She doesn't think that. You're imagining it."

Francie sips the tea, trying to force back the anxiety. She doesn't want to talk about Barbara, she wants to talk about Winnie, about their conversation earlier. But she can't, not with Lowell. She didn't tell him what happened, knowing how angry he'd be at her for bringing Will to Winnie's apartment. To make matters worse, Barbara stayed home all afternoon, her hair in furry plastic curlers, whispering into the phone in their bedroom. Francie assumes she was calling friends back in Tennessee, asking if they heard that Lowell was mentioned in the news, telling them she'd been right all along about the dangers of New York City. Barbara emerged from the bedroom only after Lowell came home, and by then Francie was too afraid to say anything at all.

"France, come on. She means well. Things were different when she had kids. She just—"

"Oh my god!" Barbara's yell from the bathroom startles Francie, and she spills a few drops of hot tea onto Will's arm. He begins to wail as Lowell jumps to his feet, bumping the table and spilling his beer, extinguishing two of the candles. He rushes down the hall toward the bathroom and knocks on the door.

"Mom!" He tries the handle but it's locked. "Mom! You okay?"

"I knew it!" Barbara's voice is triumphant. "I said it from the beginning."

"What are you talking about?"

The door bursts open and Barbara steps into the hallway, wrapped in a towel, her face a tight sheet of gray, bubbles sliding from her shins to the floor.

"They're bringing her in for official questioning," Barbara says, her mask cracking. "That friend of yours. The mother. I *knew* she was hiding something."

CHAPTER NINETEEN
NIGHT ELEVEN

I have an image of someone cutting me.

A long, thin knife penetrating my stomach, just below my navel, an easy slit, a straight line to my heart. I'm empty inside. As black as ash, my organs like dust. One touch and my heart crumbles into a million sooty specks, black powder left on the floor, leaving dark footprints wherever I walk.

I've always been this way. A bad little girl. My father said it all the time. "Leave her alone," my mom would yell at him. "Do better," she'd whisper to me when he wasn't around. "Stop giving him reasons to be mad."

I thought becoming a mother was going to change me, but I was wrong. The baby just made everything worse. And now everyone is going to know the true me. It was inevitable, right, that they're on to me? Francie, that nosy, meddling twit.

Midas's blanket. Why didn't I take care of that earlier? Why

Why why why

My thoughts are unraveling. I have to remain calm. I hear a booming voice in my head, as if it's speaking through a megaphone. I can picture the voice. It's mustached and wears a large top hat, circular wire glasses, and emerald shoes that curl up at the toes.

Hey lady, it yells through its megaphone. *You must remain calm. This is no time to get hysterical.*

(Ha, guess what, voice? I've done it. I've become exactly what my father said all women become. *Hysterical.*)

We're going to disappear. I know I keep saying that, but this time I mean it. Tomorrow. The problem is, well . . .

The cash is almost gone. I've been too afraid to look, but I did. Yesterday. $743.12. That's it.

I had no choice but to tell Joshua.

"But don't worry," I said last night, keeping my back to him so I wouldn't see the shock and anger in his eyes. "Not all of it." (For the first time in months I'm happy Dr. H isn't around. "I said it a million times: be careful with that money," he would say, his expression a study in disappointment, as if I were still a teenager.)

Then today Francie showed up, distracting me from the money, reminding me we have bigger problems. What if they don't believe me? I finally spoke that question out loud. What if they see through the story we've created?

What if I go to jail?

But Joshua just turned away from me. I know even the mention of it terrifies him. Later, as we ate our dinner in silence, I was well aware what he was thinking.

Little Miss Clever can't get us out of this predicament. Miss Tenth-Grade Math Whiz, and you still haven't figured out a solution to a very simple equation of where to go?

I can't waste any more time. Not with the way they're closing in on me. Tennessee. Montana. Alaska. We'll drive until we find where we want to be, or run out of gas. We'll settle down. I'll get a job. We'll rent a cabin. Joshua is hoping for something remote and private. Land on which we can lose ourselves, start over. Somewhere we can never be found.

I want that too. I think I do, at least, when I try to picture it. A garden in the back. Maybe some chickens.

A gun nearby for protection. Just in case.

CHAPTER TWENTY
DAY TWELVE

> **TO:** May Mothers
> **FROM:** Your friends at The Village
> **DATE:** July 16
> **SUBJECT:** Today's advice
> <u>YOUR BABY: DAY 63</u>
> It's been nine weeks since you gave birth, and it's time to talk about BALANCE. We know how it is. Taking care of the baby. Buying groceries. Getting back in shape. For some of us, preparing to go back to work. It's not easy. The best thing you can do for yourself—and your baby—is to strive for the right balance in your life. Maybe you hire a mother's helper a few hours a week, or ask a friend to babysit so you can go to the gym. Maybe you spend a little extra money having your groceries delivered. Find what works for you. After all, a happy mother, a happy home.

Nell's body feels as if it's made of cement, her legs cast in plaster. She hears the crying, but it's muffled. The baby is calling to her from under water. She tries to move, but she doesn't have enough strength.

"Nell."

She smells the trace of vanilla in her mother's hand lotion and opens her eyes. Margaret is standing over her.

"Am I late for work?" Nell asks.

"No. It's not yet seven." Her mom crouches beside her. "I hate to wake you, but you need to see something."

Nell notices the look on her mom's face. She sits up. "Is Beatrice okay?"

"Yes, sweetheart. She's fine. She's sound asleep. Sebastian just left for work. But come out to the living room with me."

Nell lifts herself from the warm sheets and follows her mom down the hall. Margaret arrived yesterday evening, leaving work immediately after Nell called, driving the four hours from Newport to Brooklyn without stopping. She slept on an air mattress in the living room, the monitor beside her, tending to Beatrice so Nell and Sebastian could have their first full night of sleep since the baby was born.

The television is on in the living room, and Nell sees that Mayor Shepherd is standing at a podium, stepping aside to give Rohan Ghosh a place at the bank of microphones.

Nell looks at Margaret. "What happened?"

Ghosh is holding up his hand. "I'll speak when you all quiet down," he says, pausing to sip from a bottle of water. "Last night, we were led to conduct a new search of the car owned by Winnie Ross, in which we discovered a blue baby blanket stuffed into the tire well. The blanket matches the description of the one taken from Midas's crib the night he was abducted. Our forensic team has confirmed that the fibers of the blanket contain traces of Midas Ross's DNA, as well as evidence of his blood."

"No," Nell says, her chest growing tight.

"What led you to look at the car again?" someone yells from the crowd.

Ghosh continues to speak, raising his voice. "At approximately six this morning, Winnie Ross was taken into custody and formally charged in the disappearance of her son, Midas Ross."

Nell gasps and her mother comes to stand beside her, taking her hand. "Did you find the body?"

"We'll have more details for you later today. Right now, I'd like to thank Detective Mark Hoyt for his diligent work on the case. And, of course, recognize Mayor Shepherd. You guys were pretty hard on these two, but everyone involved did a stellar job." Ghosh collects the papers from the podium. "That's all for right now, folks. Thank you."

Nell grips Margaret's hand as the image on the screen switches to footage of Winnie being led from the back of an unmarked SUV into police headquarters in Lower Manhattan. Winnie peers at the cameras from under her dark hair, her wrists in cuffs behind her back, a uniformed man at each of her elbows.

She enters the building, and a newscaster's face fills the television, but then the video starts again from the beginning: Winnie getting out of the car, walking toward the police station, looking up into the camera, her eyes vacant, her face like stone.

———

No. Francie bounces Will up and down the hall, saying the word out loud. "No."

She takes her phone from the counter and types. Are you getting my messages? We need to talk about this. I have an idea.

She needs Will to stop crying. She needs a moment to think. She goes into the kitchen, relieved to finally have the apartment to herself, Lowell on his way to the airport to drop off his mother. She hasn't eaten since lunch yesterday, and she's faint with hunger, but there's nothing she wants in the cupboards. She opens the freezer and takes a packet of frozen corn from the shelf, holding it to the back of her neck. The apartment is sweltering—confining—and she wants to turn on the air conditioner, but this morning Lowell asked her, his voice just above a whisper, to avoid using it to save money on their electric bill until she gets paid for the photography job she lied about having.

"No." She says the word louder this time. They haven't found his body. He could still be alive.

The doorbell rings again. It's been ringing for the last two hours. Journalists seeking a comment. Mrs. Karan, her landlady, called Francie earlier, telling her she needs to make them get off the stoop and go away, complaining that somebody knocked over her potted geraniums. Francie checks her phone, impatient for a response from Nell and Colette, and writes again, typing with her free thumb.

I'm serious. We should talk to Scarlett. I think she can help.

That woman Francie saw on the balcony across from Winnie's building, watering the plants: Francie thinks that may have been Scarlett. At first she wasn't sure, but last night, while Lowell slept in their bed and Barbara on the couch, she locked herself in their hot, windowless bathroom, studying the notebook she keeps in her underwear drawer, searching for anything she may have missed. Thirty minutes later, naked in the tub, the shower water like ice pricks on her back and scalp, her hair like curtains down her cheeks, she remembered something: the last May Mothers meeting a few weeks earlier, when Scarlett told them that Winnie was depressed. Francie clearly pictures it. They were sitting on the blankets, sipping the wine Nell brought. Scarlett said how worried she was about Winnie. How they were neighbors, and had taken walks together.

Francie places Will gently into the swing, works the pacifier into his mouth, and flips the dial to the fastest setting.

Maybe Winnie told her something, she types. Something that could help.

She hits send, and her phone rings right away. It's Colette. It sounds like she's crying.

"Francie, you have to stop. You're grasping at straws."

"No, I'm not." Francie begins to cry, too. "The blue blanket. The police didn't even check Winnie's trunk before last night?"

"No, that's not what they said. They checked it again. Someone—"

"I was awake all night, thinking about it. If Winnie confided in Scarlett about her depression, maybe she confided in her about other things, too. Maybe there's something there, something people are missing—"

"No." Francie can hear the impatience in Colette's voice. "You have to listen to me, Francie. I know this is hard. It's hard for all of us. But I'm getting seriously worried."

"I know. Me too. I've been worried—"

"No, Francie. I mean about you."

"Me? This isn't about me—"

"You need to get some rest, Francie. You're not thinking rationally. You need—"

"But they haven't said he's dead. They haven't found his body." Francie's throat is so tight, she feels as if she might choke. "Maybe he's still alive. Maybe there's still time to save him. He needs to be with his mother—"

"No!" The word is harsh in Francie's ears. "He can't be with his mother, Francie. His mother is the one who hurt him. Accept it. It's over."

———

Francie throws the phone onto the couch. *Over?*

The doorbell rings again, and then she hears footsteps on the stairs. There's a hard knock on the door. It's Mrs. Karan, coming to tell her she can no longer live with this chaos. She's come to evict them. She, Lowell, the baby: they'll have nowhere to live.

"Hello? Francie?" It's a man's voice.

She steps closer to the door. "Who is it?"

"Daniel."

"Daniel?" Her head is spinning. That name. It's familiar. *Daniel.*

She closes her eyes and presses her temples. The article she read. The interview Winnie gave after her mother died. *I've been relying on Daniel. He's the only thing getting me through the grief.*

He's banging harder.

Winnie's boyfriend? He's here, at her apartment? Did Winnie send him? Perhaps with a message—something to lead her to Midas?

"Francie, open up. Please. I have to talk to you."

She turns the dead bolt and opens the door an inch, peering into the hall. The word comes out in a whisper.

"*Token*?"

———

"You were her boyfriend?"

"Yes," he says. "A long time ago."

"And now—you're *together*?"

"No, no. It's nothing like that." Will lets out a cry, and Francie stands, but Token gets to him first, lifting him from the swing. He cradles him to his chest and begins to pace her living room.

She sits back down on the armchair, keeping her eyes on her baby. "But the two of you—"

"We're just very good friends." His gaze is on the floor, avoiding hers. "After her mom died, she ended it. She withdrew from everyone, including me. I did everything I could to change her mind, but she refused to see me."

"I don't get it. Why are you here?"

His laugh sounds strange—bitter even. "I don't know, to be honest. I just wanted to see you. You may be the only person who sees what's going on here."

"What do you mean?"

"Winnie didn't do this."

Francie is so tired; her mind is cloudy. She doesn't like him holding Will, but she feels lightheaded. "Your arrest. What—"

"How did you find out about it?"

"We saw your mug shot."

"I figured. You found it online. But why did—"

"No. Not online. It was mailed to us."

He stops pacing. "Mailed to who?"

"Us. Me, Nell, Colette."

"What do you mean, it was mailed to you? By who?"

"I don't know. It arrived in the mail. Someone sent it to Colette at the mayor's office. There was no return address."

"At the mayor's office?" He closes his eyes. "I don't get it."

"What did you do?"

"I almost killed someone."

Francie stands and takes Will from his arms. "Leave. Right now." She turns her back to him, shielding Will from him. "I'll call the police."

"No, Francie, listen to me. It wasn't like that. It was to protect Winnie. She was in danger."

She turns around. "Danger?"

"She had a stalker."

"Yes, I know. Archie Andersen. I read about it."

Token nods. "It was after Winnie and I broke up. She didn't know I was doing it, but I followed her to rehearsals, when she went back to work, making sure she arrived safely, that he wasn't following her. Winnie thought he'd lost interest, but then he showed up at Audrey's funeral. It terrified her. I wanted to make sure she was safe."

"And?"

"It was her third day back at work after her mom died. He was waiting for her on the corner, after she got off the subway. I wasn't sure it was him at first, but I stayed close. He followed her inside, and then he grabbed her and forced her into the stairwell. I was on him in a second. He didn't even see me. Banged his head into the ground so hard I cracked his skull. He was in the hospital for weeks."

"Did you go to jail?"

"Nine months. I pled guilty to a misdemeanor assault in exchange for a lighter sentence. One year in prison, got out early for good behavior. The judge sealed the case, at the request of Winnie's lawyers, and we were able to keep the whole thing out of the press. Winnie quit the show after that. Did everything she could to fade from the public eye."

"He recovered? Archie Andersen?"

"Long enough to move to West Virginia, where he killed an elderly couple in a botched robbery attempt. He's been in prison for eleven years."

Francie shakes her head. "That wasn't reported."

Token glances at her. "No?"

Francie's mouth goes dry as she presses her lips to Will's forehead. He's in jail. "Why didn't you just tell us that you and Winnie are friends?"

"Winnie's very private." Token sits on the sofa. "You may have noticed? After our kids were born, she encouraged me to come to a May Mothers meeting. But she asked me not to share our history. It would just force questions. She doesn't like to talk about those years."

"I can't believe this. You went to jail for her."

"I did." His face is darkened by a passing shadow. "And I'd do it again in a second. I'd do anything to protect her." He lowers his eyes to the floor. "And Midas."

Francie watches him for a few moments. "Listen," she says, taking the seat beside him on the couch. "I have an idea. Something that occurred to me yesterday. Something I believe can help."

He keeps his eyes on the floor but Francie thinks she detects a change in his expression. When he finally looks up, he's smiling. "Something to help her?"

CHAPTER TWENTY-ONE
DAY THIRTEEN

> **TO:** May Mothers
> **FROM:** Your friends at The Village
> **DATE:** July 17
> **SUBJECT:** Today's advice
> <u>YOUR BABY: DAY 64</u>
> When you have a baby, everyone in the world seems to have an
> opinion (Ha! Who are we to talk?). How to deal? First, take what
> you hear with a grain (or six) of salt. Nothing's going to undermine
> your confidence more than listening to every shred of advice. Also,
> realize it's well-intentioned. While we love our babies more than
> anything in the world, a lot of other people (We're looking at you,
> Grandma!) want to play a role in making sure the little one is safe.

Colette traces the shards of sunlight on Charlie's cheek. His hand
is on her waist.

"Do you know how rarely, in fifteen years together, you've
cried in front of me?"

She nods and closes her eyes, seeing the image of Winnie
being led into the police station yesterday. Another wave of grief
hits her.

"I wish we'd talked about this sooner," Charlie says, drawing
her closer. Last night, after watching the news about Winnie,
Colette broke down, admitting everything. About making copies of the police file and taking the flash drive. About how she's

been struggling to stay afloat, and her concern about Poppy, how fiercely she's been watching her, searching for any sign of improvement. How hard it's been to try to balance everything: being a good partner, a good mother, a competent writer.

"What do you want to do?" Charlie asks her now.

"I don't know." Poppy whimpers over the monitor, and Colette rises to get her, but Charlie places a hand on her back.

"Let's give her a second to work it out on her own."

Colette relaxes back into him.

"Actually, that's a lie. I do know what I want to do. I want to make sure she's okay. I want to just be a mom for a while. And at some point I'll return to writing. My own writing." She wipes her tears on the pillowcase. "Even though my brain no longer works and I have nothing to write about."

Charlie smiles. "Do what every new mother does. Write about having a baby."

"I need to get her," Colette says, as Poppy cries out again.

"I'll do it." He sits up, searching the floor around the bed for his boxer shorts. "It's Saturday. Stay in bed. Get some more sleep."

Colette clicks off the monitor and sinks back under the sheet, breathing in Charlie's scent on her pillow. Outside the window, the European starlings gather on the fire escape, eating from the bird feeder she set out a few days ago. She closes her eyes, wishing she could remain here all day, shutting out her grief and the images of Winnie being led into jail, expecting that at any moment she'll hear the news that they've found Midas's body.

Her phone rings on the table beside her. She wants to ignore it, but she knows she can't.

She sits up and reaches for it. "Hi."

"Are you on your way?"

Colette pauses. "No."

"It's almost nine. You're still coming, right?"

Colette rubs her eyes. "Nell, I'm not sure. I—"

"Colette, no," Nell says. "Don't do that. You said you'd be there. We both did." Nell pauses. "I'm serious, Colette. We have to do this. We promised her we would."

———

Charlie is making coffee, Poppy cooing cheerfully in the bouncy chair at his feet, when Colette walks into the kitchen, wearing her yellow sundress. "I need to go out for a little while," she says.

"You didn't tell me that. Where to?"

"I have to do one quick thing." She kisses him. "I'll be back soon. And guess what we're doing tonight?"

He wraps his arms around her waist and presses her hips to his. "I have one idea."

She laughs. "That. And I made us a reservation for dinner."

"The three of us?"

"No. I got a sitter."

"You're kidding. Who?"

"Sonya, from downstairs. Do you know she was a nanny to twins for two years?"

He cocks his head. "Of *course* I know that. And thank you. That'll be nice." He takes his time kissing her. "Take an umbrella, it's starting to rain. And hurry home."

———

Nell is waiting in front of The Spot, a dripping newspaper held over her head against the rain, an iced coffee in her hand.

"Sorry, I'm late," Colette says.

"Come on." Nell sips the last of the coffee and tosses it into a nearby garbage can. "Francie's called me three times already."

Colette picks up her pace to keep in step with Nell, knowing this is the right thing to do. Francie showed up at Colette's late last night, her eyes swollen, her words coming out in a flurry: Token had come to her apartment, saying he and Winnie dated in high school. Francie told him what Scarlett had said at the last May Mothers meeting, about Winnie being depressed, and her growing certainty that Scarlett was the woman she'd seen from Winnie's building.

"He thinks I should talk to Scarlett," Francie told Colette. "He thinks it's a really good idea. But I've e-mailed her several times and she's not responding. Token said I should trust my instincts and keep trying. I want to track her down. We both think this might be our last hope to find Midas and help Winnie."

"Francie, that is a crazy idea," Colette said.

"No, it's not. We didn't even realize Winnie was depressed. Plus, she's one of those women. She always knows what to do. I'm telling you. We need to talk to her."

Colette hasn't been able to shake the desperate look in Francie's eyes, and it's still with her as she hurries alongside Nell down the hill. "Okay, so what's the plan?" Nell asks.

"We'll let her drop off this letter. And then I'll suggest we go get coffee. We'll talk to Francie there, tell her how concerned we are about her."

"I wish we could skip this part and go right to the coffee. Imagine what Scarlett is going to think when she reads this letter?"

"I know, it's ridiculous, but it's the best I could do." A clap of thunder echoes around them as the rain begins to fall harder. Colette moves closer to Nell, shielding her with her umbrella. "I talked to Charlie's editor. She went through this after her first was born. She gave me the names of three therapists."

"Good," Nell says. "If Francie says she won't make an appointment, we'll call Lowell. He needs to understand there's something larger going on here."

They turn the corner, and Colette sees Francie waiting in front of a building at the end of the block. Someone is standing with her under her umbrella.

"Is that Lowell?" Colette asks.

Nell squints. "That's Token. Did she tell you he was coming?"

"No. I thought it was just going to be the three of us."

"You're late," Francie says as they approach. She holds up the envelope. "You guys want to read it? Token"—she looks at him—"sorry, Daniel thinks it sounds okay."

"I'm sure it's fine," Colette says. "What did you write?"

Francie licks the envelope and seals it. "Just what I told you last night. That we're wondering if she knows something that might help."

"Great," Colette says.

Francie takes a deep breath and walks up the stoop. Token steps closer to Colette.

"You mind?" he asks, nodding at her umbrella. Colette and Nell move aside to make room for him. His shoulder is against Colette's, and she can feel his breath on her neck as they watch Francie bend under her umbrella to look at the names on the mailboxes. "I was right! It *is* her apartment," she says, just as a woman opens the front door from inside, knocking Francie's hip.

"Sorry," the woman says. She holds the door open. "You coming in?"

Francie glances back at them, and Colette shakes her head. "No," Colette says. "Just leave it—"

Francie reaches for the door. "Yes, thanks."

"Goddammit," Nell says, under her breath.

"Come on," Colette says, watching Francie disappear inside the building. She runs up the stoop, Nell following, and catches the door before it closes. "You coming?" she calls to Token.

"No," he says, pulling up his hood. "I think it's probably better if I stay here. Just in case."

"Yes, keep watch," Nell says, and then lowers her voice to an exaggerated whisper. "If we're not back in three days, call the police."

Colette and Nell enter the foyer. "Francie," Colette calls up the carpeted stairway. "Drop off the letter and let's go."

"I seriously don't have time for this," Nell says, heading up the stairs. "My mom is leaving today."

Colette follows Nell to the third floor, where she sees Francie's wet umbrella leaning against the wall next to an open door at the top of the stairs. Colette steps inside the apartment, entering a small kitchen. Neatly stacked packing boxes line the hallway, marked in bold letters: POTS AND PANS. LINENS. DISHES. The counter is crowded with baby bottles, prenatal vitamins, Chinese herbs, and boxes of lactation tea.

Francie is standing in the living room, separated from the kitchen by a white tiled island, examining the room. "How did you get in?" Nell asks her.

"The door—it just opened."

Colette looks at the doorknob, which is battered and loose, noticing a screw on the floor. "Francie, did you force your way in?"

"No. The knob was loose."

"This has officially gone too far," Colette says. "Leave the note outside."

"I will." Francie's voice is distant as she walks past Colette, down the hallway, sliding past the boxes, toward the bedroom. "Just give me a minute."

Colette sighs and then notices Nell, who is paging through a notebook on the kitchen counter. "Check this out," Nell says. "It's a chart, tracking the baby's feeding and diaper changes." She turns another page. "God, she even writes down every time she hears a burp."

"You don't?" Colette asks.

"I do, yes," Nell says. "But only for Sebastian's burps. I have an entire storage unit of these things."

Francie walks back into the kitchen and continues past them.

Without saying a word, she opens the glass door and steps onto the small terrace. The railing is lined with potted flowers and herbs, and the beginnings of a tomato plant. She looks out across the yard for a few moments and then walks back inside, her curls misty with rain, and peeks inside a closet just off the kitchen. "You think it's possible she had a video monitor, or a nanny cam?"

"No," Colette says. She walks to the closet and shuts the door. "That is definitely not possible." Colette places her hands on Francie's shoulders. "Leave the note. It's all you can do."

Nell walks closer. "Colette's right, France. Let's go to The Spot. It's been a rough few days. Muffins are on me." Nell pinches the extra fat at her waist. "See?"

Francie wipes her nose. "You think she'll call when she gets the letter?"

"I do," Colette says. "You're doing the right thing. But it's time to go."

Francie nods. "I left my bag in the bedroom." She walks down the hall toward the back of the apartment as Colette goes into the living room to close the terrace door.

Nell peers down the hall. "Would it be weird if I use her bathroom? I shouldn't have had that coffee." But then her expression changes, and she walks closer to the door.

"What's wrong?" Colette asks.

Nell holds up her hand. "Listen." Colette hears it then: a baby crying.

"That can't be her," Colette whispers.

"I know. She's away, right?"

"Shhhhhh, baby. Shhhhh." Footsteps jog up the stairs. "We're almost home."

"Oh my god," Nell whispers, grasping Colette's arm. "It is her. She's back."

———

Colette follows Nell down the hall to the bedroom and closes the door behind them. They hear Scarlett entering the kitchen. "What are we going to do now?" Nell asks.

"I don't know."

Nell rushes to the window. "Is there a fire escape or something?"

"Francie," Colette says. "Are you paying attention? She's here."

But Francie doesn't seem to hear her. She's standing in front of a desk in the corner of the room, rifling through a drawer, her expression vacant. Scarlett sings in the kitchen.

"*Hush little baby, don't you cry. Mama's gonna sing you a lullaby.* Okay, my darling," she says. "It's time for lunch. Shhhh now. Mama's here. Let me get out of these wet clothes first."

The door opens, and the bedroom fills with the piercing sound of Scarlett's scream.

———

"Colette." Scarlett's hair is damp down her back, her face stricken with fear. She looks at Nell and Francie, her arms wrapped protectively around her baby, who is squirming at her chest under the rain hood of his carrier. "What are you doing here?"

Colette laughs nervously. "Scarlett. My god, how awkward is this? We're so sorry. This is—"

Francie steps forward. "We're here about Winnie."

"Winnie? I don't understand. Is this about the e-mails you've been sending me?"

"Yes. You didn't write back. You left me no choice but to come here." There's an alarming edge to Francie's voice and a wild look in her eyes, and then the thought strikes Colette. Where is Token? Why didn't he alert them that Scarlett had come home?

"To be honest, Francie, if I was going to write back, it would have been to ask you to stop. The number of e-mails you're sending me. It's a little disturbing."

"I saw you the other day, on your balcony, when I was at Winnie's."

"On my balcony? What do you mean? We've been away."

"No, I saw you," Francie says. "You had a watering can."

Scarlett is shaking her head. "Okay—"

"Winnie confided in you," Francie says. "That's what you told us, at the last meeting. She admitted she was depressed."

Scarlett's baby releases a soft cry of hunger, and she begins to bounce him. "Yes, and—"

"And you were home that night, right?" Her voice is rigid. "With your in-laws?"

"I spoke to the detectives about everything I know." Scarlett shifts her gaze from Francie to Colette and Nell. "I'm sorry, but whatever it is you're doing—the incessant e-mails. And now this, coming here, breaking into my apartment—it's completely out of line." Her voice is taut with anger. "Not to mention against the law."

Colette feels the heat of embarrassment at her neck. "Scarlett, we're sorry. We were going to just leave a letter—"

"How did you even get in here?"

"Your door—it was unlocked," Francie says.

"My door was unlocked?" Her face flushes. "How stupid of me."

"We didn't plan to—" Colette tries to steady her voice. "We—"

"It wasn't our intention to come inside," Nell says, walking to place a hand on Francie's elbow. "How about we just go and leave you to your day?"

Scarlett's baby cries louder. She turns to walk down the hall toward the kitchen. "Good idea."

Colette lets out her breath. "Come on."

Nell leads Francie toward the door, but Francie wrests her arm from Nell's grip and walks back toward the desk.

"Francie," Nell hisses. "This is no longer funny. Come *on*."

Francie silently takes a stack of papers from the top drawer of the desk and holds them up.

"Natural Remedies for Clogged Ducts." "Six Sleep Cues You Can't Miss."

"Francie, come on—"

Francie shows them the next pages, printouts of an online article.

GWENDOLYN ROSS ARRESTED IN THE DISAPPEARANCE OF HER SON

LACHLAN RAINE ADMITS AFFAIR WITH STATE DEPT. INTERN ELLEN ABERDEEN

Francie flips again. It's the e-mail from Nell. The Jolly Llama. 8:00 on July 4. Everyone come, and especially Winnie. We won't take no for an answer.

Francie's hands are trembling as she holds open a notebook, and they read the page together.

What if they don't believe me? I finally spoke that question out loud last night. What if they see through the story we've created? What if I go to jail?

But Joshua just turned away from me. I know even the mention of it terrifies him.

Francie flips to the next page, and a handful of folded papers falls onto the floor at their feet. Nell picks them up and unfolds them.

Token's mug shot. Three copies of it.

Colette closes her eyes, hearing only the sound of the rain pulsing against the skylight above them.

"Oh my god," Nell says under her breath.

Colette opens her eyes. *Go*, Francie mouths.

———

Scarlett is standing by the door. The baby is crying harder.

"He sounds hungry," Francie says. "Can I do something to help?"

"You can leave," she says. "My husband is parking the car and will be back any second. Trust me, he's not going to be so understanding."

Colette walks toward Scarlett. She pictures herself running down the stairs, out on to the sidewalk, sprinting through the rain, back to Charlie and Poppy, none of this real. But then her gaze meets Nell's and then Francie's, and she feels herself taking a few steps toward Scarlett.

"What are you doing?" Scarlett says, her hands at the baby's head.

Colette reaches for the rain hood. Scarlett pulls away, but Colette catches a glimpse of his hair, and then his face.

"Midas," Francie says from behind Colette as Scarlett walks brusquely into the kitchen. Colette follows, her legs weak.

His screams grow louder as Colette reaches Scarlett. She forces her hands inside the carrier and hooks them around the baby. She feels Scarlett pitching toward the sink, and sees the knife locked in her fist.

In an instant, she becomes aware of a searing flash of pain in her side. She hears the sound of Nell's voice. She sees Poppy's face.

And then it all goes black.

———

I place the knife on the table.

Francie is standing motionless. Nell is kneeling beside Colette, who has fallen to the floor. The baby is screaming at my chest. "Now look what you've done," I say, gazing down at him. "You've upset Joshua."

"Scarlett, what have you—" Francie is walking closer to me. "Give him to me. Give me Midas."

"Midas? Midas is dead. This is Joshua." I see the terrified look in his eyes, and whisper into his ear. "Don't worry, sweetheart. We're going to be all right."

The room begins to twist. The air glistens with dust. They're here to visit.

I'm hosting a May Mothers Meeting.

Nell is crying and holding her phone to her ear. I have to think quickly. I walk over and snatch it from her hand.

"No! Give that to me." She's frantic. "We have to get her help."

I calmly place her phone in the sink, turning on the faucet. "No phone calls during our meetings, ladies. It's rude." I turn to Francie. "You too."

"Me too?"

"Yes." I hold out my hand. "Give me your phone."

Francie reaches for the back pocket of her shorts, the same, pea-green, milk-stained, ill-fitting Old Navy shorts she wears to every meeting, the poor girl. "My phone? I didn't—"

I step over Colette and spin Francie around, my nails digging into her soft bicep, and grab the phone from her pocket. I toss it in the sink next to Nell's and squeeze a stream of blue gel over the phones, watching them disappear under a cloud of bubbles. I catch my reflection in the cabinet glass, noting the dark bags under my eyes, the state of my hair. I look awful.

I pinch pink into my cheeks and fluff up my hair. I really should have put more effort into looking good for this meeting. I know how much these women care about that.

"I'm sorry," I say, turning back to Francie. "I don't mean to be rude. Joshua has been a little moody and it's starting to get to me. But you guys know how *that* is, right?"

I walk to the apartment door, twisting the dead bolt into place, stringing the chain lock. Kneeling down, I summon the strength to slide a stack of packing boxes in front of the door. I'm a little dizzy when I stand. "No point in going to the park in this rain," I say, walking to the refrigerator. "Let's just meet here. It's more comfortable. And I have to feed this baby."

I take a bottle of breast milk from the freezer, nearly the last of the stash I was able to pump before my supply dried up. I know I should have been more disciplined about it, setting my alarm for the middle of the night to keep pumping, taking more herbs, drinking that awful lactation tea. Once again, I've failed.

"Sit down," I tell Francie, sticking the bottle into the microwave. "And please don't tell me microwaving breast milk destroys all its good properties. I am aware of that. I've read the same books. And I'm choosing to adhere to my own parenting philosophy. It's called *Mothers: Fuck All of You.*" I laugh and glance down at Colette, who is leaving a pool of blood on the kitchen tiles. "Maybe you should ghostwrite a book about *that*," I tell her.

I take the bottle to the couch and look at the others, noticing something. "Wait," I say. "Where are your babies?"

Francie is silent, but then something changes in her expression. She seems to compose herself. "It's girls' day," she says, sitting down beside me, her eyes on Joshua. "Remember? We said no babies. Right, Nell?"

"Girls' day?" I tug down the fabric of the baby carrier and prod the nipple into Joshua's mouth. "Sounds fun. I must have missed that e-mail. I just hope you're not hungry. This meeting is unexpected."

Colette moans from the kitchen floor, and I see that Nell is pressing one of my good hand towels into the wound at her side. "Did you bring your muffins?" I ask Colette.

Nell's face is chalky. "Her muffins?"

"Isn't that her thing? She brings the muffins, the rest of us bring the ennui." Joshua squirms at my chest, and I pull the bottle from his mouth. He lets out a burp. Barely a burp, but it will do. I stand to make a note of it in my notebook but then decide to sit back down. I'll do it later, after they leave.

"Well, how about some coffee?" Francie asks.

"Coffee? What about the clogged duct? I told you caffeine just makes it worse."

"I know. I gave up. Formula feeding now."

"Formula? Really? That's too bad." Joshua is watching me, and I know there's no use in continuing to avoid his eyes. Right away I see the scolding look, the anger. He so resembles his father right now. Asking me how I let this happen, why I haven't done a better job of avoiding this, like I promised I would. I look away. "Coffee? Let's see."

I walk back into the narrow kitchen and open the cupboards. "Nope. I've already packed the coffeepot. Lactation tea will have to do. Now where are the mugs?"

I start the water and rifle through a box in front of the door, spotting the tacky *Cape Cod Is for Lovers* cup Dr. H bought me as a joke at a rest stop during our first weekend away together two years ago. The first time we had sex somewhere other than the floor of his office, the white noise machine turned as high as possible, in case his next patient arrived early. The weekend he first said he was in love with me, and long before I discovered what a monster he could be.

I unearth a jar of unopened pickles and a can of black beans in the back of the cupboard. I pop open the pickles, pour the beans into a clean bowl, and when the water is ready, I carry them to the coffee table with the tea.

"Looks great," Francie says, but her face doesn't register appreciation for my efforts. Knowing her, she's judging me for not having baked something. She takes her tea. "Now, as you know, we have a certain way of starting these meetings," she says.

"You mean my birth story?" I laugh. "That was my idea, wasn't it?"

Francie nods. "And since you're hosting, you should go."

I urge Joshua to accept the pacifier clipped to his shirt. "Well, I delivered on Mother's Day. I lay down for a nap—"

"No," Francie interrupts. "Before that. Start with the pregnancy."

"Oh, okay. Let's see. So, Dr. H didn't want any more kids. He claims I tricked him, but I was on the pill. I'm the one percent." I laugh. "Not *that* one percent. The other one. The one the birth control package warns you about."

"Dr. H?"

"My psychiatrist. Joshua's dad. I called him my boyfriend once." I cringe, remembering that moment at the bar in Queens, next to the hotel where we'd sometimes meet. "My boyfriend will have another whiskey sour," I told the bartender, a woman in her seventies, plastic earrings dangling from her stretched lobes, a Styrofoam cup swimming with cigarette butts between the dusty bottles of flavored vodka behind her.

She turned to make the drink, and he seethed beside me. "Don't ever call me that again," he whispered in my ear, his hand gripping my thigh, leaving five purple dots I discovered later that night as I undressed for him. "We're not a pair of fucking teenagers."

"He's married," I tell Francie. "But we were together for two years." I roll my eyes. "You know, on and off."

Francie nods. "Is he the one parking the car right now? Your husband?"

"Hmmmm?" Oh right. I'd said that earlier. "No. I don't have a husband."

"So Dr. H—"

"We haven't spoken in months, since I told him I was going to keep Joshua. He's kind of nuts. Narcissistic personality disorder, if you ask me. It makes it hard for people to love others. I learned about it from him, in fact. *The only person your father was capable of loving was himself.* That's what Dr. H always said, but swear to god, he could have been talking about himself." I'm surprised to feel a lump growing in my throat. This isn't easy to talk about.

"Anyway, my parents weren't the best role models, and I wasn't planning on kids. But then Joshua came along, and I never wanted anything more. From the minute he showed up as a pink plus sign between two thin sheets of plastic, I *knew* him."

I rub Joshua's back, thinking about those days, how joyful they were, feeling him growing inside me. Reading him books in the bathtub. Taking him for walks in the morning to the new playground, promising to bring him back one day. I'd walk barefoot through the sand pit, envisioning him collecting rocks, learning to climb trees. All the things kids are supposed to do. "He was such an active little guy. Such a kicker. Always telling me what he wanted." I laugh as I tip another stream of sugar into my tea. "Remember how they talked to us from inside?"

I can see by the empty expression on Francie's face that I've veered off topic. "Sorry. Dr. H always said I talk too much and risk boring people to death." I press my fingers to my temples, trying to huddle my thoughts into order, to concentrate on what I'm saying, and not on the way Joshua is looking at me.

"Stay focused, Scarlett," I say. I smile at Francie. "I had a very specific birth plan. You know, no epidural, skin-to-skin contact, sprinkle him with organic fairy dust but don't clean him off before giving him to me. The thing is, nobody seemed to care about my plan. Before I could even hold him, they'd taken him away to that little table thing, with all the lights and wires.

"I can't remember the doctor's name, but I can hear her yelling something—barking orders at people. Then she was attaching wires, wheeling him out of the room, not even letting me see his face—to see if he looked the way I'd been imagining he would." The other doctor was there then, telling me I needed to be stitched up where I'd torn. *You need to lie down, Mom. We need to take care of you first.*

"Would you like a pickle?" I extend the jar to Francie. "No? Nell?" Nell's eyes are swollen. She shakes her head. "Anyway, hypoxic-ischemic encephalopathy. That's what a doctor told me. In other words, he suffocated during the delivery. Or, in even other words, fetal demise. *Fetal demise.* Doesn't that sound like it should be the name of a female punk band?" I begin to laugh and find that I have a hard time stopping. "Sorry," I eventually say. "I don't think this is funny at all. To be honest, I'm so racked with guilt. I was *so* careful during my pregnancy. I did everything I could to keep him safe. I don't know what happened. I didn't mean to hurt him—"

Francie touches my leg. "Scarlett. It wasn't anything you—"

"Anyway," I say, standing up and walking away from the pity in her face. "Another woman came in to ask me if I wanted to hold my son before they took him away. I didn't know if I wanted to hold him. 'Is that what people do?' I asked her. 'Yes,' she said. 'Closure.' That's the word she used. Someone had thought to put a hat on him, before they brought him to me. As if we still had the luxury of worrying that he might be cold."

I pause to finger a hill of cold beans into my mouth, aware of how famished I am. I can no longer remember the last time I ate.

"They told me I had forty-eight hours to register his death. I never did it. To be honest, it's making me a little nervous. Do you think that might be a crime?" I bounce Joshua to the balcony door, opening it. I need some fresh air. I reach for the binoculars on the bookshelf and look across the wet backyards, into Winnie's home, wondering what she's doing. I haven't seen her in two days, since Daniel was there, when I watched him open the curtains and then make her dinner, sitting beside her on the couch, handing her tissues from the box in his lap, her plate untouched on the coffee table.

Oh right, I remember, putting the binoculars back in their place. She's not home. She's in jail.

I turn to Francie. "Anyway, that's pretty much it." I laugh. "My 'birth story.' I'm glad I got my turn. I wanted to volunteer to go that night, when Winnie declined. But I don't know, I was feeling shy."

"What night?" Nell asks.

"The fourth of July. At the Jolly Llama."

"You were there?"

"Yes. I stayed inside at first, at the bar. Watching you guys. I was going to join the table, but it felt weird. I've never felt like I really fit in with this group. And then, of course, I met that guy."

I see him, standing there, watching me. I knew what he wanted. I'd just witnessed him attempt the same thing with Winnie. The blatant eye contact from his place at the bar. The smile. The way he took in my body when he finally approached. Winnie rejected him immediately, but I couldn't help myself. "I accepted his drink," I tell Francie. "One thing led to another." I feel his hands under my dress in the bathroom stall, begging me to go home with him. If only I'd said yes. I sigh and shake my head. "It had been a while."

Francie is immobile. "Was he wearing a red hat?"

"He was hard to miss, right? So handsome. But yeah, that stupid red baseball hat."

"I don't understand," Nell says. "How did you take the baby? With Alma—"

"Alma was lucky."

"Lucky?" Nell says.

"Yes. After I left the bar with the key you gave me, I was sure I'd have to hurt her. But she saved me a lot of trouble. She was sound asleep."

Tears collect at Nell's chin. "I gave you the key?"

"Yes. We spoke that night, at the bar. You don't remember?"

Nell squeezes her eyes shut. "I do—I thought I did. But everyone said you weren't there. They said it was Gemma I spoke to."

"Nope. Hang on." I stand and walk to the small closet off the kitchen, taking out the blond wig and straw cowboy hat from the top shelf. I put the wig on, but it sits awkwardly. I look inside, and Winnie's phone falls to the floor at my feet. "Oh, there it is. I was wondering where I put that thing." I put the wig back on and turn to Nell. "Look familiar?"

"It *was* you."

"Yes. I couldn't believe you recognized me. Colette and Daniel—sorry, *Token*—stood *right* next to me for like ten minutes and had no idea. Of course, they were too busy looking at each other all googly-eyed. Remember, Colette? You told Daniel about your job with the mayor, swearing him to keep your little secret between you.

"I eventually decided to push my luck, get closer, see what you guys were talking about. I stood at the railing, my face toward my phone. And then I took that photo of you, Nell, looking so wild and out-of-control." I can't help myself, and a laugh escapes me. "Sending *that* to Detective Hoyt worked out way better than I'd dreamed. I thought it was just going to lead Hoyt down your trail, buying me some time. Instead, it distracted everyone from the real issue. That the police had failed to find a baby." I fish inside the jar for another pickle.

"I watched the whole thing. Winnie leaving her phone. You deleting that app. Putting her phone in your purse. Then you barged into me on my way out of the bathroom, just when I was about to go home. 'Come on,' you said. 'Let's bum a smoke. It's been ages.'

"We went to the smoking patio where a very nice gentleman gave you one of his cigarettes. I had a glass of red wine, you had a Camel Light and a gin and tonic laced with my last four Xanax. Within the half hour, I had Winnie's phone and key. Trust me. Me and Joshua, together in the end? I didn't think for a *second* that was possible. I didn't keep going to your meetings believing I'd actually get him back."

"Our meetings," Francie said. "You came. You had a baby."

"No." I raise my eyebrows. "I had a porcelain doll inside a stroller. Hello? Thanks for never asking to hold him, by the way. The level of self-absorption in this group *really* played to my advantage."

"Oh my god. You—" Nell's words break apart in a sob.

"Followed you into the bathroom. You tried to fight, but you were pretty out of it by then. Wait a second. Listen." I hear a noise in the hallway. "Are others coming?"

"No," Francie says and holds up her mug. "My tea is cold. Can I have another?"

"I suppose." I lift Joshua to my shoulder and step over Colette and back into the kitchen.

"So, you and Joshua are moving to Westchester?" Francie asks as I light the burner. "That'll be nice."

"Westchester? I wouldn't be caught dead in Westches—" But then I remember. "That was also a lie. God, I'm terrible. I'm not sure where we're going. My mom has been dead for years and god knows I'd never stay with my dad. We were upstate for a few days, at Winnie's house, but we can't go back there."

Francie's eyes are wide. "Wait. Do you mean—"

"That Winnie knew about it? Of course not. But you can find anything on the Internet if you're willing to look hard enough. Like Daniel's mug shot. Or your real identity, Nell, if you have a flair for remembering faces and access to Lexus Nexus. The address of Winnie Ross's country home upstate was right there in the police report of her mother's death. I was sure there'd be no way she'd hide a key, but lo and behold. Under the flowerpot. The same place my mom used to hide ours." I feel a dark wave passing over me, thinking about those four quiet days with Joshua, how peaceful they were. "We'd still be there, if it were up to me. But then Hector came to mow the lawn and screwed everything up."

"Hector." Francie's expression is severe. "Scarlett, you didn't—"

"I had to. He saw us. I couldn't believe it when he walked into the kitchen as I was scrambling eggs for breakfast. 'You're supposed to be in Brooklyn,' I said. I'd been watching him. After the journalists dragged their darkened souls back home, Hector would arrive at Winnie's. Bring her groceries. Straighten up her house. He wasn't supposed to go upstate—that wasn't in my plan. But he did, and he had to pay the price, and now, so does Winnie."

I walk to close the door to the terrace, to drown the sound of sirens splicing the air. I take Francie's mug and return to the kitchen, pouring the boiling water over a fresh tea bag. "I'm being honest when I say this, but I really didn't want Winnie to go to jail. That unfortunate woman has been through enough. I tried to place the blame on others. You know how many times I called that police line, offering tips? The white guy on the bench. The sex offender down the block. Alma. Poor thing. Won't be long until *she's* deported." I place the kettle back on the stove, and then suddenly I hear a commotion behind me. Nell is sliding the boxes aside, and Francie is fumbling for the lock. Before I can make sense of what's happening, Daniel is there, forcing the door open.

"Daniel!" I say. "I knew I heard someone knocking earlier. You're late."

"I've been texting you," he says to Francie. "I saw her coming. I've been trying to get in the building, but—" He stops talking, noticing Colette on the floor. His face goes pale.

"Daniel," Francie says, quietly. "She has Midas."

He is studying me, a peculiar expression on his face. When he approaches, he seems so big all of a sudden. I feel the light changing around us: a grayness shadowing the room, like clouds rolling across the sun. My legs give out and I reach for the counter, cradling Joshua's head. I haven't felt this out of sorts since my first trimester.

"You took Midas?" Daniel says to me.

"His name is Joshua."

"Joshua?"

"Daniel, please don't stand so close to me," I say. "Go sit down. There's beans."

Francie is beside him then. "Scarlett, we just want to help. You've had a long day. Just you and the baby."

"I have," I say. "It's hard."

"I know." Francie places a hand on Joshua's back. "It is. It's hard."

I look at Daniel, and despite the hardened look on his face, I feel a wave of sadness for him. "It must be so much harder for you. Trying to do this as a guy." I manage a laugh. "I know. Educated, wealthy white guy. Boo-hoo. The burden of it. But really, being a stay-at-home dad? That can't be easy."

"Give me the baby," Daniel says. He grips my arm. His skin is smooth, his fingers strong, just as I've imagined his hands would feel on a woman's body.

"No, I won't give you the baby," I say. "You have your own." The sirens have grown louder and my back is pressed to the wall and there are footsteps on the stairs. Maybe it's Gemma, or Yuko, with her yoga mat, arriving late again. But then the door is knocked open and men in black shirts are rushing into the room.

Francie is saying Midas's name, and Daniel has his hands on

Joshua. There's so much shouting, and I can't make sense of what's happening.

I smell rain.

I'm in the stairwell, lumbering down the steps, belly first to the sidewalk, praying for the car service to hurry up and arrive. I feel the pain gripping my back, and see the look on the taxi driver's face. The liquid seeps from me and I'm lying on the hospital bed, wishing Dr. H was here. Grace, the nurse, tells me to breathe.

I feel the pain and the darkness, and I know that something is wrong. Something is terribly wrong. I know that I'm going to lose Joshua. Again.

"Wait!" I yell. Francie is holding my arms, and Daniel is wresting Joshua away from me. "I can't let you take him. Let me see his face. I want to see what he looks like!"

"Hands above your head," Grace screams. But it's not Grace. It's a police officer.

"Please don't wash him off. I want to hold him. Skin-to-skin contact immediately after the birth." I feel the pressure, squeezing my chest. "It's critical."

"Hands above your head!" Grace says, louder, her gun a straight line to my heart.

I put my hands on the wall and close my eyes.

Closure.

My fingers spider the wall, and I reach for the knife hanging from the magnetic strip. I feel the slick, cold metal of the blade and wind my fingers around the handle, pulling, aware of the magnetic fields splitting, breaking free from one another.

The sensation stays with me as I hear Francie scream; as I see the glint of light where the blade has caught a thin ray of sun streaming through the terrace window.

I close my eyes, and just before the knife meets my skin, I call for him one last time.

Joshua.

EPILOGUE
ONE YEAR LATER

TO: May Mothers

FROM: Your friends at The Village

DATE: July 4

SUBJECT: This week's advice

<u>**YOUR TODDLER: FOURTEEN MONTHS**</u>

In honor of the holiday, today's advice is about independence. Do you notice that your formerly fearless little guy is suddenly afraid of everything when you're out of sight? The friendly dog next door is now a terrifying beast. The shadow on the ceiling has become an armless ghoul. It's normal for your toddler to begin to sense danger in his world, and it's now your job to help him navigate these fears, letting him know he's safe, and that even if you're out of sight, Mommy will always be there to protect him, no matter what.

Winnie puts on her sunglasses and stuffs her short hair under a baseball cap before stepping into the small garden. She crosses the street quickly, her head bent toward the ground against the wind.

A man in a top hat is standing in front of an amplifier at the entrance to the park, a marionette strung from each hand, a line of children sitting at attention in front of him, their faces slack with awe. A gust of wind blows the hat from his head, and Winnie turns away from the crowds, heading in the opposite direction, down the sidewalk toward the break in the stone wall. She steers the stroller over the pebbles and under the arch, and when she mounts the hill and enters the wide lawn, she slows, surveying the crowd. Two young women in bikini tops lie on their stomachs, laughing at something, iced coffees in their hands, sections of the *New York Times* strewn on the grass in front of them. A soccer game is under way nearby, dozens of shirtless men running in the rising dust, yelling to one another in Creole. Winnie spots them in the distance, where they said they'd be—on blankets under their willow tree.

She walks across the lawn, averting her eyes from the flowering dogwood on her left, under which a dozen or so people are gathered; red, white, and blue balloons bob from strings tied to the legs of a plastic table. She sees herself under that tree—her mother's tree—a year ago. She hasn't returned to the park since that night when she made her way here, twenty minutes after leaving the Jolly Llama, walking aimlessly at first through the deserted streets, and then with purpose. The mosquitos circled and the oppressive heat of that July night bore down on her as she sat cross-legged, her back against the knotty trunk, writing her mother a letter.

It's a practice she kept for years, coming here with the leatherbound notebook she found the night of Audrey's death, wrapped in silver paper and left on the dining room table when her mom ran out to buy ice cream. The inscription on the front page, written in Audrey's delicate script, has mostly faded: *Today you may turn eighteen, but you will always be my baby. Happy birthday, Winnie.*

The notebook is nearly filled, with long letters Winnie has written to her mother any time she had something she needed to share: that she'd quit *Bluebird*, and she and Daniel had broken up. That she'd used some of the family money to set up a foundation for young dancers. That Archie Andersen was in jail, finally, the same week her father died from a heart attack during a business trip to Spain. It was also under the dogwood that Winnie wrote Audrey two years earlier, letting her know she'd done it: she'd found the right sperm donor. She was going to have a baby.

She hadn't initially planned to come to her mother's tree the night Midas was taken, but as soon as Alma arrived, she knew she'd much rather be alone than at a crowded bar. After stealing into Midas's room and kissing her sleeping son good-bye, she'd taken the notebook from the shelf. Later that night, as the sky sparkled with fireworks from the crowd across the lawn, she cried as she wrote under the light of a nearby park lamp about what an easy baby he was. About the way he smelled and how small he felt in her arms and that his eyes were just like Audrey's, so much so that when he looked at her sometimes, Winnie thought she was looking at her mother.

A group of people nearby break into "Happy Birthday," and Winnie sees that Nell is waving from under the willow tree. Winnie picks up her pace, trying to shut out the memory of that night, and it's only when she approaches their blanket that she realizes she was wrong. She doesn't know these women.

"Hi," one says. "Can we help you?"

"Winnie!" Francie is gesturing from the next tree. "Over here." Behind her, Colette and Nell are spreading gift-wrapped boxes on a blanket. Beatrice, Poppy, and Will dig in the dirt nearby.

"I'm sorry," Winnie says to the women as Francie walks over, her new daughter Amelia, two weeks old, asleep inside the Moby Wrap at Francie's chest.

"You're here," Francie says. Winnie detects the relief in Francie's voice. "I'm really glad you came."

Winnie follows her to the blankets. "We lost our tree," Colette says, smiling up at her.

"Replaced by younger women," says Nell. "Good thing none of us have any experience of what *that* feels like." She shakes her head at Colette, who is pulling napkins and plates from a bag. "For the fifth time, would you let me do that?"

Colette waves away Nell's hands. "I can lift *napkins*," she says. "In fact, Poppy and I both had our last physical therapy appointments yesterday. She's exactly where she should be, and"—she places her palm on her side, over the site of the wound—"I'm getting closer to feeling like myself again."

Francie is watching Winnie. "You doing okay?"

"I'm fine."

"Yeah? You getting out of the house?"

On the paved path beyond the trees, a couple flashes by on Rollerblades. "A little."

Colette pops open the lid of a large cake container.

"You got a cake with an . . . orange square?" Nell asks her.

"It's supposed to be a house." Colette licks icing from her finger. "I made it myself."

"You're kidding. I never would have guessed."

"It's gorgeous," Francie says. "That house is pretty much drawn to scale. Lowell keeps telling people it's a three-bedroom we bought, but unless he thinks someone is sleeping in a closet, he's exaggerating. It's so nice of you guys to do this for me." She pulls a napkin from the stack. "These hormones. I've forgotten how *emotional* everything feels with a newborn." She blows her nose. "I'm going to miss you guys."

Nell laughs. "Francie, you were born to move to Long Island. You'll be the mayor of that town by Christmas. Although at the rate you're going, you'll probably be a mother of six by then."

"Out, Mama." Midas is looking up at Winnie, squirming under the restraint of the straps and pointing at the other children. Winnie unbuckles him, and he slides to the ground, running to join them in the dirt.

Colette doles out the cake, and they eat in silence for a few moments. "I don't know if we want to talk about this," Colette says. "But I'd rather get it out of the way. I watched the show last night."

"I thought you would," Nell says. "So did I." She glances at Winnie. "Are we talking about this?"

Winnie smiles. "It's okay." She watched it too: *Baby Midas: A Tale of Mayhem and Modern Motherhood*, with Patricia Faith. A two-hour prime-time special, aired on the anniversary of Midas's abduction.

Daniel showed up at her place late yesterday afternoon with a bag of hamburgers and a six-pack. "I don't know if you want to watch it," he said. "But if you do, I'll stay and watch it with you."

She knew most of the details already. Mark Hoyt paid a visit to her house a few days after Midas came home, and told her everything that Scarlett had admitted to. The stillbirth. How, after coming home from the hospital, she'd spend hours sitting in her darkened apartment, watching Winnie through binoculars, fantasizing that Midas was her baby. How she'd lied and told the May Mothers that Winnie had confessed to feeling depressed, and had paid a young locksmith $300 to get inside Winnie's car, claiming it was hers, stuffing Midas's baby blanket into the tire well.

"She interviewed Scarlett," Colette says. "It's heartbreaking."

Francie stops chewing. "You're kidding. I couldn't bear to turn it on."

"She visited her in prison. Scarlett's still being held in the psychiatric ward, and yet they allowed Patricia Faith to sit her down in front of cameras for an hour. Patricia Faith, apparently, made a sizable donation to the prison."

Nell shakes her head. "Does Scarlett not have *anyone* looking out for her?"

"I'm doing my best not to think about it anymore," Francie

says. "All during Amelia's birth, I kept picturing her. Can you imagine? Lying there, not knowing what's happening. Where they've taken your baby. And then being told—"

"No," Colette says. "I can't."

"When they handed Amelia to me, I kept asking the nurses, *Is she okay? Is she breathing?* They had to tell me several times that she was fine. It was only then that I allowed myself to believe that she was real."

"She told Patricia Faith her biggest regret is that she survived the stab wound, that day we found Midas." Colette's gaze is on the circle of new moms under the willow tree. "And that she used to take that doll to playgrounds and music classes, keeping it in the stroller. Nobody ever noticed."

Winnie moves the cake around on her plate with her fork.

Do you ever feel delusional, Winnie?

Ever have any visions of hurting yourself?

We've looked at your medical records. You suffered from severe anxiety after your mom died. We hate to ask you this, Winnie, but have you ever thought about hurting Midas?

"I couldn't watch the whole thing," Nell says. "Those stories about her abusive father. And that therapist that got her pregnant? What a horrible human being."

———

They kept telling her to go out—the May Mothers, Daniel, the pediatrician—everyone arguing that it would be good for her to have a break from taking care of Midas for a few hours. But she didn't want a break. "I found this app for your phone," Daniel said, over sandwiches in the park the day before. "It's called Peek-a-Boo! You can keep an eye on him. I think they're right, Winnie. You could use a break."

But then she left the phone on the table, her key inside. A deep swell of regret builds inside of her. She closes her eyes, seeing herself at the bar, ordering another iced tea. Lucille had called Daniel, saying Autumn wouldn't stop crying and he needed to come home, and then that guy approached, leaning in too close, resting his hand on her waist. His rancid breath, the punch of the music, the pressing crowd of young men and women.

She needed to get out of there.

She knew. She was leaning against the tree, the notebook in her lap, watching the fireworks across the lawn, when she heard the police sirens. She knew, the same way she'd known the moment she looked in the eyes of that policeman who'd appeared at her front door twenty years earlier.

"Something's happened."

She searched for her phone in her purse, frantic, needing to hear from Alma that Midas was okay. She can feel the sting in her heels, her shoes chafing her skin, as she climbed the stony path, sprinting down the sidewalk, the sound of her feet on the pavement thunderous inside her head. The door was open and the police were there and Alma was sobbing, and then they were asking her questions. Where was she? Had anyone seen her leave the bar? Did anyone, as far as she knew, want to hurt Midas?

"Anyway," Colette says, "enough of that. I brought you all something." She takes three spiral-bound stacks of paper from her bag and hands one to each of them. "My novel."

Nell snatches one. "You finished?"

"Two months recovering from surgery leaves lots of time for writing," she says.

Nell flips through it. "I can't wait. What did Charlie's editor think?"

"I didn't want to say anything until I was sure, but she likes it." Colette's eyes shine with excitement. "They want to publish it."

The wind picks up, and Francie squeals as Nell pops the cork off a bottle of champagne. "I should have gotten two of these."

Nell pours them each a plastic flute, and they touch their cups together as a roar of laughter erupts from the new mothers under the willow tree.

"I have that exact same thought, *constantly*," says a woman in a red sundress. "I was getting a manicure yesterday, and I panicked, thinking I'd left the baby on the sidewalk in the car seat. She was at home with my mother-in-law. I ruined my nails. I think I'm going crazy."

Francie glances in their direction and laughs softly. "First-time moms." She takes Amelia from the Moby Wrap. "My back is killing me. Who wants her?"

"Me," Colette says, reaching for the baby. She sinks her lips into Amelia's dark curls. "Tell me one thing more delicious than new baby smell."

"This cake." Francie looks at Nell. "Are you going to read the whole thing right now?"

Nell places Colette's manuscript on the blanket beside her. "No, tomorrow. I'm taking the train to DC." She pulls back her hair, which now reaches her shoulders and is back to its natural color. "We're hosting a summit on paid leave." It's been months since Nell quit her job at the Simon French Corporation to become the executive director of Women for Equality. "Listen to this," she says, and Winnie tries her best to pay attention, but she's having trouble concentrating, her awareness pulled toward the mothers under the willow tree. The woman in the red sundress has risen from the blanket and is walking toward a nearby cluster of strollers.

"Did you guys see that article yesterday?" she calls to her group, peeking inside a stroller. "It says that swaddling is now thought to *cause* SIDS."

"That's absurd. The book I'm reading says the exact opposite."

Winnie turns back to Francie, who is reaching to cut another slice of cake, but she stops, the knife suspended in her hands, as a commotion breaks out behind them. A woman is in the middle of the lawn, shouting a child's name.

"Lola!" The woman spins in a circle, her hands cupped at her mouth.

A man jogs up to her. "I can't find her."

"Lola!" the woman yells through the wind.

"She was just here, a minute ago."

Winnie's eyes go to Midas. He's near the picnic tables, scraping the dirt with both hands.

"Lola!"

"What's happening?" Colette asks, looking in the couple's direction.

"There," Nell says, pointing up the hill. "There's a girl over there." Winnie spots the young girl in the distance, running toward the wooded path, away from the couple yelling for her.

Colette gets to her feet. "We have to go get her."

"Yes, quickly. Go." Francie drops the cake knife and reaches for Amelia. "Give me the baby."

"Lola!"

Winnie feels a rush of motion as a small brown-and-white spaniel charges by their blanket, a cracked tennis ball in its mouth. The couple falls to their knees, catching the dog, who jumps between them, clawing playfully at their chins and chests. "That is the last time we're letting you run free," the man says, clipping a leash to its collar.

Colette sits back down, her face flushed. Her laugh is forced. "I think my heart just stopped."

They're silent, and then Nell reaches for a gift-wrapped package on the blanket. "Here." She tosses it toward Francie. "Open something."

Francie unwraps her present from Colette—an expensive set of copper mixing bowls—and Winnie tries to still the tremor in her hand. As she sets her cup on the grass, she notices the figure in the distance.

It's a woman, standing on the shaded path just beyond the circle of mothers. She's wearing sunglasses, a black top, and a wide-brimmed hat. She's alternating glances between the mothers under the willow tree and the spot where Midas plays.

"To be honest, I'm more nervous about moving than I expected," Francie is saying, reaching for another gift. "I hope you'll come visit."

"Don't worry, we will," Colette says. "Won't we, guys?"

"Yes," Winnie says. She can't make out the woman's features, but it's the same thick brown hair under the hat. The same sharp cut of her jaw.

It's not her. It can't be.

Francie sets aside the baby quilt, embroidered with Amelia's name, that Winnie bought for her and takes a baby bottle from her diaper bag. "Is that *formula*?" Nell asks.

"I told you. I'm doing it differently this time. No more perfect mother." Francie laughs, and the sound of it is sharp in Winnie's ears.

"I'm going to the bathroom," the woman in the red sundress says. She climbs the path, away from the willow tree, her dress fluttering to her hips in the wind. "Someone keep an eye on her?" she yells behind her, but none of the women in her group seem to hear. Someone is telling a story. They pass around a bag of pretzels.

The woman in the hat is watching.

"Midas," Winnie calls, but he doesn't look up. The woman begins to walk toward the willow tree. Toward Midas.

"Midas!" Winnie stands. Her baseball hat flies from her head and her bare feet cut against the sharp twigs as she rushes to the tree, yanking Midas by the arm. At the sound of Midas's wail, the crowd under the willow tree looks in Winnie's direction, just as the woman reaches them. She takes off her sunglasses, and Winnie sees it's not a black shirt she's wearing, but a baby wrap.

"Hi," the woman says. "Are you the May Mothers?"

"Yes."

Midas is grabbing his shoulder.

"Oh, good. I wasn't sure if this was the right group." She throws her hat to the ground and shrugs a backpack from her shoulders, and then peels a baby from the carrier. "I'm Greta."

"Greta! You made it." The women shift, making room for her. "Finally."

"Hurts, Mama." Midas's face is streaked with dusty tears. Winnie crouches down and presses him to her. The women under the willow tree stop talking and look at her as Midas's cry grows shrill. "Too tight, Mama. Hurts."

"I'm sorry," she whispers to him. "I'm so sorry."

"Winnie." She hears someone calling her name. "Winnie."

Winnie, you really must come. We insist.

Winnie, tell your birth story.

I don't understand, Winnie. Did anyone see you leave the bar?

"Winnie, it's okay." She turns around. Daniel is standing next to her.

"You're here," she says.

"Of course I'm here." He picks up Midas, and then smiles. "Come on. Come sit down. It's okay."

She reaches for his hand. Slipping her fingers between his, she allows him to lead her back to the circle as the women under the willow tree watch, hugging their babies to their chests, their eyes clouded with concern, their blankets billowing around them in the warm summer wind.

ACKNOWLEDGMENTS

The author extends her deep gratitude to Billy Idol for his generous permission to use his lyrics in this work.